THE
PRESENCE

Books by T. Davis Bunn

The Quilt
The Gift
The Messenger
The Music Box
One Shenandoah Winter
Tidings of Comfort & Joy

Another Homecoming*
The Dream Voyagers
The Meeting Place*
The Presence
Princess Bella and the Red Velvet Hat
Promises to Keep
Return to Harmony*
The Sacred Shore*
To the Ends of the Earth
Tomorrow's Dream*
The Warning
The Ultimatum

The Priceless Collection

1. *Florian's Gate*
2. *The Amber Room*
3. *Winter Palace*

Rendezvous With Destiny

1. *Rhineland Inheritance*
2. *Gibraltar Passage*
3. *Sahara Crosswind*
4. *Berlin Encounter*
5. *Istanbul Express*

*with Janette Oke

THE
PRESENCE

T. DAVIS BUNN

BETHANY HOUSE PUBLISHERS
MINNEAPOLIS, MINNESOTA 55438

Published by Bethany House Publishers
A Ministry of Bethany Fellowship International
11400 Hampshire Avenue South
Minneapolis, Minnesota 55438
www.bethanyhouse.com

Printed in the United States of America

Library of Congress Cataloging-in-Publication Data

Bunn, T. Davis, 1952–
    The presence / T. Davis Bunn.
        p. cm.

    I. Title.
PS3552.U4718P74   1990
813'.54—dc20   90–39180
ISBN 1–55661–137–4 (original edition)   CIP
ISBN 0–7642–2301–1 (Tenth anniversary edition)

For IZIA
Who helps me listen to God.

God did this so that men would seek him and perhaps reach
out for him and find him,
though he is not far from each one of us.

Acts 17:27, NIV

T. DAVIS BUNN, a native of North Carolina, is a former international business executive whose career has taken him to over forty countries. With topics as diverse as romance, history, and intrigue, Bunn's books continue to reach readers of all ages and interests. He and his wife, Isabella, live in Oxfordshire, England.

Behold, I will pour out my spirit unto you,
I will make known my words unto you.

Proverbs 1:23, KJV

Whoever believes in me, as the Scripture has said,
streams of living water will flow from within him.

John 7:38, NIV

⊣ ONE ⊢

The first time it happened was at dawn on his fifty-third birthday as he sat in a friend's boat on Little Frying Pan Lake. T. J. Case thought he was having a stroke. He felt a brief moment of regret, a heartbeat of wishing he could tell Catherine once more how much he loved her. Then thought ended and wonder began.

The fishing trip had been his wife's idea. Two evenings ago Catherine silently packed the car while he was watching the election returns, laden with anguish for himself and dog-tired satisfaction for the young man whose campaign he had helped to manage. The next morning she bundled him into the passenger seat with a blanket, a pillow, a thermos of coffee, and a Bible. What's all this? he had asked, not really caring. Emergency aid for the walking wounded, Catherine told him. A little enforced R and R. He nodded, then asked, so where are we headed? It's all arranged, she said. Jeremy's loaned us his boat. Told me to keep you out until your head and heart are back in working order. His shoulders bounced in a humorless laugh. Jeremy said that? Catherine started the car, turned solemn dark eyes toward him, and said, you've been looking out for everybody but yourself for too long.

Seven months earlier, after weeks of sleepless deliberation, Thomas Jefferson Case—TJ to his many friends, Thomas to his wife—had decided to cross party lines and back a Republican friend for the U.S. congressional race. The local Democratic party had thrown a major fit and, when that hadn't worked, had openly sabotaged his own campaign for reelection to the North Carolina State House of Representatives. TJ lost the primary to a man willing to toe the party line, but his Republican friend went on to take the U.S. House seat from the Democratic incumbent. TJ had half-expected both outcomes. Yet his own loss hurt worse than he knew how to put into words.

The local papers made a big deal about it. In the run-up to the November elections TJ was dubbed "a man of principle" and credited for turning the U.S. congressional race around. Interviewers dwelt long and heavy on his "incredible sacrifice" and seemed to search for ways to make him squirm. TJ remained stoic, saying only that he was a lawyer first and a politician second. What was important, he told them time and time again, was what this young man had to offer.

The pain, the frustration, the endless wondering whether he had done the right thing—all this lay hidden too deep for anyone to see. Anyone, that is, except Catherine.

So when TJ awoke in the final hour before dawn he had a tough time believing he was really there; miles from the nearest telephone, snug in the cabin of the luxurious cruiser. The loudest sounds were Catherine's breathing and the lazy slap of water against the hull.

The boat was owned by his client and friend, Jeremy Hughes. Catherine called him their closet Midas. TJ called him the last of a dying breed. Everything Jeremy Hughes touched turned to gold. Everything. The man had a second-grade education, hadn't read but one book in his entire life, yet he made money as easy as other people made mistakes.

Take his last deal. Jeremy had purchased six hundred acres of worthless bottomland, the junk property that skirted three towns, and contained a rapidly sinking state road, a collective garbage dump, and a lake that had a maximum depth of four feet after a hard rain. It was land so miserable even the hunters steered clear. Jeremy bought it for fifty bucks an acre, brought in a special engineering group from Florida, convinced the surrounding towns to cough up half the engineers' fee, drained the boggy soil, then let it sit in dusty desolation for two winters and a summer. The second spring he parceled it into garden plots, hired people from as far as thirty miles away, and truck-farmed the whole six hundred acres. It turned out the land would grow okra the size of sweet corn and melons the size of basketballs. He contracted the produce out to first-class restaurants as far away as New York, charged them top dollar, and made a fortune.

When a local reporter interviewed him and asked how he had known the soil was so rich, Jeremy replied, "Smelled it."

"Speaking of the smell," the reporter said, "is it true that local townships have been trying to obtain state funds for twenty years to buy all this up and drain it just to get rid of the stink?"

"Might've stunk to some people, sonny," Jeremy replied. "Smelled like money to me."

☐   ☐   ☐

Twenty-three years ago, a younger and skinnier Jeremy Hughes had marched into TJ Case's law office one morning and announced he was looking for an honest man.

"Don't have to be smart, but smart'd sure help. More'n anything I need somebody who can keep other people's lawyers from climbing inside my wallet."

TJ stalled in what he called his best lawyer fashion, took in the man towering over his desk. And if Jeremy Hughes did anything well, it was tower. He stood six-foot-five in his muddy construction boots and weighed in at maybe a hundred and seventy pounds. He was a wiry bundle of barely contained energy, with blue-gray eyes that shot icy fire at everything they touched. Jeremy was dressed in what Catherine came to call the Hughes Formal Wear—khaki pants with a rough patch on one knee, checked shirt, and a hunting jacket with a broken zipper. His head was a shock of sandy hair that hadn't seen a barber for months. His oversized hands looked like shovels, with knuckles all bruised and broken from heavy work.

TJ asked Jeremy Hughes how he had found the law firm.

"Now that's a right interesting story," he drawled, plopping down in a chair and stretching out legs that seemed to go on for miles. "I'm sitting on a land deal that looks to make me a whole mess of money. Trouble is, you should see the old boy the other side's got working as their lawyer. Got the eyes of a snake and more oil on his hair than I use in my truck. Handed me this contract with fifty-seven pages of fine print and licked his lips. Yessir, he truly did. Eat me for breakfast is all that boy aims on doin'.

"I scampered fast as my feet could take me," Jeremy said. "Got up and out that door like my tail was on fire. Started drivin' around in my truck, didn't even know where I was goin'. Sat there at a stoplight like a dummy, watchin' the lights go from red to green and back to red, and knew I was licked. Can't do this deal without the other side, see. They own the land right around me. Want to build this humongous complex out there. They're offerin' a little cash up front, then a chunk of the development. That's all fine with me. I got no need of money right now, and these boys ain't no better or worse'n most builders I've met. They're just out for all they can grab. But their lawyer, now—he's a piece of work. He don't aim on leavin' more'n a greasy spot on the sidewalk when he gets through.

"So I bowed my head right there at that light, and I prayed. 'Help me, Lord,' I said. 'I can't do this myself. Show me what I gotta do.'"

Only four years out of law school, TJ had already developed a successful pose he used with new clients. He reacted like a tortoise sneaking back inside his shell, all watchful eyes and body armor until the fellow ran out of steam. Experience had taught him that he could take about ninety-five percent of what a client said during the first meeting and toss it out the window. His grandfather, the founder of the firm and TJ's guiding light during his early years, had put it differently. Every time he interviewed a new client, his grandfather had said, he was tempted to walk out the front door and make sure all the hot air hadn't lifted the building off its foundations.

A new client spent the better part of a sleepless night deciding what he did and did not want his lawyer to know. At the first meeting the client swept every particle of guilt or error under a monumental pile of words. TJ's grandfather had once suggested that the firm install a rack of wings and halos in the waiting room. That way new clients could stop in, try on a few pairs, find the ones that set right, save everybody a lot of time and trouble.

TJ Case's grandfather had used first meetings to clean his pipes. He had carved out the bowls, cleaned the stems, then polished the exteriors with a soft cloth he kept in his top drawer. A six-piper had been pretty standard. Anything over a ten-piper left him in a bad mood for the rest of the day.

As a fledgling lawyer, TJ had tried to stop new clients in mid-flow by asking a pertinent question. It hadn't worked any better for him than it did for anybody else. The clients stopped, looked tremendously aggrieved, said they were just coming to that, and went right back to where they'd left off.

So TJ began sketching, using his new-client meetings to draw what he called his "winged team." The first time Catherine saw one of his drawings, she laughed, clapped her hands, and said it looked like an angel that had had a head-on collision with a rocket. She began taping his best efforts to the refrigerator door, right next to their daughter's finger paintings.

When Jeremy Hughes started his story, TJ picked up his yellow legal pad, leaned back far enough to hide his artwork from view, and wrote "contract" in the upper right-hand corner. This was the beginning of a list he would review with the client once this Mr. Hughes ran out of steam. Under that he wrote "details of deal," then "bank," "quarterly audit for control," "name of lawyer and group," and "how about a smaller deal on his own?" Then he started sketching. This fellow was going to wear a football helmet with little Mercury wings for wind shear and flap control.

All this ceased when Jeremy Hughes announced that he had stopped and prayed. TJ later told Catherine that if the man had done a handstand on his antique leather chair, he would not have been any more surprised.

His secretary chose that moment to buzz him. It was an unspoken rule that whenever he was meeting with a new client, she would call him fifteen minutes into the conference and say whatever came to mind. TJ called it his escape clause.

"The neighbor's cat had eleven kitties under my cellar stairs last night," she said. "My little girl is in seventh heaven. She's got it in her head that they're all hers. I was wondering if I could sue my neighbor. Willful destruction of my peace of mind, or something like that?"

Normally he would think of something cute to say that would brighten each other's day with a shared smile. Today he simply said he would have to get back to her about it, and to hold all calls. He set the telephone down, turned his total attention back to Jeremy Hughes.

"Well, sir," Hughes continued, "I opened my eyes, turned the corner, and right smack dab in front of me stood the prettiest little grove of dogwoods you ever did see. And there beside it stood the Church of New Zion. I guess you know the one?"

TJ nodded. It was his family's church. Had been for over a hundred years.

"I won't try to make it out like something it wasn't," Hughes said. "Can't do that and expect you to give me honesty in return. Nossir. Truth is, I was a tad concerned when I saw the preacher out front, changing the Sunday announcement board. Had to stop and think when I realized where I was. But the answer to my prayer was maybe right there in front of me. So I said, Hidy, Lord, and went over to introduce myself."

Hughes chuckled. "The reverend wasn't havin' a bit of me when I first got there. Like to have froze me up solid, what with that face of his all clamped down hard as stone."

TJ nodded. He'd run afoul of Reverend Amos Taylor's "freeze 'em dead" look often enough as a child. Reverend Taylor had baptized him, married him, and buried more of his relatives than TJ was willing or able to count. For decades now the old man had been preaching and guarding his flock.

"When he decided I meant what I said and wasn't just some troublemaker, he popped out the biggest smile I'd ever seen. 'Nigh onto blinded me. Took me into his house, sat me down, and told me 'bout you. Carolina undergrad and Wake Forest Law, full scholarships to both, that's what he said."

TJ's antennae worked overtime, searching for the slightest hint of derision, found none. The man was genuine, he decided. Strange as a two-headed shoat, but genuine.

"Always had a great admiration for somebody with education. Envy, too," Hughes said easily. "My daddy was a backwoods country farmer. Never had much use for schoolin'. He said anybody who could sign his name and read the Bible knew all he needed to know. I've carried that burden with me all my life. Hardest test of faith the good Lord ever gave me was learnin' how to forgive my daddy."

A pang of old heartache struck TJ. He wondered if Reverend Amos had said anything about his own father to this man, decided not, wondered for the thousandth time if that wound would ever heal.

"Now maybe you see why I gotta find myself an honest man. I don't need just any lawyer. Nossir. Fact is, I could stand on any street corner in this city, whistle one time, and be up to my ears in lawyers. I need somebody I can trust. Somebody who'll tell me where the bear traps are. I told all this to your Reverend Taylor. He's a remarkable man, by the way. Know what he said?"

TJ shook his head. He couldn't imagine what Reverend Amos had told this gangly white man in his patched trousers and muddy work boots.

"Said he always liked to hear a man pray. Best way he'd found to look inside a man's heart. Said it was almost as though the Holy Spirit was listening with him, giving him a second pair of ears." Hughes' eyes had a luminous quality. "So that's what I'd like to ask you to do. Before I trust you with my family's future, if you see what I mean. What I'm asking, Mr. Case, is whether you'd be willing to pray with me."

It was all TJ could do to nod his head. He was too astonished to speak.

Jeremy Hughes hunkered toward the edge of the chair. "I'll just say a few words; then you can take over."

He bowed his head and began, "I thank you, Lord, for bringing me here today. It's a miracle that I'm here in this man's office. Shoot, my whole life's just one big miracle. Here I am, a hick from the backside of nowhere, sittin' in this fine office, doing deals with the best of them. It's all your doing, Lord, and I just want to thank you. Give me the strength to see what it is you want me to do with all this, and to live my life like you'd want me to. I ask all this in the precious name of Jesus Christ. Amen."

A balloon of pressure swelled in the center of TJ's chest, so big he could barely breathe, much less talk. Lord, Lord, help me, he said to himself. I have no idea what I ought to say. His heart sounded like faint thunder in his ears.

"Heavenly Father," he prayed, and heard a calm strength in his voice. It steadied him, eased the pressure, made it easier to continue. "You have brought two strangers here before you, as different as Simon the zealot and Matthew the tax collector. Yet here we are, Lord, praying to you together. We cannot be doing this ourselves. It is only your presence here with us, filling us with the Holy Spirit, that makes this prayer possible."

TJ heard himself saying the words, but he had no idea where the thoughts were coming from. None at all. It was like listening to someone else pray.

"We know that all things work for the good of those who love the Lord and are called according to His purpose. Are you calling us to a higher purpose, Father? If so, then give us the strength and the wisdom to do your holy will. Let us see clearly what must be done, and then enable us to carry out our tasks with joyous hearts and with voices that proclaim your wondrous name."

TJ paused to swallow hard. The lump was coming back to his throat. He wished he could stop, yet knew there was more to be said.

"Whenever two or more of us are gathered in your name, there you are also. You are with us here today, Lord. Be with us always. May every time we come together be blessed by your strength, your presence, your light to guide our way. In Christ's holy name we pray. Amen."

TJ raised his head in time to see Jeremy Hughes give his eyes a backhanded swipe behind the curtain of his hair. He felt like doing the same thing, but made do with a series of fierce blinks.

"Well, sir," Hughes cleared his throat, "I'm not sure I caught everything you said. I was too busy hearing something louder."

TJ permitted himself a smile. "I didn't say a thing."

Hughes laughed and whacked a dusty thigh. "Now if that ain't the truth." He inspected TJ frankly, said, "Excuse me for askin', but I'd as soon have this out in the open right now. You got anything against workin' with a white man?"

"No. Not one bit," TJ replied, glad he could answer truthfully. Holding his own gaze steady, he asked, "Do you mind having a black man for your lawyer?"

Hughes searched an inner pocket, pulled out a bulky sheaf of papers, handed them over, said, "Naw. The Lord turned me color blind 'bout two minutes ago."

□   □   □

TJ slid the cruiser's cabin door shut behind him and stepped out into the first faint hint of dawn. He knew Catherine was awake, but she would lie and doze for another hour. This was a daily gift she gave him. She guarded his hour of solitude more fiercely than he did, claimed it was all done in her own best interest. Catherine called it his hour of sanity. Remind you what's important, she would say, before you go out and let the world beat cymbals upside your head. You're what's important, he always replied. Now you're talking truth, she'd say. You just see you don't forget it.

He uncovered the portable Bunsen burner, filled a saucepan from the fresh-water container, lit the stove, and set the pan in place. From the cupboard under one of the seats he pulled out a mug, a flashlight, a spoon, a jar of instant coffee and his Bible. Catherine had arranged all the items before going to bed. Years ago, when they had first started using Jeremy's boat, TJ would jokingly ask her if she had remembered to put out his survival kit. Now it was simply unspoken habit.

The boat was far too big for the lake. When Catherine first saw it, she told Jeremy that fishing the Inland Waterway in it would be like putting a whale in a swimming pool. Jeremy replied, yeah, well, anybody who don't like it don't need to come back. That boat has more bathrooms than my momma's house, Catherine told him. But does your momma's house float, Jeremy asked. It would, Catherine replied, if she spent as much on it as you did on this. I need a boat big enough for my kids, Jeremy explained. Gotta have room for my kids.

Jeremy never went on the water without at least a dozen children screaming and scrambling over everywhere. The owner of the dock where he kept the boat called it a fisherman's worst nightmare come to life. Every time Jeremy came to pick up the boat, the fellow would stick his head out of the office and say something like, be sure to check it good for bombs.

Some of Jeremy's kids were from the two area orphanages, others were children of local tobacco sharecroppers. There were also a few local

Indians, especially the ones whose parents hung around street corners and drank up welfare checks as fast as they came in. The boat was called *Asylum,* which Jeremy was quick to point out meant "a place of refuge."

Ever since Jeremy's wife died of cancer eleven years ago, his life had revolved around his business interests and his kids. He was the unnamed sponsor of both the orphanages, as well as founder of a regional summer camp for the underprivileged. Whenever he was asked if he had any children of his own, Jeremy always replied, at last count, four hundred and sixteen.

□　□　□

TJ filled his cup with boiling water, spooned in coffee, flicked on the flashlight, and opened his Bible. He was working his way through Hebrews, but he always began his days by simply opening the Book and reading whatever passage caught his eye. He would then drink his coffee, meditate on the passage for a time, and pray. With his second cup he would begin his regular study.

The first passage he opened to was in Isaiah: "I heard the voice of the Lord, saying, Whom shall I send, and who will go for us? Then said I, Here *am* I; send me. And he said, Go, and tell this people, Hear ye indeed, but understand not; and see ye indeed, but perceive not."

TJ switched off the flashlight and looked out across the water. I haven't done enough, he thought, giving way to a familiar guilt. I have everything in the world. Everything. And I still waste most of my time worrying over things that don't mean squat. Here I am with a wonderful wife. Two angels for daughters. Five lovely grandchildren. A good job. More money than I know what to do with. The best friend in the world.

He sipped his coffee and nodded his head. I waste too much time worrying about things of this world. What I've given back isn't even a drop in the bucket.

Almost in reply, he caught fleeting glimpses of his life. The retainer Jeremy paid him was more than enough to live on. Over the years he had gradually shifted other clients to his partners and taken on an increasing number of defendants who could not pay.

A stint on the local school board had led to his election to the city council. From there to the county board of commissioners. Ten years later he was elected to the state legislature.

In moments of strength, as he had watched the destruction of this second career over the seven longest months of his life, he had felt deep in his heart that he was following the principles set out by God. In weaker moments, which were many, he could only pray that he was.

He remembered what his grandfather had told him on the eve of his first election to the state legislature, just three months before the old gentleman had passed away. I'm so proud of you I could burst, he had said, but I'm gonna tell you something I don't want you ever to forget. Don't ever look to politics as a source of income, son. Do that and you're on the road to destruction. Keep yourself on the straight and narrow, a shining example to all those pride-swollen, idol-worshiping fools. And the instant you find yourself needing the money or the position or the title beside your name, quit! Stay on, and sooner or later you'll sell your soul to the devil called compromise. Stay in the service of your people only as long as it really is service. When it stops being service and starts being a job, get out!

The first Christmas after TJ's election, Catherine had stitched a needlepoint plaque for him. It read: "Whosoever will be great among you shall be your servant," a verse from the Gospel of Mark. TJ hung it in his legislative chambers, directly across from his desk. When visitors commented on it, he told them it was his lifeline. Now it was upstairs in the attic gathering dust, along with all the other debris from his political life. Once he could look at it again without feeling a pang of loss, he would probably hang it in his law office.

□   □   □

Through the faint veil of dawn the nearby shoreline slowly grew visible. Clumps of muhly grass hugged the waterline, and a dogwood painted with autumn colors nestled between two stumpy pond pines. Beyond that, red cedar and spindly pine trees rose like ghostly sentinels in the morning mist. The air was close and breathless, the water utterly still. It was warm for November, and TJ was comfortable in his flannel shirt and jeans.

Little Frying Pan Lake was the worst-kept secret in North Carolina, and wasn't really a lake at all. It was set snug in the heart of a marsh that lay off the Inland Waterway. The place could be reached only through a very narrow, very deep passage that was impossible to find unless somebody showed the first-timer how to line up the old cedar stump, the derelict pier, and the correct point on the compass.

From the air, Little Frying Pan and its entry channel looked like a skillet with a bent handle. The body of water was a half-mile wide and lined with meandering marsh banks, muhly grass, and rotting trees hung heavy with Spanish moss. It was the best spawning ground for large-mouth bass this side of the Everglades. Trouble was, the place had simply become overfished.

Local fishing guides swore customers to absolute secrecy, took them in, and hoped for a big tip. The customers in turn brought friends they wanted to impress with their knowledge of local lore. Stories about fair-sized catches grew into legends about an Indian guide who caught a large-mouth bass so big it sank his canoe.

Jeremy sometimes talked about how it had been twenty years ago, when local fishermen would never have dreamed of entering the haven under power. Back then, they cut their motors halfway down the channel and rowed in. It was an unspoken rule, like not talking in church. A hushed silence hung over the place, and fishermen greeted each other with solemn waves and hand signals. Lifting the stringer from the water meant you had a good catch. Details were kept for the boat dock.

Nowadays on a summer Sunday the passage looked like an interstate highway. Boats swooped up and down the channel with high-powered outboards whining and rumbling, their wakes swamping the muhly grass. Fresh arrivals glared at other boats as though they were trespassing on private property. Most of the local fishermen and almost all of the fish had long since departed.

But during the rest of the year, the early mornings still held the awesome hush of a sanctuary. Jeremy Hughes loved to maneuver his boatload of kids down the passage, after first stopping and carefully explaining to all and sundry that he would personally strangle the first nonbeliever who dared disturb the haven's silence.

Jeremy always tried to arrive right at dusk, after all the fishermen had given up in disgust and gone home. He would send the kids to bed with a Bible passage and a story. He tried to instill a pride of heritage in the Indians, a wonder of history in the sharecroppers' sons and daughters, a reverence for nature in them all.

TJ and Catherine had made the trip with Jeremy and the kids once a month until the crisis of the past half-year had begun. They always departed ever humbled by the wisdom of this uneducated man.

Jeremy lavished all the love he had on these children who had been fed the dregs of affection. There's three words you're gonna learn the meaning of, he told them time and again, even if I gotta drill holes in your thick skulls and stuff it in. And what are they, he would roar. Faith, hope and love, the children would shout back, laughter shining from their faces. And what's the greatest of these, he would ask. Love, they would cry in unison. Right, he would say. I guess I don't drown you after all.

□   □   □

A distant whooping echoed through the soft autumn morning. Soon the air would be filled with a thousand birdsongs, a choir that TJ had enjoyed since childhood. He breathed a deep sigh and gave silent thanks for the wonder of another dawn.

Then it happened, and his world was changed forever.

With a grace and ease that made the power even more awesome, a silence descended upon him. It was not the stillness of the morning. It was a presence that flooded his heart, his mind, his entire being and *commanded* him:

Be still.

As gentle as it was powerful, as loving as it was demanding, the Presence was all-consuming. And the Presence was God.

The dawn became a holy fire. The lake, the sky, the shore—all were filled with a holy light.

Blinded by the all-transforming power, yet knowing without question what he was witnessing, TJ fell to his knees. He was filled with a single thought: I am unworthy.

In the mirror of this perfect light came a clear and total vision of life's purpose. He was created to worship God. All else seemed a shabby pretense of sham and indulgence. A sin. A lie.

I am unworthy.

The light and stillness intensified, and the Voice spoke.

Who will speak for Me?

There was no doubt, no need to wonder. The request was a perfect gift of total love, and in its answer was the key to life.

I will, TJ Case replied.

Then go to your rulers, the gentle Voice said to him. *They are in need of Me.*

An instant of confusion. Then a shock of understanding. Washington, TJ said. I am to go to Washington. For a moment his spirit quailed, and he asked aloud, "But what will I say?"

The light and power began to diminish, drawing down to the Bible that had fallen from his lap. Gradually the world returned to the awakening dawn, yet a passage on the open page continued to shine with a holy light.

With trembling hands TJ picked up his Bible and read:

"Behold, I send you forth as sheep in the midst of wolves: be ye therefore wise as serpents, and harmless as doves. But beware of men: for they will deliver you up to the councils, and they will scourge you in their synagogues; and ye shall be brought before governors and kings for my sake, for a testimony against them and the Gentiles. But when they deliver you up, take no thought how or what ye shall speak: for it shall be given you in that same hour what ye shall speak."

⊣ TWO ⊢

Congressman John Silverwood, the junior member of the United States House of Representatives from North Carolina, allowed his two luncheon partners to enter the restaurant before him. It was clearly expected and all part of the game.

The customary period of decompression following his recent election had been cut short by the request to come to Washington for this luncheon. His two colleagues were here because the Republican National Committee was having its first strategy session for congressional committee appointments. They had a hole in their schedules and decided it was a good time to meet with Silverwood. The possibility that the newly elected congressman might find it inconvenient to fly to Washington on twelve-hour notice did not enter their minds. They called and Silverwood came. It was that simple.

First to pass through the restaurant's entrance was the senior senator from North Carolina, Reginald Erskins, staunch defender of the right and powerful kingpin on a number of major committees. Senator Erskins was a tall man in his early sixties who hid excess poundage under carefully tailored suits. The mane of silver hair, the self-satisfied expression, the pompous bearing—it all spoke of a man most at home with the mantle of worldy power.

Following Erskins was Ted Robinson, chairman of the North Carolina Republican party, a man who had stood behind innumerable thrones for more than thirty years. When he had taken on the chairmanship, the Republicans had been, in his own words, the biggest joke in the state. Finding Republicans in North Carolina, he had once told an interviewer, was harder than finding seashells in the Blue Ridge Mountains.

But all that had changed, and changed drastically. In these most recent elections Robinson had delivered a Republican governor, fourteen new Republican state legislators, seven new state senators, and the first Republican U.S. Congressman from the eastern district in the country's history. If John Silverwood held any importance at all in Ted Robinson's eyes, it was because he represented even better things to come.

The Monocle was a smallish restaurant on the Senate side of Capitol Hill. Silverwood thought it horribly overpriced, but he was not yet accustomed to the cost of living in this city. The size of the mortgage he was going to pay for his two-bedroom Georgetown townhouse gave him nightmares.

The maitre d' bowed and scraped over the senator, barely gave Silverwood a glance, then marched them to what he announced was the senator's regular table. Silverwood wondered how on earth three people were going to sit at it. Maybe they were expected to hold their plates in their laps.

The table was about as big as a Carolina serving dish and covered with layers of starched linen. Silverwood had to suck in his belly and scrunch around to keep from bouncing the guy at the next table off the wall.

Ted Robinson was equally unimpressed. He watched the maitre d' stalk off, snapping orders at bustling waiters, said, "That is positively the fakiest, most ridiculous Italian accent I have ever heard. What is he, Persian?"

"Lebanese," the senator replied, casually glancing through the menu before shutting it and setting it down. It almost covered the table. "The fellow at The Rotunda was Persian."

"Yeah, that's right." Robinson gave a frosty smile. "What was his name, Alfredo? Alfonzo?"

"Something like that," the senator replied. "What a character."

"Not anymore," Robinson said. He looked at Silverwood and explained, "Back, what, eight or nine years ago—"

"Longer," the senator interrupted.

"Whenever. Back in the Carter administration there was this restaurant near the National Democratic Club called The Rotunda. The maitre d' was this really suave-looking Persian. He drove a forty-thousand-dollar Porsche and had a house in Georgetown."

"Not an apartment," the senator emphasized. "A house."

"Yeah, well, one day our pal was found in the back of his Porsche with a bullet in his head. He was supposedly supplying drugs to the staffers on the Hill."

"I never liked that restaurant," the senator said. "Even on the sunniest day the place was dark as a tomb."

"Nobody'd go in there after that," Robinson went on. "So they closed it down and the Democrats moved their club in there."

"On Saint Patrick's Day Tip O'Neill would come in and sing 'When Irish Eyes Are Smiling,' then dance a jig."

Throughout the leisurely lunch the senator and the party chief entertained their freshman colleague with bits of Washington lore, the latest gossip, predictions over who would be picked for the choicest posts within the new administration, and instructions about how the new boy on Capitol Hill was expected to field certain major issues. Silverwood kept his mouth shut and listened. These men could be his most powerful allies or his worst enemies.

John Silverwood was from old Carolina stock. He often pointed out that relatives still worked a tobacco farm which was a hundred years older than the United States of America. The fact that the only farming he had ever done was plant a few flower bulbs was seldom mentioned.

Silverwood was not a big man. He stood an inch under six feet, but most people thought of him as taller because he intentionally held himself very erect. He maintained a rigid workout schedule, pumping iron and playing racquetball four times a week. Those ninety minutes of unleashed fury were the only time he let himself go from the emotional armor he showed to the outside world.

The junior congressman was a patient man. It was not the patience of a calm sea, however; it was more the tension of a steel cable pulled taut by a thousand-pound load. He had waited through two terms in county politics, six years in the state legislature, and eleven of the longest pre-election months of his life to get to where he was now. Waited, listened, and learned.

He was one of the new breed, set to wheel and deal in the world of modern Washington politics. The centralized power structure, where rule of might was balanced between a strong president and the senior members of Congress, was crumbling. Nowadays power was in perpetual flux, passing from back-room staffer to newly elected congressman to assistant secretary and back again, its movement governed by the issue of the moment. Who held the reins was determined more by the media and special interest groups than by experience or seniority.

John Silverwood had studied this long and hard. He was determined to become an expert at headline-grabbing media politics. He knew that the player's identity was far less important than how the media portrayed him. He had trained to develop a solid television image. He was armed, he was elected, and as soon as Congress convened he would be stalking his elusive prey: Power.

He was careful not to let any of this show. The Old Guard was solidly entrenched in the North Carolina Republican party. They allowed no threat to the established pattern. Fresh blood was admitted only after showing themselves to be true followers of the system. Silverwood had long since developed as bland an expression as his craggy features would allow. What he really felt, what he really wanted, remained buried deep.

Over coffee the conversation turned to his recent election. Self-satisfied backslapping over the addition of his district to the Republican ranks led to optimistic predictions on how the trend might continue.

"Been a right busy week," Senator Erskins said. "What with meeting the new administration and the committee going hard on all the new appointments."

"Tough," Silverwood said, silently envying him.

"Had lunch with one of our new hotshot power-brokers this week. What was his name, Ted?"

"Jim Lockes. He's responsible for senior appointments. Slated to be Chief of White House Personnel after the January swearing-in."

"Said they were looking out for some skirts and colors."

Silverwood looked a question at Robinson.

"Women and minorities," Robinson explained. "They've got a staff over there right now, reminds me of some southern college fraternity."

"Diversity," the senator added. "Fellow said they were looking for a little more diversity in the ranks. Had this little wispy voice, like, 'Please let us know if there's anyone we should be talking to.'"

"And we thought about your friend," Robinson said.

"Or Ted did," the senator added. "I'd heard something about him, of course, but Washington's kept me so busy I don't know which way's up anymore. That reminds me, son. I hope you know how sorry I am that I couldn't make it back to give you a hand more often during the campaign."

Silverwood made some vague noise and seethed inside. The senator had shown an initial preference for a second Republican candidate, one who had previously worked for Erskins's own reelection. But the polls had shown early on that the other fellow had a snowball's chance in the Sahara of getting elected. So rather than lending his support to Silverwood, the party's chosen candidate, Erskins had hibernated for eight months in Washington. He had not shown his face a single time in Silverwood's district.

"I heard something about how this black fellow may have made the difference," the senator went on. "What was his name again?"

"Thomas Jefferson Case," Robinson replied, lowering his voice to a conspiratorial level. Credit was never voiced loudly in Washington. "And there's no 'may' about it. John's sitting here with us right now because of what that man did."

"He definitely tipped the balance," Silverwood agreed.

"Crossed over party lines in the middle of the campaign, did I get that right?" The senator patted his coiffure into place. "The man must be a fool."

"Not at all," Robinson countered. "I've met him on a number of occasions, and the man is anything but a fool. He chose to stand on his principles even when it meant committing political suicide."

"What was the issue?" the senator asked. "Something about education, wasn't it?"

"He wants to establish special programs for gifted children," Silverwood replied. "Education's been the basis of his entire political career. He finally decided that the Democratic ideal of equal education for all just wasn't working. Put an awful lot of thought and work into it. Spent over two years traveling the entire southeast, gathering statistics and talking to local authorities. The report he put together for the Democratic Party Caucus last year was nothing less than incredible."

"You've read it?" the senator asked.

"Most of it."

"So did I," Robinson said. "That was one of the issues we had to agree on before he'd give his support to John. I thought at first we were just dealing with another black who'd had his pride hurt. But not anymore."

"He took it to the Democrats not once, but seven different times," said Silverwood. "They patted him on the head, made some kind of polite noises, and sent him away. So he got involved with the local school system, monitoring the four regional high schools. Then he took it to the papers."

"Seems I recall seeing some headlines about that," the senator said.

" 'Showdown Over Educational Policy,' " Silverwood supplied. "That was back, oh, the summer before last."

"The Asheville paper dubbed him 'The Lonely Knight,' " Robinson said. Asheville was the original stronghold of the state's Republican party, and home to the only right-leaning newspaper in North Carolina.

"This was not some casual decision," Silverwood informed them. "When he finally came to see me, the man was in agony. Really at the end of his rope. He did it because he just couldn't stand there and let them destroy our educational system. That's exactly what he said."

"Seems amazing that you'd get this from a black man," the senator mused. "I'd have thought he'd believe special ed would wind up being just for the little white kids."

"That's the most amazing part," Robinson said.

"As long as the program is really open to everybody on the basis of merit alone," Silverwood explained, "his study shows that there's an incredibly high proportion of minority students who come in. His study went against every grain of Democratic policy-thinking for the past twenty years. The key issue, TJ feels—"

"That's what he's called? TJ?"

"TJ Case," said Robinson. "Mention that name in Democratic party circles these days and you'll have a dozen stroke victims on your hands."

"TJ feels that the key is not to equalize education but to equalize the availability of education," Silverwood continued. "And the way to do this is to set the gifted schools in the center cities."

"In the slums?" The senator was shocked.

"Right in the middle of minority neighborhoods," Robinson explained. "Pour a bunch of government money into renovating one of the old schools, make it into a model kind of place. They've done one in Raleigh, and it's pretty incredible. TJ walked me through it. The neighborhood has been totally transformed in just five years. I'm not kidding you. Five years. Rich families raise a stink because the neighborhood's not safe for their kids, so police protection picks up. The area gets too hot for the nasties, so all of a sudden it's kind of a nice place to live. New people start moving in. Not the really rich—they mostly send their kids to private schools anyway. Upper middle class, young professionals. Minorities living next door to whites. I tell you, the difference is incredible."

"Why haven't I seen this?" The senator looked at both of them accusingly. "You're telling me something like this is going on right under my nose and I've never even heard about it?"

"Reggie, it's one school in the whole state," Robinson said soothingly. "Four hundred kids out of how many? A hundred thousand? We only found out about it because Case made us go down and look it over."

Silverwood held his peace. There was little to be gained from stating the obvious. Senator Reginald Erskins was rock-steady and well-informed on the issues he considered primary, but he turned an almost blind eye to everything else.

Erskins gave his staffers enormous power. On secondary issues they made both the initial and final policy analyses, then simply told him how to vote. In return the senator demanded unswerving loyalty. Anyone foolish enough to disagree with him on a primary issue was given five minutes to pack.

Some senators knew every state legislator back home by their first name. They considered it a matter of principle to know exactly how each felt about issues of key interest to the state. Erskins held no such views. He had once been heard to refer to the state legislators as those folks riding at the back of the bus.

The people had elected Erskins because of what he stood for. His job was to make his stand as hard and fast and noisy as possible. Any issue not directly related to this premise was shunted aside for his staffers to handle. So it was no surprise that he had not heard of the recent developments in education, nor that he had only a vague knowledge of TJ Case. Education was nowhere near the top of Senator Erskins' list.

"TJ Case is real strong on building the equal opportunity concept into this program," Silverwood went on. "He gets pretty hot about racial bias in schools."

"What does he call it?" Robinson smiled his tight little grimace. " 'Teaching our children the absolute worst of what we are,' something like that."

" 'Showing a casual disregard for the basic teachings of Jesus Christ,' " Silverwood said. "I like that one best."

"So did the papers," Robinson agreed, adding for the senator's benefit, "He's a strong Christian and makes no bones about it."

"You really like this fellow, don't you?" the senator observed.

Robinson hedged in his best political manner. "He's impressed a lot of people, Reggie. Right across the color line."

"I seem to recall that the papers made a big thing of his endorsement," the senator said.

"Went all over the district with me," Silverwood agreed. "Introduced me to all the local leadership. Made I don't know how many speeches."

"We about worked that man to death," Robinson said.

"What are you trying to tell me? That he did all this out of the goodness of his heart?"

"All we *promised* was that we would get his ideas a hearing in Washington," said Robinson. "It could be a powerful move, though. Bring this man up to Washington, hold him out to the southern blacks as an example of how the Republican party would treat them."

The senator mulled this over, said, "The blacks sure made the difference in the last election."

Robinson nodded grim agreement. After a bitter four-month battle, the Democratic candidate had carried the state's second senatorial seat by a margin of less than two percent of the total vote. There was no question that the solid backing of the black vote had tipped the balance.

"Something like this could make all the difference the next time we go to bat," Robinson agreed.

Erskins leaned back in his chair and focused his gaze on the far wall. The other two sat and watched and let him muse in silence.

"If we put him on our staff, it'll look too much like we're making a token payoff," he said, thinking aloud. "The blacks are getting too smart to swallow that sort of thing. It needs to be something independent."

There was another long pause; then he turned to Silverwood. "So do you think we could get your friend to Washington?"

Silverwood made his expression doubtful. "I don't know. This is a real local boy we're talking about here. He's lived in North Carolina all his life. There could be some chance, but I'd have to work on him hard."

The senator nodded his understanding. "But he's a good man?"

"The best," Silverwood agreed. He hesitated, as though the thought had just come to him. "What about something in the White House?"

"Might not be a bad idea," the senator agreed. "Since he's so devoted to this education thing, we could try Special Assistant to the President for Education?"

"The White House," Robinson exuded. "Great. The blacks'd love it."

"It's perfect," Silverwood agreed. He had to clench down tight on the jitters in his belly to keep his emotions from showing. TJ Case would be his own little White House mole. He was going to pump Silverwood full of inside information. Being the first in the know was vital to gaining real power.

"I'll talk to that fellow Lockes soon as I get back to the office," the senator said. "The incoming administration and I are at loggerheads on a couple of major issues here, so there's room for a little horse trading."

"You might bring up the fact that they haven't tapped many people from North Carolina to serve on the President's staff yet," Robinson suggested. "That might be good for a couple of extra points."

"Leave that to me," the senator replied, still looking into the distance. "The President's made education a priority issue. This wouldn't be a bad place to have our own man, eh, Congressman?"

"Not at all," Silverwood replied.

"Special Assistant to the President for Education," Robinson repeated, clearly pleased. "The black voters'll eat it up with a spoon."

"It's better than I'd hoped," Silverwood agreed, impressed with this casual show of power and determined that they wouldn't overlook his role in all this. "I'm pretty sure I can get TJ to accept it. I'll have to push hard, but I think it can be done."

"Then it's settled," the senator declared, and waved for the check. "Get in touch with my secretary tomorrow. I should know by then if we can work it out."

"When you talk with this fellow Case," Robinson said, "make sure he understands what we're doing for him. We're not out for gratitude. We want his loyalty."

"And make it sound urgent," added the senator. "Easier to push a man if he thinks the fate of the nation rests on him making a decision in the next fifteen minutes."

⊣ THREE ⊢

When TJ and Catherine pulled up to the boat dock, Jeremy was waiting at the end of the pier. Beside him pranced their youngest grand-daughter, five-year-old Macon. She was waving her one free hand wildly over her head and struggling to break free, as though she wanted to jump in the water and rush out to greet them. Which was probably why Jeremy held her other hand in a death-grip.

"Her mother went home an hour ago" were his first words. "Said it was either drown her or leave her with me."

"Did not," Macon corrected. "Daddy got a 'mergency and Uncle Jeremy said he'd wait and come back with y'all." Macon's daddy was a surgeon in Raleigh, and her mother was TJ and Catherine's eldest daughter.

"If I let go your hand, do you promise to behave yourself?" Jeremy asked.

"Don't try squeezing blood from a stone," Catherine warned know-ingly. To Macon she said, "Honey, run take this to the car."

Jeremy watched Macon struggle down the pier with a suitcase slightly smaller than she was, then turned back and said, "Everything okay?"

She glanced toward the cabin of the boat, where TJ was busy shut-ting down all systems. "Yes and no."

"I didn't loan you my boat for y'all to go out there and fight."

Catherine did not smile. "Let's wait till we're home, Jem. There's a lot to talk about."

TJ chose that moment to come out of the cabin. He reached across the rail to grip Jeremy's hand. "Hello, Jem."

Searching his friend's face, Jeremy spotted something he'd never seen there before. A calm strength—and something else. There was a mighty peculiar light to his eyes.

"Y'all haven't been fightin'," Jeremy said. It was not a question.

"No," Catherine answered, still subdued, her eyes on her husband. "It's not that."

"You look all lit up like a Christmas tree," Jeremy remarked to TJ.

"Everything's fine, Jem," TJ replied quietly.

"Let it wait till we're home," Catherine repeated, handing up the cooler. "Here comes little Miss Hurricane again."

When they were packed and ready to roll, Jeremy elected to let Catherine drive so he could sit in back with Macon. That way, he told the girl, he wouldn't have to reach over anyone when it came time to feed her to the bears. He was gruffer with her than with the other four grandchildren because she was his favorite, and he was embarrassed by how much he cared for her. With her child's perception, she sensed the truth and answered with a love as strong as his own.

Jeremy divided his attention between Macon, who was giving her doll a detailed account of the weekend, and his two friends in the front seat. As he watched, he listened to his own inner voice, an old habit he relied on constantly.

Once a business associate asked him how on earth he had figured that a deal was going to come down as it did. It was plain as day, Jeremy replied; there for all the world to see. Maybe for you, the man said. You know, it just amazes me how much people don't see, Jeremy told him. It's like they're so afraid of seein' something that'll rock their little boat that they go through life with blinders on. All they hear is the storm inside their heads. Then when somethin' happens they coulda seen a mile off if they'd wanted to, they go screamin' around the place like chickens with their heads cut off. What did I do to deserve this? Why is life so cruel to me? Jeremy shook his head. I don't know what's worse—watchin' it happen, or tryin' to tell somebody about it and listen to 'em call me a fool.

So he observed the pair in front as carefully as he knew how, and he listened to what his gut was telling him. There hadn't been a fight. He was sure of that. When Catherine glanced at TJ, it was with a light of real pride, real love, real support. Maybe they had just had a special weekend—man and wife. But Jeremy didn't think that was it. Something had happened. He had that itchy feeling down his spine, the feeling that sometimes came before a big deal opened his way. Something had happened.

TJ had always been a silent kind of fellow, but there was a different stillness about him today. It seemed to overwhelm the car, touching everybody but Macon, who was the happy bundle of energy she always was. TJ sat and stared out the front window, although there was no rigidity to his frame, no sullenness, no anger. The man had changed somehow, Jeremy was sure of it, but he couldn't put his finger on why he felt that way. Back on the boat dock there had been a distance to his gaze, as though he were looking out into eternity.

Macon set her doll down on the seat between them, straightened the starchy little dress and patted the hair in place, then settled back against the door so she could look directly at Jeremy.

"Uncle Jeremy, it's time for a story," she announced.

"A story! What on earth gives you the idea I can tell stories?"

"'Cause you always do, and you never do till I ask," she replied.

"What's in it for me?"

"For us," Catherine corrected. "We all get fifteen minutes of peace from little Miss Precocious Maximus."

"That's me," Macon explained to Jeremy.

"What's that you say?"

"What Gram said. Precious something. She means I'll be quiet if you tell me a story."

Jeremy stuck his lower lip out and nodded his head thoughtfully. "And will you?"

She shrugged her shoulders. "Depends if I like it."

He leaned over close to her face and squinted at her. "Did somebody try and tell me you're just five years old?"

"Going on seventeen," Catherine said.

"Can I start it off?" Macon asked.

"Might as well," Jeremy decided. "Man's gotta be smart enough to know when he's beat."

"Okay," she replied. She kicked the edge of the seat and scrunched up her face in deep concentration.

"I know! I know!" she cried. "Once upon a time, a preacher died and went to heaven."

Jeremy silently counted off several seconds before he asked, "That's it?"

"Honey, that's the end of a story, not the beginning," Catherine told her.

"No, it's not. It's my story and I can start it any way I want to. Right, Uncle Jeremy?"

Jeremy bobbed his head from side to side and stalled with "How long ago was once upon a time?"

"Aaahboouut, threedaysago."

Jeremy drummed his fingers on the window and hummed a toneless "Three days, three days," then snapped his fingers. "But, honey child, you forgot to tell me the most important thing."

"I did?"

"Why sure. You didn't tell me where the man was from. Shoot, if'n you'd said the man was from that little podunky town in South Carolina—what's its name, Farmville—why, I'd've known in a minute what you was talkin' about."

"Make it a long one," Macon said, and curled up in her corner of the seat.

"'Course I'd heard about Father Coughlin passin' away. Whole county talked about it, seein's how he was the only Catholic preacher that side of Greenville. Rumor had it the bishop up north was having trouble fillin' the spot, on account of how a lot of the locals didn't care too much for Catholics—most of 'em bein' Baptist and all. So while the priests were waitin' for the bishop to make up his mind, they got to callin' it Purgatory, South Carolina."

"What's that?" Macon asked.

"Don't interrupt, honey," Catherine said.

"What's what?" Jeremy asked.

"Purga—I can't say it."

"Purgatory? Well, that's kinda like a bus stop in the sky. People who aren't sure where they're headed kinda sit around there and hope God is havin' one of His good days."

"Don't be blasphemous, Jem," Catherine said. "Honey, purgatory is something Catholics believe in. They say it's a place where people go after they die if they've sinned too much to be let into heaven. They stay there and wait for a while and then God lets them into Paradise."

"Did you understand what she just said?" Jeremy asked Macon.

The little girl nodded. "Cath'lics go there if they're bad. Tell the story, Uncle Jeremy."

"Rule number one in raising children," Catherine said. "If they ask you a question, tell them the truth."

"You know what?" Jeremy said to Macon. "You're 'bout the remarkablest little girl I ever laid eyes on."

She slid back in the seat, made herself smaller than normal with pleasure. Her eyes fastened on his face.

"Well, like I said, old Father Coughlin dies and goes to heaven. And when he gets to the pearly gates, Saint Peter's there to greet him. He opens up that big book of his, the one where all God's children's got their name written down, and puts a little tick beside his name. Then just before he gives the father his wings and halo, Saint Peter asks if he'd mind watchin' over things for a second.

" 'I've been sittin' here nigh on two thousand years,' Saint Peter said, 'and I'm in bad need of a coffee break.' "

"I'm not sure this is something I want my grandchild to hear," said Catherine.

"I knew there was a reason I never told stories when grown-ups were around," Jeremy said. "They don't know how to be seen and not heard."

"Not to mention the fact that my daughter would skin you alive if she heard you talk like that."

"She would not," Macon piped up. "Momma says Uncle Jeremy's got more sense in his big toe than most people got in their whole body. Momma says the world would be a better place if there was more people like Uncle Jeremy. Momma says—"

"All right young lady, that's enough." Catherine held up her hand.

"You just mind what you say, Jeremy. You're neither too big nor too old to get a piece of my mind."

"She means a spanking," Macon explained.

"I know she does," Jeremy replied. "This is about the noisiest story I ever told. Now where was I?"

"Father Coughlin's waiting for Saint Peter to get back," Macon said.

"He sure is. Feels pretty good too, he does. He hasn't had it all peaches and cream, tryin' to keep his flock together in the middle of Baptist country. But standin' there lookin' at Paradise stretched out beyond him, Father Coughlin decides it's all been worthwhile.

"He hasn't been standin' there for more'n a couple of minutes when, lo and behold, who should show up in front of the pearly gates but Preacher Jones, the minister of the biggest Baptist church in Farmville. The father pops down behind Saint Peter's desk—out of habit, you know, like he was still on earth and had to decide whether to face the preacher and feel the daggers in his back or hide behind a tree. He crouches there and watches the preacher look around, tryin' to get his bearings, and he thinks about some of the things he had to put up with. He remembers how Preacher Jones had called the father's congregation 'no-account idol-worshiping, godless heathens.' He recalls the time the preacher wrote a letter to every Catholic in town, urgin' them to become Baptists and save their immortal souls. He remembers the revivals where loudspeakers shouted out the town's shame over havin' those 'Yankee Pope-lovers with their loose morals and shameful ways come down and take away good factory jobs from the Baptist brethren.' Father Coughlin thinks about all those things and a couple of others your grandmother here won't let me mention, and he decides it was time for a little fun.

"The father kind of eases himself up, little by little, from behind Saint Peter's desk. It takes a moment for Preacher Jones to realize who it is, but when he does his eyes bug out and his jaw hits his chest. Coulda knocked that preacher over with a feather. He takes this scary look around, and you could tell exactly what he was thinkin'—like, hey, did I take a wrong turn somewhere? Father Coughlin knows it too, and says, 'If it's heaven you're lookin' for, you've found it.' Then he makes his face real stern. ''Course, we'll have to see whether it's the right place for you.'

"Preacher Jones is busy remembering the same things as Father Coughlin. You can tell on account of how he commences to sweat. But being Baptist, he decides the best thing to do is bluster. 'What d'ya mean by that?'

" 'Exactly what I said,' the father told him. Then the Catholic man makes this big to-do about turnin' a couple of pages in Saint Peter's book. He leans down close and starts squintin' his way up and down the page, runnin' his finger up and down the lines, flippin' the pages back and forth, pretendin' to search that old book. Couldn't make hide nor hair of it, of course. Peter wrote everything down in that old language, you know, Arabic."

"Aramaic," Catherine corrected.

"Just what I said. Anyway, all the while Preacher Jones is busy bein' about as scared as any man ever deserves to get.

"Finally Father Coughlin heaves this big sigh, pulls at his lower lip with two fingers, and scrunches up his forehead like he's real concerned. He flips one more page, decides Preacher Jones has cooked about long enough, and says, 'It don't look like your name is down here anywheres.'

"The preacher had to grab hold of the gate to keep his legs from bucklin'. His voice gets all squeaky with panic. 'Could you look one more time? Maybe you missed it.'

" 'I done checked it twice already,' the father said. 'I think you oughta go on down and ask by that other door. See if they got your reservation.'

"Old Preacher Jones looks about ready for his second fatal heart attack of the day. 'Couldn't you maybe just write my name in there yourself?'

"Father Coughlin gets this shocked look on his face and slams the book shut. 'Not on your life!'

"Then old Preacher Jones drops down on his knees and starts cryin'. 'I'm beggin' you, brother, one Carolina Christian to another. You just gotta let me in.'

"This was about the most fun Father Coughlin'd had in years. He gets this sublime expression on his face and says, 'Well, maybe there is one way.'

"Preacher Jones grabs for it like he was catchin' hold of a lifeline. 'Anything, brother, anything at all.'

" 'Well, it means you gotta become a Catholic.'

" 'I *what?*'

" 'Yessir,' Father Coughlin says, 'we got us a special on Catholics this week. All you gotta do is convert, then confess your sins and get absolution. After that I can let you in.'

"Preacher Jones leaps to his feet, 'I'd rather roast in hell!'

" 'Fine,' said Father Coughlin, and points straight down. 'Door's right along there. Just follow the smoke.'

"That makes Preacher Jones freeze up solid. 'You're serious, aren't you?'

" 'Dead serious,' Father Coughlin says, which I think you'll agree was in right bad taste.

"Preacher Jones thinks it over a while and decides becomin' a Catholic was maybe a tad better'n burnin' in hell for all eternity. So he sighs real long and says, 'Okay, tell me what I gotta do.'

"But just then, lo and behold, up steps old Saint Peter."

"Uh oh," Macon said.

"Uh oh is right. He isn't the least bit pleased. He storms up, turns a fiery gaze on Father Coughlin, and the poor man shrivels up like a popped balloon.

" 'You think this is a game?' Saint Peter roars.

"The father does a major cringe. Desperate don't even begin to describe the look in that poor man's eyes.

" 'How'd you like to regret this for all eternity?' Peter bellows.

"Preacher Jones, now, he's stepped back a ways, just in case little bits of Father Coughlin start flyin'. Has his eyes open all big and innocent, watchin' it all come down on the father. He has one big toe diggin' a hole in the cloud, and looks like a little kid who just found out he's gonna get a lollipop instead of a spankin'.

" 'I'd be happy to show him the other door,' Preacher Jones says to Saint Peter.

"Peter's not havin' any of that, though. He swings around and says,

'You just remember what side of the pearly gates you're standin' on and keep a civil tongue in your head!' Then he turns back to the father and says, 'Now, what am I gonna do with you?'

"Now old Peter's a kindhearted saint. He's gotta be with a job like his. But he's shrewd too. He knows he's gonna let the father in, see, but he doesn't want him knowin' that just yet. Not till he'd really seen the error of his ways.'

"Well, by this time the father's sweatin' harder'n a farmer who's just finished a day of croppin' August tobacco. He kind of gibbers a minute, then says, 'How 'bout I apologize to Preacher Jones real nice like?'

" 'No,' Peter says, 'I don't think that's gonna do it.'

"Father Coughlin realizes the time for worryin' about pride is long gone, on account of he can feel the flames around his ankles. He flings himself facedown at Peter's feet, twists the folds of the old man's robes in his fingers, and sobs fit to beat the band.

" 'Please, sir!' he cries. 'Pleeeeze don't send me down below. I been good all my life. Please don't make me burn.'

"That's all Peter wants, see, just to be sure the father is really and truly sorry. But just as Saint Peter is ready to lift the man up and dust him off and send him through to Paradise, Peter catches sight of Preacher Jones.

"The reverend's kind of sidled off to one side, thinkin' he is safe over there from Peter's eyes. He's got his hands behind his back and is rockin' back and forth on his heels, wearin' the biggest grin you'd ever hope to see. Yep, this was a dream come true for Preacher Jones. He points his nose up in the air, sniffs long and hard like he'd just caught a whiff of barbecue on the wind.

"You gotta remember now, gloatin' ain't real high on the list of things to do in Paradise. So you might say Saint Peter was as put out with Preacher Jones as he was with the father.

"Then the light dawns in old Peter's eyes. He lifts the father back up to his feet, dusts the cloud off the front of his robe, and tells him to get ahold of himself 'cause he's not goin' to hell.

" 'I'm not?' the father asks, wipin' his eyes.

" 'No, you're not,' Peter answers. 'You're goin' back to earth and convert.'

" 'Convert to what?'

" 'You're gonna have this major inspiration from your heart attack, see, and in your very first sermon you're gonna tell the world you've decided to become a Baptist.'

" 'A Baptist!'

" 'That's right. And not in just any old church either. You're gonna join Preacher Jones's church. Hey, maybe we should make you assistant pastor. How'd you like that?'

"About this time Preacher Jones comes bouncin' up all panicky-like. 'In *my* church?'

"Peter turns around, tuggin' hard at his beard to keep his mouth from turning up at the edges. 'Well, now, it ain't *your* church anymore, is it?'

"Anybody with a grain of sense could see what was goin' through Preacher Jones's head. Here he is, all dead and everything, about as far out of the picture as anybody can get, and what's old Peter gonna do but send his arch-rival back to convert and join his church. And there ain't nothin' he can do about it. This is a very worrisome development. Yep. Preacher Jones is about to become the first angel in heaven with an ulcer.

"Father Coughlin's still kinda shell-shocked too. 'You want me to go back and be assistant pastor in a Baptist church?'

" 'Yeah, see, they're a little shorthanded right now,' Peter says, 'since Preacher Jones here died so sudden-like. It won't be for too long, though. Just a couple of weeks. They'll be gettin' this bright young fellow in, and then you can come back up and take your rightful place in Paradise.'

"Father Coughlin thinks all this over. 'And what if I don't go?'

"Peter gets this solemn expression on his face and proceeds to shake his head slow. 'Oh, I don't think I'd refuse if I were you. Seems to me you could spend a right long time regrettin' a decision like that.'

"Preacher Jones decides he'd better act while there's time, so he clears his throat real loud and says, 'Ah, Mister Saint Peter, sir, seems to me like the father's real sorry for what he did.'

" 'Oh I am, I am!' Father Coughlin says, givin' the preacher a look of pure heavenly gratitude.

" 'I'm ready to let bygones be bygones and invite the good father on into heaven,' the reverend says. 'There ain't no reason to send him back to earth.'

" 'There's not, huh?'

"Preacher Jones tries his best not to squirm under Peter's gaze and says, 'Nossir. Why, I'd even be willing to go back myself and help out till the new man arrives.'

"Peter pretends to give it some real serious consideration, then says, 'No, the father's gotta go back for a while.'

" 'But I *want* to go,' says Preacher Jones, real frantic-like.

" 'Yeah,' the father says, kinda frantic himself. 'He *wants* to.'

" 'Fine,' says Saint Peter. 'That's just fine. So here's what's gonna happen. You're *both* goin' back. Preacher Jones, you're not gonna fully recover. Sorry 'bout that. Your heart attack's gonna leave you in the hospital. Father Coughlin, you're gonna feel so sorry for the preacher you'll go over and help out in his church till his replacement arrives. 'Course, you'll have to convert so's they'll let you in the front door.'

" 'And you, Preacher Jones,' Peter goes on, 'you're gonna be so overcome with gratitude that you decide to convert to Catholicism right there on your deathbed.'

" 'Ah, Mister Peter, sir, ah, that ain't exactly what I had in mind,' says Preacher Jones weakly.

" 'Me neither,' agreed Father Coughlin.

" 'Yep,' Saint Peter says, ignorin' them both, 'that's exactly what's gonna happen. Ain't it nice to have all this squared away?' He holds up his hands to stop the fellas from sayin' anything more. 'No, no, don't thank me. Y'all better be gettin' on back to earth now. Have a real good time, and we'll be seein' you both in a coupla weeks.' "

Catherine swung the car into a service station. "Pit stop, everybody. Macon, don't go running off, honey. We won't be here long."

Jeremy intended to ask TJ about the trip while Catherine was in the restroom, but his friend wandered off to the edge of the trees lining the back of the parking area. Jeremy leaned against the car and watched TJ, knowing without asking that he wanted to be left alone.

"Something big happened out there, and don't you even try and tell me different," Jeremy said to Catherine when she returned.

She gave him her gentlest smile, letting the warmth fill her dark eyes. "Our beloved Dr. Hughes," she said, wrapping a strong arm around his waist and hugging him close.

"I'm a lot of things, woman, but a doctor I'm not and never will be."

"Oh, yes," she said, giving a solemn nod. "A Ph.D. from the school of hard knocks." She hugged him again. "Sure makes me feel a whole lot better having you here, Jem."

"You're about to get me halfway worried."

Catherine was in her early fifties, but anyone who did not know would probably guess late thirties at the outside. Her *café au lait* skin remained unlined, and her tall frame was thin and shapely. When angry, which was seldom, her strong features flashed fire and she used her tongue like a lash. Her most common emotion, however, was an amused patience. She watched the world with the humor of a mother for a beloved child. She was regal in bearing without being cold or aloof, saved from being unapproachable by a heart full of love. Children flocked to her for support and a listening ear. Friends brought their troubles and were soothed. Her firmness and tough honesty were tempered with humor, perception, and real love.

She displayed all of that now as she looked over to where her husband was wandering through a grove of whispering pines. "It's not my story, Jem. You'll have to wait and hear it from him."

"I don't mind waitin' for a surprise if I don't know there's one comin'," Jeremy replied. "But I hate havin' to wait for something once I know it's there. Can't you give me a hint?"

It was as though he hadn't even spoken. "If I didn't see the change in him with my own eyes, I wouldn't believe it had happened," Catherine said. "He's been like this for four days, Jem, and still there are times when it's all too much, and I get to wondering and worrying. I can't tell you how reassuring it is to hear you say you see it too."

"See *what?*"

"Honey," she called out to TJ. "Time to go. Do you see Macon? There she is. Come on, you two. We want to be home before dark."

Then she turned back to Jeremy and repeated, "It's his story, Jem. You're going to have to wait till we're home and hear it from him."

When they were back in the car, Macon announced that her doll, Miss Priss, was very tired and needed to nap. Then the little girl laid her head down in Jeremy's lap and with both arms wrapped tightly around her doll was asleep in seconds flat.

"Miss Priss?" Jeremy asked softly.

"It's what her mother used to call her," Catherine said in a normal tone of voice. "And there's no need to whisper. That child could sleep through the Second Coming."

"If that's the case," Jeremy decided, "there's no need to wait till we're home to tell me what happened, is there?"

With his eyes steady on the road ahead, his voice calm and matter-of-fact, TJ proceeded to tell Jeremy what had taken place on that morning four days earlier. Jeremy listened in silence, glad that he was sitting behind his friend so he did not have to show any response. When TJ was finished, Jeremy looked down at Macon and watched as she reached up and curled her hand around one of his fingers in her sleep. He wished he knew what to say.

"You don't believe it, do you?" Catherine asked.

"I *know* what my best friend *thinks* he saw," Jeremy responded. "I also know this same man was sufferin' from nervous exhaustion when he left here a week ago."

"It happened, Jem," TJ said. "It was as real as—no, that's not true. It was the *most real* thing that's ever happened to me."

"Well, since the Lord's never spoken to me direct-like, I don't have any yardstick for comparison," Jeremy said, his voice flat. "What're you gonna do, just hop on a plane and pop up to Washington? Drop in on Congress and say, hey, y'all, I got a message from on high and here I am?"

"Now you wait just one minute—"

TJ stopped Catherine with a gentle hand on her shoulder. "If Jeremy'd come to us with a story like this, would we act any different?" He swiveled around to face his friend. "I don't know what I'm supposed to do or how it's going to be done. All I know is that the Lord spoke to me, and He told me I was to go to Washington."

Jeremy hesitated. That calm luminescence still filled TJ's eyes, like a candle had been lit deep within him. "And do what?" he asked.

"Whatever He tells me to do," TJ replied.

"You're about the most solid man I know," Jeremy stated. "And if you think you had a vision from God, well, I suppose maybe you did. I'm not saying I believe you. Not yet. But I'm listenin', and I'm not makin' any decision about what I hear. If He spoke to you once, more'n likely He'll do it again."

"I appreciate that, Jem," TJ said.

"You gotta admit, this ain't your ordinary experience. I mean, it's not every day your best friend tells you he's seen God. It takes a little gettin' used to."

Catherine pulled up to the stoplight at the first major intersection marking the Raleigh city limits. As she waited for the light to change, she turned to Jeremy and said, "But you saw the difference. You told me that yourself."

"I'll tell you what it's like," Jeremy said. "I feel like half of me wants to put you back out there on the boat till you get your head together. The other half is positively certain you saw what you said you did."

□ □ □

After a brief stop at the home of TJ and Catherine's daughter, where Jeremy placed the still-sleeping Macon in her own bed, the three drove the remaining blocks to the Case home.

The house was painted white and was sheltered by four ancient oaks. A large veranda encircled the entire ground floor, open in front and screened in back, and a dozen hickory rockers just begged to have friends come up and "set a spell." The windows were large and adorned with real working shutters, painted light blue to match the trim. It was a large, comfortable, happy-looking house.

When TJ's grandfather had originally built the house, which TJ later renovated and expanded, it stood in the heart of Raleigh's oldest black neighborhood. In the three quarters of a century since then, the neighborhood had changed beyond recognition.

In the early sixties the state went on a building spree and had decided that all of its new buildings would be finished in marble. TJ's grandfather called it the most awful decision the legislature ever made, but not much of a surprise. Because the land in the black neighborhood was cheaper than that occupied by the businesses, offices, and small hotels on the other side of the capitol, the state proceeded to condemn the old neighborhood and level the century-old homes. TJ's grandfather once told a visitor that the new buildings were fitting tombstones to the history that had been destroyed.

The borders of this new construction were established by three untouchable bastions of white Raleigh—the oldest women's college in the state, the capitol, and the governor's mansion. Because TJ's house was two blocks over on the safe side of the governor's mansion, it was spared from destruction, but the neighborhood was gone forever. Land prices shot up a hundredfold, apartment complexes filled every free square inch, and the old houses that remained were purchased for astronomical figures and remodeled with no regard whatsoever for cost. The street was now lined with stained-glass front doors, lead-pane windows, split-oak sunrooms with polarized glass, and heated swimming pools. Compared to its neighbors, TJ's place looked positively country.

Usually Jeremy would pace around the front yard as if he were marking off footage for apartments, shade his eyes, squint around, and say something like, Maybe we oughtta keep one of the trees and pen it in a cutsey little courtyard. Call it Oak Hills Estate. How's that sound? Today he just started unloading the car.

"You'll come in for a while, won't you?" Catherine asked.

Jeremy hefted the larger cases. "Yeah, I feel like an old hound dog that's gotta worry this bone a little longer."

When the car was unpacked and Jeremy was slumped into a chair on the back porch, Catherine brought him a tall glass of lemonade. A few minutes later TJ came walking out with an unfolded letter fluttering from his hand.

"What've you got, honey?"

He adjusted his spectacles, lifted the letter, and read, "Dear Mr. Case: Your office informed me that you were on vacation and could not be reached. I have taken the liberty of writing to your private address, as this is a matter of utmost urgency. Please call me the moment you return, as I would like to discuss a very important opening here in Washington, a position which I am sure will interest you greatly. However, there are a number of other candidates being considered, and it is therefore absolutely necessary that I discuss this with you as soon as possible." He looked up. "Sincerely yours, John Silverwood, U.S. House of Representatives."

There was a moment's silence before Jeremy said, "You sound so calm. Doesn't that scare you even the littlest bit?"

"Of course I'm scared," TJ answered. He pulled up a chair, sat down, and pointed at Jeremy's glass with his spectacles. "Honey, do you think I could have one of those?"

Catherine didn't move. "You look about the most unscared of any man I've ever seen."

"My fears all seem a little puny in the face of this," he responded, holding up the letter. "The Lord has called me, and I'm going to do what He tells me to do. It's as simple as that. Yes, I'm scared. But how I feel about it doesn't change things one bit." He reached out his free hand. "Let me have some of that, Jem."

"You know what's the strangest thing of all?" Jeremy paused for a sip before handing the glass over. "Here we are, sittin' 'round here, takin' our ease, talkin' like we would over the weather. If somebody'd asked you a week ago what you'd do if the Lord called your name, you'd have said, Dance down the aisles singin' praises."

"I'm too worried to dance," Catherine said quietly, her hands clenched in her lap. "I feel as if my life is about to go flying off in some cross-eyed direction and I don't have anything to say about it."

"You've got the right to say anything you want about this or anything else," TJ responded gently.

Catherine sighed. "No, I don't." She clasped the arms of her rocker and pulled herself erect. "I'm too tired to talk about it anymore. Good night." Without looking at either man, she walked into the house.

"I oughtta be goin'," Jeremy said, sliding forward in his chair.

But TJ waved him back. "Stay a while longer, will you? I need a little company right now."

"What about Catherine?"

"I learned long ago never to broach a difficult subject with Catherine when she's tired." TJ hesitated, then said, "I've got to do this, Jem."

Jeremy looked into the distance, blind to the brilliant sunset painting the sky. He nodded his head slowly a few times. "It's still hard as the dickens for me to accept."

"In a way it is for me too." TJ lifted the letter again. "It sure makes me feel better to have this."

"Makes it more real, you mean?"

"No, I've never questioned that. It's hard to describe, but the moment was so real it's made the rest of my life seem a little unreal. Like watching shadows. No, that's not right." TJ shook his head. "I don't know how to explain it."

"Sort of a change of perspective?"

"Yes. I suppose that's as close as you can come to the feeling in words. A rearranging of all my priorities. Like everything in my life has suddenly become a lot less important than I thought it was."

"I can't say as I've ever experienced anything like what you've just told me about."

"Neither have I," TJ returned quietly.

"Still, I've felt His guiding hand in my life so many times," Jeremy said, his eyes on some unseen point beyond the porch railing. "Not some explosion like what's happened here, but I've never doubted it was His voice."

"The still small voice that guides your life," TJ agreed. "The daily miracles we so often take for granted."

"That's for sure. It shames me to think how I ignore His presence because it's so gentle. Makes it so easy to pretend like I've done it all myself." Jeremy glanced over at his friend. "But I tell you what. All this takes my breath away."

"Mine too." TJ looked down at the paper in his hand. "It's a miracle. And this letter . . . you know, I think He gave it as a sort of reassurance. A reminder that He's going to be there with me through it all."

─┤ FOUR ├─

"Sing to the Lord, you saints of his; praise his holy name. For his anger lasts only a moment, but his favor lasts a lifetime. Weeping may remain for a night, but rejoicing comes in the morning."

The passage from Psalm 30 popped into TJ's mind as he passed through the oak doors and entered the Praise Hall of the Church of New Zion the next morning. It was a fitting note, especially after the surprise Catherine had dished up for breakfast.

His prayer time that morning had been spent mostly asking the Lord to turn his wife around. *I can't do this without her, Father,* he had said time and again. *There's nothing on earth that I can say to change her mind if she sets herself against it. And it's not enough to have her grudgingly come along. You know it's not. Whatever you've got in store for me is going to tax me to the limit. I can feel it in my bones. I can't handle such a burden without Catherine beside me. She was awfully upset last night. And worried. I've spent most of the night feeling her anger and tension stretched out there beside me. I've been married to that woman for almost thirty years, and when she's like this, there's not a thing on earth I can say to her. It's up to you, Lord. I'm turning it over to you.*

Then in typical fashion, once he had turned it over to God, TJ spent the better part of an hour worrying about possible arguments. Like his grandfather had often said, it was one thing to hand a problem over to the Lord; it was another thing entirely to let Him keep it.

He heard her clattering around in the kitchen, pouring a cup of coffee, setting the table for breakfast, putting out the frying pan, with none of her usual Sunday-morning humming and singing. His heart started a frantic beat, as though she were already standing in front of him, hand on her hip, head cocked to one side, eyes squinting in that mixture of scorn and disbelief that never failed to send him straight through the roof.

But when she appeared in the doorway, it was a Catherine he had not seen in years, a little shy and a little awkward and more than a little scared. Looking as if she wanted nothing more than to be held by her man. It was a look he had seen a great deal during their courtship days, and it was one of the many things about her that had captured his heart. With the arrival of their first daughter and all the worries and responsibilities of motherhood, those vulnerable moments had slowly slipped away.

TJ set down his coffee cup and rose to hold her, trying to remember the last time he had seen that look. And the moment he had her in his arms, all the worries and arguments fled like smoke on the wind, and all he could say was, "I can't do this without you, Catherine."

She sighed and snuggled closer, her forehead seeking the familiar crook in his shoulder. Her soft voice floated up from his chest level. "Just tell me once more, are you absolutely, positively sure that it was God who spoke to you?"

"More sure than I've been about anything in my entire life."

"You realize what this is going to do to our lives, don't you?"

He started to voice some platitude, like, it's going to work out all right, but caught himself in time. Despite a ferocious desire to protect her from what might not ever arrive, he admitted, "It worries me almost as much as thinking you might not be there with me."

She sighed. "Just when I thought we could settle down, have some time for ourselves again. The kids are out on their own, you've finally gotten away from all that political mess, and what happens?"

Something in her tone said everything was going to be all right. He offered up silent thanks as he stroked her face and said, "I need you, Catherine."

"You think I don't know that?" Her fingers traced a design down the length of his spine. "It's one thing to sit snug and comfy in church and ask God to speak through you, and something else entirely when it happens."

"I expected a lot more doubts from you," TJ confessed. "Things like, how can you be so sure, or why on earth did He choose you? I've been sitting down here for over an hour wondering what in heaven's name I could say to convince you. I think the thing that scared me most was fearing I might start doubting it myself."

"I saw your face that morning," Catherine said. "And I felt the love and light pouring out of you the rest of the time we were together on the boat. I heard your voice when you tried to tell me about it. I saw the letter waiting for you when we got home. All night I've been trying to come to grips with what all that means. There's a part of me that wants to call you a fool, honey. I feel the power inside me to destroy what you're trying to do, and I've been wrestling with it all night. You can't imagine what it feels like, knowing I've got the chance to hold on to all this and knowing I can't."

"I didn't know you felt that way about the politics," TJ said.

"It wasn't the politics." She sounded a little impatient now. "It was everything. The pressure you were under, having to stand there and watch what the world was doing to you, knowing there was nothing I could do but be there. You can't begin to imagine how helpless that made me feel." She pulled away far enough to look up at him. "And just when I thought it was finished, you're telling me it's going to start all over again."

He couldn't help it—he had to laugh at that one. "Of all the ways I could think to describe you, girl, the absolute last one I'd think of is helpless."

"Who you calling girl?" She rewarded him with a smile. "You telling me I could just say the word and make all this go away?"

"That what you want?"

"Part of me," she said, suddenly sober again. "The part I can't listen to wants to fight this as hard as I've ever fought anything in my life."

"I can't do this without you, Catherine," he said again.

"Don't I know it," she retorted sharply, and held him close in a fierce embrace, then abruptly let him go. "Now, if I don't stop with this nonsense and see to breakfast, we're gonna be late for church."

□　□　□

Church that morning was the old shell of a structure that had been the first Church of New Zion. It was a rough-hewn hall, measuring thirty-five paces long and eighteen wide. The exposed rafters were supported by five thin tree-trunks that had been cut and trimmed and stripped and laid in place lengthwise down the roof. Another seven logs, thicker and broader this time, formed the hall's supports. They were planted deep into the earth—three at each end of the hall and one in the middle, with the three central pillars cut higher so as to support the A-frame roof. The two doors at the back opened to either side of the supporting trunk. The walls and floors were split-timbered and held in place with wooden pegs; the original builders could not afford nails.

The oil-skin windows had long since been replaced by glass, but many of the first lead panes were still there, run like clear frozen molasses to thicken and broaden at the base over these past hundred and twenty years. The exterior had been sanded and repainted so often that the boards seemed to flow in curving waves. The roof had been torn up and replaced several times, most recently with untreated hickory planking closely resembling the original. Before that, the roof had been modern asphalt tile, which everyone had loathed. It had totally destroyed the feel of the place, and had lasted only nine months before passion overcame practicality, and the new one had been laid.

The simple structure, unadorned save for the whitewashed wooden cross that rose above the nave, stood in a grove of dogwoods. They had been planted the year after the church had been completed, and nowadays totally dwarfed the hall. In the springtime the sight of the simple whitewashed church standing amidst a cloud of blossoms stopped traffic on the highway and drew photographers from all over the state.

The newer church, made of brick and nine times as large, stood about a hundred yards farther away from the road. It was separated from the original edifice by the gardens and the parking lot because, as some liked to claim, it was the only way the worshipers could hear themselves think. TJ's grandfather had been head deacon when the newer church's cornerstone had been laid in 1932, and had fought tooth and nail to erect the second hall beyond the dogwoods. He had threatened to tie himself to the first tree to be cut down, and had said the only way they would harm one blossom was by spilling his own blood first.

TJ's great-grandfather had been born a slave on a Louisiana cotton plantation. When the Civil War ended, he was a boy of thirteen who had already spent five years of servitude in the fields of a white master. His family banded together with twenty-three others, a total of ninety-nine souls, and headed north, where life was supposed to be better. They had no specific goal nor a firm grasp of geography beyond the borders of the next few farms down the road. All their worldly goods were carried in two battered wheelbarrows, a pushcart, and on their backs.

The journey lasted over a year. When the band could not beg or forage enough food, they stopped to seek work. Steady labor was as scarce as money in those early Reconstruction days, and this, as much as anything, kept them heading north—always north.

Miraculously, they all survived, including one toothless old grandmother of seventy-some years. And just at the point where they were ready to give up, when the bonding force of hope was no longer enough to keep the group from drifting apart, they happened upon a ramshackle Carolina community with more land than it could farm.

It was a story repeated a thousand times throughout the South: All the white menfolk went off to fight, leaving the women to survive as best they could. With defeat came destitution, so the ladies sought out the shreds of other families with whom they could struggle for survival. Whole communities became ghost towns, leaving empty homes and untilled fields as the only legacy of what once had been.

The band of travelers had chanced upon a small farming community that had lost every male over the age of fourteen. Every single one. Four hundred acres of prime tobacco land were going begging. And despite their best efforts, the white women were slowly starving.

TJ's great-grandfather had been one of the five men sent over to talk to the white women. They wanted to live there, they told the women. They would farm the land and tend the women's homes as long as they could have enough land to build houses and plant gardens of their own. The white women made the men stand out in the pouring rain and kept three ancient bird guns trained on them. The women were clearly terrified of the newcomers. Only desperation made them listen. Finally they said that ten of the families could stay.

The men refused. They had come too far together, been through too much, to split up now. Well, the eldest of the women demanded, what was to keep them from sneaking in one night and slitting all their throats?

It was TJ's great-grandfather who replied. "The first house we want to build is God's house," he told the women. "All we want is a place to live as free men, like the Lord wants us to be."

The white women waited for the old lady to reply. She spent a long moment searching the black man's face, then lowered her rifle and turned away.

"Let them stay," she said.

They were home.

The community stood on the outskirts of a tiny village called Zebulon, thirty miles, or one solid day on horseback, from the state capital. But the new arrivals didn't know this. Nor did they care.

A few among them knew how to read, and they were told to search the Scriptures for a name for their new home. The answer was found in the sixty-second chapter of Isaiah: "The Lord has made proclamation to the ends of the earth: 'Say to the Daughter of Zion, "See, your Savior comes! See, his reward is with him, and his recompense accompanies him."' They will be called The Holy People, The Redeemed of the Lord; and you will be called Sought After, The City No Longer Deserted."

□　　□　　□

The old Praise Hall of the Church of New Zion rang with joy.

"This is truly a day the Lord has made!" A pair of hands waved in the air, soon to be joined by a hundred others, swaying from side to side in a harmony punctuated by loud amens. "I pray that I will be where the Lord wants me to be!"

"God is a GREAT God!" Catherine leapt up and shouted out, making TJ jump and shrink back in his corner. She lifted her hands and danced toward the center aisle, caught up now in the spirit of praise and worship. TJ heaved a silent sigh and sought safety in his Bible.

The Church of New Zion's original building was full to the bursting point, as it was most Sundays. The ancient floor thundered and shook to the pounding of two hundred feet as the faithful responded to the call to "dance their joy before the Lord!" The only soul who did not join in was TJ. From time to time pitying looks were cast his way. The man just didn't realize all he was missing.

There was no preacher in the Praise Hall. Those who felt they needed somebody else to talk for them were welcome in the big church across the way, the one with the pretty stained-glass windows and the choir all dressed up in robes and the reverend up there behind his fancy hand-carved wooden banister.

When the new church had been completed in 1938, a lot of time and talk was spent worrying over what should be done with the old building. Some wanted it for a church social hall, others for a little museum; but the issue never came up for a vote. Long before the talk was over, a decision had been made. It was to be a Praise Hall.

It took six years to finish the new church. They stopped every time the congregation ran out of money, started back when there was another hundred dollars in the kitty. Everything possible was done by church members, donating labor when the Depression years squeezed their purses dry. Other congregations called them fools for building in the height of the Depression; they held their tongues for the most part, saying only that bad times were the best times to praise the Lord.

At first it was only the older people who attended the praise meetings, the ones who remembered how it was back before the church had a regular preacher. In the early days a traveling preacher would stop every few months and fill the little church with the word of the Lord. The rest of the time the congregation simply had to make do.

They danced, they sang, they cried, and they prayed. Those who could would read the Scriptures, while the deacons and elders cared for the needs of the church and the congregation. During the long Sunday services, many of them lasting from dawn to dusk, those simple God-fearing people did the best they could with what they had.

Most folks were mighty pleased with the new church, to have a regular preacher come in and call their little settlement home. Still, there were some who yearned for the old days, when they did as the Spirit called them, spoke when the Lord told them, ministered as they were led. And after the newness of the church had worn off a little, this group began meeting back in the old hall. Ignoring the criticism of those who called it the way of po' black folks, their cries of joy rang out loud and clear in the Carolina air.

But it was the new preacher who finally set the seal of approval on the old Praise Hall.

"There's a certain smugness that's set in among us," Reverend Taylor said to the congregation about a year after they had moved into the new church. Amos Taylor was then a tall gangly young man, but his eyes glinted with a holy fire behind his wire-rimmed spectacles.

"Yessir," he said, "there's a lot of people walkin' around these parts with their noses stuck up in the air. Better watch out, is what I'm here to tell you, else you're gonna see the Lord come along and slap you awake. You hear what I'm sayin'?"

He stopped and looked out over his congregation. "Why don't y'all just try and sit still for a second. You're always tellin' your children to do it. Now how about a little of that same lesson for you folks. Just sit down there right quiet, stop your fannin', now, nobody's gonna faint. Just sit there and tell me what you hear. Wait. What's that? You hear what I'm hearin'? Is that joy I'm listenin' to? Is that somebody out there singin' praises to the Lord? Why, yes, I do believe that is."

The reverend's eyes were blazing now. "There's been something very alarmin' brought to my attention. Something that scares me mightily. Know what it is? It's pride. It's greed. It's the fear that freezes my belly up solid, scarin' me so bad I can't sleep at night, thinkin' that so many of my flock are gonna burn for all eternity. You hear what I'm sayin' out there? There's people out there listenin' to me that think they're better off now that they sit in some fancy church, listenin' to somebody else stand up here and do all the work.

"Listen up, you sinners. You let me do the work, the Lord's gonna know it. He don't give you salvation for comin' here. No sir. He's gonna let you in if you BELIEVE. Now tell me something. Who's the stronger believer? The one who sits in here and wishes that old fool would shut up so they can get back to their dinner, or the ones over there across the way, singin' and shoutin' their hearts out, praisin' their Lord?"

Not only did the bickering stop, but the old hall began to fill up almost every Sunday. And when the services ended, when the congregation in the new hall walked calmly out into the Carolina sunshine, shaking hands and smiling and talking politely in little groups, the doors to the old building beneath the dogwoods would slam back, and out would pour a storm of singing, clapping, shouting, hand-waving people, eyes uplifted to heaven. Laughing and embracing and praising God. And the polite small talk would dry up in front of the new church like dew on a hot summer morning.

Still there were those who sought to leave the old ways behind, to forget the horrors of the past and the old ways of worship with them. They sought to mimic the white worshipers, calling their way civilized; and in their quiet stuffy way these people threatened to tear the church apart. But Reverend Amos Taylor and his elders stopped that before the roots of destruction could gain hold.

The church continued to invite the circuit-riding preachers and traveling evangelists to visit. And every time a guest preacher was invited to fill the pulpit, Reverend Amos escaped to the Praise Hall, along with his deacons and elders. It became an unspoken rule that no one could become a church leader unless he had put in his "hard time," as it came to be known.

And so the little church in the dogwood grove remained, and grew, and taught future generations sacred lessons about their heritage.

□ □ □

"The Lord ain't *never* late. He may not be early, but He's always on time. *His* time. It's *your* time that ain't right."

TJ loved the services in the Praise Hall, especially once Catherine had exploded up to dance and shout and sing for both of them. He had never been able to let go like that. Spontaneity was not a trait he knew even on a nodding basis. But his heart was filled by what he felt and heard, and despite the disparaging looks from some of his fellow worshipers, TJ always sensed that this was what was most important.

"When Jesus came in, the devil went out!" Another sister moved to the front and faced the swaying congregation. "There ain't room for both in my life!"

"God is a great God!" another responded above the amens.

The sister started her testimony, and TJ made note of her opening words in his little book. The leather-bound volume was dog-eared; he went through a couple notebooks a year, filling them with his thoughts during worship and study, including some of his own prayers. The congregation had long since grown accustomed to his scribbling, and looked on it as one of a variety of strange habits collected and savored by TJ Case.

The Praise Hall had no podium, no organ, no hymnals, no trappings whatsoever. There were seven pews on one side, eight on the other, all scarred and bowed by years of service. The floor was worn smooth by the scraping of a hundred thousand shuffling, dancing feet. High up near the eaves, the walls were still chinked with clay for insulation and burned black with the soot of countless kerosene lanterns. The only concessions to modern convenience were the string of electric bulbs hanging from the central pillar and a cranky oil stove set against the front wall.

"They call us unlearned men," the sister finished, hoarse and sweaty from her testimony. "That's all right. They called the apostles unlearned men too."

"Say it, sister," called her husband from his place at the back.

"Listen to my man," she said, pointing out and down like a hip basketball player. "Look back there at that smiling face and tell me the Lord don't work miracles! What you see is a man transformed!"

"Praise God!"

"What you see is a man healed in body and mind!"

"Washed clean from sin!"

"What you see is a man who learned the message of love!"

"Amen, sister, amen!"

"Snatched from the brink, saved from the flames, brought back to the heart of our Lord!" She raised her arms above her head, closed her eyes, and sang to the rafters, "Lord, Lord, I do glorify you! Night and day I glorify my Father! You healed my marriage, brought peace to our family! I praise the Lord for what He's done in my home!"

Her husband's deep baritone broke out into "Amazing Grace," and the whole room took it up, singing and clapping and threatening to lift the roof from the eaves with the power of their sound.

TJ closed his eyes, humming his own tone-deaf tune. As often happened in such moments, he found himself looking back over an earlier experience, seeing it from the standpoint of one freed from earthly bonds. He listened to the music as it soared, unguided by choir or instrument, and he remembered the long-distance telephone conversation he'd had that morning just before he and Catherine left for church.

□　□　□

Congressman John Silverwood had been blunt. "You're finished down there, TJ. Finished for good, if you're thinking of trying to sneak back up some local political ladder."

TJ made some noncommittal sound and listened to him launch into what TJ called the softening-up process, a strong tool in the hands of a skilled negotiator. Make the man feel, really believe deep down in his heart, that his only hope lay in doing what the other wanted.

"The thing is," Silverwood went on, "you need to get away, make a name for yourself, and then come back. The local ladder's unnecessary. You've already climbed it. You can't stay around as a loser, TJ. You have to go away and return as a *different* kind of winner."

"I understand," TJ said. He had come to know Silverwood fairly well during the election process and had found him to be a direct man with an opinion. He was manipulative, yes, but a basic forthright honesty seemed to keep him from being shifty. He played the chess game of politics with skill, deftly maneuvering power and people to obtain what he wanted whenever possible. But he told you up front what he was after and how he felt about the issues at hand. TJ felt comfortable with the man, despite their very basic differences of opinion on so many levels.

For one thing, Silverwood was not really all that concerned about education. TJ had long since accepted that as fact. It was simply another issue that could gain him what he wanted, which was political power. Anyone with a grain of sense could see that Silverwood was determined to climb just as high as he could up the political mountain.

"You must have noticed it, old buddy," Silverwood said. "Since the election, how many friends have you lost?"

"I haven't been around enough to find out."

"You'll see soon enough then. They won't know what to say to you. You'll see that sense of shared humiliation in their eyes. They'll hide behind a barrier of hostility every chance they get. Either that or the fakiest good-old-boy grins you've ever had to put up with. It'll make you feel as if they don't even remember your name."

That's not the issue here, TJ said to himself, perhaps because he could feel the truth in the man's words and found himself drawing away from the shame of his defeat. All he said was, "That makes sense."

"Of course it does. And what's the reaction of the black community gonna be? Your endorsement of me split them right down the middle. Either you move fast and consolidate, or you lose them all. They'll turn like the tide and surge back behind the party ticket. Know where that'll leave you?"

"Left out," TJ responded, partly because he knew that was what Silverwood wanted to hear, and partly because he knew it was true. He stifled a sigh and said silently, you seem awfully far away right now, Father.

"You'll be high and dry, old buddy. Beached and left to rot. On the other hand, now, if you can just get out from under this and pull a hat trick somewhere else, you'll come back in higher than when you left." Silverwood paused, changed gears, and asked, "This is the first election you've ever lost, isn't it?"

"The first one."

"There's a delayed reaction. I know you think the worst is over and I'm talking rubbish, but it's true. I've been there, I'm sorry to say. Dealing with a political loss was the worst thing I've ever experienced. Some days I really got paranoid. Did people talk about me behind my back? Was I gonna lose my business clients because they wanted to stick with a winner? Did my family think I was a loser? It went on for over a year. I tell you, TJ, dealing with your loss would be a lot easier if you were winning somewhere else."

"It makes sense, John, it really does."

"Then you're interested." It was not a question.

"Yes, I guess I am."

"Excellent," Silverwood said, clearly pleased. Then added hastily. "But don't go making any major plans, TJ, not just yet. And for heaven's sake don't breathe a word about it to anyone. There's a lot of work left to be done. A lot. This is a major deal we're talking about here, and I'm gonna have to sweat blood to make it go."

TJ allowed himself a small smile. This was rule two in the political game. Present the deal as though you were championing the most difficult cause of the century. He would have been willing to lay odds that the appointment was already his.

And that was rule three. Never go public with anything until the deal is sewn up; then make it sound as if it was a touch-and-go effort. People would remember a favor a lot longer if they thought the giver had spent long and sleepless nights struggling to make it happen. In the perverse way of human nature, they would want it more if they felt there was a good chance of not receiving it in the first place.

"I'm very grateful for all your thoughtfulness," TJ said dryly.

"Of course you are. That's why I want to bring you to Washington as fast as I can." It was the honesty at work. "I'm up here sweating my tail off, trying to find me a few trustworthy friends in this city. You wouldn't think that'd be too difficult, now, would you?"

Silverwood suddenly sounded very tired. "I tell you, TJ, it's like squeezing blood from a stone. I don't mind helping the other guy out, and I don't mind sharing the pie. But if a man says he's with me, well, I expect him to be with me through thick and thin. You understand what I'm saying?"

"Perfectly."

"Of course you do. Okay. Lemme tell you what we're thinking about up here." There was the sound of a creaking chair, a desk drawer opening, and TJ smiled again. It was one of Silverwood's habits. He would lean dangerously far back in his swivel chair, kick off his shoes, open a desk drawer, and stick his toes into the recesses. TJ had seen him do it countless times during the campaign.

"I've been thinking a lot about this education thing," Silverwood said. "How much it means to you and how much plain good sense you made when you talked about it. Given the right position, you could really carry it forward here in Washington. You see what I mean?"

"Yes." Despite himself, TJ felt the excitement rise. Education was the issue closest to his heart, the single most important point he had championed during his political career.

"The administration's going to be under a lot of pressure to do something about education. The campaign was full of promises, you know that. The problem is, they didn't offer much in the way of solid policies to back them up. They're gonna have to scramble for new programs. If the White House doesn't hit Congress hard and fast on this one, the Democrats are going to take the ball and run with it."

"They're under pressure, aren't they?" Was this what God intended, that he go and come back a winner, with a new education bill as a feather in his cap?

"Sitting under the gun," Silverwood agreed. "And that's where you come in. I'd like to see you inside the White House, TJ. My man on the spot. Think you'd like it?"

"I'm your man, John." TJ heard the strength in his own voice and prayed that the Father would not let him be led astray.

"That's right, you are." Silverwood laughed to take the sting out of his words. "It'll be good to have a real ally up here, TJ, someone I can trust. Not just today, but as long as we're up here." He paused long enough to make sure TJ understood fully, then went on, "Well, I can't promise anything, not yet. But you can be sure that I'll be working on this like a kid on a lollipop. I'm gonna put myself on the line, see if I can't get this one for you. You stay close to the phone, old buddy. I'll be back as soon as I've got something definite."

□   □   □

TJ flicked through the pages of his little notebook, marveling at the profound wisdom gifted him by these simple people. His eyes caught on several phrases, and he felt the Holy Spirit illuminate the words.

"The race doesn't go to the swift or the strong. It goes to the one who *finishes* the race."

"He is our hope. Our *only* hope. And His line is always open. It's *you* who's got to stay on the line."

"If you're ashamed of Him, He's ashamed of you. Love Him. Serve Him. God is my everything. God is my all in all."

As though on cue, the congregation began the final hymn, the same one that closed all the Praise Hall services. TJ rose to his feet as the rear doors were flung open and the congregation flowed out, singing and clapping and filling the tiny grove with their joy: "It's not my mother, nor my father, but it's me, oh, Lord, standin' in the need of prayer."

A cold wind greeted him as he left the chapel. Bundled into his overcoat, he stood beneath the naked dogwoods and gazed at the blue-blue depths overhead. He heard Catherine's laughter and turned around.

With her was a woman he had known since childhood, Alice Neally. It was hard to look at this gray-haired matron of over two hundred pounds and recall the elfin sprite who had climbed the maples in the backyard and challenged him to see who could reach the uppermost branches first.

"You write down some pretty things today, chile?" Alice opened her generous mouth and laughed, and a bit of the childhood spirit showed through. "I swear, TJ, we's gonna have you up there in front next week, we sho' is."

"Out of the question," he replied. "You'll simply have to let me worship in my own way."

"Listen to how that man talk. You got to get in the spirit, chile! Open yoah heart to the Lawd!"

Catherine clasped his arm, drew up close, and said to Alice, "My husband wouldn't know a good time if it came up and beat him over the head with a stick."

Alice laughed loud enough to turn heads over by the new church. "That's the truth, that's the truth." She looked around. "Y'all seen that man of mine?"

"I saw him walking over toward the cemetery," TJ said.

The air seemed to go out of the big woman's body. "Three years in the grave, and that man still grieves over our little girl. They say it's the woman who misses a chile, and the good Lawd knows I do, but nothin' like that man." Alice shook her head. "I wakes up some nights and hears him talkin' to her, jes' like she was settin' there beside the bed. Like to scared me to death the first time I heard it. I turned on the light, and his eyes was all shut up tight, and I knew he was dreamin'. Near broke my heart, layin' there listenin' to him talk to his chile."

TJ and Catherine nodded their silent sympathy and walked with her to the edge of the dogwoods, where a knee-high, rusting iron fence marked the entrance to the cemetery.

Closest to the trees lay the old graves. In the summer they were covered with bright flowers, planted each spring by the older women of the congregation. Today they were quiet and brown, each ringed by bits of brightly colored glass that sparkled in the winter sun. Back in the early days the people couldn't afford tombstones, so they had marked their graves with bits of broken bottles. TJ always thought them gay and beckoning, as though those who remained behind were bent on celebrating the passage of their loved one on to a better place.

He left the women and went over to stand in front of his grandfather's grave. A tiny fence, no more than ten inches high, ran around this section of the yard, as it did around several other family plots. On one side of his grandfather was his grandmother's grave. On the other was his mother's.

He knew his mother only from pictures as dated as his birth. His favorite was one taken not long before he was conceived, according to his grandmother. It was a portrait of a beautiful woman with skin the color of sourwood honey. Her nose was soft and round and close to her face. Her mouth was full and looked liable to smile at a moment's notice. But she wasn't smiling. Her eyes were filled with a deep, deep sorrow.

His grandmother had told him that the picture had been planned as a surprise birthday present for TJ's grandfather. The day they went to the studio, however, TJ's mother had refused to face the camera. She knew, his grandmother had told him. She knew just exactly what was coming. She was just too much in love to change anything.

TJ had been eight years old the day his grandmother first brought the picture out from the bottom of her hope chest. She sat in the old rocking chair beside the big windows and motioned for him to join her, which meant he was to stand beside her right leg. It had been his very own special place ever since he had grown too big to sit in her lap. She draped one bony arm around his shoulders, showed him the picture, and said, "That's your momma."

TJ had seen countless pictures of her before. Every single room in his grandparents' house contained at least a couple of pictures of his mother. But this one he had never seen before, and the power of that photograph took his breath away.

Don't let your grandfather see you looking at this, his grandmother warned him. He wouldn't be pleased to hear I'd given it to you.

Why not TJ asked, and saw the same unending sadness in his grandmother's eyes that was in the photograph.

Your grandfather cannot abide this picture, she told him. The day your momma went into the hospital, he took it off the mantel and told me to burn it. Told me it nigh on broke his heart to see it.

With the candor of youth he had asked his grandmother, why doesn't it bother you like that?

She looked at him with unshed tears in her eyes and said, it does, child, it does. But I just have to keep telling myself that the good Lord knew what He was doing. If your momma hadn't fallen in love with that man, there wouldn't be this grandchild here beside me now.

His grandmother loved to talk about what his mother had been like as a child, and her eyes would shine with laughter as she described her daughter's saucy ways. She would glow with pride as she spoke about the honors won in the mostly white private school. Your momma was one of the first black women to graduate from that school, she told him, and the very first to graduate with honors.

The school's curriculum consisted of the last two years of high school and the first two years of college—what the proper families of that day called a "ladies finishing school." TJ's grandfather wanted his daughter to go to that school because it offered the best education in the state for young women. It was expensive, and her going there was frowned upon by some of their own people—and was certainly not approved of by most white folks. But the opinions of others never stopped TJ's grandfather once he made up his mind.

Then his grandmother would reach a point when she would grow extremely quiet, and the sadness and the tension would hang heavy in the air.

TJ had never known what to do or say when his grandmother reached that point. He usually just waited, and she usually sighed a long breath and said, if I've asked myself once I've asked it a thousand times, whether we made a mistake in letting your mother go off to that school.

There's a hundred questions I'm set to ask the Lord when my time comes, but that one's gonna be at the top of the list. Yes, Lord, once and for all you're gonna put my poor mind to rest and tell me if I did as I should.

All he had known was that she had run away and that she had later returned. Once, only once, TJ had asked his grandmother why his mother had left home to go live up north.

His grandmother turned around and looked at him as though she couldn't quite place him in her mind. The look was so full of pain and longing that it had scared him worse than just about anything that had ever scared him before or since. Then her mind seemed to focus and she asked, what was that you said, child, her voice all soft and full of love. Nothing, he said, not wanting to bring back that awful look of suffering, not ever. I was just talking to myself.

His grandfather, now, that was a completely different matter. Every time he talked about his daughter, a shadow would heave across his face for a moment; then his features would turn to stone.

His grandfather had a face that always reminded TJ of those old portraits of American Indian chiefs—full of planes and hollows and sharp angles—all set under skin the color of ebony. The nose was a hatchet, the mouth a thin line that was kept from looking cruel only by the stern integrity that radiated from the man.

His grandmother told him once that the old man was one-quarter Arapaho, one-quarter Choctaw, three-quarters saint, and one-third stubborn old goat. TJ said he didn't think that all added up right. I'm not talking arithmetic, she replied sharply. I'm talking about your grandfather. He's twice the man anybody else is, and 'bout more than I can handle the best part of every day.

His grandfather remained the memory that held him firmly to the path of the Lord. In his moments of greatest doubt and indecision, TJ always asked himself what his grandfather would have done in the same situation. It amazed him how other people were able to find their way down the twisting, winding road of life without someone like his grandfather to guide them.

☐ ☐ ☐

It startled him when Catherine came up and slipped her arm around his waist. She looked up at him with compassion and understanding. "You ready to go home, honey?"

He looked back to the grave and said, "I miss that old man."

"I know you do," she replied quietly, holding him close.

Especially now, he thought to himself. I feel so weak, so vulnerable, so unsure of what I'm supposed to do.

Deftly Catherine guided him out of the cemetery and back toward the car, helping to support his weight, surrounding him with her love.

⊣| FIVE |⊢

The taxi that brought TJ into Washington from National Airport was driven by a black man with a weather-beaten face and hair the color of dirty snow.

"Bancroft Place," the man said, giving TJ a friendly eye in the rearview mirror. "That's up Kalorama way. Nice area 'round there. Lots of embassies and 'spensive houses."

"I've got a friend up there," TJ said, staring out at the gloomy twilight of a February afternoon, wondering what he was doing here.

Congressman John Silverwood had confirmed TJ's appointment less than a month after that Sunday morning call. Following that, he had continued to phone TJ every week or so, passing on news of the new administration and its takeover, keeping TJ apprised of Washington developments and making sure his man stayed hooked.

Through November and December the new President's skeleton crew—called his Transition Team—worked out of the cavernous basement of the Commerce Building, taking up some two hundred thousand square feet of space. It was staffed primarily by people who had been with the President through the campaign. On Silverwood's recommendation, TJ did not come up to make himself known.

Chaos was how the congressman described it. Three thousand phones ringing all at once, people chasing around like maniacs. Total chaos. You might wind up in a better position by carving your niche out now, Silverwood told him, but I doubt it. Either way, you'll be entering the arena at a disadvantage. These people have been working together for as much as three years, all dreaming of this moment. Let them scream and run around in little circles for a while. Come up when the dust settles.

The first call from the White House came in early January and gave TJ another sleepless night. It was from one of the personnel officers, a mid-level staffer who stressed his importance by trying to bully TJ into arriving the following week. I have a law practice to put in order, TJ had replied. The man was not impressed. What do you have that's more important than serving your President? But TJ refused to be pushed. He told the man he'd be in Washington in two weeks, and hung up.

The next day he told Jeremy about it, letting some of his worry show through. Jeremy had been strangely silent, and then with an even stranger abruptness stood and said he was leaving town for a few days on business. What business, TJ asked. Just business, Jeremy replied. Somethin' that's been on my mind for a while. Well, TJ said, more than a little confused by this lack of concern, will I see you again before I leave? But Jeremy had remained evasive and seemed in a hurry to get going.

Nine days later, he called just as TJ was sitting down to breakfast. Got a pencil, Jeremy asked. Okay, take this down. TJ noted the address his friend gave him, asked, what is this? When you get to Washington, grab a taxi and tell the driver to bring you here, Jeremy replied. I've already made hotel reservations, TJ said. Cancel them, Jeremy said. It's all taken care of. What's been taken care of, TJ asked. Tell you when you arrive, Jeremy replied. Have a good trip.

And then the world seemed to do everything possible to stand in the way of his going. It was one crisis after another. His law office lost three secretaries and two paralegals in one week, a senior partner had a heart attack, and an associate left for a three-week honeymoon. There was simply no one to take over the work, which meant he had to do it all himself before he could leave.

Then his younger daughter, Elaine, caught a virus of the inner ear, which left her with such a severe case of vertigo that she could not stand up without support. Her husband was frantic, trying to hold down a full-time job and take care of two young children and a sick wife all by himself, which meant Catherine was needed there. So TJ had left for

Washington alone and exhausted.

□ □ □

"Nice area, Kalorama," the cab driver repeated. "Stayin' long?"

TJ turned away from the window and pushed himself into polite alertness. "I have a job with the new administration."

The driver smiled his approval. "Ain't that nice. Gonna be living here for a while, then. Well, Washington's a nice town. Got its bad areas nowadays, but still a mighty nice town. Good place to live."

"You been here long?"

"All my life. Yessir, close on sixty-eight years."

TJ nodded. "Seen a few changes, haven't you?"

"That's the truth." The man laughed. "When I was a little boy, I used to like watchin' the old men come by an' light the streetlamps. They was all gas back then, you know. Then in the mornin' they had this little cup on a stick and they'd go 'round turnin' 'em off. That's how much things've changed." Once more he glanced at TJ in the rear-view mirror. "You ever been here before?"

"A few visits. Mostly official stuff, and never for very long."

"You'll prob'ly like it fine. Color don't mean any more here'n anyplace else, and a lot less'n in some places I know. Fella got the right job, he could be green all over and not wear nothin' but big purple feathers, people'd still bow and scrape."

TJ smiled at this. "Last I heard we were living in a democracy."

The driver laughed. "Yessir, I heard somethin' 'bout that too. Tol' me we was all equal under the law, jes' some is more equal than others."

TJ leaned forward and squinted against the gathering dark. "Is that the Potomac up ahead?"

"That's her. I been drivin' this same road for nigh on eleven years, and I still do enjoy this sight. That's the Washington Monument over there, an' the Lincoln Memorial. Then up there you can see the top of the Capitol."

"What'd you do before you drove a cab?"

"Near 'bout everythin'. My first memories're all 'bout work. I was still in school, you know, an' this fella put me on a truck. That was the beginning for me. Life of hard work's all I ever knowed. Twenty-five, thirty-five-pound blocks of ice. Used to take these tongs, sling that ice over my back, and carry it up four 'n five flights of outside stairs—fire escape stairs—in all kinds of weather. Tough work. All my life's been filled with hard work."

TJ leaned back, touched by the man's words. "What'd you do after that?"

"Got a good job after that. Good for those times, anyways. Worked in a grocery store. All these fine black folks'd come in. Lawyers, doctors—mostly wives but some gentlemen too—in all their fancy white-man's clothes. Wouldn't never touch nothin'. They'd walk down the aisles, point out what they wanted, or jes' stand there at the counter and name it, brand and all.

"Old man Thompson—that's the fella what owned the store—he'd have this big ol' wad of bills in his pocket and the change on the counter in a cigar box. I'd stick all the groceries in a wicker basket and carry 'em home for 'em, walkin' behind them fancy folks. Got 'bout a dollar a day in tips. Big money for a poor boy back then."

The man kneaded the steering wheel with stubby work-worn hands. "Sounds like nothing now, don't it. Lemme tell you how hard it was. Two years 'fore I started with the ice company—lessee, I was twelve then. Biggest thing in my life was when my brother got home; he was six years older'n me. He'd count his pennies from begging or piece-work or haulin' coal, whatever. Wasn't no such thing as a steady job. Didn't have no daddy. We needed forty-five cents for him, me and momma to go down and eat our fill of soup. Kitchen down the street sold big bowls of soup with a hunk of bread for fifteen cents. When I was twelve, there was so many people out there waiting for soup some days, we stopped traffic. Had to have a policeman there to hold the crowd back. Lotsa people waiting for the kitchen to open meant a lotta work that day. Yessir. After that and the ice work that grocery job was easy street."

"Mister, something about the way you say that scares the dickens outta me."

The man chuckled. "Reckon it could scare a sensible fella. If'n it came once, sure as the sun's gonna rise tomorrow, it could come again. Problem with this world is there ain't too many sensible people 'round. . . . Hey, look over here," he said, returning to his tour-guide role. "That's the J. Edgar Hoover Building. Used to be a store there called S. Kann's. That and Lansburgh were the two big department stores back then. And right there, between ninth and tenth on Pennsylvania Avenue, was what they called Market Place. Worked there for a while too. They'd bring the fruits and vegetables in there by horse, set up these little stalls, and sell there all day."

TJ inspected the front of several high-rise buildings for a sign of the past, but found none. "You were working two jobs?"

"Two, sometimes three. Momma got sick 'bout then, and doctors gotta be paid."

How long, oh, Lord? TJ shook his head, feeling admiration for the quiet strength of this man. The matter-of-fact way he spoke of hardship made TJ feel smaller than the less fortunate of his people. His people. How seldom he thought of them in that way. He had lived a truly sheltered life, shielded from the horrors that this man and so many others had suffered. He was thankful he had never had to face such trials, but knew that because of it, he lacked something. Something only found through the pain of such a life. A fountain of strength drawn from depths he had never fathomed within himself.

"My house didn't have no electricity," the driver went on. "No furnace neither. Had a coal-fire stove in every room. Had a waist-high ice box; you stick your block of ice in there, and your perishables on the ice. Summertimes you wrap newspaper 'round the ice, keep it from melting so fast.

"Didn't have no hot water, no bathroom," the man continued. "Cold water faucet, one for the whole house was all there was. Took a bucket of water out with us when we went to the shed, washed it down good. Hot water we cooked up over the stove. Didn't have much. Knew we were poor. But we had our Lord. Yessir, Sundays was a time of settin' work aside and gettin' right with God. Only thing that saw us through."

TJ sent a short prayer heavenward. Thank you for this man, Father. I was filled with doubt when I arrived, and was plain deep-down scared to boot. But I see in this man the power of simple faith and the wondrous ways in which you work. I don't know why this man had to suffer through such a life, and I don't know why I was called to this place.

But I hear in his voice that he knows you, and I feel in my heart that he has done your will. Thank you for this example, and give me the strength to do as you want.

"Biggest things in my life back then was church doin's and the Louis fights. Fella down the street used to take the radio outta his car and bring it in his house. Radio, speaker, battery, wire, the works. Took him the best part of the afternoon. Then the whole neighborhood crowded in the room listenin' to Joe Louis fight. Yessir. *Happy* times. Folks nowadays got all this television, movies, nightclubs, you name it. Don't know what happiness is. Spend all their lives chasin' after this 'n that. Don't get 'em nothing but old. They's forgot the Lord. Don't know there ain't nothin' in this whole world 'cept Him can fill that emptiness."

He turned the corner and pulled up in front of a brownstone house. "Number forty-six, Bancroft Place. Real nice home. Your friend must be doing all right. Yessir, hope you enjoy your stay here in Washington."

TJ glanced through the window and saw a charming three-story home with white shutters trimming large windows. The house was tall and narrow, with space for just one window on either side of the front door, three on the second floor, and another tiny one under the eaves. A minuscule lawn with carefully trimmed shrubs fronted the house. A battery of gaslights flanked the front door, the driveway, and the walk. TJ decided the place must be worth a fortune, wondered what Jeremy was up to, telling him to come here.

"I surely enjoyed what you had to say," TJ said to the driver as he paid him.

"Nothin' but an old man ramblin' on 'bout things been dead and gone for too long. Don't hardly ever talk 'bout those things no more. Been nice havin' someone wants to hear 'bout 'em."

TJ found himself reluctant to get out. Beyond the safety of the taxi lay an unknown world and untold responsibilities. "What's your name?"

"Sam'l. Sam'l Jones."

"Well, Samuel, it's truly been a pleasure making your acquaintance." He stuck out his hand. "My name's Thomas Case. All my friends call me TJ."

The man's grin threatened to split his face. "Likewise, Mr. Case, sir. Likewise."

"Call me TJ. Please."

The door to the taxi opened and Jeremy stuck his head inside. "If y'all are gonna sit there jawin', slide on over and make room for me."

TJ introduced the two men and watched Samuel retreat behind a barrier of reserve in the presence of the white man. He said, "I sure would like to see you again, Samuel, once I'm settled in."

"That'd be just fine, Mr. Case, just fine," the man replied, recovering a bit of his former friendliness. "Matter of fact, I goes to a church not far from here. New Jerusalem Baptist, over on P Street, 'bout 'leven blocks thataway. You'd be mighty welcome."

TJ handed him a pen and paper. "Write down that address, will you? And put your phone number down too, if you don't mind."

"Nossir, I don't mind. You need something, you jes' call us anytime."

"I truly appreciate that, Samuel. I'm sorry, I don't have a number yet—"

"Yes, he does," Jeremy interjected. "It's 376–9924. And this is his address."

Samuel gave the house another look, took in the new gray Continental in the driveway, returned to his former reserve. "Well, that's just fine. Say, I best be gettin' along. Got a livin' to make. Been nice meetin' you, Mr. Case. You too, sir."

"See you in church, Samuel," TJ said.

"Sure thing, Mr. Case. Y'all welcome anytime."

After they had unloaded the bags and waved Samuel on his way, TJ said, "What's this about my living here?"

Jeremy lifted the two heaviest bags, said, "You sure you want to talk about that right now, TJ? You look plum wore out."

"I asked you a question, Jem."

Jeremy headed for the house, said over his shoulder, "I've taken a lease on it. 'Bout the only place I could find that'd come furnished."

"You've done *what*?" TJ hefted the remaining luggage, hurried after his friend.

"This here street's called Bancroft Place. Area's called Kalorama. Realtor lady said it means 'beautiful view,' but she couldn't say in what language. Didn't know what the view was of either. Another too-expensive house prob'ly. Or a million-dollar pothole. City's full of 'em."

"I can't live here," TJ said.

"Don't talk nonsense. 'Course you can."

"This house is worth a fortune."

"No, you got it wrong there. This house mighta cost a fortune, but it ain't worth half of what people here'd like to make you *think* it's worth." Jeremy stopped, turned around, and said, "Tell you what, TJ. Why don't you just sleep on it tonight? You look about as tired as I've ever seen you."

TJ saw the concern in his friend's eyes, felt the barriers melt. His shoulders slumped and he sighed. "I don't know if I can do this, Jem," he said, his voice low.

"Yeah, I kinda figured you weren't gonna be all thrilled about leavin' your world behind. Don't know anybody who'd be real happy about that, come to think of it. It sounds all nice and noble when some preacher says, 'Follow the Lord's will.' And you're sittin' there thinking 'bout the country ham and biscuits waitin' back home, your mind buzzin' with this 'n that. Then around He comes and tells you to drop everything and go shootin' off to the ends of the earth, to the last place you'd ever want to live. You're gonna be happy, right?"

"You don't belong here either, Jem."

"Now that's for certain. But I heard His voice too, ol' buddy. Said to hustle myself on up to Babylon and make sure His man don't get eaten alive."

"You're a real piece of work," TJ said. "You sound about ten times more hick than you really are."

"Can't let these boys know how much you know, TJ. That's lesson number one. They don't mind a fool. It's the smart ones they gotta guard against. You might shake their little house of cards. Upset the power structure."

"You saying I got a lot to learn?"

"Anything you need to know, TJ, He'll tell you. Talk when He tells you to talk. The rest of the time, keep your trap shut. I always figured that's why He chose Moses, with his speech problem and all. Lord chooses the silent ones 'cause they know when to keep quiet."

Jeremy led the way up the brick steps to a massive oak door. "I'm doin' what I gotta do, TJ, same as you. I'm your butler, your chauffeur, your bodyguard, and anything else that comes up."

"You're nothing of the sort, Jem."

"Listen to what I'm sayin'. My service to God means servin' you right now, same as yours is to be His mouthpiece." He pushed the front door open with his foot. "Now just let it drop. You're so tired you're slurrin' your words. Anything else you got to say can wait till tomorrow."

TJ hesitated, then nodded his agreement, glad in spite of himself for the reprieve.

Jeremy led him into an entrance hall that would have been better suited to a full-sized mansion. A crystal chandelier was suspended from the ceiling two floors above their heads.

"The living room is there on the left, and what I guess is going to be our den is on the right—unless you want a study all your own. The kitchen and dining room are at the back, down that hall. Catherine's and your bedroom is up at the top of the stairs. Mine's on the left there beside it."

"This is too much, Jem," TJ murmured, looking up and around. "I can't—"

"Let it ride, I said. Go on up and get some sleep. We can talk about it in the morning, once you've had a chance to get your strength back. You couldn't whip a wet rag right now."

□　□　□

After his Bible study the next morning, TJ came downstairs. The aroma of freshly brewed coffee lured him to the kitchen, a room equipped with white breakfast table and chairs, white cabinets, and all the most modern conveniences. Light streamed through floor-to-ceiling bay windows opening from the breakfast nook onto the garden.

Jeremy was seated at the table with a cup of coffee and an open Bible in front of him. TJ paused in the doorway long enough to take in the two places set for breakfast, the coffeepot on the stove, the bacon draining on a paper towel, and the eggs waiting beside the frying pan.

"I don't recall ever seeing you in a tie before," TJ said in greeting.

Jeremy did not even look up. "Catherine warned me not to expect a civil word out of you until you'd had your second cup of coffee."

"When did you talk to Catherine?"

"This morning. She said to tell you that Elaine's doing much better. She also said for you to behave yourself and remember what you're up here for. I told her that if you started to forget I'd take it as my personal responsibility to whang you upside the head with that fryin' pan over there."

"Did she say when she was coming up?"

"Directly." Jeremy stood and moved to the stove. "How many eggs you want?"

"One. What does that mean, 'directly'?"

"Exactly what it sounds like. Your daughter still isn't well enough to manage two little kids and a house by herself." Jeremy broke an egg into the skillet. "She didn't say it, but I imagine Catherine figures you're gonna have your hands full gettin' used to this new work. She'll be up after you've had a chance to settle in."

TJ poured himself a cup of coffee and sat down at the table. "I don't imagine this job is going to be so difficult that my wife has to wait to join me."

Jeremy turned around, propped the hand holding the spatula on his hip, and gave his friend a look of pure pity. "Wasn't either one of us talkin' about the job, TJ."

TJ sipped his coffee, slid Jeremy's Bible around. It was opened to Habakkuk. "What are you reading him for?"

"Now that's an intelligent question if I ever heard one." Jeremy took a pitcher of orange juice out of the refrigerator, poured two glasses, and set them in front of TJ with a clatter. "You 'bout ready to tell me what's really botherin' you?"

"All right," TJ agreed. "How long do you intend on keeping this up, Jem?"

"I kinda figured you weren't going to do the sensible thing and just let it be," Jeremy said. He scooped up the egg, placed three strips of bacon beside it on a plate, opened the oven door and brought out a plate of toast, then set it all down before TJ. "One thing I gotta do today is buy us a toaster."

"You're not joining me?"

"Be right there. Go ahead and start. We can bless it in your belly just as well as on the plate." Jeremy broke two eggs into the sizzling pan. "Times like this, I really miss Ella. She had a way with words that I always loved to hear. Wasn't much she couldn't help a person understand. I never could decide if it was what she said or the way she said it that I liked better."

TJ paused with a forkful of egg in midair. Jeremy seldom talked about his dead wife. The loss remained an open wound. "She was a fine woman, Jem."

"That she was. Better'n anything I deserved havin', that's for sure." Jeremy loaded his plate and sat down, then folded his massive work-worn hands above his plate and bowed his head. TJ laid down his fork and closed his eyes.

"Lord," Jeremy began, "I've always been better at givin' orders than at persuadin' people. Takes ten times longer and a hundred times the words, and you never gave me the patience or the knowledge. My brother here needs me, and I know in my soul this is where you want me to be. But I don't know how to make him see that. So it's up to you, Father. In Christ's name I pray. Amen."

"You forgot to bless the food."

"It's a free country," Jeremy said, digging into his bacon and eggs. "You got any complaints, you go right ahead and do your own thing."

TJ picked up his fork, laid it down again. "I just don't feel comfortable having you do this, Jem."

"Doin' it for *you* is what you mean. If you'd just get it through that thick head of yours that I'm doin' it for the Man upstairs, you wouldn't have any trouble with it at all."

"You really feel that way?"

"Never felt surer of anything in my life. Felt it in my bones the first moment I realized He really had spoken to you. Now eat your breakfast before that egg freezes to your plate." Jeremy chewed a few more bites, then said, "I've been starin' retirement in the face for a couple of years now, TJ. All those things I've been doin'—the schools and the boat and the relief program—it's all felt like I was just bidin' time. I always figured I was just gettin' ready to follow Ella on across the Great Divide. But not anymore. Nossir. For the first time in I don't know how long I *know* I'm where I'm supposed to be. Doin' exactly what the Lord wants me to do. And that's all that matters, old friend. I feel like my whole life has been leadin' up to this moment. Don't know why, but that don't matter either."

"You're too young to be thinking about retirement," TJ said mildly.

"I've got a great future, and it's all behind me. All I've got left is servin' the Lord, and where He wants me to be is right here."

"Did you talk to Catherine about this?"

"Now that's a remarkable woman. I was all huffin' and puffin', figurin' she was gonna be up in arms about me crowdin' her. Know what she did? Kissed me on the cheek and said I was a blessing. That's what she said. A blessing. Said you'd put up a fight, but that I was to just hang in there and you'd come around."

"Catherine said that?"

"The day I left and again this morning. Said you were prob'ly determined to go out there and face the world all by yourself. I was to remind you that the Lord didn't say anything about you marchin' in solitude. He just said 'go.' "

"But we can't afford this house, Jem."

"We who?" Jeremy laughed.

"I mean *I* can't."

"I thought that was gonna come up sooner or later. You think maybe you could refresh my mem'ry, tell me what the Bible says about pride?"

"What's that got to do with it?"

"Everything. You know good and well, better'n me prob'ly, how much I'm worth. What'm I supposed to do with it besides help others in the Lord's name?"

"There're others who need it more than I do, Jem."

"Don't worry, they'll get their share. I've already started workin' on that."

"You must be spending a fortune on this place."

"Yeah, I had myself a real good holler when the real estate lady told me how much this cost. In actual fact, she told me I was gettin' it for a song 'cause the owner was in a hurry to go overseas. The thing is, TJ, it seems expensive because we're used to down-home prices. This here house would fit in your basement back home, and that's a fact." He held up his hand. "I know what you're gonna say. But listen, old buddy. There's gonna be some real tough times comin' down. I can feel it in my bones. He didn't bring you up here for any old picnic."

"I've been thinking about that too," TJ confessed.

"Yeah, well, you and Catherine are gonna need a place to come home to, you understand what I'm sayin'? An island of peace. I tell you, TJ, there hasn't been anything in a whole long time that's felt as right as gettin' this house for y'all."

"You mean for us," TJ said, giving in.

"That's right, and don't you forget it." Jeremy hid his pleasure in a flurry of activity. "You best go get yourself ready for work while I tidy things up here. We need to leave extra early this morning. I've studied a map, but I swear we might end up in Kentucky before I find my way downtown."

TJ climbed the curving stairs, tried to accustom himself to the fact that this was his home. He looked around the spacious bedroom with its four-poster bed and period furniture, then stepped into the marble-tiled bath. He stood in front of the full-length mirror that opened into a walk-in closet.

His friends said TJ was a man whose age was hard to place. He could look fifty, they said, or thirty, depending on whether he was smiling. In truth he was fifty-three, and for the past few years had been struggling against a bulging middle. But in a suit he looked fighting fit, broad in the shoulders and tapering to a leanness accented by his six-foot height.

His reddish brown curls were trimmed close to his head. He had inherited most of his grandfather's face—a strong jaw, razor-sharp features, slightly slanted eyes—but there among the harshness were his mother's full lips. And the color of his skin told the whole world about his father.

TJ learned about his heritage at the ripe old age of eleven. After a long week of worry he approached his grandfather. He did not hesitate because he was afraid his grandfather would be angry. His grandfather's stern yet placid nature was one of the foundations upon which his young life was based. No, he hesitated because he knew his grandfather would be totally honest.

His grandfather had a favorite chair, a throne that was reserved for his exclusive use in the evenings. When TJ had been very young, that chair had been his favorite playground during the day. No matter how miserable he might have felt at any time, the chair was there to embrace him with the ancient strength of his grandfather.

The chair was an old winged horsehair monstrosity with a back so high that TJ could barely see over it when he stood on the seat. The chair was covered with a blood-red crushed velour that his grandmother despised. She tried on numerous occasions to get his grandfather to let her have it re-covered. You most certainly may, was his traditional reply. On the day I am dead and buried you may take it out and burn it as far as I am concerned. The chair stayed as it was.

Beside it stood an equally ancient brass lamp, an enormous edifice as tall as a man. It possessed a magnificent total of five bulbs, which could be turned on one-by-one until the brightness rivaled the sun. As a child, TJ loved to turn the switch, watching with fascination as the room became illuminated in stages. His grandfather would lift him, his strong old hands around TJ's ribs, squeezing so hard it threatened to stop his breathing as he switched the bulbs up to four. The only time all five were lit was when his grandmother sat across the room reading her Bible.

That evening he stood at the doorway for the longest time, watching his grandfather read the newspaper and wondering if he should ask. He was almost ready to turn away when his grandfather lowered the paper slightly and peered over the top of the glasses that always slid down his nose as he read.

"What you want, son?"

"I was just wondering something," TJ said lamely, wishing he could back out, knowing it was too late.

"Well, these old ears can't hear if you're gonna talk like a summer wind and stand on the other side of the room."

The old man dropped the paper to his lap and signaled him to come nearer. Standing beside his grandfather's chair, his eyes dancing all over the room, TJ asked, "I was just wondering why you don't never talk about my daddy."

His grandfather sighed. "Been waiting for you to ask me this," he said, his voice a rumbly echo and his face grave as he carefully folded his paper and laid it on the side table. "Kept wondering whether I should say something, but how's a body supposed to know? I just decided to leave it up to the Lord. I figured He'd know better than me when it was time."

His grandfather's tone set TJ's heart to hammering. He stood on legs that suddenly felt weak and wished he were somewhere else, anywhere else, knowing without knowing what was about to come.

"Son, your momma ran away to marry your daddy," his grandfather said, reaching one hand out to caress TJ's shoulder, as though feeding strength to young limbs.

"But Grandma said—"

"I know what your grandma's been saying, and I know how she's spent years tiptoeing all around this subject. She's done the best she knew how, raising a boy when most people her age are getting ready to meet their Maker. You know I never said anything when she started off on her stories, you know how I always left the room, and you know I've never lied to you in all your life. And that's why you've come to me, isn't it?"

TJ nodded, growing more scared by the minute.

"Son, your momma fell in love with a white boy when she was eighteen years old. I don't mean she was infatuated. I mean that little girl was totally head over heels in love with the man.

"We all make mistakes, son. All of us. Your granddaddy most of all. I gave that angel an ultimatum. You know what that is? Well, that's when you tell somebody they've got to either do what you say or else. I told your momma—" The old man stopped, clenched his jaw for a moment, then went on in a quieter voice. "I told your momma that she either had to leave that boy or leave my house. Two days later she quit school and ran off with him to Boston.

"We all pay for our mistakes. All of us. I lost my little girl for being such a pigheaded fool. Maybe God will be able to forgive me. I hope so, because I sure as goodness can't."

He was silent so long that TJ thought his grandfather had forgotten he wasn't alone. The boy stirred impatiently, and his grandfather turned two misty eyes toward him. He seemed to search his mind for a moment before bringing the world back into focus.

He sighed a shaky breath. "We didn't hear anything for eleven of the longest months in my life. Then a letter came, just four lines long. The boy had died of pneumonia in the coldest winter anybody could remember. She didn't have any money for food and she was pregnant. She knew that we"—the old man stopped, fought for control, went on—"she knew that we hated her, she said. She asked for pity for the sake of her unborn child.

"I drove up to Boston and brought her back. Child wasn't nothing but skin and bones. Your grandma spent what time she had putting some meat back on her. But she never came home. Not really. The light in her had died with that boy."

He looked down at TJ, tears flowing freely now, not the least ashamed of crying. "It was love that brought you onto this earth, child. That's the one thing you got to remember above all else. Your momma loved your daddy with all her heart and soul, and she never got over losing him. When she went into labor, the doctor saw at once that she was too weak. Said he'd have to do a Cesarean to save you. That's when the doctor cuts a hole in the mother's stomach and takes out the baby. But while he was doing that, your momma just slipped away. He did what he had to do, son. He brought you into this world and made sure you were all right. Then he tried to save her, but it was too late. She was gone."

TJ clung to his grandfather and cried, and the old man held him close, rocking him gently. "It was hate that killed your momma, son. I've waited these eleven years to tell you how sorry I am, and to say I hope one day you'll be able to forgive me for what I did. Hate and fear are the devil's tools, son. White against black, black against white, it don't make the tiniest bit of difference. It's a sin big as all creation. And I promised God there wouldn't be any of it in the way I brought you up. It's too late to do anything about your momma, son, but sure as tomorrow's sunrise, this is one lesson you're gonna learn from me."

□   □   □

Jeremy pulled up to the Old Executive Office Building entrance on Seventeenth Street. Beyond the gate and the uniformed guard the building loomed like a palace, all lofty towers and spires and turrets and gray granite carved in gingerbread shapes.

"Got that letter in case they ask?" Jeremy inquired quietly.

"In my briefcase," said TJ, making no move to leave the car.

"Well, if there was ever a time for prayer, this is it."

"You start," TJ suggested.

"Heavenly Father," Jeremy prayed, "all-powerful Lord, we stand here before you and ask for your help. We are dwarfed by the might of this world. It is so big and fancy and impressive. It makes us feel so small. Help us remember who you are, Lord. Help us remember that all power comes from you.

"I'm prayin' for my brother here, Lord. He's answered your call, and he's come to a place far from home. Watch over him, Father. Guide his footsteps. Give him the strength he needs to do your will."

TJ remained silent a moment, then began to pray. "Lord, everything in my heart has been spoken by my brother. Thank you for sending Jem to enrich my life. It is at times like these that I realize how truly important friendship is, and what it means to be brothers in Christ. Make us vessels of your love and mercy. In Jesus' name I pray. Amen."

The two men raised their heads and knew a moment of embarrassed silence, as most men will after letting their hearts be seen. TJ studied the misty rain that had begun trickling down the windshield until he saw Jeremy stick out his hand. With effort he met his friend's gaze.

"Go get 'em, TJ."

He found himself reluctant to let go of that rock-hard hand. "Why do I feel as if I'm about to be fed to the lions?"

Jeremy smiled. "Prob'ly because you are."

⊣| SIX |⊢

Breakfast at Au Pied de Cochon had become a daily ritual for Congressman John Silverwood. "At the Foot of the Pig"—he remembered enough of his college French to translate the name—was an all-night cafe possessing a sort of low-life charm. It was also the only neighborhood place open at six in the morning, which was when he normally wanted breakfast. At that hour the clientele consisted of groggy lovers just ending a night of revelry and early risers trying to get a jump on the competition.

The restaurant was a three-block stroll from Silverwood's small Georgetown house. Actually "small" did not begin to describe it, especially when he thought of what he had left behind in North Carolina. This place was four cramped rooms on three floors, with bathrooms so squeezed under stairways and eaves that he could not stand up straight in the shower. From the outside the house was quaint, and the address and location were what he'd been looking for, but none of the rooms were large enough to give him any breathing space. And the price was simply staggering.

It was a pleasure to escape the claustrophobic atmosphere and walk to the restaurant through the early-morning air. After a few weeks he knew all the waiters by name, and it gave him a sense of belonging to walk to his accustomed spot, dump his newspapers on the table, and spend a few minutes exchanging political gossip with the locals. They treated the freshman politician with the carefully studied nonchalance of any true Washingtonian, but he could tell they were pleased by his attention. He anticipated the early meal with the eagerness of a deeply lonely man.

His wife, Suzanne, was not going to join him in Washington. Her decision troubled Silverwood more than he wanted to admit, even to himself. Suzanne was an audit partner with a major accounting firm, and her position gained him bonus points with the local feminist groups. But she hated politics, hated the disruption it caused her career, and loathed the role of dutiful wife called for around election time.

Silverwood did not know whether the clients who refused to turn over their work to another accountant were the real reason for her not coming. Nor did he care. All he knew was that he felt like the low man on his wife's totem pole.

He did what he could to ignore the gnawing ache of loneliness during those first nights in Washington. Thankfully there was enough challenge to keep him fully occupied, so he threw all his energy and emotion into his work. During their daily phone conversations, however, he fought a constant desire to yell and scream at her.

The truth was, he needed her. He needed her more than he had ever needed anyone in his entire life. Sometimes he felt as if he were suffocating in the alienness and the conflict and the petty backstabbing of the Washington political jungle. He kept waiting for Suzanne to say that she was ready to move, that missing him was a voice speaking louder to her heart than her ambition. He tried to find the words to express his own need, but he could tell she did not want to hear them, did not want to be tempted, did not want to come. And he burned with the anger and the shame of being second to a career in his wife's eyes.

The glass walls of Au Pied de Cochon's patio looked out over Wisconsin Avenue. Despite the misty rain blowing like wayward fog, the street vendors were busy setting up their stalls. He sipped his coffee and thought of his wife and watched with blind eyes as the hawkers fumbled with trinkets and watches and scarfs and sunglasses, stomping their feet to keep warm. Why couldn't Suzanne see how much he needed her? Why couldn't he express that need? He was a politician, for heaven's sake! He could convince an entire district to back him for public office. Why on earth couldn't he communicate with his own wife?

He pushed away the thoughts and rattled open his papers. On top was *The Washington Post,* and under that *The Washington Times.* Though he would never say it to anyone else, he always thought of it as *The Post* for facts and *The Times* for bias. The latter was the city's right-wing paper, and it often skewed the facts violently. Still, it was essential reading if he wanted to fathom the right-wing position on any major issue.

On top of these he opened the half-size *City Paper,* a weekly local filled with little besides gossip. Having these tidbits of useless information at his command gave him a sense of security when making idle conversation with the locals and longtime residents. It made him feel a little less the outsider in this strange, big town.

At the bottom of the *City Paper's* inside cover was a quarter-page ad for erotic garments, featuring a woman in a leather and chain outfit. A white slash announcing a major sale discreetly covered her breasts. He read the description of rubber and leather items on sale and wondered who on earth would be willing to shell out good money for such trash. He turned the page, spotted Chuck Shephard's column, and read: "In May, a Yonkers, New York, eighth-grade boy broke his teacher's nose with a flurry of punches after the teacher demanded that he pledge allegiance to the flag. The boy said it was against his religion."

Silverwood snorted his disgust and wished he had been there to defend the teacher. What the child needed was a taste of his own medicine. He imagined a snuffling, bloody-nosed kid being led through the Pledge of Allegiance by the threat of further punishment. Yes. Make the punk stand there and say it a thousand times.

His breakfast arrived, and he laid down the paper and dug into Eggs Benedict without the Hollandaise sauce—basically two poached eggs with cheese and Canadian bacon on two halves of an English muffin. An overpriced Egg McMuffin, he thought.

□　　□　　□

In the taxi on his way to the office, Silverwood opened his briefcase, spread out his work, and did his best to ignore the early-morning traffic snarl. The trip took over half an hour; thankfully this morning he was not required to share the cab, as often happened.

Politicos deemed it best to keep taxi fares as low as possible by doing away with the meter and allowing cabs to charge by the number of city districts they passed through. It was also agreed that the drivers could pick up a second fare, provided both passengers were going in the same direction.

Silverwood disliked the strange closeness of a shared cab. He was still new enough to become outright angry at the stone faces and cold silence of people sitting right beside him. Washington political staffers were the most arrogant, impolite upstarts he had ever met.

Three mammoth buildings of marble and granite and statues and pillars flanked Independence Avenue across from the Capitol. In Silverwood's opinion the most magnificent was Longworth, the middle building, where his suite of offices was located. It still gave him a thrill to pass beneath the massive columns and enter the marble portico, where the guards greeted him with a respectful nod, no longer needing to check his badge. As he stood and waited for the elevator with the small lighted sign "Members Only," he felt he had really arrived—a member of the exclusive club of political power.

The rabbit warren that was his third-floor office was an entirely different matter. There was simply not enough space. There was never enough space in Washington. He had been warned of this before he arrived, but nothing could have prepared him for the cramped quarters his staff was forced to endure. They accepted it because they had to and ignored their working environment as much as possible. The only time he had heard them disagree was over space. Normally his office was filled with the good-natured cynicism of young staffers thrilled over the chance to stand close to the throne and help shape policy. But let anyone dare threaten their tiny fleck of floor space, and bombs began exploding.

His office was a suite of five rooms, counting the antechamber where two secretaries were separated by a sofa and two chairs. His personal assistant and secretary shared the room next to his own, while the other seven staffers hung themselves from coatracks and perched on the windowsills, as far as he could tell. With everyone seated at a desk—which was seldom—the air seemed too close to breathe.

The doors opened at his floor and he strode purposefully forward, almost colliding with a young woman walking down the hall. When she saw who he was the flash of irritation changed to eager friendliness.

"Good morning, Congressman Silverwood," she said, giving him her number-one smile. Her blond attractiveness was powerful, and the message in her eyes was clear. "I'm Sally Watkins, Congressman Hesper's secretary? He's on the housing subcommittee with you?" A lilt made every sentence into a question. "I saw you at the hearing last week?"

"Of course, how nice to see you again." Hesper was a crass old warhorse who habitually slept through all but the first five minutes of every hearing unless the press was out in force. Silverwood vaguely recalled seeing this breathtaking beauty at the subcommittee's opening session.

"I thought your comments were great, really super."

Silverwood's appointment to the new subcommittee investigating the Department of Housing and Urban Development had been a mixture of chance, timing, and skillful maneuvering. He had overheard a couple of journalists at a Washington cocktail function discussing the HUD investigation, and one had predicted that it would be the Watergate of the new administration. At that time Silverwood had known nothing except that discrepancies had been found and an investigation was imminent. Misuses of federal funds were fairly common, and investigative subcommittees were burdens to be avoided at all cost—unless they could result in political mileage.

A few phone calls the next day uncovered the fact that what initially had been only a few questionable items was turning into an avalanche. As a policy analyst with the ultra-conservative American Enterprise Institute put it, the feds turned over a rock and the roaches scattered for cover. Is it big, Silverwood asked. Depends on what you mean by big, his friend replied. It won't bring down the government. But by the time the investigation's finished, HUD'll probably look like somebody let off a grenade in a dump truck.

So Silverwood visited with the Minority Whip and a couple of new allies and discovered that a seat was still open on the subcommittee. He jumped at it, and the day after his name was put down, the Washington papers exploded with front-page headlines on HUD improprieties. The Whip later said that his secretary fielded three dozen calls from various congressmen offering everything from their seats on the Finance Committee to their daughters for a place on the subcommittee.

Recalling that opening hearing, Silverwood glanced briefly at Sally Watkins's shapely form, then back to the long white-blond hair, sparkling blue eyes, and inviting mouth. She glowed with youth and good health and eagerness. He recalled the words of a senior senator who had told him about the Washington girls who chased after elected officials. Power groupies, the man called them, and mighty nice, if you get my drift. Silverwood laughed, thought the man weak for risking a life's ambition for a moment's pleasure.

What he had not realized was that they could be so beautiful. "Maybe we could get together for lunch sometime," he found himself saying.

Her look made his toes curl. "I know how busy you are during the day. Why don't we have a drink after work?"

He agreed, and watched her sway down the hall, wisps of hair streaming out behind her like blond beckoning hands. With a shake of his head and a frown to cover awakened desire, he turned and walked to his chambers.

His assistant, Bobby Hawkins, was perched on the arm of the sofa in the outer office, listening to a man in sunglasses. Silverwood walked on through quickly, knowing that if the visitor was unimportant or had not made an appointment, Bobby would take care of it.

The second office was a tiny afterthought where his secretary, Marge Daley, and Bobby worked in claustrophobic circumstances. He stopped at Marge's desk to check the mail.

"Who's the guy with Bobby?" he asked.

"Your first appointment," Marge said, handing over a typed copy of the day's schedule. She was gray-haired and efficient and a jewel beyond price as far as Silverwood was concerned. She had stood by him through the worst of the campaign, working impossible hours and proving herself time after time. She was married to her work and totally loyal to him. She was also prickly as a cactus with most other people. His staff had nicknamed her Miss Horney Toad and called her office The Little Shop of Horrors. Bobby was the only person she approved of completely, probably because he was as loyal as she was.

"I call it inertial advocacy," came a dry voice from the outer office.

Silverwood thought the man sounded three days dead.

"Not bad," Bobby replied. "Did you key that one up yourself?"

"I did indeed. It means a lobbyist who's out to stop change of all kinds. I personally believe it's an idea whose time has come. Think of all the people out there who are terrified of change. The man who champions such a cause should reap enormous benefits."

Marge rolled her eyes toward the ceiling, and Silverwood smiled. "Tell Bobby to come in alone first."

Bobby Hawkins was a chubby cherub in wire-rimmed spectacles. His clothes were always wrinkled, his glasses always sliding down his nose, his tie always loosened and slung over to one side, his shirt pocket always full of pads, slips of paper, and numerous pens. He never walked; he slouched from place to place. But he had a photographic memory and an awesome ability to assess the political winds. He was indispensable.

Bobby slid himself into the chair opposite Silverwood's desk. "What do you think of our walking cadaver?"

Still glancing through papers, Silverwood asked, "Why does he keep his sunglasses on? He's twenty feet and three rooms from the nearest window."

"Probably afraid of the light." Bobby fished through his pocket, pulled out a calling card, and tossed it on the desk. "Anthony Shermann, senior partner with Shermann, Blinders and Bledd."

"You're kidding. Is that really what they're called?" Silverwood dropped the papers and picked up the card. "You'd think with a name like that they'd have starved to death."

"Ted Robinson set up the appointment."

That made him look up. "Robinson called?"

"The man himself," said Bobby. "I did some checking. Shermann and Company are one of the biggest corporate law firms in DC. The senior partners don't practice much anymore, though. They spend their time walking the halls of power."

Silverwood gave a low groan. "Lobbyists."

Bobby nodded. "Loyalty for sale. I've just about decided I'm in the wrong business, Congressman. Know how much that boy charges? A thousand bucks an hour. One of his assistants let it slip."

"So what does he want?"

"He didn't say." A steely glint appeared in Bobby's eyes. "But I can guess."

"The HUD investigation," Silverwood said.

"Too right. There must be a lot of guys out there who're not happy over having their honey jar taken away."

"Maybe you'd better sit in on this one."

"You kidding?" Bobby stood and dragged over a second chair. "I wouldn't miss this for the world."

Anthony Shermann's handshake was as dry as parchment and as lifeless as his voice. "Such a pleasure to finally meet you, Congressman Silverwood."

"Likewise." Silverwood debated about whether to ask him to take off the sunglasses. "Take a chair."

"Thank you so much." The man eased himself down as though afraid a harsher movement would break something.

"So you're a friend of Ted's."

"Oh my, yes. Mr. Robinson and I have worked together on a number of issues over the years. I have very few regular clients, you see. Too costly. Most people don't want to pay unless there's a crisis. But when there's an urgent problem, why, they come running to me." Shermann laughed, a sound like dry husks rattling in the wind. He waved a hand vaguely, said, "And then I have need of good men like Mr. Robinson."

"And you have a crisis now, I take it," Silverwood said, thinking the man sounded positively reptilian.

"Rather a large one, I'm afraid. There's a construction firm that stands to lose a great deal of business from this HUD investigation."

Silverwood resisted the urge to give Bobby a confirming glance. "I see."

"Oh my, yes. Such a lot of business. And a great deal of it is in your district. They employ over a thousand people in eastern North Carolina, and all on HUD-related projects."

"And you're afraid there have been some unlawful activities?"

"Not unlawful, no, such a harsh word. Nothing unlawful, I assure you. All we have here is a solid, respectable builder trying to make a living in a horribly competitive market." Thin fingers raised to fiddle with his glasses. The lenses were clear at the bottom, darkening to completely opaque halfway up, hiding the man's eyes. "I wonder how many of us could come up squeaky clean under the microscope of a congressional investigation?"

Silverwood felt his hackles rise. Was the man threatening him? Whatever the case, he had heard enough. "Mr. Shermann, I can assure you that all of our investigations will be as thorough as the due process of law allows. And if your client is found to have been involved in criminal activities, I will personally see that he is prosecuted to the full extent of the law."

"Well, I suppose that's all I can do today, then, isn't it?" There was no change in expression or tone. His words had the depth and feeling of a machine. Shermann rose to his feet. "I just thought I should make you aware of the situation. Good day, Congressman."

When he was gone, Bobby grimaced. "I wonder if he catches flies with his tongue."

"That was too easy," Silverwood said.

"He got what he was looking for," Bobby agreed.

"But what good is that going to do him?" It worried Silverwood that the man had gone to all the trouble of making an appointment and then left without a fight.

"Maybe all he wanted was to be able to show his client that he could put the issue up before somebody on the committee. Show that his contacts are strong enough to justify his fee."

"No there's something else here, you mark my words," Silverwood said. "We haven't seen the last of that one."

□   □   □

"Yes, sir, can I help you?" One of the Old Executive Office Building foyer guards turned his attention to TJ. The voice was quiet and well trained, the eyes missed nothing.

"I'm supposed to begin work here today," TJ said. "I'm sorry, but I don't know the routine."

"Can I see some identification, please?" The guard pulled out a clipboard and ran his finger down the roster. "Yessir, Mr. Case. Here it is. Room 202. I'll give you a temporary badge for today, and someone upstairs'll take you down for a permanent one. Sign in here, please."

The guard passed him a plastic badge hung from a thin metal chain. "Slip that around your neck, please, and keep it out where it can be seen at all times." He gave a practiced smile. "Welcome aboard, Mr. Case."

TJ thanked him, passed through the metal detector, and stopped in front of a large display of photographs showing details of gloriously ornate rooms, hand-finished ceilings, and detailed iron scrollwork. He stooped to read a placard:

> Next door to the White House, the Old Executive Office Building (OEOB) commands a unique position in both our national history and architectural heritage. Designed by Supervising Architect of the Treasury Alfred Bult Mullett, it was built from 1871 to 1888 to house the growing staffs of the State, War, and Navy Departments, and is considered one of the best examples of French Second Empire architecture in the country.

TJ looked around. He was the only one looking at the display. The hall was crowded with people, but they all hurried by with blind eyes, intent on internal issues and pressed for time. Saying little, seeing less.

Once he was away from the entrance, the hallways were tall and broad and nearly empty. The marble-tiled floors were grooved and worn by a century of scurrying footsteps. Ornate brass lamps that must have originally been gaslit were suspended from the ceiling. People he passed would look, search for recognition, smile a blank hello, and move on.

The door to Room 202 was locked. TJ looked around, saw no one to ask, and decided to try the door to the right. He knocked, heard nothing, tried the handle, then pushed the door open.

An attractive auburn-haired young woman looked up from her desk. "May I help you?"

"I'm sorry to disturb you. My name is TJ Case and the door to my—"

"Oh yes, Mr. Case." She stood hastily, calling over her shoulder, "Joan, Mr. Case is here." And to TJ, "My name is Ann Crenshaw, I'm one of the secretaries assigned to your office."

"How nice to meet you," he replied, then turned to greet the young woman who appeared in the doorway. She was probably in her mid-twenties, but her fragile features, framed by pale-blond curls, left him thinking of her as a child.

"Mr. Case, I'm Joan Sammons, your assistant," she said, holding out her hand. Her voice was quiet, almost resigned, but her eyes were bright with intelligence and a hard, assessing quality that belied the fragility of her face and voice.

It surprised him that his secretaries and assistants had already been chosen, but he hoped it didn't show. "Pleased to meet you, Ms. Sammons."

"Call me Joan." She glanced at her watch. "I was supposed to tell Blair Wellesley up in Presidential Personnel when you got in, but I'm not sure he's there yet." She gave him a wan smile. "We work Washington hours here, nine or ten in the morning to midnight."

"Or until nine or ten the next morning," Ann added. "Depends on when your item comes up on the President's agenda."

TJ nodded. "Are you both coming from Education?"

"No," Joan replied. "I was with a computer consulting firm in Phoenix, and Ann was with a bank in Fairfax County. We both quit our jobs a year and a half ago to help with the President's campaign."

"Everybody in the office was on his campaign staff," Ann said.

Except me, TJ thought, and asked, "How many are we?"

"Five, with two slots still unfilled. One guy's supposed to start next week. There's been some holdup with his FBI clearance. The other one I haven't heard about yet from Personnel."

TJ searched for the proper response. "It certainly is nice to know that I have some experienced people working with me. I'm afraid I don't know a thing about how Washington works. Or the White House."

Joan and Ann exchanged a glance. "It's pretty much a club atmosphere," said Joan. "Almost everybody in the building was active in the campaign. People gave up their jobs, their careers—"

"Their families," Ann added.

"Some of us," Joan admitted. "There were a lot of sacrifices made during the campaign. This is sort of the payoff."

"The money's not much, but it's fun being right at the seat of power," said Ann. "And exciting."

"I'm sure it is," TJ agreed, glancing around. The L-shaped outer office was jammed with two desks, a computer work station, book-shelves, filing cabinets, and two armchairs covered in some kind of Chinese fabric. A small radio on the floor was playing rock music at a low and insistent level. On the wall behind Ann's desk was a blowup of a Far Side drawing—skulls planted on poles in the front yard of a ranch-style house, with the caption "Suburban Headhunters." The other walls were bare except for a couple of pictures of the President.

"Why don't I show you around," Joan offered, and said to Ann, "Call down to Personnel and see if Blair's come in yet."

Joan took him through what had clearly been an antechamber but now contained a shoulder-high partition blocking off space for a desk and a second computer terminal. "This is my office," she said.

The third room was long and narrow and as crowded as the others. Two desks faced each other, separated by a row of filing cabinets and another computer terminal. A plaque on one desk read, "The Washington Golden Rule: He who has the gold, makes the rules."

A high ceiling accented the room's cramped dimensions. Slender windows at one end opened onto a small balcony; TJ craned, glimpsed the White House through the bare tree limbs and falling mist.

"John Stuart was a lawyer with a firm in Boston," she said, pointing to the desk with the plaque. "And the desk over there is for the guy who hasn't been cleared yet. I don't know what we're supposed to do with the fifth person. Stick a desk out in the hall, I suppose."

"Or stuff them in a drawer," TJ agreed. Every inch of space seemed occupied.

She led him back through the secretary's office, where Ann was just hanging up the phone. "Blair's on his way over," she said.

Joan nodded, opened the doors across from the unoccupied desk, said, "This is your office."

The room was more spacious than the others, but not by much. The desk was large enough to look cramped; the bare conference table seemed totally out of place. The nicest aspect was the set of large, old-fashioned window-doors that opened onto the balcony. The view of the White House was stupendous.

Trying to keep his voice casual, TJ asked, "Does anyone here have experience in education?"

Joan's eyes turned hard as stone, but her voice was as soft as ever. "You do," she replied. "The rest of us have experience in politics."

TJ nodded. "Beautiful view," he said.

"There are some chairs and a little table on the balcony, they're pushed over to one side," she said. "It's going to be a nice place to work in the springtime."

TJ moved close to the glass and looked down on the parking lot that separated their building from the White House grounds. Joan came up beside him.

"That's the West Wing," she said, pointing to the side closest to them. "The President's office is on the other side, overlooking the Rose Garden."

Beneath them, a police officer was leading a German shepherd from car to car. The dog circled each one, carefully sniffing tires and underbody. For bombs, TJ decided.

"Blair's going to have you pretty busy for a day or so," Joan said. "But we need to meet as soon as possible to go over some urgent matters. The President's made education a priority issue, and they want us to get to work on policy as quickly as possible." She gave him another wan smile. "We can't let Congress get the jump on us, can we?"

"No, we can't," TJ replied, turning away from the windows.

Joan led him back to the outer office, where a young man now sat perched on the edge of Ann's desk.

"I told him I wanted a signed picture of the President," he was saying. "And I didn't want any fakey signatures. I've done enough of 'em in the campaign to be able to tell the difference."

"Blair, this is Mr. Case," Joan said.

"Hey, hey, welcome to Washington, Mr. Case." The young man walked over with outstretched hand and a smile that meant absolutely nothing. "Blair Wellesley, Presidential Personnel. I'm the one assigned to show you the ropes."

"Nice to meet you," TJ said, wondering if everyone here was as young as this trio. And as casual.

"Yeah, same here." He turned to Joan. "You tell that cowboy of yours he pulled in a lot of favors on that last one. The ball's in my court now."

"I'll tell him," Joan promised.

"You've got a hotshot from Boston on your team who's out to solve all the world's problems in one day," Blair said to TJ. "Well, you ready to go? A lot to get done this morning."

"By all means," TJ replied, and motioned for him to lead on.

Outside the office, Blair stopped and pointed at the doorknob. "Seen that? Here, take a look."

TJ bent down, saw that the brass knob boasted an ornate anchor-and-stars design.

"I love showing these things to visitors. When this place was built, it housed almost half the entire government. The knobs tell what the rooms were used for. This was part of the Navy Department."

As they walked down the hall, TJ ventured, "Everybody certainly does seem young."

Blair laughed. "There're seventeen hundred employees here and in the White House, and I'll bet you money that two-thirds of them are under thirty. See, the money's pretty awful, so those who take the lower jobs have to be young enough to live on bread and water for a while. The payback is intellectual. People give up four years of pushing their careers forward so they can have the chance to play with power."

"And most of them were with the President's campaign staff?"

"Yeah. You're a real exception to the rule. Most of us have either worked together or known about each other for a couple of years now. We pretty much lived in each other's pockets during the campaign." Blair glanced sideways at him. "Some people'll be kinda cool toward you at first. You know, the new kid on the block. It'll pass. Especially with you working on a high-priority item like education."

TJ decided he might as well ask it now. "What's the policy on hiring and firing within my section?"

That sobered his guide immediately. "Why, do you have any complaints?"

"Of course not," TJ said. "I was just a little surprised to find my section already fully staffed."

"They're good people in there," Blair said flatly. "The best. They've given up just about everything for the past year or so to get the President elected. Shoot, Joannie's husband ended up divorcing her, she was spending so much time away from home. They know politics, and they know what the President wants. You'll be glad you've got them, believe me."

□   □   □

TJ followed Blair Wellesley downstairs and along the whitewashed hall, a bit dazed and bewildered by too much too fast. First they'd gotten his ID, which had to be a temporary one because TJ's FBI clearance had not been completed. Blair explained that until he had his permanent ID, he would have to be escorted inside the White House or met at the entrance by a West Wing staffer. Then came an excruciatingly boring conference with a serious young man from the Legal Affairs section who droned on for over three hours about what TJ could not do while in office and after leaving government service. TJ had listened and nodded and tried to pay attention, but found his mind going back to the ethics class he attended in law school.

□   □   □

I'm sixty-seven years old, Professor Seers had told them that first day. I've seen the laws that govern this nation go through changes I would not have believed possible when I qualified forty-four years ago. But this class isn't about those changes. You'll have all your lives to study and learn about them. What we're going to study is the foundation, the rock, the one thing that can't change, not if we intend to keep this nation alive.

He was a tall man who wore his wisps of gray hair like a crown. His body was stooped and clearly feeble, and movements came with a great deal of hesitant shakiness. But his voice was firm, and the light in his eyes brilliantly clear. TJ remembered him as the best professor he'd ever had.

"Ethics is the rarest word in the legal vocabulary," Professor Seers told them. "Most of you here think law has to do with right and wrong. That is true only in the rarest of cases. Most of the time, law is about limiting freedom. Law is about defining what you can and can't do. Law is about prohibitions. Law is about punishing. We *hope* for right and wrong. And that's about all we guardians of the law can do, hope. And pray for guidance.

"The only way we can be sure that right or wrong is followed in the law is if our nation comes to know the Lord in its heart and mind. For the makers of law, it gives them guidelines to follow. For the average citizen, it teaches that *nobody is above the law.*

"That is the single biggest problem with our society today. People consider themselves safe from the law so long as they think they won't get caught. They see the law as something valid only for others, and only applicable if it suits them.

"It is impossible for someone who has not had a personal experience of God, that deep-down heartfelt transformation, to accept that laws can be truly eternal. And without this belief born of personal experience, law will remain something to scramble around, rather than something to strive to uphold.

"It is impossible for anyone to remain totally within the law. The Bible is full of this fact, as anyone who has studied it can testify. It is a three-thousand-year legacy of man's weakness. But with an acceptance of God, we can be assured that man will at least try to follow the law. And that, ladies and gentlemen, is all we can hope for. That man will try.

"Man has developed a myriad of terms to describe a government without God seeking to rule a people without God. And how many words are in our vocabulary because of man's inhumanity to man— communism, pogrom, anarchy, dictatorship, military coup, Stalinism, concentration camps, civil rebellion, prisoners' suicides. How many of us are doomed to a hell on earth because of the absence of God from our lives?"

There were fifty people who listened to the professor that first class. By the time the next class met, forty-three of the students had opted for other courses. One of them had made his opinion very clear in a conversation that TJ had happened to overhear. What's the point, the student had told a friend, of listening to five months of some religious nut? His friend had agreed and added, it's hard enough to make a living out there anyway, without carrying around this extra burden of guilt.

□   □   □

On their way to lunch, TJ listened with half an ear to Blair's determined chatter. The people moving past them were mostly male, mostly white, and most looking urgently important.

The cafeteria was a clutter of noise and people and tables of various sizes. Blair led him through the serving line and over to a larger table that still had two empty places. From the expression on Blair's face he clearly knew everyone.

TJ set his tray down, but before Blair could follow suit a large woman with bright red hair shouldered past him and jammed her tray down with a clatter. Dull eyes in a face caked with makeup dared him to argue.

Blair hesitated, his confidence clearly shaken. He said, "It's okay, TJ. I'll see you after lunch."

TJ watched his only acquaintance in the room turn and walk away. He decided to excuse himself and follow, but the other black man at the table stood and extended his hand.

"Carter Williams," he said. "You look about as lost as I did my first day here."

"TJ Case. Nice to meet you." He shook the proffered hand. "I'm sorry it shows."

"Don't apologize. Everybody's got to start sometime." He looked at the redheaded woman who had taken Blair's place. "Right, Bella?"

"Don't ask me," said a voice made from equal parts gravel and boredom. The woman did not even look up from her food. "I just work here."

Williams gave the top of her head a sardonic look and rolled his eyes at TJ. "Come on, sit down. I'll introduce you so you can get busy and forget everybody's name."

Swiftly he introduced the other six around the table, giving brief anecdotes about their background and positions. TJ saw a group of intelligent, carefully casual people who inspected him intently. No instant judgment here. Just caution. They were all good at what they did, he was positive of that. Very good.

"And this is Bella Saunders," said Williams, completing the circle. "She's one of the top OMB liaisons with White House staffers on that most important of policy instruments." Carter was giving special emphasis to his words, his eyes losing their gleam as he gave TJ a warning look. "I'm talking about money."

"Without which nothing gets done," a woman across the table added, her eyes carrying the same warning.

"I see," TJ said noncommittally.

They were clearly not satisfied with his reaction. "The OMB approves all the funding proposals coming out of the various agencies," Williams continued. "Including the White House and all OEOB policies. And anytime a White House staffer, *like you*, has to testify before a congressional committee, your testimony has to be approved first by the OMB."

"Extremely powerful," a young man said from the far end of the table, speaking into his coffee cup.

"Bella's been here longer than anybody, haven't you, Bella?"

"I've seen 'em come, watched 'em go." She looked at TJ with eyes as devoid of emotion as her voice. "Thomas Jefferson Case, late of Raleigh, North Carolina. Seconded by senatorial recommendation to the position of Special Assistant to the President for Educational Affairs."

The man on the other side of Bella snapped his fingers. "Case. Yeah, now I remember. You're the guy who switched parties to help that congressman with his campaign. What was his name?"

"Silverwood," TJ said, impressed with their knowledge and feeling even more the novice.

"Yeah, that's it. Silverwood." The man said to the others, "Brought over half the black vote. First time in history we've got a Republican congressman from that district."

"Special emphasis on education of gifted children," Bella went on in her whiskey-and-cigarette rasp. "Answers to Mason Whitfield." She turned to TJ. "Bet you haven't even met the man yet."

"Bella knows everything about everybody," one of the women broke in. Her voice laid the compliment down heavy, but her eyes were saying something else entirely.

"It's my job to know," Bella said.

Thankfully the conversation turned to lighter topics, and TJ did what was clearly expected, which was to watch and listen. He felt it was all a theater put on for his benefit.

"I saw a good one today," said the young man seated across from

Bella. "A sign on somebody's desk over in Commerce says, 'The First Law of Bureaucracy: The first 90% of a job takes 90% of the time. The remaining 10% takes the other 90%.' "

"That's nothing," said the woman across from TJ, shaking her head. Her spiky brown hair, stiff with mousse, didn't move. "I had to go over to Senator Jenson's office yesterday, and his secretary's got this sign that says, 'The more garbage you put up with, the more garbage you're going to get.' "

"Yeah, I know her," Bella said. She had the weariest eyes TJ had ever seen. "She tried to steal my coffee cup the last time she was in my office."

"The one that says 'The first guy who makes a sexist remark gets this hot coffee in his lap'? "

"Yeah, I love that little grin the lady on the mug is wearing," someone remarked.

"And that line on the reverse side, 'Have a nice day.' It's perfect. Where'd you ever find it?"

"It's a limited edition of one," Bella replied smugly. TJ glanced at the other faces, realized they were paying her homage.

"You still liking your new job?" someone asked the woman across from him.

"It's great," she replied. "I landed in a real California-type agency. I feel totally at home. It's so laid back you'd think the receptionist was passing out Valium."

"Wow."

As TJ listened to the empty banter, a change came over him. It was so gradual, so quiet in its approach, that he was not even sure when it began. But he did not question its arrival. It felt like a milder form of the sensations he had known that morning on the lake.

"It's totally broke," the woman was saying. "We get these daily memos asking if anyone wants to take early out, get pregnant, or sign on for a year's leave of absence."

"Sounds incredible."

He was having difficulty concentrating on the conversation around him. His chest filled with some silent power—a living presence, a sense of higher awareness so strong that the scene before his eyes withdrew to a vast distance. The empty faces, the calculating eyes seemed like a dream. Only the sense of power growing within him was real.

"Yeah, just goes to show," Carter Williams said, giving TJ a wink. "Dreams really do come true in Washington."

"I guess it's too early to ask what you'll be doing?" one of the men asked TJ. The question was placed casually, but all eyes were on him now, ready to probe, study, and judge.

"I'm not exactly sure what my responsibilities will be," TJ replied. He had real difficulty in saying the words. There was something else that needed to be done. He understood a growing purpose, a calm urgency, a need to be fulfilled. It did not matter that the sensation was illogical. The presence of the Holy Spirit was real. Guide me, Father, TJ prayed, and waited.

Bella finished her coffee and set her cup down with a clatter, as though demanding that attention return to her. "Well, you've just joined the only organization on earth that doesn't discriminate," she remarked.

The group was locked into an immediate embarrassment. Carter Williams looked straight at TJ, said nothing.

"Oh, there's discrimination, all right," one of the men said, trying to make a joke. "In Washington, though, it's based on who's got power and who doesn't."

"That's not discrimination," Bella declared flatly. "That's politics." She refused to see that she was making everyone thoroughly uncomfortable. "Black people here are just like anybody else. We don't follow the slave mentality you still find in the rest of the country."

Silence engulfed the entire table. The Presence within TJ reached out to Bella in unearthly tenderness, searching for her heart, seeking to fill the void mirrored in her eyes. It was as gentle as it was powerful, and the words simply came to him.

"Discrimination doesn't begin with white against black," he said quietly. "It's a basic part of American society. The white lawyer looks down on the white truck driver. And the truck driver needs to look down on someone else just so he can feel a sense of worthiness too. You don't have to go back to slavery to find the basis for discrimination. It's everywhere. Here. Today. If you see yourself as superior to someone else for whatever reason, then you're discriminating. If someone covets power as a means of showing superiority, he is discriminating."

The table seemed frozen solid. TJ had the impression of several faces staring at him in openmouthed surprise, but all he could be certain of was the love he was feeling for this poor woman. The Presence within him simply poured itself out.

"The answer lies in the Bible," he continued. "The apostle Paul tells us that we are all equal. All of us. If we can't abide by this, then we are sinning. And the very worst kind of sin is the one which we don't or won't or can't admit to."

He stood and picked up his tray, and he felt all eyes at the table follow him. Before turning away, he said quietly, "It was nice meeting you all."

As he was walking out of the cafeteria, Carter Williams caught up with him. "Man, I really admire what you said back there. But if you're not out to commit professional suicide your first day on the job, you got to find some way to apologize to the Dragon Lady."

"I have nothing to apologize for," TJ replied.

"Did you hear me say anything about a cause? No, you didn't. I'm not talking about logic here. I'm talking about revenge." The man was clearly worried for him. "Bella's been here since before the Civil War, and her only love in life is making hamburger outta staffers. Somebody told me she even did in a deputy secretary back in the Carter days. Absolutely neutered the guy."

" 'And they went their way,' " TJ quoted, " 'joyfully proclaiming their thanks for being able to suffer in the name of their Lord.' "

"What's that? Something from the Bible?"

"Acts," TJ said.

"Yeah, well, all I got to say is, you better have the funeral service down real good. 'Cause if you don't find a way to get back on Bella's good side, you're gonna need it." He patted TJ on the shoulder. "Be seeing you around. That is, if Bella leaves anything besides the bones."

⊣| SEVEN |⊢

After supper that evening TJ told Jeremy what had happened during his first day on the job and about the doubts that were now working their way to the surface. He did not mention the unusual sense of God's presence he had experienced in the cafeteria. Now that it was no longer evident, it was hard to believe that something unseen could have felt so real. But he did tell Jeremy about his encounter with Bella Saunders.

"I wonder maybe if I should have avoided it," he concluded.

"Don't seem to me you had any choice at all," Jeremy replied.

"I could have stood up and walked away. Or just sat there and kept my mouth shut. I could have done a hundred different things, all but stand up and beat my chest."

"If you came up here plannin' on buryin' your head in the sand, yeah, I suppose you coulda run away. But I recollect there bein' somethin' else that needed doin' up here."

"What's that, Jem?" TJ ran an uncertain hand over his cheek. "Can you remember what on earth we're doing up here?"

"Far as I remember, it had somethin' to do with followin' His lead."

"I feel about as out of place here as a fish on dry land."

"Seems to me the Bible says somethin' about blessed is the man who doesn't feel like he belongs here on earth."

TJ smiled. "You've got an answer for just about everything tonight, don't you?"

" 'Bout these things there ain't much room for doubt, old buddy," said Jeremy. "While I was listenin' to you talk about that scene at lunch,

I was thinkin' to myself, man, I'll bet you there's been a lotta times the Lord's tried to work through people like He did through you. Tried to get in there and help somebody. But we're just too busy listenin' to the voices of the world to pay any attention. Too worried about our jobs or our reputations or what people're gonna say behind our backs. So whoever it was that needed help right then got nothin' but empty words. You know, if I was God, I'd be kickin' holes in walls right about then."

"I heard somebody call her the Dragon Lady," TJ said idly. He got up and refilled both their coffee cups from the pot on the stove. "People kept sticking their heads in my office, not saying anything, just looking in like you'd stop and look at an animal in the zoo. I could kind of hear what they were thinking. You know, there he is, the guy who committed hari-kari in the cafeteria his first day on the job."

"If there's one thing I'm not worried about, it's whether the Lord is watchin' over you," said Jeremy, stirring sugar into his coffee. "You just keep on tryin' to do His will. Let these other turkeys take care of their own selves."

□   □   □

TJ had hardly been at his desk for five minutes the next morning when Bella Saunders appeared, trailing cigarette smoke and stale perfume. "Mind if I come in?"

"Please do," he said. He stood and scooted around to hold her chair. When he looked up, Ann was standing in the doorway.

"I guess you don't want to be disturbed," she smirked.

"Thank you, no."

She shut the door with a knowing smile, and TJ wondered what it was going to be like trying to work with people in his office who weren't really on his side.

"A real gentleman. I like that," Bella said. "Got an ashtray?"

"I think I saw one here yesterday." TJ glanced around, spotted one on the conference table. It was pewter and stamped with some official insignia.

"Thanks." Bella set the ashtray in front of her on his desk and dragged deeply on her cigarette. "It was real interesting what you said yesterday about the lawyer looking down on the truck driver." The smoke poured out with her words. "See, my father was a truck driver."

TJ sat down, felt his stomach sink a notch. "I didn't mean anything personal—"

"He was always real defensive about the way people looked at him," she plowed through his apology. "He was a real proud man. Real proud. And hard."

She paused for another puff, a shaky one this time. "He'd get so excited watching the news or reading the paper he couldn't sit still. There wasn't anything he loved more than hearing about some big-time politician or businessman being dragged through the mud."

Her mouth tasted a smile. "I can still hear what he'd say, almost shouting it out. 'Sweet revenge. Yessir, all those good times are over. Revenge, baby. How sweet it is.'"

As she spoke, TJ felt the same inward connection as the day before. Perhaps because he was not caught so flat-footed by its arrival, he was able to listen to Bella and watch his own inward transformation at the same time.

"He was a hard man. I've said that already, haven't I? He was hard on us children and hard on my mother. Especially when he'd been drinking. He could get so mean then, he used to scare me something awful. It was like some devil got out and took over his body when he'd been drinking.

"There were a couple of black men who drove trucks for the same company as my father. We'd all get together sometimes, and he was always real nice to their faces. But the things he said behind their backs were just terrible."

She stabbed her cigarette out with an angry motion, clearly fighting hard to maintain control. "I don't know why I'm telling you all this. I stayed awake half the night thinking about what you said and remembering things I hadn't thought of for years. But I don't know why I'm sitting here running my mouth like this."

He felt the Presence extending outward like a rising sea of calm, washing words into his mind. "You're here because you're tired of carrying these burdens," he said quietly, reaching through her anger and distress with compassion.

Suddenly she was weeping softly. "Look at me," she sniffled. "I can't even control the faucets."

"You're tired of feeling the emptiness, tired of running from the pain. In all those years of running, you've never escaped. And you know you never can. Do you know why, Bella? Because you carry what you flee from in your mind and in your heart."

With that, she broke down completely. "I'm so alone," she sobbed.

"How wrong you are," TJ said softly. "You've never been alone."

"I'm old, I'm alone, and nobody cares. Nobody." She looked at him through eyes streaming tears and mascara. "What are you doing to me?"

" 'Verily I say unto you, Unless a man dies and is born again, he can never enter the kingdom of heaven.' Have you ever heard those words before?"

"I don't know. Maybe I have. I can't remember." She crumpled her hanky and dabbed at her eyes. "I must look a wreck."

TJ spoke, his words a gift from somewhere beyond his earthly limits. He felt the Spirit moving, touching, teaching, praying. He held a gift he could only know by giving it to another.

"It's a verse from the New Testament, and it means that you must allow the worldly self with all its pains and fears and doubts and struggles to pass away," he told her. "First you must see this old self for what it is—nothing but a lie. A lie seeking to convince itself and others that it's real.

"When you see it honestly for what it is, you can recognize it as worthless. It is not a treasure to be guarded. It is not worth fighting and hating and hurting others to keep intact. It is a burden. The heaviest one you can ever know. Do you feel the weight?"

"It's like a stone on my heart," she said, with hopeless eyes and a trembling voice.

"You can be free," he said, his voice still soft, the words still a gift. "Let that burden of sin and guilt go."

The tears came anew. "But how?"

TJ smiled with a tenderness that reflected the love in his heart. "By turning it all over to God. By accepting His Son Jesus as your personal Savior."

She was crying so hard now that the words were barely a whisper.

TJ asked her, "Would you join me now in prayer?"

☐   ☐   ☐

When Congressman John Silverwood arrived at his office, his stomach churned from another argument with his wife. He had accused her of caring more for her position than for their marriage, and she had accused him of being blind to everything but his own political ambition. There was no mention of love, not even a casual questioning of how the other person was feeling.

In the cab on his way to work, Silverwood decided he would stop calling her every day. All they did was argue anyway. It left him feeling sick.

He did not bother to make polite conversation with his secretary. Marge knew him well enough to understand his mood. She offered him only one small smile with his telephone messages and mail.

Bobby was in Silverwood's doorway before he sat down. "Ted Robinson's called you five times already this morning. Says it's urgent. Want me to get him?"

"Go ahead," he said dully, sorting through messages and letters, scribbling notes to aides on most, setting some aside to handle himself. A few he threw away—lobbyists and busybodies who pestered him constantly, offering him nothing but exhaustion, frustration, and illogical ideas.

His hand hesitated over the last telephone message, from a Ms. Sally Watkins, asking him to call her back. Sally Watkins? Where had he heard that name before? Then he remembered. The beauty he had met in the hall yesterday, the one who worked for Congressman Hesper. He felt his blood sing as he remembered her look. The gloom he had carried into the office lifted.

The phone rang. It was Bobby, saying he had Robinson on line two. Silverwood pushed the button and heard, "What say, John? How's it going this morning?"

"Fine," he said, still staring at the phone message from Sally Watkins.

"Got anything we need to discuss?"

"You called me," Silverwood replied.

"Yeah, that's right." The head of the North Carolina Republican party seemed unsure of himself. "Listen, ah, how're those HUD investigations moving along?"

Silverwood put the message slip down. "You want to know about the investigation or about the meeting I had with your man yesterday?"

"He's not my man." Robinson hesitated. "Listen, John. Gotta be careful with this Shermann."

Bobby appeared in the doorway, and Silverwood waved him away. "What're you doing, sending me somebody like that, Ted? The man didn't even tell me who his client was."

"I'm not talking about the client. I'm talking about Shermann." Robinson sounded almost frightened. "Just take it easy with him, John. Humor the guy."

Silverwood opened a side drawer, leaned back in his chair, pried off his shoes, slid his feet into the recesses. "How am I supposed to humor somebody who basically admits that his client has been up to criminal activities?"

"He said that?"

"More or less. Bobby was sitting in the office with me."

Robinson thought it over. "Well, I guess there wasn't anything else you could have done."

"Who is this guy?"

"He's a menace," Ted Robinson replied, his voice showing spark for the first time. "I'm surprised the grass doesn't wither under his feet."

"Then what on earth are you doing sending him to me?"

"I didn't have any choice. Don't ask me anything more, because I'm not going to tell you. Just listen to what I say, John. Be careful around this guy."

"Thanks for nothing," Silverwood replied.

"Afraid you'll be hearing from Reggie on this one."

"Erskins knows him?"

"Most people who've been around Washington for any length of time know Shermann. He has a habit of getting around."

"It gave me the creeps just being in the same room with him," Silverwood replied. "He looks like walking death."

"That may be," Robinson said. "But just remember, when you know that guy's involved, stay on your toes. And don't cross him if you can help it."

As soon as Silverwood put down the receiver, Bobby poked his head around the door again. "Hearing starts in fifteen minutes."

"Be right there. Shut the door, will you?" Silverwood picked up the telephone message slip and dialed the internal number. When the voice answered, he felt his heart speed up.

"Oh, how sweet of you to call me back." Sally seemed genuinely pleased. "I was so hoping I could catch you before your day got too busy."

"What can I do for you?" It was a new sensation to be pursued by a woman as attractive as this.

"Well, I was just wondering if maybe we could get together for that drink tonight?" That attractive little lilt was still in her voice.

"Let me check." Silverwood drew his calendar toward him and was astonished to find his evening schedule booked solid for the next two weeks. "I don't believe this."

"What's the matter?"

He flipped through the pages again. A series of formal receptions he had already agreed to attend stretched out like some endless barrier. He wondered for a moment if something wasn't trying to keep them apart, then swiftly pushed the thought aside. It was suddenly very important that he see her, that she not think this a polite turndown.

"I'm really sorry, but I have something on every night for the next two weeks. My first free evening is a week from next Sunday."

"Oh." She sounded disappointed. "Well, if that's the earliest we can get together, I suppose it'll have to do."

In an attempt to make it more definite in her mind, he asked, "Where shall we meet?"

She brightened at that. "Let's see. Do you know the Four Seasons Hotel?"

He hesitated. The Four Seasons was a mammoth brick structure with outrageous prices—a single room cost over two hundred dollars a night—situated in the heart of Georgetown. He debated whether or not he should be seen there with an attractive single woman. Then it struck him that, in all honesty, he really didn't care whether Suzanne found out or not.

"Yes," he replied. "As a matter of fact, I live only about five blocks from there."

"You live in Georgetown?" Suddenly she sounded like an excited teenager. "Oh, I've always dreamed of having a home on one of those little cobblestone streets. There's nowhere else on earth I'd rather live."

It was on the tip of his tongue to invite her to his home, but he was saved by Bobby's impatient knock on the door. Silverwood dropped his feet to the floor and said, "Sorry, but I've got to get to a committee hearing. What time shall we meet?"

"Would seven o'clock be all right?"

"Perfect," he said, smiling into the phone. "See you then."

□   □   □

TJ arrived late the next morning, slowed down by Friday traffic and fitful snow showers. The big flakes fell wet and heavy, slowing traffic to a snarling crawl. The roads were solid streams of blinking lights, steaming manhole covers, honking horns, and heavily bundled pedestrians moving faster than the cars.

Bella was waiting for him in the outer office. TJ's staffers were clustered around her, glancing from her face to the Bible tucked under one arm and back to her face again.

She lit up at his entry. "I was afraid the weather would keep you away this morning."

"Not on your life," he said, returning her smile. "Sorry to have kept you waiting."

"That's all right. I've just been telling your people what a wonderful boss they have." She held up her Bible. "Look what I bought."

"Excellent, excellent," he murmured, pleased. "Shall we get started?"

"I'd love to."

TJ ushered her into his office. As he closed the door TJ noticed his staffers still standing there, watching him. He said, "Any of you who wish would be most welcome to join us."

Bella chuckled. "I've been getting that same reaction from everybody."

TJ pulled up a chair beside her, said, "Just so long as you don't let them turn you back."

"Not a chance. I can't remember the last time I've felt so good." She turned shining eyes toward him. "I feel as though a mountain's been lifted from my shoulders. And the crazy thing is, it wasn't until yesterday that I ever really acknowledged that the weight was there. Oh, I suppose I've known all along that it's been with me. The pain, the frustration, the loneliness. I'm so much in the habit of pushing that stuff away I guess I just forgot that's what really was inside me. That and this aching emptiness I never wanted to face up to."

"Being honest about the emptiness is the hardest step a person can take," TJ agreed.

"I guess I'd just about given up on ever finding anything that would give my life meaning." She gave him a shy smile. "I can't tell you how much this means to me."

"Don't thank me," TJ told her. "Thank God. This is very important, something the apostle Paul talks about. You have to understand that no one can come between you and your Savior—not a teacher, not a friend, not even a cause."

"I've never really studied the Bible. My mother used to have a big one up on a shelf in the living room, but I can't ever remember her taking it down and reading it."

"I'm glad you bought one for yourself," TJ said.

"I was looking through it last night. There's a place in front for someone to sign when they present it." Her voice became very small. "Would you sign mine for me?"

"Of course." He took out his black pen and wrote on the presentation page: *To my dear sister in Christ, Bella Saunders. May you ever draw strength and comfort from these words. May you ever draw nearer to your Lord. TJ Case.* Underneath he wrote *John 17:20–26.*

He handed the Bible back to her. Bella held it reverently, read the inscription, said nothing. The expression on her face told it all.

TJ cleared his throat. "Well, there are two ways we can go about this. We can take a book of the Bible and study a few verses every day. Or, if you like, we can take a particular theme or idea and see how various passages in the Scriptures address it."

"Oh, I like the second idea much better," she said. "I can study the individual books at home, but I don't know enough about the Bible to fit the different pieces together."

"All right," TJ agreed. "But when you read at home it is important to study each verse and ask yourself how it applies to your life today. Remember, the Bible is not simply a book written two thousand years ago. It is the living word of God. It is His message to you, a personal gift to help you understand His will and to guide you through this life."

Bella's expression was solemn, her eyes very wide. TJ felt his heart go out to her, and silently prayed that this dawning of new light would not dim, but would grow and strengthen and remain with her forever.

The day's topic came to him so clearly, he knew it was another gift. Though there was no sense of great power accompanying it, he knew the Lord was directing him again.

"What I like to do is to combine passages from the Old and New Testaments when I am studying an idea," TJ began. "In that way I get a sense of the continuation of God's will throughout all time. You see, He did not change His law with the coming of His Son; He *built* upon it. He *fulfilled* the Old Testament teachings."

He opened her Bible and said, "Let's look first at a passage in the Old Testament book of Isaiah, chapter fifty-five, verses six through eight."

"Wait, wait, let me write it down." Bella scrambled in her purse for pen and paper. "Okay."

TJ read:

"Seek the Lord while he may be found; call on him while he is near. Let the wicked forsake his way and the evil man his thoughts. Let him turn to the Lord, and he will have mercy on him, and to our God, for he will freely pardon."

TJ looked up, said, "The greatest freedom God has given us is the freedom to choose which road we will take through life. We can walk the path of darkness, or we can ask Him into our lives and walk the path of eternal life. It is that simple. This Bible passage is important because it says that the time of choosing is not always with us. In my own life, I have found that there are times of tremendous growth, followed by times of calm, as though He is giving me a moment to catch my breath. I think it might be that way for people who do not yet know the Lord. There come moments when the door to faith stands directly in front of them. It is their choice, whether to open it or keep it shut.

"Now let's look at what happens when someone turns away from this opportunity." He turned the pages. "I am going to read from the New Testament, the first chapter of the book of Romans, verses twenty-one, twenty-two, twenty-four, and then twenty-eight through thirty-two."

"For although they knew God, they neither glorified him as God nor gave thanks to him, but their thinking became futile and their foolish hearts were darkened. Although they claimed to be wise, they became fools.... Therefore God gave them over in the sinful desires of their hearts to sexual impurity for the degrading of their bodies with one another.... Furthermore, since they did not think it worthwhile to retain the knowledge of God, he gave them over to a depraved mind, to do what ought not to be done. They have become filled with every kind of wickedness, evil, greed and depravity. They are full of envy, murder, strife, deceit and malice. They are gossips, slanderers, God-haters, insolent, arrogant and boastful; they invent ways of doing evil; they disobey their parents; they are senseless, faithless, heartless, ruthless. Although they know God's righteous decree that those who do such things deserve death, they not only continue to do these very things but also approve of those who practice them."

"He lets them do it," Bella commented, still bent over the passage.

"If it is what they want, the Lord does not stand in their way," TJ replied. "And in that last sentence we see what they receive."

"Death," she said quietly.

"Eternal damnation, a timeless void of death. The Lord has never sent anyone to hell. But if people insist on ignoring His call and continuing to walk the path of darkness, He will allow them to go their own way. The consequences are based on their personal choices."

He leafed through more pages. "This final passage is a warning from Jesus Christ to those who seek the way. It comes from the thirteenth chapter of the Gospel of Matthew, verses three through eight, and then nineteen through twenty-three."

TJ read the parable of the sower, concluding with these words:

"But what was sown on good soil is the man who hears the word and understands it. He produces a crop, yielding a hundred, sixty or thirty times what was sown."

Bella looked at him with solemn eyes. "This is really important."

"There's nothing more important in all your life."

She studied the passage. "How do I grow roots like this?"

"By studying the Bible, praying, searching your heart with honesty, asking the Lord daily to strengthen your faith, finding a church that speaks to your heart, and giving to others with love. All these things help. And a lot of other things that we can talk about in future days."

"Did you mean it when you said we could do this every morning?" Bella asked.

"I would be delighted," TJ replied. "Perhaps we should start a little earlier if we're going to make this a daily practice."

"That's fine with me."

They shared a smile; then TJ said, "Why don't we bow our heads and pray before closing."

When the silence enveloped them, TJ prayed, "Heavenly Father, we give thanks for this moment of worship at the start of our day. Our hearts are filled with your word and we see with a clarity that is only possible when you are leading us. We were not made for sin, Father. That is so very clear to us at this moment. We were made for love. Our primary task in life is to love you, and our second is to love each other. We have this capacity. You have given it to us. So long as we keep our minds and hearts fastened upon this, we can resist sin. We can resist the false choices. We can see that the darker ways are wrong, and dangerous, and utterly without hope. We thank you for the gift of hope that comes to us when we follow your word. Guide us through this and every day. Fill us with your hope, your joy, and your love. In Christ's holy name we pray. Amen."

Bella thanked him, gathered her things, and walked to the door. She looked at him with eyes made young, said, "I can't wait until Monday."

─┤ EIGHT ├─

"Hey there, Mr. Case." Before TJ had even gotten out of the car, Samuel Jones, the airport taxi driver, was there to greet him. "Sure is nice you could make it this mornin'."

"Good morning, Samuel." TJ found himself very grateful to see a friendly face. He had always disliked entering a church for the first time. Church to him was a second home.

"I'm very sorry we didn't make it last Sunday," TJ told him. "I've got a sick daughter, and I decided to go home for the weekend. You remember my friend Jeremy Hughes, don't you?"

"Yessir, Mr. Hughes." A little strained this time.

"Good mornin', Mr. Jones," Jeremy said. If he noticed the man's reserve, he did not show it.

Samuel turned back to TJ, his face showing concern. "Sure hope your daughter's doin' better."

"Not as well as I'd like," TJ replied quietly.

"Say, I'm sure sorry to hear that. Sure am. I'll be sayin' a prayer for her today, Mr. Case. Never known it to hurt," he concluded with a smile.

"Thank you, Samuel." TJ was touched by the man's simple warmth. "That's very kind of you."

"My pleasure, Mr. Case. Always glad to do a service. Y'all come on with me, want to introduce you to the reverend."

☐　　☐　　☐

TJ had feared mightily that his daughter was not getting better. Although Catherine kept insisting that it was only a matter of time, TJ worried that she had been keeping the worst from him. So he traveled home, and found his daughter just as Catherine had said, weak but on the mend.

Catherine was delighted to see him, but was scared at the same time. I've spent a lot of time wishing I didn't have to go up to that city, she told him his first night back. But the more I pray about it, the surer I am that this is where He wants us to be. It's hard having you back because it makes it easier to ask if we maybe wouldn't have to go. I'm just about worn out, looking after this sick girl and her two little children. So you gotta promise me if I'm weak and ask for us to stay, you just won't pay me any mind. TJ held her and promised as she asked and wondered at how he'd ever been blessed with such a wife.

He and Jeremy had returned to Washington directly after church on that previous Sunday.

TJ's meetings with Bella that second week continued to go well. They remained the one bright spot in an otherwise troubled time. Work in the office moved at a snail's pace. His days were filled with "Orientation Meetings"; they had little to do with policy and nothing whatsoever to do with education. TJ felt he was being initiated into an exclusive club dedicated to politics and power. Service to the people was not mentioned once the entire week. Not once.

□   □   □

Samuel Jones led them around to the back of the church. A tall, stern gray-haired patriarch in flowing black robes stood listening gravely to several women all talking at once. He noticed Samuel Jones standing with the two strangers, and he excused himself and walked over.

"Reverend Wilkins," Samuel Jones said, "this here's TJ Case and a Mr. Hughes."

"Good morning." The reverend shook hands, said, "Samuel tells me you're going to be around here for a while."

"Yes, sir," TJ said, liking the man's face. It was hard and strong, brooking no nonsense. The reverend reminded him a little of his grandfather—strength and inner solidity, dedicated to God with single-minded purpose. "It looks that way."

"Something to do with the government, I understand. Samuel wasn't too clear on that."

TJ hesitated, said, "I've been appointed Special Assistant to the President for Education."

There was a little murmur from Samuel, but the only reaction from Reverend Wilkins was, "A mighty important position. Congratulations."

"I'm just trying to do as the Lord leads me," TJ replied quietly.

"Now those are nice words to hear on a Sunday morning," Reverend Wilkins said.

Jeremy spoke up for the first time. "Nicer when they're put into action during the week."

Reverend Wilkins turned and inspected the white man. "Yessir, they certainly are. Only way I've found of giving words like that any meaning." He looked back at TJ, said, "I'd be pleased to invite y'all 'round for lunch if you don't have something else planned."

TJ glanced at Jeremy. "That's very kind of you, Reverend," he answered. "We'd be delighted."

"Fine. We live right back over there, the little red-brick house on the corner. Just come on back when we get through." The reverend gave them a nod, walked toward the church.

The Jerusalem Baptist Church filled every single inch of its P Street lot. TJ intuitively knew its history as soon as he saw the church. The building was built with the first flush of wealth that infused the black community toward the end of World War Two. Scraping the bottom of the barrel, they had just enough money to buy property and put up the church. The lot was probably the only thing available for a reasonable price in their neighborhood, and they had designed the church around it. There was a strip of grass two feet wide bordering the edifice itself. The entrance stairs emptied directly onto the street. There was neither garden nor sidewalk; such things were for rich white churches with money to burn. These people wanted the biggest church their money could buy, a space for all their people to come and gather and worship God. Gardens could wait for the hereafter. Right now it was more important to have help to make it through this day.

Since that time, the neighborhood had gone through a total transformation. Back when the church had originally been built, Georgetown was largely black and mostly poor. Then had come the gentrification of the sixties and seventies, when the housing prices of that area had shot up to the moon.

The result was that the parishioners sold and moved and lost all connection with neighborhoods and friends and a way of life that was no more. All that survived was the church. It had been the church of their fathers, and remained a magnet for the children today. It was a gathering point for families who traveled from as far away as Maryland and Virginia, all coming together once a week to worship their Lord in the house their fathers had built.

All the windows right the way around the church were stained glass. Each was a story of a family's scrimping and saving to beautify their church and glorify their God. TJ knew without asking that the windows had at first been plain glass. One by one, they had been taken by families and re-designed around a favorite Bible passage. And at the base of each was a dedication to a dearly departed, in memory of someone who had raised them and helped them and taught them to respect their Lord.

"We got our littlest granddaughter stayin' with us right now," Reverend Wilkins began his sermon. "Beautiful little thing, apple of her daddy's eye. Can I have me an Amen?"

There was a feeble response, the sound of a congregation warming itself up gradually. There was no rush. They had a long way to go. It was the way they wanted it, a day truly given to the worship of their Lord.

"Well, sir, yesterday mornin' I was right tired. Night before I'd sat the deathwatch with old Mrs. Simpkins. Y'all remember Granny Simpkins. Got seven of her offspring out here today. Yeah, she's gone on to higher ground. Lemme hear a Praise God for the departed woman."

The chorus was stronger now, the people touched by the nearness of their own passing, their own judgment.

"Granny Simpkins' last prayer was for her boy Julius. Y'all see Julius out there on the streets today, tell him his own sweet mother saw him standin' at the gates of hell, and with her last dyin' breath prayed that her boy'd have the sense to turn around." The fiery eyes glared out over the congregation, and the voice rumbled, "Yeah. Praise God. Old Julius thinks he's okay, man on the street, playin' 'round with drugs and sex and such. His momma saw where he was headed. So did I."

"Say it, brother!" cried a woman's voice.

"I'll say it," the preacher said, the sound carrying the power of an approaching summer storm. "Say it long as the Lord gives me strength, loud as I can. You people gotta turn around. Turn! Turn! That's what Isaiah says. Turn from your wicked ways!"

"Amen!" came the chorused reply.

"Yessir, had my little granddaughter stayin' with us," he said, his voice softer. "When my wife told her yesterday that her granddaddy was goin' to lie in for a spell, girl decided to come up and keep me company. I heard her comin', decided to play possum. So when the door opened I shut my eyes up real tight, lay there all still, and heard those little feet come paddin' up to the side of the bed. Opened my eyes just a bit so's I could see that cute face peerin' right up close to mine. Well, she stood there kinda inspectin' me for a while; then she went over and crawled into my rockin' chair. She loves that chair, yessir. Never known a chile who didn't love to be rocked, but that girl just adores to crawl up in her granddaddy's lap. Stay there all day if I let her."

Appreciative murmurs flowed toward him, and his tone gentled further.

"Right 'bout then, the sun peeks up over the house next door. Comes streamin' in through my window every mornin', just lettin' me know the Lord's given me one more chance to go out and do His will. I could hear the rocker creakin' kinda funny like, so I turned over quiet as I could and opened my eyes just a crack.

"Well, my granddaughter was standin' up in the rocker, leanin' on the back of the seat and stretchin' out one hand toward the sun. She was kinda hummin' this little tune; then she says, 'Good mornin', God.' "

Preacher Wilkins' gaze out over the congregation held the moment silently. "Don't you know, I'd give anything to be able to see God like that again. Simple and happy as a little child watchin' the risin' sun."

"Praise *God!*" came a voice from the back.

"It'd be possible, don't you know. Yessir, it really would. Fact is, when our Lord walked this earth that's just exactly what He said. Gotta see the world like we was lookin' through the eyes of the little ones. But it's so difficult, Lord, oh my God, it's hard. How on earth's we supposed to do such a thing?"

"Tell us, Preacher," called a voice.

"All right, I'll tell you. It's possible, you know it is, our Lord's not gonna tell us to do somethin' we can't. All we gotta do to hear His voice is release ourselves from the chains of guilt and sin."

"Free us, Lawd, free us!" came the reply.

"Be cleansed by the blood of the Lamb," sang out the preacher.

"Lawd God Almighty," called a deep baritone, "cleansed forever more!"

Reverend Wilkins reached into his pocket, drew out a handkerchief, mopped his face, said, "Ain't nobody ever *wants* to be ruined. 'Course not. Nobody *wants* to be lost. We's surrounded by friends and family, every blessed one of us, all wantin' to be saved. Yessir. *Good* people. And you ask 'em, yessir, every one of 'em'll tell you, why 'course they believes in God. Problem is, they don't do nothin' about it. Nossir. They's worn out. They's lazy. They gots so much to do, family needs this and that, why, life's just too hard to have time for the Lord."

"Time, Lawd, Lawd, gotta take time for God!" came the response.

"They don't look to the things that really matter. Don't think 'bout what really concerns them. Lotta these people, they don't sin, not really. Not in the beginnin'. They just don't do *anythin'*. They just sit there, lettin' life pull 'em every way but loose. And sooner or later, they start to wander."

"Help us, Lawd," called a woman. "We's weak, so weak, stay with us."

"From that point, the next step is a sure thing. Y'all hear 'bout sure things every day of your life. This here is the surest thing of all. Don't matter when or where, but there'll come a day when your eyes and your heart, they're gonna deceive you."

The congregation groaned a denial.

"Yes, it will. The thought of sin is there in all of us. All the time. And the step from doin' nothin' to doin' sin is so tiny you can't even feel you've taken it." The preacher paused, wiped his face, looked out and rumbled, "Can't see it, nossir, not 'til it's too late."

"No, no, don't let it happen," pleaded a older man. "God, don't let it happen again."

"When we start to sin, we never think of how far it's goin' to go. But one step leads to another, yessir, we all know that, don't we?" Reverend Wilkins chuckled without humor, his eyes raking the gathering. "Yes, ain't one of us who's not been fooled. Or tried to fool ourselves 'bout sin.

"The ol' sin just keeps on mountin', and right there beside it rises that first cousin to sin, guilt. The burden just keeps gettin' heavier, don't it? More sin, more guilt, and before we know it, we're lost. We get so caught up in the burden we forget what it's like to walk like free men. So we start lookin' for some way to hide. Drugs, alcohol, sex, anythin' at all, yessir, anythin' to make that burden easier to bear."

Here and there faces among the congregation showed the agony of unbearable burdens, of mistakes made, of people they knew who had been lost to the darkness. The sounds they made were not words so much as cries of raw emotion.

Reverend Wilkins wiped his face once more, paused long enough to let the congregation quiet itself, then went on, "All seems so easy at first. So fine. Yessir, we just don't want to face up to where it is we're headed. Y'all get out your pencils, now, I got somethin' I want you to write down. Want you to put this up somewhere so's you'll look at it and read it every time you start thinkin' on that first little step. Yeah. Next time you want to walk off the narrow path, next time you think ain't nobody's gonna know when you play around, I want you to remember this."

The preacher fumbled in a pocket, brought out a pair of reading glasses, slipped them on his nose, said, "This here's what I call the Twelve Stages of Sin. Y'all ready to write? Okay. First comes *pleasing*, then *easy*, then *delightful*. That first big turnin' from the path comes with the next step, *frequent*." He repeated the four words as paper rustled and pencils recorded them.

He peered over the tops of the lenses, said, "There must be at least a few of you out there who know what happens after that. Yeah. C'm on, all you sinners out there, what comes next? Or by the time you get to this point, are you so blind you can't see anymore where you're headed?" He leaned over the pulpit, rasped in a half whisper, "Or maybe you just don't want to see. Yessir. Maybe that's it."

No one dared venture an answer, so Reverend Wilkins went on. "All right. After frequent comes *confirmed.* And then the next big turnin' is made, when you slip into *impenitent.* Y'all know what that is. That's just a big word for not bein' sorry. Naw. Y'all don't care it's against God's will. Y'all want to do it, don't you? Yeah. That's all that matters. Yessir. Ain't nothin' more important than doin' that little sin just one more time.

"From there the sinner becomes *obstinate,* then *resolute.* And with the next turnin' he just doesn't bother to fight anymore—not with himself, not with others, not with Satan. He's just *resigned.* And once he's resigned to sin, well sir, it's just a small step to the end. *Ruined."*

The silence in the church was total.

The pastor slipped off the spectacles, his hands visibly shaking with emotion. "Ruined!" The word was a hoarse shout of pain. "Ruined! Lord God Almighty, there goes another sinner lost to Satan! How on earth did he ever get so far away from your path, Father? How could we let a loved one get so lost in darkness?"

He ignored the answering cries of his congregation, thrust a trembling finger out over their heads, called, "How many of you are gonna be layin' there on your deathbed, prayin' for a lost loved one? How many'll look back to that first little step and wish, 'Oh, Lord, how I wish I could've stopped it 'fore it got too far'?"

Reverend Wilkins dropped his voice down to a dusky rumble, asked, "And how many of you're gonna have to pray for your own poor souls? How many're gonna be makin' that final stand, knockin' on the door of the heavenly kingdom, and quakin' in your boots 'cause you've got caught up in the path of sinnin' against your God?"

The congregation followed his lead, quieted to the occasional moan, the occasional half-whispered prayer.

He let them sit and think on it for a long moment before finishing with the solemn words, "So far from where we sit back to that little girl raisin' her hand and wishin' God a blessed good mornin'." His eyes closed. "So far, Lord, and yet so *close.* All it took was just one step. All it took was just settin' you aside and gettin' lost in the cares of the world.

All it took was lettin' ourselves forget what was important. All it took was openin' our lives to sin. Just one step, Lord, all it takes is just one step."

He opened his eyes to gaze once more over the group. "So when y'all see old Mrs. Simpkins' son Julius out there dealin' his drugs and sellin' his women, you stop and say a prayer for that poor ruined child of God. Don't you condemn him, nossir, don't you even start to judge that poor man. You're walkin' the same path as him every time you give in to that first easy, pleasin', delightful step of sinnin'. You're walkin' right there alongside him, temptin' fate and close to losin' your place in heaven. Y'all remember that. Let Julius be a livin' example of what can happen if you don't keep your eyes fastened on your Lord."

□　□　□

It was not until they were almost on the little parsonage's front porch that Jeremy said, "My, but that man can preach a sermon."

"It's certainly nice to know we've got this to look forward to on Sunday," TJ agreed, hoping Catherine would feel the same.

"Yessir," Jeremy said. "Sure is fine, knowin' you've found a home."

TJ hesitated before knocking on the door, said, "You don't think you'd be more comfortable in a, well, a church farther uptown, Jem?"

Jeremy faced his friend, said, "You know, the only time you ever get uptight around me's when you start goin' on about color."

"I just said—"

"I know exactly what you said and I know exactly what you *meant.* Now stop with your nonsense and knock on the man's door."

A very large, very black woman opened the door, gave them both a big smile. "Hello, I'm Rose Wilkins."

"Very nice to meet you, Mrs. Wilkins. I'm Thomas Case, and this is my friend, Jeremy Hughes."

"Mr. Case, Mr. Hughes. A pleasure to meet you both."

"Thank you for having us in your home, ma'am."

"Y'all come on in. The reverend's in the den. Lunch'll be ready in just a few minutes."

Their progress down the hall was slowed by nine screaming children who poured out of the back passage and raced around them. Mrs. Wilkins swiped the air over their heads, said sharply, "Quiet down and mind your manners!" Slightly subdued, they giggled their way out the door.

She gave an apologetic smile, said, "My two eldest daughters are here with their families."

"Children are the same right the way 'round the world," Jeremy replied. "Quiet only when they're asleep or stuffin' their faces."

She gave him a shrewd glance, said, "I don't believe my husband mentioned what you did, Mr. Hughes."

Jeremy decided those arms of hers could fell an ox. "I'm up here workin' as Mr. Case's servant, Mrs. Wilkins."

Beside him TJ breathed a silent sigh and examined the carpet at his feet.

"I see," she said, clearly not believing a word of it. "Well, y'all go say hello to the reverend. We'll be callin' you in just a few minutes."

The lines on Reverend Wilkins' face were etched more deeply than before the sermon. TJ remembered his grandfather had once said that the way to tell if a preacher had his heart in his message was by seeing if he aged ten years while he was up at the pulpit.

But the strength was still there, and the deeply centered determination. He accepted their compliments with a solemn nod, as though more intent on whether it had a useful effect than on whether they enjoyed it. TJ took the seat facing out the back window and onto the yard's single tree, gazed out at its bare leafless limbs, and decided that here was a man he could trust.

"I have a problem I'd like to discuss with you," TJ began. "It's a personal one, and I know we don't know each other very well, but I'd like to tell you about it anyway. That is, if you have the time."

"Why don't we go ahead and start," Reverend Wilkins replied gravely, not seeming to be the least surprised by the request. "We can always finish up after lunch if need be."

"You want me to wait outside?" Jeremy asked.

"No, no, it's nothing you haven't heard already." TJ took a breath, hesitated, said, "I don't even know how to start."

"Try at the beginning," the reverend suggested. "Just take your time, Mr. Case. Ain't nobody in any hurry on a Sunday afternoon."

So TJ began back at the lake, worked his way through the vision, described the letter and the conversation with Congressman Silverwood, and had just arrived in Washington when Mrs. Wilkins opened the door.

"I been callin' and shoutin' now for fifteen minutes," she said, the massive body thrust forward with indignation. "What on earth are y'all up to so's you can't hear me say lunch is on the table? I got nine childrens that're just about ready to drive me crazy."

"Go ahead and start, darlin'," Reverend Wilkins told her gently. "It looks like we may be here a while yet."

She gave them an uncertain look, said, "I'll put your plates in the oven, but don't you be any longer than you have to," and left.

The reverend turned back to TJ, said, "Just you go on right where you were, Mr. Case."

"These have been some of the most confusing and frustrating weeks of my entire life," TJ said. "Ever since I've arrived here I've felt like a cog that's been plugged into the wrong machine. The people I'm supposed to work with are as far removed as they can be from what I'm used to. I don't even have an idea what I'm supposed to be doing professionally, much less for the Lord."

TJ weighed the air with his hand, searched for a way to make himself understood. "It's not that I doubt the vision, or my call to come here. I just wish, well, I wish I had some kind of reassurance. I look back at what I've done, uprooting myself and my family, traveling to a strange place, taking on a job and responsibilities which quite frankly seem a little unreal, and I just wish I could be sure that I've done what's right.

"I'm praying for some kind of confirmation, some indication that this is as it's supposed to be, and all I hear is silence. Quite frankly, I'm worried. Very worried. It's not that I doubt the Lord. I doubt myself."

Reverend Wilkins was silent for a while. He swiveled his chair around so he could see out the back window, but his eyes did not focus on anything visible. TJ was content to sit and feel the release of getting it all off his chest. Jeremy waited in utter stillness.

When the reverend turned back around, it was to Jeremy that he spoke first. "I'm not sure I understand what you're doin' up here in Washington, Mr. Hughes."

"I've come up to be this man's servant," Jeremy replied, not hesitating an instant. "Whatever he needs, that's what I'm there for."

"I see," he said, not showing any surprise. "And have you had a vision too?"

"No sir, Reverend, never have."

"And yet you're willin' to drop everything, pick up and move to another city, just like that? I find that very interesting, Mr. Hughes. I hope you don't mind me saying this, but I find it very interesting."

"Well, sir, Reverend, it's like this. I've known TJ Case for almost twenty-four years. We've worked together, on and off, for all that time. And we're friends. Been friends ever since the first day I met him, seems to me. I don't recall havin' met all that many folks in my life who could say they'd worked with a person for six months, much less two dozen years, and stayed friends. But there you are. I know his wife. I know his family. And I respect them. No, respect's not the right word—I'm sorry Reverend. I'm not an educated man."

"You're doin' just fine, Mr. Hughes. Just fine. Please carry right on."

"From the first day I met TJ, Reverend, I knew I was standin' in the presence of an honest man. I can't tell you why I felt like that, but I did. I *knew* it. Here was a man who was honest with himself, with his family, and with God. He loves the Lord, Reverend. You just stay 'round him for a while and you'll see it for yourself. TJ Case is a gentleman who truly loves his Lord. So when my friend told me he'd had a vision that called him to Washington, I knew in my heart that I had to go with him.

"It wasn't all that difficult, I've got to admit. My wife's been dead quite a while now, and I've got some young folks in the business who run it better when I'm not around to poke my finger in the works and get in their way. So maybe I was just lookin' for an excuse to move on, but I don't believe so. I'd like to think that the Lord's just helped to make my way up here a little straighter."

There was a warm glow to Reverend Wilkins' gaze as he nodded in time to Jeremy's words. "It takes a strong man to follow the quieter voice of our Lord."

"I wouldn't say that, Reverend," Jeremy replied. "Seems to me the Lord uses the voice He wants for the message He needs to get across."

They shared a long comfortable gaze before Reverend Wilkins said, "We're certainly glad to have you join us, Mr. Hughes. I hope we'll be seein' more of you around here."

"That's very kind of you, Reverend. Thank y'all very much."

Reverend Wilkins turned to TJ, said, "Mr. Case, havin' a vision ain't nothin' that unusual. It's not somethin' that happens every day to everybody, but that don't make it not real. Paul was clear as day 'bout that in Romans.

"Now the first thing I look for when one of my people come in here and starts talkin' 'bout visions is, am I talkin' to a person who's listenin'? You see, Mr. Case, when a person gets all excited and starts runnin' 'round talkin' 'bout how the Lord's done come down from heaven and spoke in their ears, screamin' up a storm and all set to go out and tell the world how great they are, you know what I'm talkin' about? Well, sir, when that happens I just tell 'em to go home and take two aspirins. Don't matter how real that vision was, long as that person wants to go 'round blowin' their own trumpet, they's no chance the Lord's work is gonna get done.

"This is not what you're on about. I've been sittin' here listenin' to you with my ears and with my heart, if you see my meanin', and my heart's been tellin' me this is a man who really believes the Lord's done talked with him. And I believe it too, Mr. Case. I really do. It ain't no matter of logic. I just feel like the Lord's called you to do a service.

"And I understand what's botherin' you. Least, I think I do. You're not doubtin' the Lord. No sir. You just haven't found any purpose big enough to justify you being called to drop everything and come to Washington."

"That's it exactly," TJ said, enormously relieved that he had found someone who understood. And who believed his story. It was incredible how much that meant.

"That's entirely natural," Reverend Wilkins said in his deep, hoarse voice. "But you got to remember, now, that maybe you don't need to know what that purpose is. The fact that you're here, doin' whatever comes up in front of you, may be all the Almighty wants you to know. You do what is there to do. The Lord'll open the doors when He's ready. You see what I'm sayin', sir?"

"Yes, sir, I certainly do," TJ replied.

"That's fine. Now the other thing you got to keep in mind is, be patient. Wait upon the Lord. Let the Lord tell you what He wants, when He's ready to tell you. Maybe you're just not ready, did you ever think of that? Maybe you need to get your feet on the ground, get yourself some experience. God may be preparin' you. When He's ready, when He thinks *you're* ready, He'll let you know. You can count on that, Mr. Case. He'll let you know what it is that needs gettin' done. You just concentrate on gettin' yourself ready."

─┤ NINE ├─

Early Monday morning TJ entered the empty outer office, opened his own door, stopped cold. "What on earth?"

Bella was there to greet him. "I thought it needed a little dressing up."

There were two hanging plants at each corner of his window, an orchid blooming in all its glory from a terra-cotta bowl beside his desk, and a vase of fresh flowers beside his telephone.

He looked at Bella.

She pointed to the sign on his desk. "I found that yesterday in a religious bookshop. Passed by and felt like there was a hand pulling me inside." Her chuckle rasped from a thousand cigarettes. "Guess you never get too old for miracles."

The sign was a polished wooden slab with a brass front reading: "Carpenter From Nazareth Seeks Joiners."

He turned to her, said softly, "No, I guess you don't."

She shared with him the quiet joy of giving and being appreciated, said, "I've invited a couple of friends to join us this morning. Hope that's okay."

"Fine with me," TJ replied.

"I think they mostly showed up out of curiosity. Or disbelief. You know, what's got the Dragon Lady smiling?" She gave another of her coarse chuckles. "I smiled at somebody in the hall on Friday, and looked back to find him standing there with his jaw on his chest."

TJ laughed, said, "Well, praise the Lord."

"If you're ready, they're all waiting down in the conference room."

"All?" TJ picked up his Bible, followed her out. "How many are there?"

"At last count, just over a dozen."

□ □ □

The numbers at their morning sessions continued to grow, slowly but steadily. Tuesday it was fifteen, Wednesday around twenty, and by Thursday they had the table in that large conference room almost full. TJ did not want to let the people think he was counting prizes, so he did not take an exact number; but he would have guessed the total at over two dozen. It was gratifying to see so many faces returning day after day, especially with all the difficulties TJ was facing with his work.

There was a note on his desk Friday morning from Bella: "Spoke with a few more friends about your devotional. Invited them to show up. Hope it's okay. If even half do come, it'll be too many for the conference room. Got permission for us to use the small cafeteria."

As he walked downstairs, his main concern was that Bella would not be too disappointed if the number was small. Anyone who had set up prayer groups or Bible studies knew how tough it was to bring people in, especially in the beginning. Like a little seedling, the plant first had to grow roots and take hold before the blossoms could come forth. This was tough for new converts to understand, as TJ knew from bitter experience. Still flush from that first miraculous contact with the Holy Spirit, they realized that here lay the answer to all the world's problems. Here was what the whole world had been waiting for. All they had to do was just let people know how wonderful it was, and everything would be fine. Nobody would dream of turning down something as great as this.

Wrong.

It was a sad and painful experience at times, this first confrontation with this lack of concern. TJ had struggled many times with new believers who felt so crushed by the world's rejection that they too felt pulled from the Way. He was so worried about finding Bella in such a position that he could not concentrate on what he was going to say.

The hubbub was clearly audible before he reached the downstairs landing. He walked toward the small dining room, the one usually reserved for private luncheon meetings, wondering what on earth was going on. Then Bella popped out of the main cafeteria laden with a trayful of cups and saucers, nearly colliding with him.

"I thought the least we could do was wake them up first," she said, fire in her eyes.

TJ tried to count the cups stacked almost to her chin, said, "You've got this many here?"

Her chuckle was something out of a thirties' movie. "Honey," she said, briskly leading him down the hall, "this is the third tray."

The room was jammed. People mingled and chatted and watched him curiously as he entered. He followed Bella up to the front where a table stood loaded with a coffee urn, cups, saucers, milk and sugar. He put his Bible down and busied himself over coffee. Anything to fill his hands and keep from needing to meet anyone's eyes.

He sent a swift little prayer heavenward, panic hovering around the edges of the words. Lord, what on earth am I supposed to tell all these people?

Bella's preamble was as abrupt as everything else about her, and the room fell silent. "This is TJ Case, the fellow I was telling you about. I know everybody's got a busy day, so we won't waste any more time."

TJ looked up, saw that more than half the people had no chairs and that everyone was staring at him. There was a lot of skepticism in their expressions, a lot of cynical little half-smirks on their faces. He set his cup down, trying to still the sudden shiver in his muscles, and picked up his Bible. He did not know what he was going to say.

"In my church back home we used to have a little morning prayer group that met most days," he said, and felt a sense of calm enter him with these first words. "We never met for more than a few minutes, just long enough to have a Bible reading and a little prayer. The idea was to kind of anchor the day with a moment of fellowship and communion with our Lord."

He stopped. It was not a conscious pause, rather one that seemed somehow called for. *Be still,* a silent voice seemed to say in his head, and TJ stopped.

And the Holy Spirit came into the room.

He could see that it was not just for him. The change was in all their faces. *All* their faces. Not only were they listening. They were *joined*. The group felt the silence. They were brought out from behind their masks of fear and cynicism and illusions of worldly power. They were *listening*.

TJ knew what was to be said. Not a conscious thought, it was a gift that came with the presence of the Spirit. There was no room for doubt, no need to question. He opened his Bible to the book of Mark, found the passage, and looked up.

"It has always helped me to see the Bible as one unified whole," he began. "It does not stand as separate passages, but rather as building blocks that together form a single structure. They all support each other, just as the individual bricks of a building are built one upon the next. For this reason, we can choose a single theme and see how it is woven throughout the entire Bible. Together these individual passages, these separate little bricks, build a holy shelter. If we can learn to dwell within this House of God, we are protected from the dangers and temptations that constantly swirl around us."

He looked down, continued. "I am going to read three passages this morning. They are from three different books, but all deal with one particular theme. Watch and see how they strengthen and support each other.

"The first one is from the twelfth chapter of Mark:

> "One of the teachers of the law came and heard them debating. Noticing that Jesus had given them a good answer, he asked him, 'Of all the commandments, which is the most important?'
>
> " 'The most important one,' answered Jesus, 'is this: "Hear, O Israel, the Lord our God, the Lord is one. Love the Lord your God with all your heart and with all your soul and with all your mind and with all your strength." The second is this: "Love your neighbor as yourself." There is no commandment greater than these.' "

Quickly TJ turned the pages, found his second passage, noticed that the room was totally silent. There was not even the sound of clinking cups.

"The second reading is from the thirteenth chapter of First Corinthians:

> "Love is patient, love is kind. It does not envy, it does not boast, it is not proud. It is not rude, it is not self-seeking, it is not easily angered, it

keeps no record of wrongs. Love does not delight in evil but rejoices with the truth. It always protects, always trusts, always hopes, always perseveres.

"Love never fails."

TJ searched, found, said, "The final passage comes from the fourth chapter of First John:

"Dear friends, let us love one another, for love comes from God. Everyone who loves has been born of God and knows God. Whoever does not love does not know God, because God is love. This is how God showed his love among us: He sent his one and only Son into the world that we might live through him. This is love: Not that we loved God, but that he loved us and sent his Son as an atoning sacrifice for our sins. Dear friends, since God so loved us, we also ought to love one another. . . .

"God is love. Whoever lives in love lives in God, and God in him. Love is made complete among us so that we will have confidence on the day of judgment, because in this world we are like him. There is no fear in love. But perfect love drives out fear, because fear has to do with punishment. The one who fears is not made perfect in love."

TJ closed the Book, felt the Spirit strengthening and intensifying in him. It is only by giving that I can receive, he thought. Thank you, Father, for this chance to give.

"Let us pray," he said, knowing the words were there for him to speak, to pray, to give.

"O Lord, Heavenly Father, we are so weak and so afraid. To love in a world like this means to take a terrific chance. We don't know how it's going to work out, or how the other person is going to react. Yet you do not tell us to think of such things. You tell us to love. How is this possible in such a world, Father? How can there be hope for the world unless we learn to love, yet how can we love when all about us there is only hate, and when there is so much fear in our hearts?

"The answer is so very clear, so perfectly visible if only we are willing to see. We are incapable of loving without your guidance, without your presence in our lives. We cannot do this alone, Lord. We must turn to you. It is only in you that love is possible. It is only when you are in our hearts and lives that the impossible is done, and the fearful know love."

He had to stop. He could not go on. There was such a burning in his chest that for a moment he could not breathe. It seemed as though a beam of light was extending out from the center of his chest, bathing the room in a holy fire. He loved, and yet it was not he who was loving. The divine flame of love rushed through him, filling him with an intensity that immobilized him.

He could not move, he could barely concentrate on his own voice. But the words were again there in his mind, and they needed to be spoken.

"Heavenly Father, help us to know love. Help us to know your healing embrace, the presence of the Holy Spirit in our lives. Let us be filled, and in so doing know the inexpressible joy of giving with love to others. With love, Father. With love. Let us know your divine love. In Christ's holy name. Amen."

The group remained very quiet. People moved with reluctance, standing and walking slowly from the room. TJ fought back the urge to turn and flee, knowing his place was by the door, meeting the people's eyes, shaking hands, thanking them for coming. The gazes were thoughtful, the voices subdued. Someone asked if he was going to do it again on Monday, and the entire room paused to listen to his response. I would be happy to, he said, and he was blessed with a grateful smile.

He started to help Bella and a few others gather cups, but was shooed away. As he departed, a man fell into step behind him, asked if he minded a little company. TJ recognized Carter Williams, the black man who had walked with him from the cafeteria that first day.

"Man, I gotta tell you," Carter said. "I came because I was curious. You know, here the Dragon Lady herself starts smiling at people and spouting all kinds of wild stuff. Coulda knocked me over with a feather. Lotta people here this morning, they're like me, gotta find out what you did to make the change."

"I didn't do a thing," TJ said mildly.

"Yeah, yeah, I kinda see that." Carter Williams sobered. "My grandmother was real religious. She tried to knock some of that stuff into me, but you know, I just wasn't into it. Never really gave it much thought. Too busy trying to prove I was as good as the next man, white or black."

"The whole world's out there screaming for our attention," TJ agreed. "And only one little voice in our heart is whispering, the answer's not out there. It's in here."

The man nodded several times, clearly wanting to take it all in. "I like the way you say that. Makes a lot of sense. You say you're gonna do it again Monday?"

"Every day anybody wants to listen," TJ replied.

"Yeah, well, count me in." Carter slapped him on the shoulder, turned away, said in parting, "It's nice to know somebody's up there who cares. Been a long time since I felt this good."

Congressman John Silverwood entered the congressional hearing rooms that Friday afternoon a very troubled man. He had expected the luncheon with TJ Case to be a power play. The new man was to be shown who held the keys to turn policy into legislative reality. TJ needed reminding how much he owed Silverwood, and in whom his first loyalty rested.

On the surface, all went as planned. Underneath, however, Congressman Silverwood was not so sure.

He met TJ at the Occidental, the restaurant in the Willard Hotel just a block down Pennsylvania Avenue from the White House. Although he did not often have an opportunity to come here, it was fast becoming one of Silverwood's favorites. The entire place had been renovated to the grandeur of an earlier era and reeked of political lore. Julia Ward Howe was said to have penned "The Battle Hymn of the Republic" there. President Ulysses S. Grant would come over and sit in the ornate lobby, smoking his cigar and drinking a brandy, and try to escape from the pressures of running a nation. He was said to have created the term "lobbyists" right here, for all the characters who used the opportunity to bend the President's ear.

The wood-lined restaurant was filled with murmuring voices, the air heavy with the smells of rich perfume, richer food, and power. It was a heady mixture. Silverwood felt a satisfying thrill in going through such restaurants nowadays—to be recognized and need to stop and chat with people along the way gave him a sense of belonging, of importance.

When TJ joined him and declined his offer of a drink, Silverwood recalled the man's religious bent. The discussion began immediately, with TJ offering very clear and intelligent assessments of the political and the structural difficulties he would need to overcome in making his assignment work.

Nonetheless, as the luncheon progressed, Silverwood became increasingly perplexed. TJ did not discuss these matters as though talking to a confidential ally. Regardless of how sensitive the information might have been at this stage of policy development, Silverwood was convinced that TJ would have said the very same thing to anyone who had asked.

Silverwood tried to discuss the need for secrecy, the essential fact that political power was won by being the first to present a new idea. The media focused on one person, the leader. All spotlights turned his way. If a foe was to hear of this and steal the limelight, TJ would gain nothing for all his hard work.

TJ listened intently, nodded occasionally, said nothing. Silverwood was left with the feeling that the man disagreed in some fundamental way. But for the life of him, Congressman Silverwood could not understand why. Like himself, TJ Case had everything to lose and nothing to gain by premature disclosures.

Upon mentioning the fact that TJ owed him for both the job and for the furthering of his future career, TJ replied with a very solemn note of thanks. He promised to do the very best job possible. But even with this, Congressman Silverwood remained unconvinced. TJ Case had seemed like a man who really, deep down at heart, did not care.

When Silverwood finally asked him if everything was all right, TJ replied, I was just about to ask you the same thing. Silverwood, surprised, asked, what do you mean by that? Well, Case said with a voice of eerie calmness, you seem a little concerned about something. I was worried that maybe you were facing something you didn't know how to handle.

For a moment, fear clutched at Silverwood. He wondered if there was some way the man could have known about the problems he faced with his wife. If one person knew, all of Washington would be discussing it over breakfast the next morning. Silverwood pushed it away with a short laugh. Stress and pressure are always a part of this job, he said. TJ Case answered, yet peace and fulfillment are always a part of God's plan. It is those who know the greatest stress that remain in the greatest need.

Before Silverwood could recover, a man approached their table. When Silverwood realized who it was, his shock deepened.

Senate Minority Whip Richard Atterly was a tall angular man in his late sixties, ramrod straight and impatient to the point of curtness with anyone he felt was wasting his time. He looked down at Silverwood's luncheon companion, said, "You're TJ Case, aren't you?"

TJ removed his napkin, stood respectfully, said, "Yes, sir, I am."

"Thought so. Heard so much about you I figured it must be you. You fit their description exactly."

"I don't believe I—"

"Atterly. Richard Atterly. Senator from Rhode Island. I've got two secretaries and four staffers who went to your prayer meeting this morning. Came back determined to make every one of them from now on, even if it means crawling off their deathbeds. Even got me to wrangle passes out of Personnel so they won't have trouble getting in from now on."

"That's rather flattering," TJ said mildly, "but there must be some group meeting in their own building."

"That's right, there is. A Bible study every Thursday. I was one of the people who got it started. Haven't had time to get to it recently, what with one thing and another."

"What could be more urgent than giving time to prayer and studying the Lord's Word?" TJ's voice was respectful, yet direct.

Senator Atterly regarded him from under bushy eyebrows, laughed a short bark. "You're just exactly like they say. Have a way of making the impossible swallowable."

"Nothing the Lord wills us to do is impossible," TJ replied.

"I wonder about that sometimes," Atterly said, growing somber. Then, "What is it you're doing here in Washington?"

"I am Special Assistant to the President for Education."

"Well, I'm not on the Education Subcommittee myself, but some people think I do have a little clout. You run into any problems, come by and see me."

"That's very kind of you, sir," TJ said, showing no emotion over an offer that would have sent any other Washington insider into orbit. "Perhaps you would do me the honor of joining us for one of the prayer meetings."

Piercing blue eyes regarded him steadily for a moment before Atterly replied, "Why not? I've got some meetings over there Monday morning. I'll see if I can't get there early enough." He looked over to where Silverwood stood waiting to be recognized. "Haven't I seen you around?"

"Congressman Silverwood, sir. We met at the Republican party meeting last month."

"Ah yes, the young man from North Carolina. Heard some nice things about you." They shook hands. "Well, don't let me disturb your lunch. Hope to see you on Monday, Mr. Case."

Congressman Silverwood had watched the senator stride away, and decided that clearly he was dealing here with something which he did not understand.

☐ ☐ ☐

Silverwood eased himself into his seat at the hearing table with a nod to Bobby, already in his place directly behind Silverwood, and another to the congressmen on his right. He pushed the thoughts of TJ Case away. The HUD investigative hearings required a clear head and all of his attention, especially on a day when he intended to seize the lead in the questioning.

It was becoming increasingly easy for him to switch off the emotions and thoughts of one conflict, problem, or event, and train his total attention on the next item. It was a requirement of this job. Literally hundreds of issues clamored for attention every day. It was impossible to deal with them adequately unless he brought his mind to an ever-tighter focus.

Congressman Silverwood opened the file case before him and extracted the documents related to the next witness. As the gavel banged the meeting to order, television lights switched on.

Press attendance had been sporadic the first few days. The media surfaced only when there was a tip-off in anticipation of a fireworks display. Nowadays, however, the explosions were fast and frequent.

Rarely did a session pass without something occurring which was worth mentioning in the evening news.

Even a young freshman congressman reaped the benefits of the growing attention. Silverwood had been interviewed so often that he no longer bothered to keep count. All he had to do was delay his own departure from the hearing room long enough to allow the senior heavies to leave first. He didn't mind, as it gave him a moment to collect his thoughts and to select a few one-shot items that would fit well into the thirty-second mentality of television news. Because he was earning a reputation as someone who gave usable quotes, he was in increasingly greater demand.

There had been some debate as to whether these hearings should be declared confidential and the press left outside. The further the investigation progressed, the more widespread the abuse of funds and power seemed to become. There were political reputations to be made, however, and a hungry press to be fed. So the hearings remained open, and the news people multiplied.

The congressional committee assigned to investigate possible HUD wrongdoing had been forced to change venues twice, as the audience continued to grow. In the beginning they had been in a hearing room barely large enough to hold the oval conference table and three rows of spectator seats. Now they were in the second largest hearing room in all of Longworth Building. The congressmen sat at a slightly curved table facing an amphitheater with rising banks of seats. A long front table for the witnesses and their attorneys faced the congressmen. Against the right-hand wall was a small desk for the technician with recording equipment. The television cameras and light tripods were behind the last row of audience seats and along the left-hand wall, so that both the congressmen and the witnesses could be covered.

This afternoon, officials from one of the largest construction companies in the United States, the Atlas Group Incorporated, would be questioned. Two senior executives sat at the center of the opposing table, flanked by a battery of dark-suited lawyers.

Congressman Silverwood carefully reviewed his list of questions, hammered out with Bobby the day before. He felt a thrill of anticipation. There was every indication that this Atlas company had been heavily involved in the misallocation of funds, and possibly even the bribing of government officials. Bobby and Silverwood had spent long hours poring over the contracts supplied them by HUD. The conditions this company had received were incredible, and the projects they had worked on absolutely beyond belief. One was a massive public swimming pool, ostensibly for the underprivileged, yet built in a New Jersey community with the highest per capita income of the entire state. Another was a camp in California, originally built during World War Two to house interned Japanese-Americans. The houses were to be converted into apartments for migrant workers. The contract was on a cost-plus basis. The final bill came to $85,000 per apartment unit.

The investigation was continuing at a very rapid pace. There were two factors involved here. First, the issue was so new and the proportions of the scandal were expanding so swiftly that neither party as yet had developed a comprehensive position on the matter. Both parties were walking on eggshells as the issue of adequate housing for the homeless became more politically sensitive. Whatever policy was presented would have to both condemn the abuse of funds and suggest a solution that would put more money into the hands of those who needed it the most. At the same time the big contractors would be fighting like crazy to keep as much of the HUD funding directed toward luxury projects as possible; there was very little profit in housing the poor.

The second factor was simpler. There was a rumor that the Senate was planning to set up its own investigation. The potential for political glory was too great for them to leave it to a House subcommittee. This meant that the more ground the congressmen covered before this happened, the more the press and the public would continue to look to them as leaders in the unfolding drama. The Senate would simply be following in their footsteps, along a path already laid out by the House.

Because of these two factors, only a minor amount of petty squabbling was heard between committee members representing the two parties. In fact, there was an impressive amount of cooperation. For the moment, the two parties were working together, and the speed at which they dispatched witnesses was remarkable.

The committee chairman was a Democrat, as the House majority was Democratic. The chairman composed his face as the television lights came on. He droned through his opening statement, the same address he used to begin every hearing. Congressman Silverwood shuffled quietly through his papers and worked to shut out the voice. The only reason all the committee members were present and seated for the opening remarks was because of the television coverage. If a network other than C-Span was covering a hearing, the cameras would normally shoot only the initial ten to fifteen minutes, from which a sixty-second filler would be used as a backdrop while the reporter summarized what had taken place. No politician dared miss this coverage, or risked having the nation see his committee seat empty on the six o'clock news.

"I cannot tell you what a moral outrage it is," the committee chairman concluded, "even to contemplate that the agency responsible for providing housing for the homeless has instead been lining the pockets of major developers."

At this Congressman Silverwood drew himself erect in his seat. That final sentence was what was known as a "media bite," a hard-hitting, fast-grabbing phrase that the reporters could take and run with. The same one was used at every hearing, and it became a signal for the cameramen to pan the entire committee.

Congressman Silverwood's favorite media bite came from Senator Cranston, when he had chaired the Senate Foreign Relations subcommittee hearings on revisions to the Foreign Corrupt Practices Act. Senator Cranston daily lamented a law which "had a loophole big enough to fly a Lockheed through."

His attention was drawn to the sight of a wraith-like figure descending the stairs and entering the light behind the bank of television cameras. Congressman Silverwood felt an unexpected chill as he recognized Shermann, the lobbyest. The man gingerly seated himself in the first row behind the witnesses' table, and fastened his shaded gaze on the committee chairman.

The chairman seemed to hesitate momentarily as he bent his head and shuffled through the papers strewn before him. He raised his face to the cameras, cleared his throat, said, "Ah, in view of his keen interest in our first witness, I would like to invite my honorable colleague from the state of North Carolina to open the questioning. Congressman Silverwood?"

The announcement surprised him so greatly that Congressman Silverwood turned and gawked openmouthed at the chairman. The man refused to meet his gaze. Silverwood collected himself swiftly, conscious of the cameras, yet not understanding at all why this was happening. Anyone who had taken even the most fleeting glance at the material would have *known* that this company had its hand in the federal till. Why on earth was the chairman passing up such an opportunity, and turning the plum over to a member of the opposition at that? Silverwood had been pressuring the man for over a week to be allowed second position in questioning the witness, hoping that the chairman would leave at least a couple of stones unturned. To be given the green light with no prior questioning at all was beyond his wildest expectations.

Mentally he shrugged off the confusion, set a stern visage for the cameras, and asked his first question. "Mr. Tompkins, you are senior vice-president of the Atlas Group, is that correct?"

The gray-haired gentleman seated at the middle of the seven-man witness group leaned toward the microphone, said, "Yes, sir, that is correct."

"Then could you please give the committee an explanation of the events leading up to your company's being awarded a public housing contract by HUD for Princeton, New Jersey, in January of last year?"

The man glanced down at the typewritten page in front of him, replied, "Congressman, this matter is one best answered by our counsel."

The lawyer seated immediately to the left of the Atlas Group senior vice-president leaned toward his own microphone, said blandly, "Congressman, Mr. Tompkins is unable to supply the committee with that information at this time as the events and the contract in question lie outside the direct line of his responsibility. However, if you would be so kind as to allow us adequate time, we would be most happy to gather all the necessary documents together and present you with a very precise explanation of everything related to this specific contract."

Congressman Silverwood waited for the committee chairman to criticize both the lawyer and Mr. Tompkins for such a blatant attempt to avoid the question. The committee's subpoena had specifically instructed the company to produce both the documentation and the officers responsible for this and other questionable contracts. When the chairman remained silent, Silverwood turned toward him. He saw that the man's face had taken on a waxy sheen, and was literally covered with perspiration. The chill returned to Silverwood's belly as he realized that the chairman was truly afraid.

□   □   □

The peace of sharing Bible passages and a morning prayer did not erase the concerns TJ carried with him throughout the remainder of his workday. He returned from his lunch with Congressman Silverwood determined to get away from the incredible distractions that surrounded him. He was looking for ways to anchor himself upon a clear direction, ways to define and clarify his role. It was an absolute necessity, yet it seemed as though the entire world was out to confuse him and to fill his days with frantic unproductivity.

His telephone rang constantly. And not only his. The offices' cramped quarters were a chaos of jangled nerves and brassy voices and calls to answer three phones at once. Computer terminal printouts spilled onto photocopying machines that spewed papers all day long. Mail came in by the canvas-bag load twice a day. Other letters were rerouted and transferred up or down the halls, with scribbles in the corners clamoring for immediate response. His in-box was lost under an avalanche of position papers, newsletters, hearing documents, and interagency policy analyses. Staffers popped in and out in a constant stream, grabbing his elbow, asking his opinion, seeking him for a meeting, requesting updates. And everything was always, always urgent.

His own staff was made up of hard-line campaigners. They lived by the creed that power was solidified and votes guaranteed through making contacts. They spent an incredible amount of time in meetings that TJ Case considered unproductive and they called essential. They liked that word a lot, essential. It was *essential* that he meet with a well-connected gentleman who had no direct tie whatsoever to educational policy-making. It was *essential* that he be on best terms with senior-level members of the Department of Education, even if it meant backpedalling on the issues he considered most important. It was *essential* that he develop personal links with key committee staffers, *essential* that he attend endless briefing sessions where men and women droned in tired voices from prepared statements that left his head full of cotton stuffing, *essential* he fill his calendar through appointments with lobbyists from a plethora of coalitions and interest groups. It was *essential* that he agree with them, or at least let them feel that he was on their side.

TJ found it terrifically difficult to sift through the rubble and the noise and the clamor and the stress and locate the truly essential. His staff were of little help. Their perspectives were so *different* from his own. They viewed everything from the political angle; what a memo contained was much less important than how much power its author wielded. What an individual represented was secondary to how much political clout his group possessed. For TJ the crucial element remained, how to seize the initiative, how to put his educational policy in place.

Discussions with his staff soon degenerated to the level of petty politics. None of them had a background in education, none of them had the depth of experience he sought. For them, education was one of a multitude of interchangeable topics to which their new-found political influence could be applied.

He was constantly amazed at the game-playing, the scorecard of favors owed and revenges sought that his staff carried around in their heads. They judged others on the most trivial of points, from tardy arrival at a meeting three months before to supposed slights whispered behind their backs, from luncheon privileges in the White House to the color of their badges. This ruled his staff's opinion of whom he should meet, which letter should be answered first, which reception attended. Were it not for the seriousness with which they viewed it and the amount of time they wasted daily on it, TJ Case would have laughed out loud.

From their side, his staff clearly did not know what to make of him, nor of his faith. They had never known so much as a flicker of the moral and spiritual laws that guided TJ's direction. That became very clear to him every time he made reference to any sense of higher responsibility. They were afraid to work on issues with him, because they were fearful of his direction. TJ did not need to discuss these points outright. It was there in their faces for all the world to see. They did not trust him. He was not one of them.

He himself felt besieged by unanswered questions. How could he cope with so many competing demands for his time? Nothing in state legislature had ever prepared him for the sheer number and diversity of organizations that now had him targeted. How could he respond to every one of them fairly? How available should he be for the *hundreds* of invitations he received—to lunches, dinners, receptions, seminars, group meetings, working breakfasts? The demands were constant. How could he discern their agendas and their hidden agendas? When should he be diplomatic, and when should he be bluntly outspoken?

And how did all this tie in to serving God, and doing what he was here for?

Numerous times he pushed his work aside, bowed his head and prayed for guidance. The answer was both clear and calmly present. Wait.

Earlier that week, TJ had begun retreating to the familiar. He called it going back to the basics. His first responsibility was to God, his second to the President. He was not sure how the multitude of lobbyists and hand-shakers and elbow-grabbers and smilers and talkers fitted into this, but he knew it was somewhere further down the line. So he assumed his old role of lawyer and legislator.

His office was not quiet enough to concentrate, so he found another work place, a hidden alcove within the OEOB Law Library. It was three floors of book-lined alcoves, with circular balconies bordered by delicate cast-iron railings. The floor was mosaic, the ceiling ornate. It was a perfect place to sit in solitary refuge and *work.*

There he studied the reams of background material he found amassed in his office filing cabinets. He researched the cases and statutes related to education, pulling down book after book from the library stacks until he had built his own little barrier against outside distraction. He outlined arguments in favor of and against each of the major educational issues he felt were confronting the administration. This, he decided, was the *real* essential. This to him was *vital.* He hammered his statements out as though working on a key court case, preparing himself for possible queries from the President as though anticipating points from the prosecution. It was the only time in those overcrowded days when TJ Case felt that work was really getting done.

Early in the evening TJ returned to his office. He could tend to his mail and messages in peace, knowing that the two secretaries with their sullen gazes and rock music and cynical humor had already gone for the day.

That Friday evening he opened his inner door to find a man sitting at his conference table, bent over a writing pad.

The man stood up immediately. TJ recognized the Oriental face as belonging to one of the people who had attended every prayer meeting that week. TJ asked, "Can I help you?"

"I'm sorry if I surprised you," the man said, "but your secretaries told me I could wait in here."

"That's quite all right," TJ replied, thinking how unusual it was to hear such a strong American accent coming from those Asian features before him. "I'm TJ Case."

"Yes, I know," the man shook hands. "I've been attending your prayer meetings."

"Won't you sit down?" TJ went around behind his desk. "I hope they've been helpful."

"More than that. Much more. They're a real inspiration. There hasn't been a single one where I haven't left feeling in tune with God." The man waited for TJ to sit before seating himself again. "My name is John Nakamishi. My friends call me Nak." He pronounced it to rhyme with "knock."

"What can I do for you, Mr. Nakamishi?"

The man regarded him with dark, unreadable eyes. TJ guessed him to be in his late twenties or early thirties, but it was difficult to tell. There was a solid strength to the man that belied his years, a sense of deep awareness. He wore wire-rimmed glasses and a dark three-piece suit. His hair was as black as his eyes and neatly cut. His skin was tanned the color of old leather; TJ wondered where he had been to get sun in February. Certainly not here.

"I was assigned to the Political Affairs Division back in December," John Nakamishi began. "But the person I was supposed to answer to brought his own man. I've been kind of like a third leg for the past couple of months. So I took my wife and family on a vacation and got back last week. Ever since then, I've been hanging around Presidential Personnel and praying that something else would come up.

"This morning your assistant, Joan Sammons, had a meeting with the Director of Personnel. I know because his secretary goes to my church. It was their third meeting, and this time Joan basically told him to find her another place to work. She was not coming back here another day. I just checked her office. It's cleaned out."

TJ nodded, trying to take it in, feeling a little as though he had failed. "I see."

"I would consider it a real honor to work for you, Mr. Case," John Nakamishi said. "I think I would make you an excellent assistant."

The announcement was made with no change in inflection whatsoever. John Nakamishi's voice remained calm and flat, as though he were discussing the weather.

"Tell me something about yourself," TJ asked.

"I've been in Washington for five and a half years, and in the OEOB for two. I was one of a handful of people asked to stay over from the last administration, primarily because the policy issue I was working on is still being pushed. They want to keep me around for advising on continuity, but the guy who's responsible now feels more comfortable with his own man as assistant.

"Before coming to Washington I was Advisor to the Governor of California for Education for three years." At that, TJ sat up straight. If John Nakamishi noticed the change, he did not show it. "All my work here has been on the political side, but I've tried to keep up with educational policy issues in my spare time. It's where my heart has always been."

He crossed his legs, looked down at his hands for a moment, seemed to come to a decision. He looked TJ straight in the eye, said, "My grandparents immigrated to the United States from Japan at the end of World War One. My parents are both Buddhists. I was raised in the Japanese Zen tradition until I was sixteen, when I accepted Jesus Christ as my Lord and Savior. I haven't had contact with my family since then. My father banished me from his house, and erased my name from the family scroll."

TJ marveled at how calmly the story was told, as though John Nakamishi were speaking of another person. "It must have been very difficult for you."

"In some ways, but it forced me to rely totally on the Lord. I think we are given what we need to have, and looking back I can see how this separation forced me to come to know Him at a very deep level."

TJ thought it all over, realized he really needed some help. "I'm not sure how my staffing is going to shape up, but I'd like you to join us on a temporary assignment at least."

"That would be fine, sir. Thank you very much."

TJ bent over his calendar, thought a moment, said, "I have some research I need to finish Monday morning. Then Monday afternoon I'm scheduled to meet with the Secretary of Education for the first time. Do you know him?"

"I know of him," John Nakamishi replied.

"Why don't you meet me in the Law Library around three o'clock and we'll go over together. We can talk some more on the way." TJ rose and extended a hand. "John, it's been a real pleasure meeting you."

─┤ TEN ├─

"My heart's on fire today, on fire for my Lord." Reverend Wilkins paused to wipe a steaming brow. It was approaching the end of the service, and the reverend was showing the strain. "Can I have me an Amen."

"Amen, brother."

"Say it!"

"My heart's on fire, now, for all those poor souls out there who're doomed to never know my Lord!"

"Tha's the truth!"

"I don't know which would be worse, the agony of the fire, or not knowin' our Lord. And these poor souls are gonna know both!"

"Lawd have mercy!"

"Yes, they's a lotta poor folks out there, Jesus knows how my heart reaches out for them." He wiped his face again. "Got a call from Brown's Funeral Home the other day, man asked me to come over and officiate at a funeral. Fam'ly passin' through Washington, you know the story. Didn't have no regular home, or if they did they'd lost it. Traveled from place to place lookin' for work. Had a baby girl get sick and die. Girl was only four years old."

There was some rustling in the church, a few groans from mothers with young children of their own.

"Coffin was awful small," the preacher went on. "Awful small. I said the words, not so much for that little soul, 'cause I knows she was on her way to a higher place. Knew she's gonna be restin' in the arms of

Jesus tonight. No, I was tryin' to find something to say to that couple so's to help them feel a little peace. There we stood—the man, his wife, three gravediggers and me. All there to see this little girl off to be gathered in the arms of our Lord.

"When it was all over, the man came up and tried to offer me money. I told him it was the last thing I wanted from him. Wished there was somethin' more I could do, I told him. The man was bunchin' his old battered hat in his hands and cryin' soft like. Not makin' any real noise, just had these tears streamin' down his face. The woman, now, she couldn't even talk, she was so broke up.

"So the man stuffs the money back in his pocket and says to me, 'Reverend, the thing that just eats at me so is how my little girl never heard her daddy pray.' "

The church was so quiet the entire congregation seemed to hold its breath. The reverend paused again to wipe his face, then went on in that hoarse, revival-broken voice.

"The woman snuffles and tries real hard to collect herself. She walks up beside me so's to be able to look her husband right square in the face. She takes this long shaky breath, and says real low, 'Neither have I.' "

The preacher took a long moment to gaze out over the silent gathering. "Lot of folks gonna be callin' His name on that day. 'Lord, Lord,' they're gonna say. We know it's gonna happen 'cause Jesus told us. And we know what He's gonna say to them. 'Be gone,' He's gonna tell 'em. 'Be gone, I know thee not.' "

His face a mass of sharp angles and dark shadows, he looked at them with dire warning in his eyes. "I'm tellin' you, people. I'm tellin' you the only way I know how. Get right with God while there's still time."

☐ ☐ ☐

Jeremy did not get out of the car once they were home. "Reckon I might as well hit the road."

TJ offered his hand, said, "Have a good trip, Jem. Be careful."

"Always am. Too many crazies out there not to be careful."

"When do you think you'll be back?"

"Tuesday or Wednesday. I'll call you once I see how much trouble that burst pipe's caused."

"It's kind of you to help, but I don't want to trouble you," TJ said, feeling vaguely guilty that it was Jeremy and not he who was traveling back to pick up Catherine. "You could just call in a plumber and have one of the children look in on it."

"Not with an old house like yours, TJ, and you know it. Never can tell what damage's been done. Gotta have somebody go down under there and check real careful." Jeremy offered him a calm smile. "Don't fret yourself, TJ. Spent a lifetime crawlin' around in the dirt. One more time ain't gonna hurt none."

"Well, give both the girls and all the grandchildren a hug from me."

"Sure will."

"And tell Catherine I'll be awfully glad to see her again."

Jeremy chuckled. "Know what that old girl said to me last night? Said, Jem, I believe I've slept alone just about as long as I can stand." He shook his head. "Washington won't know what hit 'em."

□   □   □

Congressman John Silverwood met Sally Watkins that Sunday evening in the lobby of the Four Seasons Hotel and decided that he had been totally foolish to worry about being seen. But before they sat down, he had also decided that the vast expanse of the hotel bar was not what he wanted for atmosphere, so he asked her if she would mind a little walk.

They went to Nathan's, a bar and restaurant located on what was considered to be *the* intersection in Georgetown—Wisconsin Avenue at M Street. It was expensive and dark, lit by candles and flickering lamps, lined with leather and hand-rubbed wood, filled with interesting people and laughter and murmured conversation. Silverwood had fallen into the habit of stopping there almost every night on his way home. He found it a pleasant way to put off entering an empty house.

Tonight was the first time he had entered the bar in the company of someone else. He felt a certain pleasure at seeing the reaction of other patrons to Sally Watkins' beauty.

Just the same, he didn't like to think of it as a date. Something within him rebelled against the term. Even though the quarrels with his wife continued to worsen, he didn't want to see himself as going *out* with another woman. He was simply meeting an attractive colleague for a drink.

She allowed him to help her off with her coat, gracing him with a brilliant smile. "It's so nice to go out with a gentleman."

A sky-blue silk blouse with matching wool skirt set off the white-blond hair that hung like a fringe across her shoulders. Her pale blue eyes held a sparkling eagerness that made his chest tight.

"You look ravishing," he said.

Full lips that seemed ever ready to laugh turned up to reveal tiny white teeth. "It's nice to have someone to look good for," she said softly.

He laughed and led her toward the bar. "I doubt seriously that a girl like you has much trouble finding escorts."

"Depends on how choosy the girl is," she replied.

Drinks were ordered and arrived swiftly. She sat on the corner stool; he stood beside her so that she faced him and the wall. He looked out over the room, occasionally nodding at acquaintances and familiar faces. Her attention remained totally focused on him. There was seldom a moment when her knee was not pressed upon his leg. Her hand settled on his sleeve, her shoe traced a pattern along his shin.

As their conversation flowed smoothly and laughter came more frequently, Silverwood found himself thinking about his wife. This morning there had been the first reference to a legal separation. Looking into Sally Watkins' eyes, he could not recall whether he or his wife had brought it up. He gave a mental shrug, decided it did not matter.

"Is something wrong?"

"No, why?"

"Your expression turned so serious all of a sudden." She laid a concerned hand upon his, squeezed gently, asked, "Are you sure you're all right?"

He was filled with the desire to kiss her. She saw it in his eyes. She parted her lips slightly, looked at him quietly. He felt as though a flame soared through him. Yet something held him back. Silverwood reached for his glass with uncertain fingers, took a sip, realized that the move was entirely up to him. When he wanted it, she was ready. He had never been unfaithful to his wife, though. There had been other opportunities, but this was different. Very different. He realized that he wanted her as badly as he had ever wanted anything in his entire life.

And his wife was so very far away—and not just in distance.

"You're so quiet," she said.

He turned to her, saw the welcome still in her eyes. "I was just thinking."

Sally opened the tiny purse hanging from her shoulder, fished around, brought out a penny, handed it over with a smile. "Payment in advance."

He hesitated, decided that he wasn't ready yet, sought another subject. "I was thinking about a committee hearing Friday afternoon."

Sally Watkins laughed, a delightful sound. "You were not."

"All right," he confessed, smiling back. "You're right. I wasn't. But I am now. Can I tell you about it?"

She settled back, the welcome in her eyes replaced by a light of clear intelligence. "Sure."

"You mean it?"

"Why not? I love talking shop. It's one of the reasons I'm so happy here. I love politics. I love everything about it."

"Then you're an incredible girl," he said, comparing her reaction to the cool indifference he faced when attempting to discuss politics with his wife.

She laughed again. "I don't know about that. I was born and raised in Ruford, Virginia. Have you ever heard of it?"

"I think so. Isn't it up in the Blue Ridge Mountains?"

"That's the one. Sixty miles or six thousand light-years away from civilization, depending on whether we're talking distance or mentality. Population four thousand, or so they say. I think they must've counted the dogs, chickens, and the bodies buried in the cemetery. The only thing I ever wanted from Ruford was to never see it again. The place bored me to tears."

She sipped her drink, continued. "My birthday present to myself when I turned nineteen was a one-way ticket to Washington, D.C. I've never been back."

"How old are you now?"

"Twenty-four."

That young. "Do you realize I'm fifteen years older than you are?"

She shrugged her unconcern. "Older, wiser, and an awful long way ahead. I like older men. They know what they want out of life, and they know how they're going to get it." She gave him a steady look. "I know what I want, too. And I'm not going to get it tagging along behind some guy my age."

"Why not?"

"Because I don't have the patience, for one thing. I feel like I've spent all my life waiting around. And I like being with somebody who knows enough to tell me what to do. I've got to have a lot of confidence in a fellow to trust him like that. I can't put that kind of trust in a guy my age. Why should I? He doesn't know any more than I do."

"You're an amazing woman," he said. It was the first time he had not thought of her as a girl.

"I'm just a girl who knows what she wants," Sally Watkins replied. "I know what I have, too, and I'm looking for the right kind of guy to give it to."

They shared another long look, until she clinked her glass against his, said, "I thought you were going to tell me about a congressional hearing."

He shook his head. "You really do listen, don't you?"

"When the talk's about politics, you bet. This stuff is great. I know which hearing you're talking about, too. The HUD investigation."

He stared at her, scarcely able to accept that she really *wanted* to hear what he had to say.

The eagerness was shining through. "That was a great move, getting into the investigation. I bet you it's going to blow sky high before much longer."

"This is incredible." He had to laugh. "Do you know how nice it is to talk to somebody about this and have them enjoy it?"

She grasped his hand, spread out the fingers, laced them together with hers, set it in her lap, said, "So go on, tell."

She listened with attentive silence. He struggled to describe the hearing, worried at first that her attention would wane as he got bogged down in trying to sort it out in his own mind. But she waited patiently as he went back several times and corrected himself, reconstructing the scene, describing his initial question.

He stopped and signalled to the bartender with his empty glass, realized that she was waiting for him to continue.

He had to smile. "You've got this incredible sense of knowing when to stay quiet. You don't even realize what a gift that is, do you?"

Sally Watkins squeezed his hand, spoke reams with her eyes, said, "Tell me the rest."

When the bartender had freshened their drinks and left, Silverwood described the look he had seen on the chairman's face, and the realization that the man would not be offering the proper direction.

"So I had to take it over myself," he went on. "And as we continued, I realized that the committee was quieter than I had ever seen them before. Here we were, facing a corporation that had pretty much lived by graft, and I had the spotlight all to myself. No, that's not true. There were a couple of the others who were with me all the way. Smith and Hancock. Democrat and Republican. I can't figure it out. All the others should have been at those guys' throats. But they hardly let out a peep."

She remained silent, attentive, listening. Her eyes were clear, her expression beautiful. Silverwood had never known a woman who could listen as well as she could. He never knew it could mean so much to have someone who truly shared his interest in politics and power.

"There was this guy," he went on. "I don't even know why I mention him. He didn't say a word all day. Just sat at the end of the witness table, parked behind these two-tone shades. You know the kind, the bottom half's clear and the top part's totally opaque. Motionless as a cadaver. He's some big lobbyist. I think he's got some kind of hold over an acquaintance. He tried to put the moves on me last week."

"Who is he?"

"Guy called Shermann. Can't remember his first name. He really gave me the creeps, sitting there. I don't know why, but I feel like he's connected to what went on in there today."

Sally Watkins frowned slightly, disengaged her hand, and trailed a finger around the rim of her glass. "His first name's Anthony," she said quietly. "Anthony Shermann."

"You know that guy?"

She hesitated, nodded her head, kept her eyes on her slowly rotating finger. "He's one of the best-known lobbyists in town. A real power behind the throne."

"Maybe so," Congressman Silverwood said. "But he's still one weird guy. He gives me the creeps."

She kept her eyes on her glass. "I don't know. He's got a lot of friends here. Powerful friends."

Silverwood thought again about the committee chairman, said dryly, "I'll bet."

"Staffers on the Hill always rely on lobbyists for information," Sally said. "It's incredible how knowledgeable Shermann is about issues."

He laughed, said, "The man's a paid mouthpiece. For a thousand bucks an hour I could be knowledgeable too."

"I sometimes think a congressman's job is kind of like that of a judge," she went on. "He's got to listen to both sides before making a decision."

He nodded over the logic of that, took a sip of his drink, said, "So?"

"These people can be very valuable allies," Sally said, looking at him. "Washington's a town where you can't have too many friends. Especially around campaign time."

For some reason he found himself thinking of the last time he had tried to talk politics with his wife. It had been just before he had left for Washington, a conversation he had known would fail before he started. It had been a sort of last-ditch effort, a hope against hope that she would show an interest and agree to come with him to share his new life. Instead, she had yawned repeatedly before finally begging fatigue and asking if they could continue the next morning. Sure, he had replied, mightily depressed by her reaction and angered even more by the fact that she didn't even care how much she had disappointed him. He had moved up his departure to the next afternoon.

"You've got that look on your face again," Sally Watkins said. "What are you thinking?"

He focused on her white-blond hair, her eyes, her face, said, "It's really nice, being able to talk with you about these things. You seem to have a lot of solid advice."

Her look deepened. "I can't think of anything I'd like more than being Special Advisor to Congressman Silverwood."

He smiled, said, "You're here to take care of me, is that it?"

Her hand settled upon his arm. "If you'll let me," she replied.

⊣| ELEVEN |⊢

Congressman John Silverwood pushed his way through the revolving doors and paused a moment to take in the lobby's elegant splendor. That Senator Erskins had chosen the Promenade Cafe in the Mayflower Hotel for their meeting came as some surprise. It was quite a ways removed from the normal haunts of the Capitol Hill crowd. The hotel was situated up Connecticut Avenue, almost at Dupont Circle. Silverwood had been there only twice, once to a reception and once to lunch with a wealthy constituent. He thought it very ornate and desperately European.

Senator Reginald Erskins was waiting for him. His carefully coiffured silver hair caught the light as he rose and gave Silverwood a politician's smile. "Right on time. First mark of a professional."

"Good to see you again, Senator."

"Please, John, call me Reggie." He waved Silverwood to a seat, asked, "Drink?"

He saw that the senator had a glass in front of him, so said, "Scotch, thanks."

Senator Erskins signalled the waiter. "Don't usually indulge at midday. Doctor's orders. But there's always room for an exception, especially on a day as important as this one."

Silverwood smiled politely. "What are you celebrating?"

"Your future, my boy." The Senator stood abruptly, said, "And here comes the guest of honor."

Silverwood turned in his chair, tensed as he recognized the lobbyist,

Anthony Shermann. "I thought this was supposed to be a private meeting."

"It is, my boy, it is. Tony won't be staying but a few minutes. He's an old friend and essential to the matter at hand."

Anthony Shermann approached the table, his face hidden as always behind those opaque sunglasses. He extended a hand. "How very nice to see you again, Congressman."

Gingerly Silverwood accepted the hand. There was no strength to it whatsoever. No strength, no warmth, no sense of life. "Do you ever take off those sunglasses, Mr. Shermann?" he asked, surprising even himself.

Shermann didn't seem put off by the question. "Very seldom, Congressman. Very seldom indeed."

But Senator Erskins was not the least bit pleased. "You've got some nerve, son, insulting an important man like Tony Shermann."

"I prefer to see a man's eyes when I do business with him."

"Certainly, Congressman, I do of course understand." Shermann's toneless voice rasped a chuckle. "I've always felt I kept my glasses on for the other person's benefit. If you would like them off, however, just say the word."

"No, you don't," the senator interrupted. "John, leave Tony alone. His eyes've been sensitive to light for as long as I've known him. How long's that been, Tony? Twenty years?"

"I'm sure I don't recall, Senator."

"Here comes the waiter. Tony, give him your order. Sit down, everybody."

Silverwood hesitated, then sat down, feeling trapped.

"Now listen up, son." Senator Erskins waited until he was sure he had Silverwood's attention. "Tony's one of the most useful friends I've got here in Washington. He gives as good as he takes, my boy, you can rest assured on that point."

"You're too kind, Senator," Shermann said, his voice like wind passing through dead autumn leaves.

"Tell him what you've got in mind, Tony."

"It's very simple, really. You see, Congressman, I consider myself one of the last true Washington power brokers. We're a dying breed, I'm sad to say. Most of these so-called lobbyists nowadays haven't the slightest idea how the game is played. They're caught up, body and soul, in one cause or another, and have nothing to offer in return but a misguided sense of destiny."

Silverwood waited in silence. He found that if he fastened his attention on a point just to the left and slightly above the man's forehead he could feign concentration and not have to watch his own reflection in those two-tone shades.

"Power broker," Shermann repeated in that ancient voice. "It's a very simple concept, Congressman. I have power. I broker it."

Silverwood glanced at Senator Erskins to see how he took it. The silver-haired senior statesman was nodding agreement, a satisfied smile playing across his lips.

"My clients come to me because of the power that has been entrusted to my care. With caution and careful judgment, I assist these gentlemen in presenting their cases."

"Like Atlas," Silverwood said flatly.

"Precisely, Congressman. Our friends at the Atlas Group are a perfect case in point."

"You sure didn't have much to say at the hearing."

"Oh, there was no need to intervene, Congressman. Very little is accomplished in a public forum like that one."

"I think we're accomplishing a great deal in those hearings," Silverwood replied.

"My words referred to my own responsibilities, I assure you. For work such as mine, an intimate gathering away from public scrutiny is so much more useful."

"Like this one," Senator Erskins said.

"Precisely, Senator, just like our little meeting here." He turned an expressionless face back to Silverwood. "If I might be permitted, Congressman, I'd like to take this particular example one step further. I am in a position to offer you a seat on the House Ways and Means Committee."

Silverwood's jaw dropped. "That's impossible."

"I assure you it's not, Congressman."

"I just heard the news yesterday," Senator Erskins confirmed.

"Strictly confidential, of course. Stanley's had another seizure. The doctor says he's got to take it easier if he wants to see Christmas. He's resigning from the committee. They'll have to appoint another Republican, and fast."

Congressman Stanley Brubaker of Arkansas was the number-two ranking Republican in Congress, and minority leader of the most powerful committee in the House—the Ways and Means Committee. It controlled the cash, and thus oversaw the work done by all other committees. Nothing done by Congress—no new law, no departmental change, no pressing issue—could be acted upon until money was appropriated. In Washington political circles, the chairmanship of the Ways and Means Committee was considered the third most powerful position in the government. There were members who had gladly traded chairmanships of other committees just for a *seat* on Ways and Means.

"They'd never give that job to a freshman congressman," Silverwood replied, excited despite himself. "Never."

"Believe me, my boy," Senator Erskins told him, "if Tony says he can do it, whatever it is, consider it done. The man's as good as his word."

"Well, I must be off," Shermann said, pushing himself erect. "I have quite literally a million things to do today."

He nodded to the senator, extended his hand to Silverwood. "I do so hope we shall have an opportunity to see more of each other, Congressman."

Silverwood willed himself not to show a reaction as he grasped the limp fingers a second time. "There's no way I'd agree to anything based on some airy promise like that."

"Naturally not," Shermann agreed. "You wouldn't be expected to lift a finger until—or unless, if you prefer—the position was yours."

"And all you want in return is for me to lay off Atlas? That's it?"

"A small price to pay for such a prestigious position, I'm sure you'll agree, Congressman." He nodded once more to the senator, said, "Good day to you both, gentlemen. Congressman, it would delight me to no end to hear from you soon."

□   □   □

John Nakamishi was in the OEOB Law Library at exactly three o'clock. "That was a wonderful Bible lesson this morning, Mr. Case."

"Thank you," TJ replied, not sure what else he should say. He was having trouble getting used to the increasing size of their gathering.

"It wasn't just me you touched, sir. I never thought three hundred people could ever be so still."

Three hundred people. Bella had left him a note that morning saying their meeting was moved to the building's main conference hall. Its rows of gradually rising seats faced a small stage, where TJ had stood feeling very alone and exceedingly vulnerable. Three hundred people. Bella had told him the number. It had seemed an endless sea of faces.

Once settled in the taxi, TJ decided it was time to test the merit of this new man. "I'm a beginner at this, I'll be the first to admit it. I need your wisdom about what I'm going to be facing here. I don't even know enough to ask the right questions. I'd be very grateful for any insight you can give me."

Still facing forward, John Nakamishi gave a single nod, almost as though he had been expecting the question. In a voice as flat and bland as his expression, he said, "Secretary Edwards has a reputation as a real aggressive hothead. I've never met him, and these things get blown out of proportion in the early days of a new administration. But I think this assessment's pretty close to the mark.

"If it's true, then you're already starting out with a couple of major strikes against you. You were appointed to a position in the White House without any input from his side. He's going to resent this. A lot, if his personality is really like I've heard. You're too close to the seat of power for his liking, you have your own contacts in Congress, and you're there to develop a specific policy issue. He's probably heard something about it, but exactly how much is going to depend on how good his own sources are inside the OEOB."

TJ sat back, sort of leaning against the door so he could study the impassive face beside him, and decided that this man was an absolute godsend.

"His first concern is how close your policy objectives are to his own," John continued. "If you're going against the grain, then he's going to want to crush you fast. These early days of the new regime are crucial to him. They'll determine what policies are earmarked as top priority for this administration."

TJ nodded in silent approval, thought to himself, the man sounds as if he's ticking points off a checklist.

"If your policies are in line with his department's, then the major objective on his mind will be to make sure you know who's boss. His message will be, 'There's only one advisor to the President on education policy, and that's me.' "

TJ waited, realized there was no more coming, asked, "So what would you do?"

John turned to look at him for the first time, answered, "Stall."

The taxi let them off at a tiny triangle of grass that was struggling against the frigid weather to maintain a hint of green. TJ stepped out, saw they were across the street from the NASA exhibition and the Botanical Gardens, wished for a moment he could take time out to play tourist.

As with most Washington government buildings, the imposing marble and granite exterior of the Department of Education gave way to sullen dinginess inside. A black woman in uniform left no question in their minds that she was singularly unimpressed by their having an appointment with the secretary. With total unconcern she pointed out the elevators and went back to her magazine.

Upstairs the hallway was poorly lit and decked out in black linoleum flooring. The air had a musty odor, and many of the ceiling panels were stained and rotting. The only flash of color was the wood-grained seal above the spread of doors leading to the secretary's office. They entered a room flanked by a receptionist's desk and a set of government-issue sofas, gave their names, and were told that the secretary was expecting them.

The Secretary of the Department of Education's inner office was as opulent as his outer office was tacky. Rosewood panelling matched the massive desk and low-slung coffee table. Pictures showing the secretary with various dignitaries, including several past presidents, decorated the wall. Heavy drapes framed floor-to-ceiling windows, and rust-colored carpet muted the sound of their entry. The black receptionist gave TJ Case a measuring gaze and a professional smile, asked if he would like a coffee, said the secretary would be right with them, closed the door as she left.

Before they had time to choose between the sofa and chairs by the desk, the door opened a second time. A short, beefy, bullet-headed man walked in chewing on an unlit cigar. "You Case?"

"Yes."

He stuck out a stubby hand. "Phil Edwards. Nice to meet you."

"This is my assistant, John Nakamishi."

"Right." With studied reluctance Secretary Edwards shook the proffered hand. "I always prefer to have these first meetings in private."

"This is only my third week on the job," TJ replied, refusing to let the man ruffle him. "John has been a big help in getting me settled."

"I'll bet." Secretary Edwards moved behind his desk, took out the cigar, set it in a polished crystal ashtray, sat down in his chair. "You need some help, let me send one of my boys over."

"Thank you for the offer," TJ said.

Secretary Edwards stared across the desk with gray-blue eyes as cold as two glass orbs, pressing the fingers of his hands against one another.

Edwards picked up the phone, pressed a button, said brusquely, "Jane in the building?" He waited, said, "Tell her to come in here."

To TJ, he said, "I hear you're pushing special classes for gifted children."

"I haven't had an opportunity to push much of anything yet," TJ countered, blessing John for his advice.

The door opened, and Secretary Edwards shot to his feet. TJ and John quickly followed. "Like to introduce my Special Assistant for White House Liaison, Jane Patterson. Jane, this is the guy we've been talking about, TJ Case."

The woman was a rather hefty gray-haired lady in her mid-fifties, as solid as a brick wall. Her gaze was as icy as that of her boss.

Once they were seated, the secretary said, "Jane's been a primary schoolteacher for twenty-three years."

"And every child I've ever taught has been gifted in one way or another, Mr. Case," her voice as cold as her eyes. "How much teaching experience have you had?"

"Only Bible study, I'm afraid," TJ replied.

"Strange how a man with such little experience can feel he's expert enough to advise the President on such a sensitive topic."

"Perhaps not being so directly involved allows me a more objective outlook," he said mildly.

"I fail to see the logic in that," she snapped back.

"Why don't you tell us what you've got in mind," the secretary demanded.

"To serve my country, my President, and the children within our educational system to the best of my ability," TJ Case replied.

Secretary Edwards stabbed the air in front of him with one finger, said, "There's one thing I want to hear from you, Case, and that's whether you're going to be a team player. If some jerks in Congress think they can make some side-run on me, they've got another thing coming. There's one policy this administration is going to have on education, and that's the one formulated by this department. Too much is at stake here for some—" Secretary Edwards clamped down on what he was going to say, finished, "I gotta know whether you're with us or not."

"I have no intentions of operating in secrecy," TJ replied. It was amazing, he thought, how protected he felt at that moment. There was literally nothing that could breach his barrier of peace. "If I have learned anything in twenty years of public service, it is that men of honest principle can come to agree on anything, no matter how divergent their opinions may be at the beginning. All it takes is a willingness to join in prayer and honest discussion."

His reply took the wind out of their sails. Both Secretary Edwards and his assistant stared at him openmouthed. TJ decided it was a good time to take his leave.

He stood, guided John Nakamishi up with his eyes, said to the secretary, "We have a little group that comes together every morning for prayer. If either of you are over our way, I'd be honored to have you join us."

They were in the elevators before doubt began to set in. TJ felt the calm slide, leaving fatigue and worry in its place. He asked his assistant, "Well, what do you think?"

John Nakamishi met his gaze with steady black eyes, said quietly,

"That was about the bravest thing I've ever heard anyone say."

TJ covered his embarrassment by changing the subject. "So what happens next?"

Once again it was as though John Nakamishi had been waiting for him to ask the question. With that steady low-key style, he replied, "He's going to go straight to the President's Chief of Staff. Have you met him yet?"

"No."

"It doesn't really matter; you're new on the team and so you'll be at a disadvantage anyway. Secretary Edwards and Chief of Staff Norman Greenbaum did their graduate work at the same university and have worked together off and on ever since. Edwards will go to him and say, we can't have two education advisors. We have to have one person making one cohesive policy for this administration. And I'm that person. So the only way to keep from having conflict is for your special assistant to go through me on *everything*. He has to report through me."

TJ thought it over most of the way back to the White House. It was not until they were at the OEOB entrance that he asked, "What do you think we should do?"

John Nakamishi looked at him, asked, "Do you want to answer to Edwards?"

TJ shook his head. "He doesn't seem to be someone interested in rearranging his opinion about anything."

"He's not."

"I don't suppose he's a Christian, is he?"

John Nakamishi shrugged his shoulders slightly. "It's not for me to say, but I don't believe you would call him a very devout man."

"Since we're not likely to see eye to eye on either education policy or faith, I don't suppose it would be a good thing," TJ decided. "So what do we do?"

His assistant showed the security badge to the guard, said, "Pray."

When TJ entered the outer office, two young women he had never seen before jumped up from behind their desks. TJ halted and wondered for a moment if he had entered the wrong door.

"This is Amy Lou Sinclair on your right," John Nakamishi said from behind him, indicating a woman of perhaps twenty-five with long auburn hair, a very sincere expression, and an attractive face. The other desk was occupied by a black woman of perhaps the same age, slender and sharp-featured and equally serious in demeanor. "And this is Linda Harris."

TJ mumbled something about how nice it was to meet them, then noticed that the cartoons and the radio were no longer visible.

Linda had a Bible next to her dictionary and thesaurus. On the bulletin board behind Amy Lou's desk was a placard of the broken fish—the sign used by Roman Christians seeking entry into the Catacombs.

"The two other girls decided they might be more comfortable somewhere else," John Nakamishi said matter-of-factly. "And these two ladies were very eager to work for you."

"Were they really," TJ murmured, trying to take it in.

"This is a real honor, Mr. Case," Amy Lou said.

"I've been going to your study sessions every morning since I heard about them," Linda said. "We both have. It's been like an answer to a prayer."

"They've been a real inspiration," Amy Lou agreed.

TJ nodded his thanks, thought a moment, looked around, pointed at the wall above Linda's desk, said, "I've got a little needlework plaque my wife made for me. It's one of my favorite Bible passages. I think it's going to look fine right about there."

Once they were in his office, TJ said, "I'm grateful for the change, but not for the way it was done. Next time you want to do something major like that, ask me first, please."

"Yes, sir." There was a total lack of resentment or defensiveness in the calm voice. "I would have, but I didn't find out until this morning after the prayer session that your two secretaries had packed up and left. I ran down to Personnel. They knew about it, of course. Didn't seem very bothered about it, though. And they didn't have anybody ready to take their places." John Nakamishi shrugged. "I think maybe your reputation is growing around here. Lines are being drawn."

TJ settled behind his desk, waved John into a chair, was very glad that he had not been curt with the man.

"These two ladies have been unhappy with their bosses ever since they got here," John Nakamishi went on. "Amy Lou's been kind of subtly harassed, nothing you could put in words, but the message has been clear. The others in her office are young and pretty loose, and she's not been made real welcome. Linda's boss just plain doesn't like blacks."

"So you told them about our little problem," TJ said.

"It was like a dream come true to them," John Nakamishi said. "They've been running around all day trying to work things out. I was going to tell you first thing, but with the meeting and all I decided it could wait."

"You decided right," TJ said. He wondered how he could tell this quiet man with his unruffable calmness how much it meant to have him there.

John Nakamishi saved TJ the trouble by changing the subject. "Chief of Staff Greenbaum was head of the President's campaign. I guess you already know that."

"There's a lot about this place that I don't know," TJ admitted. "Too much."

"Secretary Edwards was one of the chief policy makers. He wrote a lot of the President's speeches, developed positions the President took on a lot of the major issues."

"It's like a den of thieves," TJ commented.

John Nakamishi did not deny it. "In their eyes, you're a newcomer to the club. You're going to be kept out of a lot of the major policy meetings. Access to up-to-date information will be hard to come by, especially if Secretary Edwards decides to stand in your way. From their standpoint, they've earned the badge of courage during the campaign. They see themselves like old warriors with ribbons on their chests, talking down to this unbloodied officer who's just stepped out of training camp."

"Sounds as if I don't have much of a chance to break in," TJ said.

"A lot of these people have mortgaged their homes, uprooted their families, suffered through separations and really bad traumas for this campaign," John Nakamishi said. "They've paid their dues, or at least that's the way they see it. Their payoff is the opportunity to shape public policy and play with national power."

"Power," TJ muttered, leaning back in his chair. "I hear a lot about power, and almost nothing about service."

"It's hard to keep your head when you've been set down on the top of the mountain," John Nakamishi agreed. "And once they're here, they've still got to fight among themselves to keep what they feel is their slice of the pie."

TJ asked him, "Is there any hope at all of getting our programs through?"

"Only if we can make it seem like it's of strategic importance to the President," John Nakamishi replied. "That's the central rallying point for everybody. Appeal to the man on top, show that what we're doing will advance the President's popularity."

"That's not it," TJ said, more to himself than to John. "That's not the way I'm looking for." He looked up, said, "The central rallying point is God Almighty."

"Not in Washington," John Nakamishi said.

"We are here to do His will," TJ stated flatly. "It's up to Him to show us what to do, and how to do it."

His phone rang. He picked it up, heard Amy Lou say, "There is a woman who wants to speak with you. She says she's with WBTV News."

He asked his assistant, "Do you know WBTV?"

"The strongest station in the area," John Nakamishi replied.

TJ pressed the button, said hello.

"Mr. Case? This is Sandra Hastings of WBTV News." It was an eager, young, insistent voice. "I was wondering if I might be able to stop by and ask you a few questions."

"What about?" He glanced up at John, who was watching intently.

"We've heard about the remarkable Bible study you've started in the White House. It sounds like something that would interest our viewers."

"It's not really a Bible study," TJ replied. "More like a small prayer meeting."

"From what I've heard, Mr. Case, this is anything but small."

"I mean brief," he corrected himself, feeling cornered for no reason he could logically explain. "We only meet for about fifteen minutes, perhaps even less than that."

"Would it be all right if I came by and asked you a few questions about it?" she pressed.

Unsure of what he should do, he glanced at his watch, said, "I'll be leaving for home very shortly, I'm afraid."

"Fine," she replied, clearly satisfied. "We'll see you there." Before he could stop her, she had said goodbye and hung up.

He put down the phone, confused, said to John, "Do you know what that was?"

John Nakamishi smiled for the first time, said, "Who knows? Maybe a miracle."

□   □   □

Jeremy put the last case in the backseat, then slid into the driver's side to make sure he could still see out the back window. He shook his head at all the things a woman considered indispensible. Besides the three big suitcases and four little ones, there were a half dozen boxes of various sizes, three hanging bags, two extra totes, and fourteen framed pictures of the family.

He rose from the car, stretched sore muscles. It had been a long day. First there was the busted pipe in the basement—three inches of water to mop up, plumbers to call in and push to get the job done fast and right the first time, a careful check to make sure there was no structural damage. Then the car was packed. And repacked again, when Catherine couldn't remember whether she'd put in her Sunday go-to-meetin' hat. Naturally it was in the last case they checked.

He would be sorry to leave the next morning. It was hard to believe the difference between here and Washington. While the nation's capital lay wrapped in a cold and wet and miserable climate, North Carolina was enjoying the warmest winter in decades. He stood there in short sleeves and took a moment to savor all he would be giving up.

Jeremy looked over the car, saw Catherine standing beside the trimmed hedges that marked the entranceway. She stood with shoulders all hunched over and fragile-looking. He walked up beside her, started to reach out, then hesitated. Grief was every person's privilege, and if there was anything at all etched deep upon that good woman's face, it was grief.

Jeremy waited until he was sure she was aware of his presence, then asked, "Sister, are you all right?"

She took a moment for a shaky sigh. "I don't know, my head says it's silly, but my heart is crying like I'll never see my home again."

Jeremy looked up at the old place, spent a moment wondering what he could say, started discarding things left and right, decided on honesty. "We're in the Lord's hands, Catherine."

"I know," she said, her voice so very, very quiet.

"You still feel like we're doin' the right thing?"

She was silent for a time, then said, "Every morning I ask myself that, Jem. It's the first question I have every single day. And it gets clearer all the time. We've got to do it. TJ does, you do, I do. It's His will. I can question the why's and how's all I want, but it doesn't change a thing. I know in my *bones* that this is His will."

"So do I," Jeremy agreed.

She looked at her friend, asked, "Then why do I feel so bad?"

Jeremy laid a comforting hand on her shoulders and searched for words. "Having it be God's will doesn't always make it easy," he told her solemnly. "It just makes it *right*."

□   □   □

TJ had not been home long enough to take off his tie before the doorbell rang. He opened the door to a beautiful young lady with shining violet eyes and honey-colored hair.

"Mr. Case?"

"Yes." TJ noticed the van in his driveway and the two bearded young men pulling gear out of the side door. He felt the first tremor of nerves.

"I'm Sandra Hastings of WBTV News, we talked on the phone this afternoon. May I come in?"

As she was already shouldering past him, TJ let his inbred manners take over, and ushered her into the den.

"What a lovely home. It certainly is nice of you to let us meet you here."

"I'm not sure—"

"We could set up right here in your study, and be through in less than an hour," she said, her pretty eyes pleading.

"I thought you just wanted to ask a couple of questions," TJ stalled, alarmed by the prospect of facing a camera and discussing his faith.

"Well, that's right, I do." She gave him a practiced smile. "But we have to get your answers down on film, don't we?"

"I suppose so," he said, defeated.

"Wonderful," she said. Hurriedly she signalled to the crew waiting by the door before TJ could raise another objection.

"Excuse me for a moment," he said, and fled to the bathroom.

Once the door was shut and locked, TJ leaned against the wall, covered his eyes with one hand, prayed as directly as his pounding heart and frantic mind would allow. Television, Lord, oh Lord, what on earth am I supposed to say? That you called me up here? They'll laugh me right out of town, are you listening to me? I know you've set this interview up for a purpose. It's too crazy to think about any other way. And I know I've been on television before, but that was politics. That was in another life. This is now, Lord. What am I supposed to say?

The answer was silence. No inspiration, no guiding light, no comforting presence. Nothing. TJ uncovered his eyes with a sigh, felt a thousand years old.

There was a knock at the door. "We're ready any time you are, Mr. Case."

Shoulders bowed, he opened the door. She greeted him with another smile, but this one did not cover the steely glint in her eyes. She was clearly looking forward to this.

"May I?" She reached up, straightened his tie, put a small hand on his arm and guided him forward.

Two tall tripods supported enormous television lights, glaring eyes focused on the two chairs flanking the coffee table. She waited for TJ to sit down, settled herself, all business now.

A technician fitted a lapel mike on both of them; the cameraman did a light check and set his focus; the technician asked for a sound check.

"Test, one, two," she said crisply, nodded to TJ to do the same, sat straighter when he complied.

"Ready," came the signal.

"Oh!" TJ sprang from his chair as though propelled by an invisible hand. It startled everyone. "Just a moment." He walked toward the bookshelves, and in doing so pulled off his microphone.

"Hey!" The technician ripped off his headphones, hurried over, picked up the mike, inspected the wiring.

"Excuse me," TJ apologized, searching frantically. "Here it is. I'm sorry. I forgot something important."

The technician looked at the newscaster, shrugged, said, "Seems okay."

TJ came back over, sat down, waited while the technician refitted his mike, endured the newscaster's exasperated look in silence.

"Could you say something again, Mr. Case? Make sure your mike still works."

"I thought I might need a Bible," he said, and set it down on the table between them.

Her sharp retort was cut off by the technician saying calmly, "Loud and clear."

TJ could sense her desire to dominate. She had an impressive force, this young woman, and she used it with consummate skill; first to manipulate him into agreeing, and now to overwhelm the interview itself. He felt lost, carried by their professional ease like a leaf floating downstream.

The cameraman made a final focus on her face, said, "Rolling."

"This is Sandra Hastings for WBTV News, here at the home of Mr. Thomas Jefferson Case. Mr. Case, recently appointed Special Assistant to the President for Education, is currently at the center of a most remarkable development."

It was very different this time. There was no physical sensation at all—no thrill, no sense of Presence, no filling of his being with some divine force. It simply was. As the newscaster began to speak, TJ knew he was not alone. There was no room for doubt, for question, for concern over what was to be said. It did not matter what she asked. He knew.

"Mr. Case, a lawyer from North Carolina, has brought a bit of the Bible Belt up with him to Washington. In the short time he has been here, he has managed to establish an astonishingly successful prayer meeting within the White House itself."

She turned to him, and the camera swung with her. "Mr. Case, how many participants do you have right now?"

"At our meeting this morning, there were around three hundred," he replied, his voice solid, strong. He was so sure of what was to be said that there was no need to even speak loudly. The Spirit was with him.

Ms. Hastings was clearly not expecting such quiet confidence from him under the gun. She hesitated, asked, "And how long have you been here in Washington?"

"This is my third week."

"Don't you find that somewhat remarkable, three hundred White House staffers gathering every morning for prayer?"

"No more remarkable than the fact that the Lord would choose me to act as His servant."

"I see." She seemed momentarily at a loss, then, "And you feel sure that this is the Lord's work here?"

"How else would you explain the gathering of three hundred members of the White House staff?" TJ replied in the same calm voice. "What I find remarkable is that so many people could witness such an event and still doubt the power of our Lord."

Sandra Hastings reacted as though slapped. The glint of steel hardened her gaze. "Tell me, Mr. Case. Do you believe that the Bible still holds relevance in the face of all our modern-day difficulties?"

He did not need to hesitate. No search for an answer was required. It was as though the reply was prepared and presented to him before she even spoke. "I believe the Bible, as God's divinely ordained message for mankind, is the *only* relevant guide to today's problems."

"You say, then, that there is an answer to all of today's complex problems in the Bible?"

"Every one of them," he replied quietly, instantly.

"Could we discuss a specific example?"

"Certainly."

She leaned forward, homing in for the kill. "How would you feel the Bible answers the problem of, say, the plight of the homeless in America?"

The answers did not appear gradually. The books, chapters and verses *surged* into his mind. He picked up the Bible, wondered for a moment why he had chosen his seldom-used Living Bible version, then understood.

"I am going to use a modern-day translation," he said, opening the

Book, "because it may have more meaning to many of your viewers."

He found the first passage with a minimum of page turning. "Zechariah, chapter eleven, verses sixteen and seventeen. 'I will give this nation a shepherd who will not care for the dying ones, nor look after the young, nor heal the broken bones, nor feed the healthy ones, nor carry the lame that cannot walk; instead, he will eat the fat ones, even tearing off their feet. Woe to this shepherd who doesn't care for the flock. God's sword will cut his arm and pierce through his right eye; his arm will become useless and his right eye blinded.' "

He looked up, said, "It is very common in biblical terms for worldly leaders to be cast in the role of shepherds. We don't have to look any further than the morning's paper to see what effect the policies of our government and business communities are having on our less-fortunate citizens."

TJ flipped over a section, was barely surprised to find he had turned to the page he sought. Truly it was a day for miracles. "Isaiah, chapter five, verse eight, says, 'You buy up property so others have no place to live. Your homes are built on great estates so you can be alone in the midst of the earth.' " He raised his head long enough to say, "I realize that this describes many people in our society. However, I also think that it is a straightforward description of how many of our landlords and developers live, don't you?"

Again he turned to the Book, found the place, and said, "Micah, chapter two, beginning with the first verse, reads, 'You rise at dawn to carry out your schemes; because you can, you do. You want a certain piece of land, or someone else's house (though it is all he has); you take it by fraud and threats and violence.' Verses eight and nine read, 'You steal the shirts right off the backs of those who trusted you. You have driven out the widows from their homes and stripped their children of every God-given right.' "

He looked up, facing both the newscaster and the camera. Ms. Hastings seemed to have turned to stone. "The Lord's judgment of these wrongdoers is equally clear." He looked down, turned, said, "In Zechariah, chapter nine, verses three and four, we read, 'Though Tyre has armed herself to the hilt, and become so rich that silver is like dirt to her, and fine gold like dust in the streets, yet the Lord will dispossess her, and hurl her fortifications into the sea; and she shall be set on fire and burned to the ground.' "

"Zephaniah, chapter one, verse eleven, is even more explicit when it says, 'All your greedy businessmen, all your loan sharks—all will die.' "

He closed the Book, looked her square in the eyes, quoted from memory: "Zechariah, chapter one, verse eleven, answers your earlier question about whether the Bible still applies to today's society. It says, 'Your fathers and their prophets are now long dead, but remember the lesson they learned, that *God's Word endures.*' "

There was a long, long moment of silence while the camera watched the two watch each other. Finally the newscaster turned reluctantly away, faced the camera, said in a subdued voice, "This is Sandra Hastings, for WBTV News."

⊣| TWELVE |⊢

John Nakamishi was waiting for him in the hall after the Tuesday morning prayer meeting. "Did you see the 10 o'clock news last night?"

TJ shook his head, said, "I could scarcely keep my eyes open long enough to find my bed."

"They showed your interview right at the beginning."

"Did they?"

John nodded, his face as impassive as ever. "You really ate that girl alive."

He smiled. "That's not the way it felt at the time."

"I taped it. You can see for yourself. When the camera zoomed in for that closing shot, you could see that you really got under her skin."

"I was scared to death before it started," TJ confessed.

"Were you really?" John was surprised. "It didn't show at all."

"Not while it was going on. Before. Once it started, well—" TJ wondered how he could explain it.

"The Spirit was upon you." He nodded calmly. "Yes, that was clear too."

TJ cast a startled glance at his assistant. Here he was, trying to find some way to describe what still embarrassed him tremendously, and John Nakamishi treated it like some everyday occurrence.

"Yes," TJ agreed quietly, "I suppose it was."

"What's it like? I can see it on your face during the prayer meetings too. I feel it myself, of course, but I don't think I've ever known it to happen so intensely."

TJ struggled to find the words. "When the Presence is there, it is the most natural thing in the world. And the most real. The more powerful the inner impression, the more detached I seem from the world around me."

"There isn't room inside us for the Spirit and the world both. Not at the same time."

What a remarkable young man, TJ thought. "Sometimes when it's over I question the experience. It's hard then for me to believe that it really happened. I try halfheartedly to convince myself that it was just my imagination."

"I do the same thing," John Nakamishi agreed, quiet and calm as ever. "The old self fights like anything to maintain control. I love that passage in Colossians, I don't know how often I've read it. The trouble is, it's not as easy to put off the old self as Paul makes it out to be."

"He didn't say it was easy," TJ said. "He just said do it."

"Maybe so," John Nakamishi conceded. "But he didn't tell us it was something we'd have to keep doing every single day for the rest of our lives."

TJ paused at the door to their offices, asked, "John, how would you like to come home for dinner with me and meet my wife?"

"Call me Nak, please," he replied. "I'd like that very much."

"Fine. She'll be coming in today, so I'll see if she feels like having company tomorrow evening."

TJ opened the door to their offices, heard Linda say, "Oh, just a moment, I think he's coming in now." She cradled the phone, said, "It's a Mr. Roberts from ABC in New York. He saw a tape of your interview and wants you to appear on the *Good Morning America* show."

TJ faltered. He hated being interviewed, avoided it whenever possible. And this time it was national television. He turned to Nak, pleaded for advice with his eyes.

The young man's calm remained unfazed. "Perhaps we should talk."

"He says it's really urgent," Linda said.

"They always do," Nak told him. "Everything's a crisis for television people."

"Tell him I'll call back just as soon as my conference is over." To Nak he said, "Come on in."

Once they were seated, Nak said, "I think a decision has to be taken here. If you go ahead and speak to them, you may be jeopardizing your career."

"It sounds like you've been thinking this over for days," TJ said.

"This is a pretty standard Washington issue," he replied. "You as a White House staffer have one primary responsibility, and that is to support the President. All publicity is supposed to go to him, not to you. Wherever possible, his people are expected to stay behind the throne and out of the limelight. If you agree to appear on national television without express permission, the administration may decide to let you go."

TJ thought it over, asked, "So you're telling me not to do it?"

"No," he paused a moment, shaking his head. "I couldn't advise you like that."

"Why not?"

John Nakamishi chose his words carefully. "Because I'm not sure what it is you're supposed to be doing here."

TJ leaned back in his seat, waited for him to continue.

"I've watched you up there in those prayer meetings, and I've seen the Spirit at work." Nak shifted in his chair. "But it wasn't until I saw you last night on television that I understood."

"Understood what?"

"That you're here for a higher purpose. I don't know what it is, but it hit me yesterday that I had kind of unconsciously been accepting this ever since we met. There's something else going on here, something more important than whether you get this education policy through or not."

"I don't know of anything much more important than the education of our nation's children," TJ said.

Nak leaned forward, said, "Sir, that's not important. Or rather, it's not *the* most important thing. What you need to be sure of is whether it's what the *Lord* wants you to be doing. That's what you have to decide."

TJ regarded him for a moment, said quietly, "Now I understand why the Lord brought us together."

"I think now might be a good time for us to pray," Nak replied.

When they had bowed their heads, John Nakamishi began, "Dear Heavenly Father, it is an awesome moment when we realize that your hand is at work. It is also a hard moment, for we are filled with our own desires and our own goals, and they seem so incredibly important to us. We want so much for our goals to be yours, so much sometimes that we have trouble seeing what it is you want us to do."

As Nak prayed, TJ felt the Presence build within him, a gentle, comforting hand, one that communicated in ways beyond mere words. TJ heard Nak's prayer and he heard the Spirit within his heart, and he knew what had to be done. He *knew*.

"Help us to understand, Father," John Nakamishi went on, "that your own perspective is infinitely higher than ours. What we see is such a tiny piece of the whole. We cannot fathom your divine purpose, it is beyond our human understanding. Help us to accept this, and give us the strength to turn our goals over to you. All of them, Lord. Even the most precious, the ones we have worked on all our lives. Help us to turn them over to you, and see you transform them so that they too fit your divine will. Give us this ability to trust you, Father. Open our ears and our eyes and our hearts to your direction, and let us accept your will and your goals as our own. In the name of Jesus. Amen."

TJ opened his eyes, said to his assistant, "I want you to call the television producer for me. If I call, there's too great a chance that he'll argue. Tell him that I will do the interview, but only if he agrees, in writing, to limit the questions to educational issues."

"He won't like it," Nak replied.

"No, he won't," TJ agreed. "But he'll do it."

"You know?" Nak's eyes widened slightly.

TJ hesitated, pushed his doubt aside, trusted in the memory of the Spirit's guiding presence. "Yes," he replied quietly. "I know."

□   □   □

It started raining soon after they crossed the Virginia border, and by the time they drove into Washington the rain had turned to snow. When they arrived at Bancroft Place, Jeremy slithered up the path behind Catherine, carrying the two heaviest cases. Catherine carried nothing but her cosmetics case. She wanted to see the house first, was what she told Jeremy.

Catherine fished the keys out of Jeremy's coat pocket and opened the front door. She took one look inside, said, "Land sakes, Jeremy Hughes, what on earth have you gone and done?"

The big man suddenly felt very bashful. "I just wanted y'all to be comfortable," he mumbled.

She stopped long enough to pull out her hatpin and take off the hard blue traveling hat with its miniature blue veil. She started to set it down on the little table by the front door, hesitated, looked closer. Its inlaid surface and rich sheen spoke of great age and greater cost. Catherine put her hat down very gingerly.

She took one step farther, spotted the delicate chandelier with its hundreds of hand-cut crystal baubles hanging from the high-domed ceiling, and stopped cold in her tracks.

"I rented it furnished, Catherine," Jeremy said, a little worried by her demeanor. "All this stuff just came with it. I haven't bought a thing. Hardly moved anything around, either."

She walked another couple of steps, peered into the living room, looked long at the enormous Persian carpet and the antique furniture and the leather chairs and the lead-paned windows and the hardwood floor, and said very softly, "Will you just look at this."

TJ's arguments he could handle, but not this. Jeremy Hughes looked at the expression on her face and felt like a fool. "You don't like it, do you?"

She turned back to him, gave him that deep honey-coated chuckle, said, "It's just fine, Jem. You've done real good. I just wish you hadn't spent all this money, is all."

"Just wanted you to be comfortable," he said. "And I got me a good deal," he added, relieved that it was going to be okay.

"We'll do fine here, Jem." She patted his arm, gave him that special smile from way deep inside. "You're an absolute angel, you know that? You exasperate me more than all my grandchildren put together sometimes, but I suppose I'll just have to put up with that, won't I?"

"It's all just part of the package, is what I used to tell my wife," he said, returning her smile. "Can't cut me up and take out the parts you don't agree with. Wrecks the guarantee."

She laughed at that, turned back to the living room, went, "Mmmmm, mmmmm, honey, does the rest of the house look like this?"

"Pretty much," he said, looking in over her shoulder. "Except y'alls bedroom. There's all these mirrors hangin' from the ceiling."

"That'll do, Jem," she said in her best Sunday-school teacher voice.

"Seemed an awful funny place to put up a mirror. Have to lie down to straighten your tie."

She started to scold him, stopped, laughed, put one arm around his waist. "I can't tell you how glad I am you're here."

"Don't even try," Jeremy said, returning the hug. He turned and started up the stairs, sure now that it would all work out all right. "Can't think of anyplace on earth I'd rather be."

Jeremy worked on making them a real down-home meal that night. Despite Catherine's determination to put the move behind her and get on with her life, it was clear to both men that she was homesick. TJ reflected his wife's mood, looking tense and concerned and ten years older than he had that morning. So Jeremy left them talking quietly in the living room, and finished preparing what he hoped would help to make it better—spareribs basted in molasses and hot mustard, black-eyed peas, mashed potatoes, corn on the cob, and fresh scratch biscuits. He'd become a fair hand in the kitchen during his wife's illness and kept it up after her death; he loved country cooking and there were few restaurants nowadays that went to the trouble of using fresh produce. Everything was out of a can, and tasted of metal and chemicals and overcooking.

He walked into the living room, saw them sitting in the two leather chairs and struggling to make conversation, pushed aside his concern, said, "Y'all can sit in here and get reacquainted after dinner. C'm on and sit down, I'm gettin' ready to put it on the table."

"It smells marvelous, Jem," TJ said.

Catherine stood, quipped, "Jeremy's got everything under such good control, you sure you two need me up here?"

"Yes," TJ replied emphatically. "Don't even joke like that."

"The man's said it all," Jeremy agreed. "Come on back."

Tension entered the kitchen with them. TJ held her chair, patted her shoulder when she was seated, looked very worried. Jeremy started loading the serving dishes and searched his mind for something to lighten the mood.

"Jem, that smells wonderful." TJ walked to the stove, leaned over his friend's shoulder, said, "Spareribs, corn on the cob, black-eyed peas, man, is that lemon chess pie I smell?"

"Ain't no reason a body's got to starve to death up here, is there?" Jeremy moved from chore to chore with the deceptive ease of one long accustomed to such work. "Sure is a shame Catherine ain't hungry."

"Watch out, now," Catherine said, making an effort to join in the banter. "You're not too old to get one upside the head."

"No molesting the chef," TJ warned.

"TJ, there's ice tea in the fridge," Jeremy said. "Here, pour me a refill and then set the pitcher on the table."

"Sounds almost like you," TJ said to Catherine. "Bossing everybody around."

"Cook's privilege," Jeremy said. "Did I ever tell y'all about the time I raised chickens?"

"I don't believe so," TJ said, pouring tea for himself and Catherine, then sitting down beside her.

"We'd always had a few hens runnin' about. Don't know any farming family that didn't look to hens and hogs for most of their dinners. Anyway, Pappy decided to raise a flock when I was six or seven, I forget when. Bought a whole mess of chicks. Cutest little things you ever saw. Little yellow fluffballs. We built this addition to the henhouse and before long the whole farm was full of the sound of chickens. Full of the smell, too, when the wind was right."

Jeremy started setting steaming platters on the table, went on, "The next winter, Pappy got a buyer for the whole flock. Musta been six, seven hundred birds. Took us two whole nights to kill and dress 'em. Slept all day, worked all night. Soon as it got dark and those hens quieted down, Momma'd slip into the hen house. I'd come up and whistle real soft, and this here hand'd slip outta the door, real quiet, holding four hens upside down by their feet. They were still asleep, see, and I'd slip one pair of feet between each finger, then take another four and put them in my other hand. Then I'd set off across the fields to the killin' shed."

Jeremy came over with a basket of hot biscuits, sat down, bowed his head, said, "Lord, we thank you for all this bounty. Please bless this food to our bodies, and all your gifts to the doing of thy holy will. In Christ's name, Amen."

He started passing dishes, said, "Bout halfway across the field, those chickens'd wake up. I don't know if they maybe figured out where they were headin'. Or maybe they just objected to being carried upside down all bunched together like that 'cross a strange field in the middle of the night."

"I know I would," Catherine agreed helpfully.

"Yeah, well, those chickens'd wake up. And when they did, my arms'd go from down by my side to straight up over my head. I was just a skinny runt of a kid, and those eight chickens like to've pulled me into orbit. I'd go skippin' along, hittin' the ground 'bout every six feet or so, scared half to death I'd lose my grip before I reached the shed."

"Didn't they scratch up your hands?" Catherine asked.

"Naw, I had on work gloves. Trouble was, though, those old chickens'd let loose with everythin' they had, if you get my meanin'. I wore this floppy old hat, so my head stayed pretty clean, but come mornin' the rest of me was pretty well covered."

"I'm not sure I want to hear this story while I'm eating," Catherine said. "Honey, put back one of those ribs and take some more greens. You don't need the calories, you need the vitamins."

"Once a mother, always a mother," TJ said, doing no such thing, pleased that she seemed to be pulling herself out of it.

"Pappy'd take the chickens from me one by one, and once he'd topped and tailed 'em, he'd hand 'em over to Jacob." Jacob had been Jeremy's older brother. He'd stayed on the farm and died in his early forties. According to Jeremy, the cause of death was a terminal case of hard work and hopelessness.

"Jacob had the worse job of all, no question about it. He'd dip the chickens in this big vat, see, full of boilin' water. Then he'd stand in front of this roller, 'bout two feet thick and covered with little rubber fingers. The fingers'd pull the feathers off and then be scraped clean by this metal wedge. The feathers'd fall into this big cage, or most of 'em, anyway. All the big ones. The little ones'd stick to the rubber fingers, dry off after a couple of turns, and kinda fly up in this fuzzy cloud right in Jacob's face. Come morning, that boy'd look like a walking pillow. There'd be these two little bare spots where he'd keep his eyes clear, and the rest of him was pure feather."

"I am positively certain this story is going to disturb my appetite," Catherine declared.

"Not mine," TJ said, his mouth full. "Jem, you outdid yourself."

"I have yet to find anything that puts a dent in your appetite," Catherine told him. "Nice as it would be."

TJ laid down his sparerib, said, "Are you implying that I overeat?"

"I'm not implying anything," Catherine said. "I'm talking fact." She looked at Jeremy, asked, "What would you call a man who can sit down and eat three helpings of everything, then two hours later be back in the kitchen finishing off all the cold biscuits?"

Jeremy turned to TJ, said, "What do those guys say when they're afraid if they open their mouths they'll hang themselves with their tongues?"

"I plead the Fifth Amendment," TJ replied.

"That's the one," Jeremy said, and to Catherine, "You got any questions, take 'em up with my lawyer here."

□   □   □

Jeremy returned from taking TJ to work the next morning, saw Catherine was already dusting the front rooms, and got busy in the kitchen. Catherine came in a few minutes later, gave a careful inspection to his work, then climbed the stairs to make herself ready.

She reappeared a half hour later, giving a last tug to the hem of her skirt. She was visibly nervous. "I've never met a big-city preacher's wife before."

"I hope we didn't make a mistake in tellin' the lady to come on by," Jeremy said. "TJ was just concerned with you not knowin' anybody yet."

"No, no, it's fine." She patted jittery fingers over her hair. "Do I look all right?"

He smiled at her. "I've got a problem with that one. I look at you,

I see a woman I've known most of my life. You've *always* looked good—
and you sure do now. And anybody with eyes to see farther than skin-
deep's gonna know they're lookin' at somebody special."

She walked over, patted his shoulder, said, "Old Dr. Hughes. Always
knows what a body needs to hear."

The doorbell rang. Catherine straightened, pulled one last time at
her skirt, said, "That must be her."

Jeremy stayed by the stove, heard her step briskly down the hall and
open the door. "Good morning. Mrs. Wilkins?"

"That's right, honey. You must be Mrs. Case."

"Call me Catherine. Please come in."

"Thank you, sister. My, what a lovely home." Jeremy heard her enter
with heavy tread. "This is my sister's daughter, Anna."

"So nice to meet you. Won't you come in?"

They entered the main hallway and stopped. The rich sounds of
Mrs. Wilkins' voice reached easily back to the kitchen. "Good heavens.
Would you look at that?"

"It came with the house, I'm afraid."

"How on earth do you clean it?"

Jeremy reached for a towel to dry his hands, entered the hallway
from the kitchen, saw they were looking up at the chandelier, said, "Aw,
I just get me a broom and give it a good shake every day or so."

The only person who smiled was Catherine. "I believe you've met
Mr. Hughes."

Mrs. Wilkins' was too busy coming to grips with this white man
really working for people in her congregation to reply. Jeremy decided
the apron he wore over his shirt and tie was just the right touch. His
face perfectly straight, he said, "Good morning, Mrs. Wilkins."

She shook herself awake, said, "How're you, Mr. Hughes?"

"Other than too far behind in my housework, just fine, thank you."
He saw Catherine roll her eyes, turned to the niece, said, "I believe I
met you in church on Sunday."

"You did indeed." The tall, handsome girl regarded him with calm
strength. Jeremy decided she was a long step ahead of the aunt.

"Would you like to come in and sit down?" Catherine indicated the
living room.

"Why thank you, that's very—" Mrs. Wilkins took one step toward the entrance, stopped in her tracks. Jeremy watched her gape at the hardwood floor, Persian carpet, oil paintings, antique furniture, and remarked to himself that she looked just exactly like Catherine had the day before.

Mrs. Wilkins turned back to Catherine, said, "Honey, why don't we just go on back to the kitchen."

"That's fine," Catherine agreed, understanding her completely. "I believe Jeremy's prepared us a little something."

"He has, huh." Mrs. Wilkins clearly was not impressed with that prospect. She allowed Catherine to lead her down the hall, only to stop once more when she caught the first whiff. "What's that I smell?"

"Oh," Jeremy replied as casually as he could, "just some greens and fatback in pot likker. And there's some cornbread that should be just about ready by now. And a big pot of Maxwell House, of course. It's already on the table."

Mrs. Wilkins turned and stared hard at him, as if she'd just spotted some strange animal and was trying her best to decide what exactly it was.

Catherine was working very hard to keep a straight face. She gave her nose a good rub, said, "Won't you ladies come in and sit down?"

Jeremy waited until the two visitors were seated, said to Catherine, "If you won't be needin' me for a while, Miz Case, I do believe I'll go out and stretch my legs. Scrubbin' them floors was right hard on my po' old bones."

"Why don't you do that, Jeremy," she replied, bending over the steaming pot, a warning in her voice. "It might not be too healthy around here."

Jeremy walked back to his room, heard Catherine set a couple of plates down on the table, go back and return with silverware. "Y'all just go ahead and start," she invited. "Please help yourselves to the coffee. I'll just see to the cornbread and be right with you."

"My, but don't that stew smell nice," Mrs. Wilkins said.

"Wait'll you taste it," Catherine replied, opening the oven door and sliding out a tray. "Jeremy seasons it with a touch of Jack Daniels and a hot sauce he makes from scratch."

A fork clattered. There was a moment's silence, then, "Can he hear us?"

"Ah, I believe he was going out," Catherine replied.

The voice lowered, said, "Honey, where on earth did a white man learn to cook like that?"

"From his wife," Catherine replied, a smile clear in her voice. "Here, try this cornbread. Jem roasts an ear of corn and puts the kernels in the batter. He mixes in 'bout a half cup of fresh cream and two tablespoons of molasses."

There was another pause, then, "This his wife's recipe too?"

"That's right."

Mrs. Wilkins became even quieter. "Was she black?"

Catherine laughed outright, scraped another chair back from the table, said, "No, she wasn't black. She was just a fine woman. One of the finest people I've ever met. A real country saint."

Very quietly, Jem closed the door to his room. When he had changed clothes, he tiptoed down the corridor, eased the front door open, and let himself out.

The door reopened behind him and a voice said, "Mind if I come along?"

He turned around, saw it was Anna, Mrs. Wilkins' niece. She stood on the narrow ledge, clearly not willing to move or let her face show any expression whatsoever until he declared himself.

"I was just goin' out for a walk," he said.

"Where to?"

He pointed in a vague direction, said, "Still tryin' to get a feel for the neighborhood."

"Have you been down to Adams-Morgan yet?"

"Not so I'd notice," Jeremy replied. " 'Course, half the time I don't even know where I'm at once I get there."

Her eyes flickered a spark of humor. "Looking for anything in particular?"

Jeremy decided on honesty. "Now that's a right interesting question. Sometimes I feel like I'm being led around by the hand, but I can't for the life of me figure out what I'm supposed to be seeing."

"Maybe I can help," she offered.

Jeremy decided he liked her voice. It had a deep honeyish quality to it, with a tiny spice of burr. "You think your aunt can get along without you?"

"Those two'll be in there for hours. Aunty Rose won't let go till she's squeezed that lady dry."

"Then I'd be right obliged to have you join me."

She walked down the steps and pointed with a languid hand. "Let's head down that way."

He matched her long stride, said, "I don't believe I caught your last name."

She ignored the question, said, "While you were in the back my aunt asked Catherine why she was living in a white man's museum." She drew out the final three words with a broad black twang. "Know what Catherine said?"

"I can imagine."

"She said it was on account of how you were giving it to her and her husband, what's his name? Some initials, right?"

"TJ."

"Yeah, that's right, TJ Case. She said your home back in North Carolina was as spartan as a prison cell. Said you'd never learned how to give anybody anything but the best you could afford. Said if she had to fault you on anything it was on how you sometimes let your generosity run away with you."

"That lady does like to talk," Jeremy replied, and changed the subject. "How come you talk like that?"

"Like what?"

"I don't know as I can describe it. You don't have any accent. Maybe a little, but surely not like your aunt."

"I went to school up north," Anna replied, pleased by the question. "Columbia. I guess whatever accent I had I lost."

"What'd you study?"

"Biology undergrad, then a master's in nursing and public health."

They stopped at Connecticut Avenue to wait for the light. Jeremy glanced her way. At close inspection the dark skin was lit with a healthy luster. She was a big girl, standing almost as tall as he and holding herself proudly erect. Her hair was cropped short, shorter than he'd ever recalled seeing on a woman. Jeremy decided he liked it on her. He guessed her age at mid-twenties. The strength he felt radiating from her would have better suited a person twice her age.

He asked her, "Where'd you get that earring?"

She fingered the large silver object that dangled from one ear. "It was a gift from a Nigerian woman I know. She lives in the area we're walking toward."

"It looks good on you," he said, and meant it.

She thanked him politely, still holding back. Jeremy decided the reserve was not just pretense. She was a calm, intelligent woman who had a strong grip on who she was and where she was going. Jeremy decided he liked her, thought there could not be two people more different than Anna and her aunt.

The light changed, they crossed and continued down beside the Hilton on Florida Avenue. Jeremy followed her lead and enjoyed being able to gawk without worrying over where he was or how he'd find his way back.

"What did you mean back there," she asked him, "about maybe being led around by the hand?"

"I dunno," he said, jamming his hands into his pockets and lowering his head. "I know I'm needed up here right now. TJ's gotta have somebody else besides his wife who he can trust with this work of his."

"What business is he in?"

Jeremy hesitated, decided on, "The power and light business."

"Didn't I hear he was doing something with the government?"

"That too," he agreed, and hurried on. "The problem is, I just don't have enough to keep me occupied. Back home, I was pretty much on fourteen-hour days, six days a week. Now that Catherine's here, my housecleaning's gonna be about as welcome as a third batch of kitties. The lady's nice as she can be, but she wants a home to run. I just keep feelin' like there oughta be somethin' else I'm supposed to be doin'."

Within the space of four blocks, the world was transformed. The crisp winter air still sparkled, but the buildings became increasingly tired, the stores decrepit, the people tattered. Two blocks later they passed an abandoned storefront where four middle-aged blacks sat huddled together against the cold. They shared a filthy blanket laid across their legs; ragged scarfs were wrapped around their ears. A Styrofoam cup sat forlornly on the sidewalk before them. The men's eyes did not even bother to lift to the people passing by, as though they had long since accepted their plight as hopeless. Jeremy bent and slipped a bill into the cup, met the one pair of eyes that raised to meet his, saw that his gesture was truly meaningless.

He straightened and walked to where Anna stood waiting. He searched her face, could find nothing evident behind the stone mask and blank eyes.

Knowing he was going to sound extremely ignorant, he asked, "Are those crack victims?"

She shook her head, said, "Victims, but not of crack. Lack of hope, yes. Jobless, homeless, hopeless."

They walked on, respecting the other's silence, and with every step Jeremy watched the city deteriorate around him. Liquor stores multiplied rapidly, as did ruined structures with bricked-up windows and signs forbidding entry. The sidewalk was a jumbled mass of crumbling stone, the street little better. Eyes that looked his way scarcely seemed to see him. They were too clouded with ancient rage.

Anna pointed across the street, said in a voice that seemed to mirror his own dull sadness, "There's your crack victim."

Jeremy's first thought was, he looks like those pictures of concentration camp victims. The man was so thin it hurt Jeremy to look at him. He walked down the street on feet that seemed to search gingerly for a foothold, as though afraid if they were set down too hard the body they carried would shatter.

He wore a shiny black suit and a dirty T-shirt, and seemed totally unaware of the cold. Numb to the cold, blind to the stares, oblivious to everything but some screaming inner drive.

It was hard to believe that anyone could be that thin and still live. The skin was stretched taut over his skull, and the clothes draped shabbily on his scrawny frame did nothing to hide the lack of flesh on his bones. His hands were skeletal, his limbs without strength, his eyes blank holes in his face. He seemed to float on the breeze, lacking the power or the interest to chart a course for himself.

Jeremy watched him drift around the corner, realized he'd been holding his breath. He said shakily, "I don't believe I've ever seen Death that close up before."

"The legion of the lost," Anna said quietly.

They moved on slowly, Jeremy praying for the young-old man, saying the words in his mind, his heart knowing nothing but pain. Anna led him down another block, turned right, and stopped.

"There's something in here I'd like to show you," she said.

Jeremy inspected the building, saw nothing to distinguish it from its poverty-stricken neighbors save a tiny sign that read, "Community of Hope." Anna took his silence for agreement, and led him up the walk.

As they approached the front door, an ancient black woman walked out and broke into a delighted smile when she recognized Anna. "How you doin', chile?"

"Just fine, Mrs. Timmons," Anna said, as cultivated as ever, as warm as she could be. "How's your back?"

"Oh, them new pills is just what I needed." The old lady was clearly eager to hold her there. "I don't hardly feel a thing once I've made it outta bed."

"That's fine," Anna said, "but don't you forget to use that heating pad at night."

Rheumy eyes sparkled as a wrinkled hand reached out to grasp Anna's. The woman turned to Jeremy, said, "Ain't she just a little angel?"

"She is indeed," Jeremy replied solemnly.

"Mr. Hughes, this is Mrs. Timmons. She injured her back a few weeks ago, but she's much better now, aren't you?"

"Thanks to my little angel here," she said, giving the hand another squeeze. "Y'all goin' up to see Tom?"

"Is he there?"

"I believe I saw him up there." The old lady cackled. "Gettin' so I can hardly remember my own name, but I still get around okay."

"You take care, now," Anna told her. "And be sure to let me know if you need anything." The smiles they exchanged warmed the winter air.

Jeremy and Anna went inside and passed a receptionist crammed against one side of the narrow hall. The black lady looked up from her wheelchair, smiled at Anna as she continued to talk on the telephone, nodded to Jeremy, motioned them through. A woman even older than Mrs. Timmons sat in front of the desk leaning on her cane as she watched the receptionist ask someone for money. She did not glance up as Jeremy and Anna passed.

The hall smelled of age and industrial-strength cleaner. Strips of worn linoleum plastered to the floor alternated with freshly sawed planks. Light came from old frosted globes high overhead. The walls were plain and gray, save for a brightly colored collection of children's drawings.

Anna led Jeremy to narrow stairs leading to the floors above. Jeremy heard voices murmur and laugh as he mounted steps that alternated between ancient warped wood and new boards. He looked over the banister, spotted the remains of what had once been a mosaic-tile design set in the ground-floor landing. He wondered how old this building really was.

The secretary occupying the second-floor landing lit up at the sight of Anna. "Girl, what you doin' here on your day off?"

Anna smiled, said, "Guess I must be hooked."

The black lady laughed, a rich sound. "Hooked or crazy, take your pick." Her gaze, open and very friendly, rested on Jeremy. "How you doin'?"

Jeremy basked in the lady's warmth, said, "Just fine, ma'am, thank you."

She lifted her eyes to Anna. "A real gentleman. Ain't that nice."

Anna laughed, asked, "Is Tom around?"

"Partly." The woman appeared to Jeremy to be smiling even when her face was serious. "His body's in his office. His mind's flittin' in and out like a hummingbird. You want me to tell him you're here?"

"Please." Anna said to Jeremy, "Come on in here, I want to show you something." She led him into a small, crowded hallway now occupied by a desk, two sorry-looking filing cabinets and a secretary.

The secretary's scruffy desk was piled high with what clearly were government forms. She said to Anna, "There's about three hundred calls for you. I gave them to Tom."

"This is Jeremy Hughes," Anna said. "Rachel is the glue that holds this shaky house together."

The woman laughed from the heart, said, "Honey, you better look for something stronger than me, if you want to come back tomorrow and find it still standing."

Anna led them through ancient double doors into what had once been a formal dining room and which now held a large conference table. Around all four walls was a collapsible metal stand holding perhaps fifty black and white photographs.

"This was our first building," Anna explained. "We started here, at least Tom Nees did, with a homeless shelter about five years ago. Tom used to be pastor to a big white church down near the Capitol. He gave it up, spent a year just walking the streets down here, then started this."

A graceful hand pointed out beyond the room's front wall. "The shelter's been moved across the street. The downstairs rooms have been made into a medical treatment center. I run that with a doctor and two other part-time nurses. This floor and the one above are administration."

Jeremy listened, but his eyes were snagged by one picture after another. He moved over to give the photographs a closer inspection.

"The next project Tom took on was a condemned building over next to where the shelter is now. He raised seventy-five thousand dollars and organized a group from his old church to come down and rebuild the interior. It took over a year, but now it's a housing co-op with thirty-seven apartments. First time any of the tenants have ever owned their own home. You wouldn't believe the difference it makes in their lives."

Each of the photographs was a silent cry, a voiceless appeal for compassion. Jeremy stared at a young black child running with such unleashed excitement that he seemed ready to take flight. He was wearing his father's ragged T-shirt and a pair of tennis shoes without laces, and he was springing up from a mound of rubble surrounded by sooty tenement blocks. Yet the expression on the child's face was one of untrammeled joy.

"We're working on a couple of things right now," Anna went on from behind him. "The shelter needs to be expanded into a place where homeless families can come and live for anywhere from six to eighteen months. A family that's lost everything usually's not in any shape to set up house for themselves, even if public housing were available. We've got to start getting them out of those awful old hotels and into places that help them find their feet again."

Jeremy turned to the next picture, saw a white mother and four children sitting on a mattress and box springs set upon a sidewalk, surrounded by all their possessions. The mother had the dull look of utter, hopeless defeat. The children ranged from an infant in diapers to a boy of perhaps eleven, and all mirrored the same look of terrible emotional pain. The eldest boy, his face scarred and twisted by inner turmoil, had eyes set back in their sockets like a man of eighty.

"One big problem is all the government assistance programs have offices that are split up and spread all over town. A single parent dragging four or five kids from place to place by bus hasn't got time to cook, to take care of a sick child, or even to look for work. And if she has problems with reading and writing, there's just no telling how many times she's got to go down and work over their forms."

The faces pulled at him, tugged at something deep in his gut. The poverty and the hardships described in the photographs were nothing but frames for the faces. The children made him want to weep.

Anna's voice remained hidden behind that cool reserve. "We need to set up an assistance program inside the shelter that will take over all this paperwork for them, give them the chance to look for jobs and take care of their families."

Jeremy moved to a placard set among the photographs and read, "I don't accept poverty and despair as part of God's plan. Instead, I believe they result from greed and injustice. I believe God has a special concern for the poor and dispossessed." Underneath was written, "Jim Hubbard, Photographer."

Footsteps heralded the arrival of another. Anna said, "Jeremy Hughes, I'd like you to meet Reverend Tom Nees."

Jeremy turned and shook the hand of a white man whose lined face shone with a calm inner strength. Jeremy looked toward Anna, said quietly, "I believe I've found what I was looking for."

⊣ THIRTEEN ⊢

When they arrived home Wednesday evening, TJ kissed his wife, took Nak's coat, said, "Catherine, Jeremy, I'd like you to meet John, er, Nak Nakamishi."

"How nice to meet you—Nak, is it? You're our first dinner guest."

"I hope I'm not too much of a bother, Mrs. Case. I understand you just arrived yesterday."

"No bother at all. We're all going to have dinner anyway. Would you like a glass of tea? I've just made some fresh."

"Thank you, that would be great."

Jeremy extended a work-worn hand, said straight-faced, "And no knock-knock jokes, right?"

"If it's not too much trouble," Nak replied seriously.

"Jeremy Hughes," Catherine said sharply. "You're 'bout this close to wearing my skillet upside your head."

"Is that what I think it is?" TJ sniffed the air, smiled at Nak, said, "I do believe Catherine's cooked us up a mess of fried chicken."

"May smell like fried chicken to you," Jeremy said. "But to an old country boy like me that smells like Sunday afternoon."

Catherine came back with two glasses of iced tea. "Young man, I hope you like chicken."

"Yes, ma'am, I love it."

After the blessing, while the meal was being passed around, TJ told them he was going to be interviewed by a network show.

"On television?" Catherine's expression was a mixture of pride and concern.

"He's already been on television here in the city," Nak answered for him. "This is for *Good Morning America*."

Catherine's eyes squinted. "I don't recall you telling me about being on TV."

"I thought it was best to give you a chance to get adjusted," TJ replied mildly. "I didn't see it, but Nak said it was on television the day before yesterday."

"What was?"

"An interview they did while Jeremy went down to fetch you."

"He was great," Nak confirmed.

"What happened?" Jeremy asked.

TJ looked a plea toward Nak, who proceeded to give them an almost verbatim report of what was said, all in that calm, quiet voice of his. When he was finished, nothing broke the silence except the tinkle of silverware on plates.

"This is delicious, Mrs. Case."

"Call me Catherine. I'm glad you like it." And to TJ, "I can't get over it. I missed my man being on Washington television."

"It wasn't all that much," TJ said.

"Yes, it was," Nak said.

"I guess it's started, then," Jeremy said.

Catherine looked at him sharply. "What has?"

Jeremy shrugged. "Whatever the Lord brought him up here to do."

"I think so too," Nak agreed. "I mean, I don't know exactly what brought you up here, Mr. Case—"

"Call me TJ, please."

"Well, sir," Nak hesitated. "Out of the office maybe. I don't know what brought you up here, but after what happened yesterday I know there's a higher purpose behind all this. I just *know* it."

"Tell us about it, son," Jeremy said.

With a nod from TJ, Nak proceeded to sketch for them their discussion after the prayer meeting, the telephone call, and the prayer. "So I went back and did just what TJ told me to do," Nak went on. "This Mr. Roberts from the network first says they'll cancel it because they don't accept restrictions being put on them by the people being interviewed. Then so help me if five seconds later he doesn't turn around and say, okay, everything's fine. And their affiliate stations are all going to run segments of the Washington interview as a lead-in to next week's show." Nak looked at TJ, ended with, "Just like you said would happen."

TJ watched Catherine's face throughout. It was a lot to be hitting her with, so soon after arriving. When Nak had finished she reached across the table, took one of TJ's hands in hers, and said, "If it's His will, then let it be done."

"Amen," Jeremy agreed.

"I can't tell you how happy I am to have you up here with me," TJ said, not caring who heard him.

"Everything's gonna be just fine," Catherine replied, patting his hand with her other one. "You'll see."

"Before we have us a prayer," Jeremy said, "I think it's time this young man hears what brought you to Washington."

TJ looked a question at his wife, who nodded. "If he's gonna be with us on this, honey, he has a right to know," she said.

So he nodded his head in return, took a breath, turned and told Nak what had happened on the boat that dawn. It pleased him to see the young man register surprise for the very first time.

□　□　□

Congressman John Silverwood turned from the work that cluttered his desk that Thursday afternoon, and watched the snow fall outside his window. He could hardly believe his own good fortune.

He had met a beautiful woman who truly loved him. It baffled him sometimes to think that Sally had chosen him above all others, but it was so. She *appreciated* him. She admired him for who he was and what he did. She shared his love of politics and looked up to him for making it to the top in a truly tough profession. Well, fairly near the top. And it seemed as though he would be reaching up even higher very soon. John Silverwood watched the heavy flakes drifting earthward, and saw Sally as she had been when he had left her that morning.

When sleeping she looked like a little girl. Her lower lip pushed out in a tiny pout, making her look vulnerable and appealing. Her blond hair lay scattered across her pillow like a halo. Slender fingers curled under her chin, clutching the sheet to her. She was a lovely girl, and she seemed to have nothing more important in her life than to make him happy. The thought of that childlike face and the adoration he had seen in it last night stirred his desire again. Silverwood sighed, pushed the thought away, turned back to his work.

He had simply stopped calling his wife. It felt as though an enormous burden had been lifted from his shoulders. Their last talk had been Monday night, when she had accused him of seeing someone else, and he couldn't stop himself from laughing. So what, he had said once he had recovered. Do you really think you've been very much of a wife? She had started to break down then, struggled to keep control, asked him if ten years of marriage meant nothing to him. A lot more than it does to you, he had replied. If you'd been capable of seeing beyond your credits and debits, you'd have realized a long time ago that I needed you here with me. By then she'd been crying full out. You never needed anyone in your life, she had sobbed over the phone. That's where you're wrong, he had replied. It's the most perfect example I can think of, of how little you know me, and how little you really care. Silverwood had hung up and not spoken to her since.

When he told Sally about it, she was all sympathy and practical advice. I know it's hard to think about, she told him after holding him tenderly and telling him how it hurt her to see him suffer. But if it's over between you, then you need to take action immediately. Even though it's hard, you have *got* to think about your career. Silverwood had nodded morosely, knowing she was right, hating to hear it stated in such starkly practical terms.

If she files action against you, Sally went on, then it could really hurt your reelection chances. But if you file for a legal separation yourself, you can claim abandonment as the reason, and in the eyes of the press you'd have the upper hand.

Each evening, Silverwood planned to call a lawyer the next morning and get things moving. Every morning, however, he found it very difficult to take that first step. It was one thing to say their marriage was over. It was another thing entirely to make it so.

So he kept putting it off, not really hoping for a change, just not wanting to see it all down in black and white. And now that he was not in contact with Suzanne, it became easier to push the unfinished business aside. Sally made him happier than he had ever been in his life, and his political fortunes were climbing skyward like a missile.

Silverwood's reverie was interrupted by his secretary, who called in to say Mr. Shermann was on the phone. The lobbyist normally called at about this time every day. It was simply a polite reminder that he was waiting for Silverwood's decision, never pressing, always understanding. For the past several days Silverwood had left instructions to say that he was not in when the man called. This had pleased his secretary mightily. He had not spoken to Sally about the offer or his deliberations at all.

Today he decided to pick up the phone. "Good afternoon, Mr. Shermann."

"Ah, Congressman, what a pleasant surprise to find you in. I hope I'm not disturbing anything important."

Silverwood ignored his rising unease over the man's toneless voice, and concentrated on the matter at hand. "I've been contacted by several people about this Ways and Means appointment. More than several, as a matter of fact. The *Washington Post* fellow, what's his name, the one who covers the White House, he told me he'd heard a rumor that the position was as good as mine."

"Yes, well, I thought it wise to begin putting the wheels in motion, Congressman. Not assuming anything, I hope you understand. I just wanted to show you that I truly am as good as my word."

"I also noticed that the Atlas questioning had been tabled for a few days."

"Yes, I was fortunate enough to be able to have that set aside for the moment. There are so many other aspects of this investigation that require your committee's urgent attention, I'm sure you agree. How many construction companies are now being considered for indictment?"

"Seventeen," Congressman Silverwood replied after a moment's hesitation.

"That's right. Seventeen. My goodness, you would hardly think that one company more or less would make any difference, would you?"

"Well, I just wanted you to know that I am giving the matter my most serious consideration, Mr. Shermann."

"I am so very grateful, Congressman. Indeed I am." There was no satisfaction evident in the rasping voice, no emotional response of any kind. "I believe I heard somewhere that the Atlas people are scheduled to reappear before the committee next Monday."

"You heard correctly, Mr. Shermann." The man's sources were very good, Silverwood conceded. He had only heard about it himself at that day's hearing.

"That gives us until tomorrow to reach an agreement, Congressman. I would then be able to have your Ways and Means appointment locked up by Monday morning, before the hearing starts, with a formal announcement coming in due course."

"You're that sure of yourself, are you?" Silverwood could still scarcely believe that the offer was real.

"I assure you, Congressman, I would not consider wasting your time otherwise."

"Well, I'll be back in touch with you by tomorrow at the latest."

"Should you decide to accept my offer, Congressman, I would be most grateful if you could please allow me to stop by for just a few moments. I always prefer to make such agreements in person, I'm sure you understand."

"Not here," Silverwood said sharply, not caring if the man was offended. "I don't want any more contact with you here in my chambers. If I decide to accept, I'll come down to your offices."

"Whichever you prefer, Congressman," Mr. Shermann replied, not in the least put out. "I look forward to hearing from you."

By Thursday evening, the snow had settled in as though making itself at home for the duration.

TJ scrunched along snow-covered sidewalks and enjoyed the air's biting briskness. It helped to clear his mind of issues that had burdened him throughout the day.

The major streets were cleared, but smaller offshoots were a disaster. Georgetown was clogged and hopeless. Abandoned cars lay under drifts as though blanketed for a long winter's nap. TJ had taken the Metro home from work; the walk from the Red-line station was less than half a mile. That afternoon the mantle of clouds and their perpetual gloom had finally rolled away. But TJ had heard as he left the building that more clouds and snow were predicted by morning.

As usual when out walking in Washington, TJ carried a pocketful of small change. A couple of coins were given to each panhandler in turn. There were always a number of them around Dupont Circle and up Connecticut Avenue. TJ tried to offer a little prayer for them as he left the money, but sometimes it was difficult to put his heart into it. Like today, when their presence just aggravated the concerns he carried with him from the office.

There seemed to TJ to be this incredible gap between educational policies and the children they were supposed to serve. Yes, serve, he thought, as he stepped through the snow. It was so much easier to think clearly out here, away from the conference room's stale air and the sideways glances that were cast around the room every time he opened his mouth. It all came down to service. The founding principle of democratic society was this: The government's sole purpose was to serve the people. If the policy area was education, then these policy makers were bound by their nation's heritage to serve the needs of their children.

At the committee meeting that day were several staffers from other OEOB departments. It had been clear from the outset that more than a few had been clued in by Secretary Edwards' Special Assistant for White House Liaison, Jane Patterson. It had also been clear that they were closing ranks against TJ and his ideas.

The gentleman from the office of the Special Assistant to the President for Legislative Affairs had stated it outright. Such ideas belong more to a preacher than a national policy maker, the man had said. The lawyer from the Office of White House Counsel had agreed and added, had Mr. Case ever heard of separation of church and state? TJ had refrained from confronting the man directly, and tried to steer the conversation back to the question of policy formation. Now as he walked the snow-silenced streets he wondered if he had done the right thing.

The catchphrase today was "nonreligious interference" in the schools. TJ had read it time and again in his research. It still dismayed him. The nation's first schools had been run by churches, not by the state. The local pastor had generally served as the school principal. The Bible, as one of the prime textbooks, had been referred to constantly.

It seemed to TJ that society was now determined to substitute its own pseudo-scientific theories in the place of God's eternal truth. The Bible was all but banned from public schools, and it was the children who suffered most from this blind self-importance of their elders.

Children rarely were mentioned in the committee meeting. The discussions were all appeasement and politics. This person needed to be brought in to assure support, this fence needed mending, that required passing through budget committee for funding, this nose would be bent out of shape unless he was called immediately, somebody needed to make sure this program was in line with somebody else's general policy directive. Several times TJ had bitten down hard against the desire to cry out, what about the children? Do any of you really believe structuring education policy around the current political winds will ever satisfy the fundamental needs of our children? Isn't a more permanent moral base required?

TJ stomped the snow from his feet loudly on the doorstep, was surprised to hear no welcoming hello. He left shoes and coat in the hall closet and followed his nose back to the kitchen. Jeremy, dressed in a filthy one-piece construction coverall and paint-stained work boots, was stirring some pots on the stove.

TJ smiled, said in greeting, "Decided to dress up for dinner?"

Without turning around, Jeremy replied, "This is the most comfortable I've been since I got here."

"What have you been up to?"

"Just helpin' some friends. Tryin' to get a few people off the streets and outta the cold. We got some families out there worryin' about their kids freezin' to death. Gotta get some shelters finished fast as we can. Had seventeen families crammed in a teeny little basement last night, wasn't hardly room to swing a cat."

TJ noticed that Jeremy had paint spackled in his hair. The only clean part of the big man was his hands. TJ asked, "Why are you still dressed like that?"

"Just got in a coupla minutes ago. Catherine wasn't feelin' well, so

I sent her upstairs and told her I'd look after things." He lifted another lid, said through the steam, "You maybe oughtta go check on her."

Jeremy's reflection in the stainless steel fan above the stove caused TJ to look more closely. "Jem?" he said.

Reluctantly Jeremy turned, allowing TJ to see the lump of gauze held in place by two ragged strips of tape above his left eye. The gauze was bright red.

"Dear Lord, Jem, are you all right? What happened?"

"Fellow wasn't lookin' where he was goin'," he said briefly. "Swung around with a length of pipe and whacked me good."

"I've got to get you to a doctor."

"I'm all right," he said. "It ain't the first time and won't be the last. Been on some sites where this'd be called a love-tap."

"But you're bleeding, man."

"Naw, it's pretty much stopped. Maybe you can tape it up better before we sit down to dinner."

"Well, why don't you sit down, let me get you something."

"I'm all right, I tell you. I got to see to dinner."

"What's the matter with Catherine?"

"Best let her tell you. She's upstairs in the bedroom. Go on, TJ, I'll be all right. She's the one who needs you right now."

He climbed the stairs, his fatigue forgotten, and found Catherine sprawled across their bed. Her shoes were off, her stocking feet tucked up under the hem of her dress. The handkerchief balled up in one fist had seen plenty of use. She did not move, did not turn his way as he entered the room. When he sat down on the bed he saw that she had been crying.

"Honey, what on earth's the matter?"

"I'm all right now," she said, her voice very low. "I just had a bad day, is all."

Fearful of holding her until she was ready, he grasped her hand, stroked her arm, said, "Can you tell me about it?"

She shook her head. "There's no need to bother you with it. You've got enough on your mind right now without having me load you down with my troubles too."

"Baby, baby, how can I sit here and see you in pain and not know what's going on?" He stroked her cheek with gentle fingers. "Tell me what happened, Catherine. Please, honey. Not telling is about the worst thing you could do to me."

She gave a hurtful sigh, slid over so she could put her head in his lap. "I decided I'd go out for a walk, down in the area where Jeremy's been working." Her voice was barely above a whisper. "It's not all that far from here, less than a mile, but the difference is like night and day."

TJ stroked her forehead, listened in silence, made a mental note to find out more about this new work of Jeremy's.

"I'm walking around, just enjoying the day and the snow and how clean everything looks all white and fresh. And there's a couple of children laughing and hanging on their mother's arm, and I'm watching them, but kind of notice a police car pull up to the curb ahead of me. You know how you can see something, but your mind's on something else, so you really don't think about what you're seeing?"

TJ nodded, aching over the pain he saw in her eyes, having no idea at all where she was taking him.

"It didn't even dawn on me, honey. I was in la-la land. And I see these people all gathered around, so I come sauntering up, and I see it's a body laying there in the snow."

Catherine swiveled around and sat up, resting herself on the headboard. Her eyes no longer saw anything inside the room.

"It was a young black man, I don't know, maybe twenty, twenty-five. And silly old me thinks, that's an awful young, good-looking man to be drunk in the middle of the day. Then one of the policemen picks up the boy's arm and kind of rolls him over. You know what I thought? That was a kind man, that policeman. That's what I was thinking. He was so gentle, just like a father switching a child to a more comfortable position.

"Then it hit me. Wham. This is a body that life has left. That boy there in the snow was *dead*. You know, I've seen and touched the shells of people all my life. Been to I don't know how many funerals. But when I see a body there in a funeral, I always know the person's not there. They're gone." She looked at him for the first time. "You know what I mean?"

"I know, honey, I know." TJ stroked her arm, pained inside to hear her say these things, glad just the same she had a chance to get it off her chest.

"It hit me awful hard, looking down and realizing all of a sudden-like that the person wasn't *there* anymore. He was gone, and I didn't even know it. I stood there and just cried my heart out. I could not get control of myself. I stood there and watched the coroner come up and feel around the top of the man's head. I looked around at all the other people, and I tried just as hard as I could to stop crying."

The tears started to form again in her eyes. She grasped TJ's hands with both of hers, said, "Honey, there was mothers there with babies on their hips and little kids standing there holding on to their momma's skirt. You know, I could just hear what they were thinking. I've got to go out and see what's happening there on the street, but I can't leave my babies in the house, so I'm gonna bring my babies with me. All these small children, with those big innocent eyes, looking down at this body. I just broke down and cried harder than before."

"Aw, Catherine, honey, come here," TJ murmured, and pulled her close. She sank against his chest, crying softly, holding him with fierce need.

"I know they're seeing all this stuff on television," she sobbed. "And that's bad enough. Now it's happening here in their community, and they're brought out to *look* at it. You know what those poor little things are gonna grow up thinking? It's *normal.* This is a regular part of life. They'll expect it. It's like their momma's telling them, see, life doesn't have any meaning, look here at this dead body. It's so sad, honey. So *sad.* These children are growing up so scarred, so calloused. How're they ever gonna learn to hope?"

Over dinner Jeremy told them about the Community of Hope and the work he was doing. "The city's got all kinds of houses down there that haven't been touched since the Depression. You see all these home-less people on the streets, makes you wonder why it's taken 'em so long to go in and do something. I mean, the houses are condemned, they belong to the city. But there they sit, all the first-floor windows walled up, with people sleeping on the sidewalk out in front."

He looked at Catherine, said, "You know, they got themselves a group that works with children."

She brightened visibly. "You think they might use another old lady down there?"

Jeremy smiled. "Don't see why not. Can't hurt to ask."

"All I know is I've got to do *something* for those children. I've just got to."

They cleaned up swiftly and moved into the living room. A fire was soon burning and the chairs pulled up close to it. "I can't think of anything I like better than a fire on a cold winter night," Catherine said.

Jeremy rose to stir the ashes and put on another log. "Don't know of many things that even come close," he agreed.

They watched in silence for a time, until TJ looked over and found his wife smiling faintly. He felt the band of pressure around his chest ease. "What's so funny, Catherine?"

"Oh, I was just thinking about one of Jem's stories. You remember the day we were coming back from the boat and he told us about the two preachers going to heaven?" She looked up from the fire, said, "I bet you don't even know what I'm talking about."

"Of course I remember."

"I bet Jeremy doesn't."

Jeremy feigned shock. "How in the world do you expect me to forget something as earth-shakin' as that?"

She laughed. "You tell so many stories I doubt you remember any of them from one day to the next."

"Now that is just plain not true. Fact is, I've been thinkin' a lot lately about those two fellows."

"You have not. I'll bet you can't even remember their names."

"Preacher Jones and Father—Father Coughlin. Lately of Farmborough. What you think of them apples?"

"Farmville," TJ corrected.

"Just what I said. Now, do you two wanna hear what happened or not?"

Catherine slipped off her shoes, slid her feet up under her, reached over and took her husband's hand, said, "What was it that baby said to you that day?"

"Make it a long one," TJ recalled.

Catherine chuckled from somewhere deep down inside. "That's

right. Make it a long one. Go ahead, Jem, honey. Paint us a pretty picture."

"Now as y'all will remember," Jeremy began, "ol' Peter's sent the two gentlemen back to kinda try on the other fella's shoes for a while. Well, the next thing you know, Preacher Jones wakes up and finds himself in a strange white bed in a strange white room. His vision is kinda blurry, like it is after a too-long nap on a hot summer afternoon. He's tryin' to sort out all this jumble in his mind, and slowly the world is comin' back into focus. He swivels his head around and sees the wife of his assistant pastor, Sister Bertha, sittin' there beside his bed.

"She looks like anybody does who's been sittin' the death watch on a friend, only to have them come back to life. Half of her wants to stand up, raise her hands over head, do a little dance, and praise the Lord of miracles. The other half figures that if she does, the pastor's gonna get shocked out of his recovery and be gone for good.

"So the lady leans over and says real quiet and trembly, 'You're in the hospital, Reverend. You've had a heart attack.'

"Preacher Jones opens his mouth and says something that sounds like 'Ngmmnghaagh' on account of his tongue being cemented to the roof of his mouth. What he meant to say was, 'It wasn't a dream after all.'

"Sister Bertha gets the message, takes a cup from the side table and helps the reverend drink. Raisin' his head like that makes him dizzy, so he leans back and closes his eyes. Sister Bertha does what most people do when they're flustered, which is chat away all casual, like the reverend has a heart attack the first Sunday of every month.

" 'Everybody's been askin' 'bout you,' the good sister says. 'The church held a special prayer meetin' for you last night. Reverend Lee,' which is the way she always refers to her husband, 'Reverend Lee preached the Sunday sermon and everybody says he did a real fine job.'

"Then she realizes the reverend might not be pleased to hear that his assistant's already steppin' into his shoes. So she does what most people do, which is speed up her talk to about a hundred miles an hour.

" 'You just wouldn't believe all the people's been askin' 'bout you,' the sister goes on. 'Why, the Catholic minister even stood up in his church yesterday and said he was gonna convert just so he could help out. Whole town's talkin' about it. Hasn't been anything like that happen since—since I don't know when. Our deacons didn't believe it at first. Nobody did, what with the way you used to carry on about Catholics. Rightly so, of course. Anyway, the deacons musta talked with him half the night. I think he's called Cacklin or Conklin or some Yankee name like that. The deacons finally decided he meant what he said, and they were so impressed they're talkin' 'bout making him some kinda special assistant pastor till you get better.'

" 'Course, Preacher Jones was laying there and listenin' to this and feelin' like an anchor headed for the bottom of the ocean. Nope, it wasn't no dream after all. The reverend knew what he had to do, and knew he had to do it quick 'fore his nerves failed him.

"He motions for Sister Bertha to help him drink again; then he manages to croak out 'Catholic.'

"Naturally, the good sister doesn't have the tiniest notion what he's talkin' 'bout. 'Of course he's Catholic,' she tells him, thinkin' the man must be soft in the head from the attack. She starts talkin' real slow and loud. 'He's gonna convert, Reverend. Wants to become a Baptist quick as he can. I hear the deacons've already called a special baptismal service for Wednesday night.'

"Preacher Jones shakes his head, gathers his strength, and whispers, 'I want to convert to Catholicism.'

"Well, that 'bout knocks Sister Bertha outta the stadium. Which is quite a feat, seeing as how she weighs close on two hundred and fifty pounds. The sister looks at him a moment, realizes her chin is hangin' down 'bout a foot below her knees, and closes it with a snap. Bam. She stands up, pats Preacher Jones on the arm and smiles real syrupy-sweet.

" 'I'll just go fetch the doctor,' she says with her mouth. Her eyes say she thinks he's flipped his noodle. She leaves fast enough to stir up a fair-sized breeze.

"Coupla minutes later the doctor comes bustlin' in with Sister Bertha wavin' her arms and flutterin' around. She's tryin' to lead him and walk behind him and whisper in his ear all at the same time. The doctor's actin' real official-like and not showin' how worried he is she's gonna step on his foot and put him in intensive care for a coupla weeks.

"So he thanks the sister real firm-like and tells her to sit down right there and he'll be with her in just a minute. Then he steps around to the end of the reverend's bed and puts on the know-it-all mask that all doctors get when they graduate from medical school and carry in their back pockets.

"He flips open the reverend's chart and stands there pretendin' to study it real good. When he's sure he's the center of attention he snaps it shut and looks down at the reverend with a smile almost as fakey as Sister Bertha's. In his best doctor's voice he says, 'Now, what's all this I hear about you hallucinatin'?'"

"Now just about that very same time, while old Preacher Jones is passin' the time of day, Father Coughlin was havin' some real interesting conversations with a bishop. After that there was a couple of his congregation, and then another bishop, then a couple of cardinals, then the bishop again. They all said basically the same thing, which was that they weren't too happy to hear the father's plans. 'Bout what you'd expect. So the father goes off to bed that night kinda wore out from havin' just gotten over a stroke the week before and now havin' a whole mess of bishops and cardinals and what-not breathin' down his neck.

"Seems the father was the first priest in history to want to become a Baptist, and the church wasn't real pleased 'bout it. The father wasn't quite clear on the details, but it seems he was somehow endangerin' the souls of millions of little South American children. Or at least that's what the cardinal said the third time he called. Or maybe it was the fourth.

"To top it off, there's this phone call that wakes him up in the middle of the night, and when the father finally manages to find his glasses and answer the thing, there's all this hissin' an' poppin'. Then this real faint voice comes on and says, 'Iza thees Father Cockleena? Roma calling-ah. Wait-ah moment, pleeze, for-ah Monsignor Giuseppi.'

"Well, the father drops the phone like it was scalding hot and goes tearin' outta the house in his nightclothes. See, Monsignor Giuseppi's the Pope's private secretary, and the last thing the father wanted to hear was how he was breakin' the Pope's heart. So he races across town, which wasn't very far, and pounds on Deacon Tait's front door till the lights come on.

"The father's gotta stop a minute and catch his breath, which ain't surprisin', seein' as how he's just run ten blocks. And only five days out of the hospital. So he stands there and pants and sweats and finally manages to tell the deacon that he can't wait one more minute, he's gotta get baptized right then and there.

"By this time, a' course, the Baptists've realized what a prize they got on their hands. See, they've been gettin' calls all day from churches as far away as Nebraska, telling 'em it's the most incredible missionary work since John Smith converted Pocahontas. You gotta remember, now, the father don't look all that hot. His hair's standin' straight up, he's breathin' like a busted bellows, he's all sweaty and trembly, and his face is red as a beet. The deacon imagines the father havin' another stroke right then and there, and then where would they be? I mean, the father don't look like he's gonna last till mornin'. The deacon figures now's a time for some fast action.

"So the deacon runs across the street and wakes up Reverend Lee, and it don't take the reverend more than a coupla minutes to see they gotta move quick. So the two of 'em run down to the end of the block and wake up Deacon Smith. Then the three of them run back for Deacon Peters, who's a deep sleeper, so they gotta make a lot of noise poundin' on the door and shoutin' up at the second floor. Which wakes up Deacon Drysdale there across the street. Not to mention 'bout fourteen neighborhood dogs and three babies. Who all naturally commence to howl.

"So by the time the four deacons and the reverend start back toward the front stoop of Deacon Tait's house, most of that side of town is up and wonderin' what in tarnation is going on at three o'clock in the mornin'. Lights're blinkin' on up and down the streets, windows're openin', and people're shoutin' back and forth 'cross the street at each other. Somebody says somethin' 'bout calling the police, but nobody hears 'em on account of all the dogs.

"Sister Bertha's out there in a nightgown not much bigger'n a circus tent. Deacon Tait's wife, who weighs in at fifty-five pounds, is wavin' her arms in time to Sister Bertha's and runnin' around in circles for the both of them. The father's just sittin' there wishin' he could die a second time and leave the whole mess behind him like a bad dream. Then up come the deacons and hold a quick conference while the neighborhood dogs kind of get together in a huddle and try to smother the poor father, who ain't got the energy to push 'em off.

"The church elders decide there's enough light from the moon for them to go on down to the creek. It's about then they realize the whole neighborhood's watchin' and wonderin' at why all the Baptist deacons are standing there on the front stoop in their nightclothes at three o'clock in the morning. Naturally they begin to feel a little foolish. But Sister Bertha, being the pistol she is, decides the best defense is a good offense and shouts out for everybody to start singin'.

"Well, the first song that came to Sister Bertha's mind is 'The Battle Hymn of the Republic,' and before anybody can object, she's into it full-on. The others join in kinda halfheartedly, but the dogs just love it. So off they go, down to the creek at three o'clock in the morning, and the dogs are all mighty sorry to see 'em leave.

"When they get down there Father Coughlin sinks onto his knees and collapses, on account of all the commotion. 'Course, everybody thinks he's going down for the third time, so they pick him up and proceed to race down the slope to the creek. Naturally, it being pitch black, and the way bein' just a path through the woods, there are some right interestin' accidents. Deacon Smith made the acquaintance of a stump and lost his bifocals. Sister Tait got whipped by a tree limb sent back by her husband, and spent a while trying to locate her teeth. Sister Bertha got right intimate with a pine tree, and when they lost the path Brother Tait found it again by rollin' down the rest of the way and fallin' in the creek.

"I guess that's why they were all in a sorta panic by the time they made the water. So Brother Tait crawls up the bank and Sister Bertha says goodbye to her pine tree, and they each grab an arm and a leg of the father, and they proceed to start swingin'. Reverend Lee catches his breath just as they get to the third swing, which meant he was kinda rushed to get in all the words. But not too rushed, 'cause they tossed the father right high. Anyway, there was just enough time for a quick 'IbaptizeyouinthenameoftheFathertheSonandtheHolyGhost' before Father Coughlin hit the water. Everybody agreed afterward it was a right nice baptism."

⊣| FOURTEEN |⊢

Friday morning dawned gray and cold. On the way out to the car, Jeremy took one look upward and called it perfect snow weather. TJ thought it looked like the sky was going to fall.

As they approached downtown, Jeremy said, "My last birthday before she took ill, Ella gave me a clock."

As always, TJ felt a little helpless when Jeremy mentioned his wife. "You never told me that, Jem."

"Never did run worth a durn. Ella'd bought this cheap little alarm clock and taken it apart. I always figured when she put it back together she left out the mainspring or somethin'. It'd run fast for a coupla days, then spin around and go slow as molasses. Ella just loved it. She kept"—Jeremy stopped, swallowed, went on—"had it there beside her bed right to the end. Said it was the first clock that kept time she could understand."

TJ searched for something to say, lit on, "Well, why'd she take it apart?"

"That's the thing. See, I'd been goin' through this right tough time in the business. You remember, it was in the middle of that Kerr Lake mess."

"I remember," TJ said, and he did. There had been a lot of sleepless nights over that one, a lot of wondering if Jeremy was going to lose his shirt.

"Afterwards I worked it out. Ella knew right along she was ill. But she figured I already had enough on my plate, so she just kept quiet about it."

TJ nodded, imagined how he would feel if he missed out on Catherine's last healthy days because of business pressures. All he said was, "That sounds just like her, Jem."

Jeremy was quiet for a long time, so long that TJ thought maybe his friend was going to let it drop. His voice was very rough when he continued, "I guess the clock was Ella's way of tellin' me that her time had come. She wouldn't do it for herself. She never said why and I never asked. Wasn't any need."

TJ understood, said, "She didn't want you punishing yourself afterwards."

"Crazy clock had a face with twenty-six hours. Ella said she knew how busy I was, but she'd missed me somethin' awful. So for my birthday that year she was gonna give me two more hours in my day. Only thing she asked was that one hour be spent with her, and the other one with the Lord."

"She was a fine woman, Jem," TJ said quietly, aching for his friend. "One of the finest."

"Been thinkin' a lot about her ever since I got up here," Jeremy said, stopping in front of the Old Executive Office Building. "Dreamed about her last night for maybe the fourth or fifth time in the past coupla weeks. Like to think it's because I'm movin' closer to the Lord through doin' His work."

TJ decided he would match his friend's honesty with a little of his own, asked, "Jem, do you think I've made a mistake, asking Catherine to come up to Washington?"

Jeremy kept his eyes forward, nodded as though expecting the question. "Ain't nowhere else that lady wants to be, TJ. Just give her a little time to get adjusted. I'll be takin' her down to the Community this mornin', maybe that'll help." He turned and gave his friend a warm smile. "Now how's about a prayer 'fore you go out to meet Goliath."

□   □   □

Congressman John Silverwood was a very nervous man. He had not felt like this since his first campaign speech, more than fifteen years ago.

But this time, he could not for the life of him figure out why he was so afraid.

He stepped through the elevator doors and faced a circular receptionist's desk, located in the middle of a circular room. Doors were placed evenly along the walls, with vibrantly colored modern paintings decorating the spaces between them. The carpet was thick and cream-colored, the walls were papered with what looked to be water-stained silk, and the round reception desk was in polished rosewood. Brass letters attached to the front of the reception desk announced that these were the offices of Shermann, Blinders and Bledd.

Lighting was recessed, lobby furniture was leather and light wood, and the receptionist was as spectacular as the room. "May I help you, sir?"

"I'm here to see Mr. Shermann."

"Of course, sir. Would you happen to be Congressman Silverwood?"

He nodded, very embarrassed that she would know who he was. It made him wonder how public the knowledge of their deal was.

"Mr. Shermann left firm instructions to have you shown right in." She stood, gave him a hundred-watt smile, said, "Would you follow me please, Congressman?"

The man's office was simply enormous, a blatant reminder of the perks available to people working in the private sector. The desk was large enough to house a family of six. The coffee table, obviously an antique, appeared to be carved from one solid piece of burl. The beige-leather furniture looked as soft as a baby's bottom. Floor-to-ceiling windows framed by silk drapes stretched across the entire back wall, and overlooked an inner courtyard and tiny Japanese garden.

"Mr. Shermann, Congressman Silverwood is here to see you."

"And just exactly on time." Mr. Shermann did his gentle little push from the seat. "I have the greatest respect for busy men who follow closely to their time schedule. It shows they have concern for the time constraints of others."

Mr. Shermann extended a nearly translucent hand. "So nice of you to drop by for a visit, Congressman."

"My pleasure," Silverwood replied, hiding his distaste as he shook the dry, delicate hand. "Nice place you have here."

"I am so glad you like it. Please, won't you have a seat? How about some coffee?"

"No thanks. I really have to be moving on very shortly."

"I do understand." Mr. Shermann sat down, waited for the door to close, said, "Then perhaps you will permit me to get right down to business."

"By all means."

"I cannot tell you how honored I am that you would agree to accept my offer."

"Just a minute," Silverwood said. It suddenly occurred to him that the man might be recording the conversation. He felt a moment of real panic. What am I doing here?

"Yes, Congressman?" Mr. Shermann showed no reaction from behind his two-tone shades. He seemed prepared to wait in utter calm all day if necessary.

"There is no deal, there is no offer, and I haven't accepted anything."

"Ah." Mr. Shermann nodded his head once, an almost imperceptible movement. "I quite understand. Of course there isn't."

"I am simply paying a courtesy visit to one of Washington's most important lobbyists." He felt a trickle of sweat slide down his spine.

"Of course you are, Congressman. And I cannot tell you how grateful I am for this honor."

Silverwood's mind raced forward, could find absolutely nothing more to say that would not incriminate him if brought to light. So he stood. "Well, it certainly has been a pleasure, Mr. Shermann. Sorry the visit has to be so short."

"Not at all, Congressman, not at all." Shermann lifted from his seat as though drawn on invisible pulleys. "The most important thing is that you stopped by."

Silverwood nodded. "Just as I said I would."

"Indeed, Congressman. It is certainly clear that I am dealing with a man of his word."

"I hope you won't take offense, but I really am very busy. I don't see how it's going to be possible for us to visit again in the foreseeable future."

"There is no one in the city who has a greater respect for your time than I, Congressman." Mr. Shermann walked him to the door on stick-like legs. "And of course I would never presume to impose myself upon you."

Silverwood stopped in the doorway, said firmly, "Goodbye, Mr. Shermann."

Mr. Shermann gave a slight bow of accord. "Thank you again for coming, Congressman."

By the time Silverwood had arrived at street level, his nerves were back in order. All in all, he decided, it could have been a lot worse. He had agreed to nothing, he had said nothing. Had he been in other sur-roundings, he might not have thought about recordings until it was too late.

He smiled ruefully, and was amused to see an attractive young lady who was walking past him smile back. Yes, actually it had all worked out rather well. For an amateur, especially well. Silverwood gave a slight shiver at the thought of how close he had come. The man could have had him with a noose around his neck if Silverwood had thought of it five seconds later. He wondered if Shermann had noticed it, decided not. There was nothing in the conversation to suggest that Silverwood had not been in control from the very first moment. Any recording would indicate a totally innocuous discussion. Nothing incriminating. His mood lightened considerably, and he felt himself springing down the sidewalk. Yes, this really might all turn out for the best. And from the sounds of it, once he had eased up on his questioning of Atlas, he'd be rid of that Shermann for good.

□　　□　　□

When TJ arrived home that night, he wondered if maybe he had somehow walked into the wrong house.

There must have been two-dozen children in his living room, and more in the den. He stood for a moment, watched the screaming, laugh-ing, racing little bodies.

TJ saw a young black woman with a shining, intelligent face seated at the edge of a circle of children. He vaguely recalled her from church, recalled she was named Anna and was the minister's niece. Then it clicked; she was the one who had helped Jeremy get started with his work at the mission. The children gathered around her were laughing and playing a hand game.

She waved, smiled, said, "Hope you don't mind. We decided it was a good day to play invasion."

Catherine joined him, her eyes sparkling. She gave him a welcome-home kiss, said, "Their heat just up and died. Jeremy said it'd be late tonight before they could fix it."

"Sure will give your neighbors something to talk about," Anna said. "I believe there're some Arabs over next door. You could pretend I'm your fifth wife and all these kids are yours."

A little girl came running up, grasped the hem of Catherine's dress, hid most of her face, and peeked shyly up at TJ. Catherine bent over and scooped the child up. "This is Mary Lee," she said conversationally. "According to Anna, this girl's had at last count four live-in daddies. Isn't she a little angel?"

"I just got a new tooth," the girl pronounced solemnly.

"Show him, sweetheart," Catherine said, then, "Now, have you ever in your life seen a prettier tooth?"

"It'd win prizes," TJ agreed. He looked at his wife, saw a woman who was truly happy. Tired, but happy. He told her, "It certainly is nice to see you smiling again."

"Why don't you go on upstairs and relax," she said. "We'll be bundling these little ones off shortly and it'll be safe to come back down."

"We're just trying to instill in these kids a sense of their own self-worth," she said from the bathroom as they were getting ready for bed that night. "Most of them don't have a daddy, never had a man who stayed around for more than a few months at a time. Don't have any real sense of home. Kids and teachers at school tell them and show them that they're not expected to perform, so they don't."

"I'm glad you had a nice day," he said.

She came out of the bathroom, switched off the light, said, "I hope you didn't mind the noise."

He put down the book he was pretending to read, said, "Well, it was a hard day, and it would have been nice to have come home to some peace and quiet. But it was nicer to see that smile on your face this evening. I don't remember when I've seen you so happy."

"It sure is nice to be needed," she agreed.

"And I really like that look you're giving me right now," he added.

She came over, turned back the covers on her side of the bed, slid in between the sheets and moved over to lay her head on his chest. "These old bones are tired tonight," she sighed.

He stroked her cheek, said, "Who you talking 'bout old to, woman? You're nothing but a spry young thing."

She chuckled tiredly, said, "You lie, you lie like a dog."

"Not me."

She gave him a gentle hug and snuggled closer. "I guess it's just one of those lessons you've got to relearn every day. Is for me anyway, 'cause I sure can't seem to remember it."

"What's that, honey?"

"There's no joy like the joy you get from giving in the Lord's name, is there?"

"None that I've found."

"I guess that's why we're here, though, isn't it?"

TJ reached over to set his book on the bedside table, muttered, "I'm not so sure exactly why I'm here right now, if you want to know the truth."

She raised up and gave him a sharp look, said, "You know. That ain't nothing but tired talking. You know."

He settled back, said, "Yes, I guess I do. It's just hard to remember sometimes. You want to remind me again?"

"You're here to serve your Lord," she said, still looking him in the eye. "What better reason could there be? You're here to serve your Maker. He'll take you where He wants you to go, and tell you what He decides you need to know. And that's it. Everything else is second-rate and not worth worrying over."

He kissed her, said, "I sure am glad you're here, honey."

"Now, where on earth do you suppose I'd be besides here?"

He turned off the lamp, searched for her hand, said, "Oh, back in your own home near your own family, instead of up here in a strange bed in a strange house in a city that's just about as strange as a city can get."

"Now you're just talking foolishness," she said huffily. "Maybe I oughtta shake you up real good, knock some sense into that stubborn old head. There's no place I'm supposed to be but right here, and don't you forget it."

"I need you," he said softly, his eyes staring into the darkness, his arms holding her close.

"Difficult as it is," she went on, "this is about the nicest thing that could've happened to me, you know that? There I was, surrounded by a house full of silence and memories of kids that've grown up and left their momma alone. And what happens but my man gets this vision and runs off to Washington." She gave a deep-throated chuckle, drawled, "Yessir, Washington, D.C. Our nation's capital. The Lord's done told my man to work in the White House. Sometimes I can hardly believe it's all real."

"Oh, it's real all right," TJ said, the worries returning.

She rolled over and kissed him softly. "Now don't you worry none, you're just exactly where you're supposed to be, doing just exactly what He wants. I know you need me, honey, and you know what? It's a gift, knowing I'm needed. Just like those kids need me. Just like those folks need you up there in that prayer service every morning. We all need each other. And that need is what binds us together, just like it's our need that binds us to our Lord. All we got to do is learn how to give to that need in love, in His name."

─╢ FIFTEEN ╟─

TJ fumbled with the buttons on his shirt, guardedly watched Catherine from across the room. She remained silent and reserved, as she had been all that morning. He did not need to ask why. TJ and Jeremy liked the church, but it was even more important that Catherine feel at home there.

She made a final dab at her face, muttered, "Like trying to take the wrinkles out of the Rockies."

TJ knew better than to offer a compliment when she was suffering from a case of nerves. "Now if you don't like this place, we can always change and go somewhere else."

"That's the fifth time this morning you've told me," she said. "Come over here and zip me up."

He knotted his tie and moved into the bedroom. When the little clasp at the top of her zipper was fastened, she lifted her face, said, "Kiss me before I put my lips on."

He kissed her, watched her expression in the mirror as she ran the lipstick over her mouth, said, "I'm really glad you're up here, honey."

She gave herself one more critical glance. "Don't be so worried. I've been going to the same church since I was old enough to walk. This is just something new to me, and it's going to take some time to get used to it."

"I just want you to be happy."

She rummaged through her purse, said quietly, "I'll be happy when all this is over and we can go home." Catherine raised her head, her eyes hard, her chin set and determined. "Ready to go?"

□   □   □

"Gonna talk about the fifteenth chapter of Luke today. Can I have me an Amen?"

The congregation called out their response. It was already warm, the air close and sweet with hair oil and perfume. Fans sporting various advertisements were waving from the hands of older members.

The reverend was a sinewy man, there was no other word for it. He moved with strength. When he shot his hand up in the air and the robe fell back, the exposed arm was taut and wiry. When he gripped the podium's dark wood, the hands clenched and tightened and seemed ready to tear chunks out of the sides.

"Jesus gave us three parables, stories about the lost ones in this life. Let me hear an Amen. Yes. Weren't no verses and chapters when these stories were told. Nowadays we let these things get in the way. Yes. The Lord told these three parables together, and that's the way we're gonna look at them today."

At a nod from the reverend, a deacon rose from the front row, walked to the microphone by the altar, read from his Bible:

> "What man of you, having an hundred sheep, if he lose one of them, doth not leave the ninety and nine in the wilderness, and go after that which is lost, until he find it? And when he hath found it, he layeth it on his shoulders, rejoicing. And when he cometh home, he calleth together his friends and neighbors, saying unto them, Rejoice with me; for I have found my sheep which was lost."

When the deacon was finished and seated once again, Reverend Wilkins went on, "We get all silly when people talk to us about being sheep. Yes. Think that's some kind of compliment. Folks, let me tell you, there ain't no animal in this whole wide world that's dumber than a sheep. Can I have me an Amen. Yeah. The Lord wasn't complimentin' us, He was tellin' it like it is."

The church's first row was filled with men, mostly heavyset and somber—deacons ready to get down in the pit and struggle and sweat and fight as the devil was brought out and banished. The second row was filled with the deaconesses, mostly wives of deacons plus a few others of special merit and years of service, attired in white and full of the

THE PRESENCE ■ 235

Spirit. They led in song, led the responses to the reverend, ministered to the weeping women who brought their troubled selves forward.

"Some of us get lost just like sheep. Blind, dumb, helpless, and too weak to get out of trouble once we've gotten in. Most of 'em don't mean to get lost, nossir. They just wander off, nibblin' at this piece of grass, seein' something else they like, wanderin' over a little farther. Just movin' from one pleasure to another, nibblin', nibblin'. He ain't doin' no wrong, no, Lord. He just ain't payin' attention.

"Then before he knows it, he looks up, yes, you listening out there? He looks up and sees it's gettin' dark. He don't know where he's at. He's lost, Lord, lost and lonely and the flock ain't anywhere to be found."

TJ started to feel Catherine tremble beside him. He shot a quick glance over her way, saw that her eyes were alight and her lips parted, totally immersed in the message.

The reverend leaned far over the podium, waited until the congregation had quieted, growled, "And then, you know what happens? Yes. All us sinners know, don't we? He hears a wolf howl out there in the darkness. And suddenly the poor little sheep is scared right outta his wool."

The congregation rewarded him with laughter and clapping and calls. The reverend was having none of it. He stood and glowered them into silence, then nodded for the deacon to come forward once more.

From the front row the heavyset man with his wreath of graying hair and three-piece suit and gold watch-chain rose and came forward and read in a sonorous voice:

> "Either what woman having ten pieces of silver, if she lose one piece, doth not light a candle, and sweep the house, and seek diligently till she find it? And when she hath found it, she calleth her friends and her neighbors together, saying, Rejoice with me; for I have found the piece which I had lost."

The congregation was caught up now, filled with the thrill of the Word. Yet the more vocal they became, the more sternly Reverend Wilkins spoke to them. He was their anchor, their hold on the Truth. I don't want you to just fly up and forget, his arched brow and frowning demeanor seemed to say. I want you to learn. To remember. To act.

"Coin gets lost from someone else's carelessness," he said, having to raise his voice to make the words clear above the congregation's groaning chant. "Somebody else is responsible here. Somebody else had to make sure it was safe. You folks listenin' to me? When our Lord walked this earth, Roman coins carried the imprint of Caesar. Y'all know that. Yessir. Just like you know how your child's gonna carry your imprint." He leaned far over, growled, "All his life."

A voice rose above the general clamor, crying, "Tell it, Jesus, yes, tell it."

"I'm tellin' it, I just wonder if anybody's listenin'," Reverend Wilkins retorted. "You folks out for a good time, out for a little Sunday high 'fore you go back to your week of sinnin', you better wake up and pay attention."

He reached into his pocket, brought out a sheet of paper, said, "Got a letter here I want to read you. Found it on my desk last Sunday after the service was over. Y'all better be listening. Yes, Lord, all you parents out there, want you to listen like it was your little girl who wrote this.

> Dear Reverend, You know me, but I'm not going to tell you who I am. I come to Sunday school and church here all the time. I've been listening to you preach, and I know I ought to make a profession of faith. But I sit toward the back with my friends, and in order to come forward I would have to walk past my father.
>
> I know that people here think he is a great man, but you don't know him like I do. He comes home drunk, and my mother sends me next door to hide so he won't beat me. He beats my mother and uses terrible language. I cannot walk by him because he is in my way. Please pray for me.

Reverend Wilkins raised his head, his look truly terrible. "It's signed, 'A Teenager.'

"Wish I could have five minutes with that father," he said, ignoring the plaintive moans rising from the congregation. He searched the people with his eyes, hunting, hunting. "Lord in His wisdom keeps that man hidden, 'cause He knows I'd endanger my very soul if I found him. All I can do is pray for that poor fool, yessir. Pray he comes to his senses and realizes where he's headed. Y'all better be listenin'. Ain't just him I'm talkin' to. Every one of you better be sure you don't stand in nobody's way.

"Child don't learn the meaning of love from a parent. Christian fails to witness to a person in need. Somebody out there don't set a proper

Christian example. Teacher don't teach a class what Christ taught. Man afraid for his job don't stand up for Jesus. Now just how many people you think this describes? How many people you figure here have failed our Lord at one time or another?"

His face glistening with perspiration and clenched with the effort of driving the message home, Reverend Wilkins leaned far over the podium. He waited a long moment, the only sound in the church a whimpering baby, then rasped slowly and heavily, "All—of—us."

He straightened, gave his face another wipe, asked them, "Does the Lord give us what we deserve? Are we gonna be punished for all eternity?" The reverend shook his head. "First He sends His Son to die for our sins, since He knows we'll never get ourselves outta this mess alone. And then what does He do? Does He cry about it? Does He moan about how tough it was to bring us back, how long He had to fight and struggle and suffer and sacrifice? Look at these stories. Look at them. How do they end? Rejoice! Brothers, sisters, rejoice! What was lost has now been found!"

Catherine raised one hand over her head, cried, "Yes, Lord, yes!" She raised her other hand, clapped them above her head, cried, "Praise God!"

TJ leaned back with a small smile on his face, fairly certain now that everything was going to be just fine.

⊣ SIXTEEN ⊢

Congressman John Silverwood's Monday was a typically frantic day. Far too much to do in far too little time. Nothing received the attention he would have liked to give it. Quite simply, almost every issue required a full-time commitment.

He was dictating a letter to an irate constituent and giving less than half an ear to the television on his coffee table. A midwestern congress-man on the screen was taking overly long to come to the point. He was playing to the House, only most of the House wasn't there. They, like Silverwood, had already decided how they were going to vote and were using the speech as an opportunity to do some pressing homework. Silverwood figured the man was good for another fifteen minutes min-imum, time enough for three more letters and, if he was lucky, a couple of calls.

Bobby stuck his head through the door, mouth pressed out of shape by the ever-present pen. He wore his bug-eyed expression, which marked something urgent. Silverwood stopped the dictation machine, looked a question.

"Senator Atterly's on line one," Bobby said.

"You're kidding," Silverwood said, dropping his feet to the floor and reaching for the phone.

"Afternoon, Congressman. Thought I'd find you in. It's the farm bill's third reading this afternoon, isn't it?" Even over the phone the senator had a commanding presence.

"Almost finished, sir," Silverwood replied, eyeing the TV set. "I'd give it another half hour at the outside."

"Won't keep you, then. Just called to say some friends and I are getting together for a prayer circle tomorrow evening. Thought you might like to join us."

"A prayer circle," Silverwood repeated dully. He watched Bobby roll his eyes and slide from the room.

"That's right. A good friend's been going through a right hard time recently. Rather not say who it is over the phone. You know him, or at least know of him. Some people from my Bible study group had the idea of getting together, having a Bible reading and praying for help and guidance. You'd be surprised how much that can do for someone in need."

"I'm sure I would, sir," Silverwood said, trying to sound interested. "I'm honored that you would think to invite me."

"Well, ordinarily I wouldn't, you know, invite a comparative stranger to something like this. But I've found myself thinking quite a lot these past few days about your friend Case. Then it struck me this afternoon that I ought to see if you'd be interested. I've learned to follow these hunches. Some call them 'the leading of the Spirit.' "

Silverwood kept his voice casual, asked, "Have you been seeing much of TJ recently, Senator?"

"Try to make every one of his morning prayer meetings that I can. The man's—well, I remember how I felt when my own staff told me about it. You've got to see it to believe what goes on there. I tell you, the Holy Spirit is there in that room. Man, is it ever."

"I see," Silverwood said, toying with a pencil on his desk. "You're probably right, sir. I really should try to make it over there one morning."

"You do that." The voice was once again brisk and in command. "Now then. About tomorrow evening. We'd planned to meet here in my office at half-past seven. Should be through by eight, eight-thirty at the latest."

"Just a second." Silverwood glanced at his diary, saw the evening was clear, said, "Senator, I'm terribly sorry, but tomorrow night is just not going to be possible."

"What a shame," Senator Atterly seemed genuinely disappointed.

"Tell you what. Let's get together after one of the morning sessions, I'll introduce you to a few of my Bible study group. At least a handful are there most days."

"That's very kind, Senator. Thank you for the invitation. This week's kind of tight, but I'll be sure to make time just as soon as I possibly can."

They exchanged goodbyes, and Silverwood hung up the phone. Morning prayer sessions, evening prayer circles, Bible study, probably church on Sunday too. Silverwood shook his head, turned back to his dictation, wondered where a man that busy found the time.

□   □   □

The taping of TJ's interview for *Good Morning America* took place late Monday afternoon.

First someone called and obtained his agreement not to appear on another network's program until theirs was aired, in exchange for limiting their questions to educational issues only. With the pressure off, they decided to do a nationwide build-up by playing segments of the WBTV interview on the news programs of ABC affiliate stations. TJ kept waiting for someone from higher up to pounce, call him in, ask him what on earth he thought he was doing giving unauthorized interviews to the media. But he heard nothing.

John Nakamishi drove him to the WBTV studios, the Washington station where the interview was to be taped. "Nervous?"

"Not yet." TJ felt a strong sense of the Spirit's presence, which left no room for pre-program jitters. It was getting so he could say, to himself at least, that it really was the Spirit, that he really was being used by the Lord, that it really was His will at work here. "I keep waiting for a nerve attack. I hate giving interviews. Always have."

"I'm sure you'll do great, sir."

"I wish you wouldn't call me 'sir.' It makes me feel about a thousand years old."

"I say it with the greatest respect, sir." John pulled into the studio parking lot, said, "I can't tell you what an honor it is to be a part of all this."

TJ opened his mouth to reply, saw Jeremy getting out of a nearby car. "What on earth is he doing here?"

"He wanted to join us, but said he probably wouldn't be able to make it to the OEOB in time. Something about trouble with some plumbing they had to install. I suggested that he meet us here."

TJ got out of the car and squinted his eyes at the sunlight. The day held an almost springtime warmth—quite a change from the previous week.

He spotted a bloodstained bandage wrapped around Jeremy's left hand. "Good grief, man, what have you done to yourself now?"

"Hammer slipped. Thought I'd try to nail with my knuckles for a change." He nodded to Nak, said, "How you doing, son?"

"Just fine, Mr. Hughes. Sorry about the hand."

"Ain't nothing that hasn't happened before. Always like to leave a little blood on a project. Kind of atoning for all those thoughts I have when the board I measured six times ends up being two inches too short." He looked at TJ, asked, "All set for your big show?"

"I suppose so. I keep waiting for a bad case of jitters to set in. I can't believe how calm I feel."

"That's because the Lord's walkin' right alongside you, TJ. Take it from me. Something big's goin' on. I can smell it."

"Me too," Nak agreed.

"Well," TJ said. "Ready to go in?"

"Not us, old son. We won't be any use to you in there."

"So what do you intend to do?"

"Get back in the car where it's nice and quiet, and pray just as hard as we know how." He held out one hand to TJ, the other to Nak, said, "Maybe we oughtta bow our heads for just a minute before you take off."

TJ took a light grip on the bandaged hand, lowered his head, and closed his eyes.

"Lord God, we sure do appreciate your lettin' us be here today," Jeremy began. "It's not necessary for us to know what you're plannin'. Just bein' a part of all this is enough. I can't tell you how long it's been since my heart's been so full. Or when I've been so sure of anythin', either. Thank you, Father, for usin' us. Thank you for lettin' us know how great it is to feel your presence so close. We ask you to give special guidance to your servant, our brother TJ. He's a good man, Lord. You chose well. Show him what it is he needs to do, and give him the strength to carry it out. In Christ's holy name do we pray. Amen."

TJ stood for a moment, holding on to their hands, giving silent thanks for the support of friends like these.

"Catherine said to tell you she always did her best prayin' when she was on her knees beside her bed, which is right where she'll be till I call her," Jeremy said.

"Thank you both," TJ said quietly.

Jeremy let go of TJ's hand, whacked his shoulder, smiled, said, "The Lord be with you."

◻   ◻   ◻

TJ sat in the stiff-backed leather chair surrounded by mirrors. A young black man silently and efficiently applied cosmetics to his face. TJ endured it quietly, was amazed at how calm he remained. Nothing seemed to faze him—not the curious glances cast his way, not the laughter behind his back, not the smirks on some of the faces of people meeting him oh-so-respectfully, not the endless waiting and shunting and prepping. He was there, yet totally detached, untouched by their petty games and cynical humor. He truly felt as though he was not of their world.

There was a knock on the door, and a woman's voice said, "Mr. Case? May I come in?"

"We're just finished in here, Sandra darling." The rather effeminate young man whipped the towel off from around TJ's neck. "He's all yours."

"Thanks, Andy." The young man left without a word or backward glance; his place was taken by Sandra Hastings. "No, no, please don't get up. How are you today, Mr. Case?"

"Just fine, Miss Hastings. It's very nice to see you again."

"May I?" She sat down beside him, gave him a wry smile. "You know, I haven't been able to get your interview out of my mind."

"It's certainly given you a great deal of publicity, hasn't it?"

"Yes, all over the country, and there've been some rumblings about bringing me to New York, thanks to you. But that's not what I meant."

TJ nodded. He knew, but felt it important that she be the one to say it.

"I've never read the Bible much. Well, hardly ever. My parents weren't really churchgoers, and I guess it was something I always figured was for, well, weaklings. I hope that doesn't offend you."

"Not at all."

"You know, people who couldn't make it on their own, people who needed some sort of crutch. It didn't really matter whether God existed or not, just so long as I could get on with my own life. And the Bible was full of boring old stories that happened too long ago to mean much to anybody." She laughed. "I guess that must sound horrible to you."

"No," TJ replied. "Tragic, perhaps. And certainly something that too many people today believe is true. But I admire your honesty. There's always hope for someone who's willing to have an open mind and heart, and the first step toward this is to be honest both with yourself and with others."

She regarded him frankly, said, "I'll bet your prayer meetings are something else, Mr. Case. Would there be any chance of my attending the one tomorrow?"

"It would be an honor to have you," he replied. "I'll have my assistant meet you at the entrance and escort you upstairs."

She glanced at her watch, said, "It's about fifteen minutes until you're scheduled to go on the air. If you're ready, I'll take you up to the studio."

She led him down a hallway, past more people who did double-takes as they saw him. TJ imagined that any locally done interview given airtime nationwide would have attracted a lot of attention. He could feel their eyes probing his back, and yet still remained detached from it all.

Climbing the stairs, Sandra told him, "It turns out that the New York office had just decided to give this religion thing greater coverage. Our interview came in at the right moment."

She pushed open the door marked with an enormous 4, said, "Good luck, Mr. Case." Her smile did not erase the worry in her eyes. "Vic can be pretty tough sometimes, especially about religious stuff. Be on your toes in there."

Two men wearing headsets came over, shook his hand, guided him away from Sandra and toward the lone chair placed center-stage. They sat him down, straightened his coat, pointed out the television monitor where Victor Morgan could be seen studying a script. There was a camera set and lights, each with technicians, on either side of the monitor. The men stepped back, asked him to look directly at the screen. Minute adjustments were made to the lights overhead and to each side. The cameras raised, ran closer, slid back minor distances. TJ sat and waited and wondered if anyone else could feel the growing Presence.

"All right, Mr. Case." A woman's voice came from directly overhead. TJ decided she was one of the people seated behind the smoked glass that covered the wall in front of him. "Can you hear me?"

"Just fine," he replied. He could not recall if the physical sense of the Spirit had ever been this strong before. The Presence seemed literally to be filling the room. He had no idea what he was going to be saying, and no concern about it whatsoever. His gentle and powerful Lord would guide him. There was no room for doubt.

The disembodied voice reached him as from a great distance. "This interview's being taped for tomorrow morning's show, Mr. Case. You'll be hearing Victor Morgan's voice just like you can hear me now. Please try to keep your eyes on the monitor throughout the interview. It makes a much better appearance if your eyes remain as steady as possible. Do you have any questions?"

"No, thank you."

"All right then, three minutes, everybody."

It came to him then. There was no single perception of individual words. It was a *vision*. In the span between heartbeats the totality of the interview was laid out for him. The questions, the answers, the power. It was *there*.

"Ten seconds."

He was *ready*.

The ON AIR sign lit up. Victor Morgan was facing directly into the monitor. "Our next guest is coming to us from our Washington studio. His name is Mr. Thomas Case, Special Assistant to the President for Education. Mr. Case has made quite a name for himself recently with his evangelizing efforts within the White House itself."

Victor Morgan turned so that through the monitor it seemed as though TJ were watching himself from behind Mr. Morgan's shoulder. Then the picture switched, and Victor Morgan was staring directly at him. "Good morning, Mr. Case. Thank you for joining us."

"It's my pleasure, Mr. Morgan," TJ replied.

Even seated and seen from the waist up, Victor Morgan looked tall. Arms long and lanky, his body slightly arched in the way many tall people greet the world, his face knife-edged and very intelligent, his smile a flickering gesture that touched only his mouth. "Mr. Case, as many of our viewers are aware, you have organized massive prayer meetings with top level government officials. Yet there are obviously times when presidential policy conflicts with religious belief. In such a case, where does your loyalty lie?"

"The only place it can," TJ Case replied. "I base my entire life upon the rock of faith in God."

The smile flickered, a bit derisive this time. "Do you really feel that the future of our nation should be entrusted to people who put faith first and their country second?"

"The tragedy of any nation is when it is entrusted to someone who would feel otherwise."

This was clearly not the answer Morgan was expecting. "Are you saying that people currently in positions of authority, in your opinion, should not be there because they do not share your beliefs?"

"My opinion has nothing to do with it," TJ replied, his voice eternally calm. "You yourself are a perfect example. Do you consider yourself to be a Christian?"

"We are discussing people in national office," Victor Morgan rapped out.

"I can think of no better way to describe your own position," TJ said. "You hold responsibility for shaping the perspective and thinking of millions of Americans. And yet a question of faith makes you extremely uncomfortable."

"You are saying, then, that everyone must feel and think exactly as you do," Victor Morgan said, tightly controlled anger in his eyes and voice.

"I am saying that people should be willing to discuss matters of faith publicly. You call yourself objective, when in truth what you mean is that you hold yourself aloof from any heartfelt contact with the issues at hand. You hide behind barriers of cynicism and intellectual analysis. The question of faith is treated as meaningless because it is not something that you can hold and manipulate and turn to your professional advantage."

TJ Case turned away from the monitor and faced the camera square on. "What I am saying is that people should have a choice. People should be able to turn on the television or look at a newspaper and know that here, in this instance, they are dealing with an atheistic approach to life and to events of this world. And, if they prefer, they should be able to turn the channel and find a station that is directly and overtly Christian."

Victor Morgan's face on the monitor seemed turned to stone.

"The same is true with our schools," TJ went on as he knew he should. "People should be given a choice. A true, direct, honest choice. If they wish to educate their children according to Christian principles, they should be so permitted.

"It is clear to anyone who has had contact with today's school system that the current method has failed, and failed miserably, to provide this choice. Why? Because it is now a stated purpose to take this right of choice away. Unless a family can afford the staggering costs of private education, they are forced to send their children to schools where the overt practice of Christian faith is *forbidden*."

There was no movement anywhere within the studio. Victor Morgan appeared to have stopped breathing. The people behind the cameras, and those on the other side of the darkened glass wall were utterly still. The Presence overwhelmed the room.

"I am therefore proposing a fundamental change in education policy," TJ continued, still talking directly to the camera. "I am proposing that the American people be given the right to choose for themselves the way their children are educated. If they want an overtly Christian approach, then they should have it. Clearly the Department of Education has not supplied this alternative, so the people of this country should be permitted to set up their own schools.

"For every child sent to these new Christian schools, the taxpaying parent should be allowed a tax credit—a deduction not from his income but from his actual tax liability—equal to the total cost of educating his or her child. Of course, there must be a limit. This figure should not exceed what the federal, state and local governments are currently spending per pupil."

TJ leaned forward in his seat, said, "But this per-pupil expenditure limit should not be based upon any hypothetical figures used today. *The federal government must be forced to take the total budgets allocated for primary and secondary education, and divide it by the number of children in the public school system.*"

He leaned back, kept his eyes trained directly on the camera, said, "There must be a federal system to carefully monitor these schools, especially their academic levels. Each school must have an appropriate percentage of minorities to be eligible for this program. And a minimum of ten percent of all places must be held for students from needy families. These children will be awarded grants from the federal government according to the income level of their family. The federal government loses no money—it would be spending the same or more to give the child a place in the public school system. But simply because a child comes from a background of poverty should not mean that his or her choice, or the choice of the parents, must be restricted."

TJ turned back to the monitor, said, "Mr. Morgan, this nation was founded upon the principle of individual freedom. All I am saying is that the time has come for this freedom to be extended to the education of our children. Without penalty. Without burdening the family with additional costs. If a family chooses to hold fast to a strong Christian faith, they should be allowed to entrust their children to schools and teachers who share this faith."

TJ turned back to the camera and finished, "If there are viewers who agree with this, do not write me. Write your congressman. Write your senator. Write to the President himself. Let them know how you feel. It will probably take a constitutional amendment to make this reality. The work must be done by you. Every person who feels strongly about the education given his or her child must accept the responsibility, and *act.*"

He stopped, his talk completed, turned his attention back to the monitor, and waited.

Victor Morgan's voice sounded strangled when he spoke. "Thank you for joining us, Mr. Case. We will pause now for a word from our sponsors."

□   □   □

There was an impromptu party in the parking lot after TJ had removed his makeup. Sandra Hastings supplied the Dr. Pepper and the warmest smile. "I can't believe how Vic let you go on like that."

"Believe it," Jeremy said, toasting TJ with his can.

"I mean, sure, I saw it, but he *never* does that. He's always interrupting, dominating the interview."

"I'm not sure old Vic had much choice in the matter," Jeremy said.

"The White House is going to go bananas when they hear about this," Nak predicted.

"Yeah, well, I suppose that's all part of the plan," Jeremy said, and to TJ, "Sounds like you did good in there, old son."

"He was fantastic," Sandra said. "It was an incredible performance."

"I just did as I was told," TJ said, feeling totally drained now that it was over. "Do you really think they'll air it?"

"No question," Sandra Hastings replied. "Victor Morgan made a lot of enemies in his scramble up the ladder. Even if it was awful, they'd show a piece that puts him in his place like this. Your interview has the additional advantage of being really good."

"Dynamite, from the sounds of it," Nak replied. "The earth is going to shake over on Pennsylvania Avenue."

"What's it like?" Sandra asked TJ. "Is it some voice out of the sky?"

"More like out of my heart," TJ replied tiredly.

"Looks to me like you better sit down before you fall down, TJ," Jeremy said. "C'm on, everybody. The show's over. Sure was nice meeting you, Miss Hastings."

She seemed reluctant to let them go. "I look forward to hearing you tomorrow morning, Mr. Case."

"I'll be sure that someone is there to meet you," TJ said, and wondered if tomorrow's prayer session might be the last one he would give.

⊣| SEVENTEEN |⊢

The West Wing was in truth a small separate building connected to the White House proper by a long covered promenade. It housed the working quarters of the President and some of his senior staff, as well as the Cabinet Room, White House mess, security, press pool, a second conference room, and a few other offices. The Oval Office, so named because that was exactly its shape—oval—stuck out of the back left-hand corner of the West Wing like a man-made egg, facing unto the Rose Garden and connected to the promenade by private doors and two small patios. Between it and the Cabinet Room, which also faced the Rose Garden, was an office that under some administrations had housed the President's confidential secretary. Nowadays it housed the President's Chief of Staff, Norman Greenbaum, a slick Boston lawyer and former legal advisor to the board of a Fortune 500 corporation. Usually a man of great polish and almost unruffable cool, today he was sweating mightily.

It was his habit to arrive in the West Wing no later than six o'clock. He rarely needed more than five hours sleep, and the ninety minutes of quiet before the other staffers began to arrive were usually enough to complete his correspondence and do an itemized rundown of the day's major activities. This morning, however, he had scarcely had time to sort through the morning's messages before his phone rang.

"That you, Norman?"

"Yessir, Mr. President. Good morning." Though he had known President David Nichols for more than twenty years, it would not have occurred to him to call the man anything else.

"I want to see you," the President said. "Now."

Norman Greenbaum gathered up the file containing the most crucial matters to be covered that Wednesday morning. There were a number of urgent issues, especially as President Nichols had been in New York and Boston all the day before. But as Norman Greenbaum hurried down the promenade and entered the White House proper, he was fairly sure that the reason for this early call had nothing to do with the ongoing international monetary crisis.

The President was sitting in his breakfast alcove, an untouched meal shoved to one side, several morning newspapers scattered across the table in front of him. "You seen these?"

"Yessir." There was no need in asking which particular item the President meant. It had made the front page of almost every single paper in the nation.

"Do you have any idea how many calls the White House has received over the past twenty-four hours in regard to this?"

"I haven't spoken with them since last night, but—"

"Over nine thousand," the President said. "At last count, running fifteen to one in favor of what this man proposed."

Norman Greenbaum whistled softly. The kitchen door swung silently open; he nodded a greeting to the staff waiter, pointed to the President's coffee cup. The door closed.

President David Nichols was a born and bred New Englander, from the tip of his aquiline nose to the surprising strength of his slender hands. Political cartoonists often portrayed him as a weakling carried into office by the continued tide of pro-Republican sentiment. Those who worked with him closely knew otherwise. He was a brilliant man, not always the case with people who held the necessary charisma to become president.

His political work was incisive, his acumen sharp and direct when it came to major policy work. He knew exactly what he intended to have completed during his reign. He demanded complete and unswerving loyalty from his "troops," as he called his staffers. What was more, he received it.

The staffers considered President Nichols a good man to work for.

He made an effort to ensure that compliments filtered down to those who had actually done the work, a rare event in Washington. He allowed no end-runs around his senior men; all contact and all information had to come through proper channels, via the appropriate Cabinet official to the Chief of Staff and then on to him. Public squabbling was absolutely forbidden and was one of the few things that stripped off the President's normally friendly demeanor and exposed a scathing temper.

The majority of his staff respected his orders, and in truth liked knowing exactly what the score was. Staffers who preferred snaking along more circuitous routes were dealt with swiftly. Lesser mortals whose passing caused no public hue and cry were out with thirty minutes' notice. Those whose ousters might have generated negative publicity simply found themselves buried under mounds of bureaucracy, their access to higher officials denied, and all confidential information kept out of their grasp. The proper term for this act of isolating a disloyal staffer was "layering."

"Nine thousand," the President repeated. "I've just called downstairs again. The calls've already started up again. The switchboard is flooded. At six o'clock in the morning."

Norman Greenbaum fiddled with his glasses, started, "Mr. President, I can't tell you—"

"I want to know two things," the President continued. "First, I want to know exactly who this man is. And, second, I want to know how this disaster is going to be neutralized before it gets any worse."

Norman Greenbaum opened his file, extracted the first sheet of paper, more to have something in his hands than because he needed to refer to it. "Thomas Jefferson Case is an attorney from North Carolina, black, fifty-three, served five terms with the state legislature, gave up his political career to switch parties and back a Republican candidate for Congress."

"I remember that. What's the young congressman's name again?"

"John Silverwood, sir."

"Yes, that's right. His name's come up recently in regard to something else, I believe."

Once more Greenbaum was amazed at the President's grasp of minute detail. "That's correct, sir. There seems to be a rising tide of support for him to take over the open seat on Ways and Means."

"Incredible that they'd even consider giving that to a freshman congressman. But that's off the subject." The President paused while the waiter served Greenbaum coffee and freshened his own cup, said, "Tell me about this Case."

"He was brought up here on the basis of his work with gifted children. Made quite a name for himself locally, pushing various educational programs specially designed—"

"This has nothing to do with gifted children! Do you realize what this madman has done? He's gone out on national television and demanded the dismantling of the nation's school system! How in the dickens did this thing get started?"

Norman Greenbaum ran a nervous hand over his bald spot. He could not recall ever having seen the President so upset. Not with him, in any case. "I really don't know, sir. From what I can gather, it seems he's been involved in a prayer group over in the OEOB."

"A *prayer* group!"

"Yessir, I know it doesn't sound like much, but from what I can gather, it's grown rather large."

"How large?" The President had grown ominously calm.

"Reports vary, sir, but I think it's close to five hundred people."

"Five hundred of my staffers attended a prayer meeting held by this Case? Where?"

"In the main conference hall, sir." He swallowed nervously. "But it wasn't just once. They do it every day."

"Five hundred White House staffers meet every morning right here under my nose, and this is the first I've *heard* of it?"

"They're not all White House. I believe some come from other agencies and Capitol Hill. I think it's five hundred, sir. That's how many the room seats, and from what I understand it's usually full."

President Nichols turned and looked out the window, his jaw muscles jumping. "And the press caught wind of it."

"I—I understand so, sir. They did an interview with him last week, which I've been told went over very well."

"Who did?"

"WBTV News. It went so well, in fact, that it received quite a bit of coverage nationwide."

The President turned back toward his Chief of Staff. "Why wasn't I told of this earlier?"

"Mr. President, sir, I—"

"You've had your chance to contain it, and you've failed. Don't try to deny it. This thing is burning like a prairie fire." He leaned across the table, his eyes boring holes in his Chief of Staff. "I told you the first day we came together, and I'm telling you again now. If there's anything I hate it's not being absolutely certain that my entire team is behind me one hundred percent. This isn't even an end-run, Norman. The man's so far out in left field he isn't even playing in the same game."

"Mr. President, I'm sure—"

"Yes, and that's your problem. You're so sure of how the whole shooting match is under your thumb that you don't see a major political time bomb ticking away right there in front of your eyes!" He slammed his fist down hard enough to spill coffee over the papers. "I didn't become President of the United States to be outmaneuvered by some religious twerp!"

Norman Greenbaum mopped up the worst of the spill with his napkin and held his reply to a quiet, "Yes, sir."

The President stabbed a finger at his aide, ordered, "Now you get out there and find me a way to turn this thing around!"

□ □ □

TJ Case walked down the OEOB hall, his footsteps echoing hollow and lonely in the early morning emptiness. He had not slept well the night before, waking every hour or so to wracking doubt and worry. It was hard to face up to the fact that whatever chance he might have had to develop an education policy designed specifically for gifted children was now wiped out. He knew politics well enough to realize that anything he proposed would now be shot down simply because it came from him. The rebel. The man who spoke out of turn.

The evening had held a few bright spots, however. Jeremy had manned the front door, and Catherine the telephone, as dozens of well-wishers had called or dropped by to thank him for what he did that morning on television. It seemed a very large number of devout Christian parents were truly worried about the education given their children. The question they raised was universal: how can we combat the wickedness of this world if we are forced to hand them over at such a young age to people who simply do not know the Lord nor even care about His existence?

The press had also been very insistent, demanding interviews for radio, magazines, newspapers and television. It seemed that clips of both the initial interview and the ABC broadcast had received wide exposure. There was even some rumor of it having been shown overseas. In any case, calls came in from all over the country, requesting interviews and guest appearances on talk shows. Catherine had taken their names and numbers, telling them that they would hear from Mr. Case once the dust had settled.

The only call he himself had accepted was when Catherine had told him that Reverend Wilkins was on the line. The man had been unusually polite. "Sure do apologize for bothering you at home," he'd said. "Man deserves a little rest after a hard day."

"Don't give it a second thought," TJ replied. "What can I do for you?"

"Nothing much. Saw your interview on the morning show, had several people tell me about it during the day." Wilkins paused. "This part of your vision?"

"Yes," TJ replied quietly. "Yes, it was."

"Thought so. Felt like I was caught up in an act of the Spirit just watchin' it." His tone softened. "Guess there'll be some serious mess comin' down after what you said."

"I would imagine so."

"Might even cost you your job, I 'spect."

"Yes," TJ agreed. "That's a very real possibility."

"Well, I know you must be doubting yourself and the Lord. Know I would. Just wanted you to know there's lots of folks prayin' for you right now."

"That's very kind," TJ said, deeply touched. "Please thank them all."

"Oh, they'll all get their reward, I'm sure of that." Wilkins bore down. "So will you, Mr. Case. Now's not the time to be forgettin' that."

"It's hard not to sometimes," TJ confessed.

"Had me a right interesting talk with Sister Carla this afternoon," Wilkins said. "You 'member Sister Carla?"

"No, I can't say that I do."

"Well, her boy just started high school this past fall. Robert's his name, folks call him Bobby. Right smart boy, real respectful and quiet. Family had a big dinner for Bobby, one of the relatives asked him what he wanted to be when he grew up. Know what that boy said? Alive. Yessir, just that one word. Alive. Fourteen years old and he's worried about living to see tomorrow."

Reverend Wilkins paused long enough to let the words sink in, said, "You just keep on doing what the Lord calls you to do, Mr. Case. There's people out there with childrens like Robert in mighty desperate need of the Lord's help."

Wilkins' words echoed in TJ's thoughts as he turned the corner to the conference room for the morning prayer meeting. He saw people milling about in the hall up ahead. As they caught sight of him, they surged forward. He steeled himself and walked on. The first ones approached, reached out, shook his hand, murmured a few words, patted his shoulder, his back, reached hands over the ones in front as the crowd grew in size and tried to touch him.

Nak pushed his way through, grabbed his arm, told those in front to give them room, and led TJ into the chamber and down toward the podium. People already in their seats stood; people nearest to the aisle reached out gentle hands. TJ felt tremendously embarrassed until it struck him that they weren't paying him homage. They were just saying goodbye.

Bella was waiting for them at the stairs leading up to the stage. "That was wonderful, what you said in the interview. Really wonderful."

"Thank you, Bella," TJ replied, touched more by the look in her eyes than by the words.

"There are two Cabinet members, three senators, and five congressmen—"

"Six," Nak corrected her.

"Is it six now?" She smiled. "Who would have thought it'd come to this when we started?"

TJ climbed up on the stage, set his Bible on the podium, kept his eyes down as he waited for the people to settle. Nak remained at his side long enough to murmur, "Mrs. Nichols is in the third row."

That startled him. "The President's wife? She's here?"

"Almost directly in front of you," Nak said, patted his shoulder again, and walked from the stage.

TJ bowed his head, afraid to look up and see her and not know what to say. Fill me, Lord, he prayed. Guide me. Tell me what it is you want me to say to them.

In time to his words, the Presence descended and granted him peace.

All doubt, all worry, all concern for the past or the future simply vanished. In that moment of transition TJ realized that all of his fears were simply cries of his humanness. So long as his being remained one with the Lord, so long as he lived the life of the new self, joined with his Savior Jesus Christ, things were clear. It was not a question of *knowing* all things. He did not *need* to know. He knew the Scriptures. He knew the presence of the Holy Spirit. He knew that the Lord's plan was unfolding. That was enough. That was sufficient in all things, in all ways.

He lifted his eyes, wished the quieted room a good morning, opened his Bible.

As always, it became utterly clear what was to be said that morning. And, as was true with every message, he realized that the words were meant as much for him as anyone.

"We are in positions of power, of leadership," TJ began. "This means that we must set an example for all people throughout this land. We must walk the paths of light, not of darkness. If we search after power, if we work for our own gain, how can we condemn others for doing the same thing? These are questions we must raise to ourselves every day. It is the only way to avoid being trapped within the illusion of worldly power. Why are we here? Whom do we serve? Where does our ultimate responsibility lie?"

He picked up his Bible, and said as he searched, "Our first reading this morning comes from the sixth chapter of Matthew." He heard pages rustle, lifted his head, smiled encouragement to those who fumbled through their own Bibles, said, "We'll start with verse nineteen:

"Do not store up for yourselves treasures on earth, where moth and rust destroy, and where thieves break in and steal. But store up for yourselves treasures in heaven, where moth and rust do not destroy, and where thieves do not break in and steal. For where your treasure is, there your heart will be also.

"The eye is the lamp of the body. If your eyes are good, your whole body will be full of light. But if your eyes are bad, your whole body will be full of darkness. If then the light within you is darkness, how great is that darkness!

"No one can serve two masters. Either he will hate the one and love the other, or he will be devoted to the one and despise the other. You cannot serve both God and Money."

TJ looked up, said, "For the past several mornings we have been seeing how the first means of serving God is through faith. Let's now consider a way this faith can be seen." He began turning pages, went on, "Our second reading comes from the tenth chapter of Romans, beginning with the second part of verse twelve." As he waited for the others to find their places, he told the gathering, "This is sometimes known as the Missionaries' Creed:

"The same Lord is Lord of all, and richly blesses all who call on him, for, 'Everyone who calls on the name of the Lord will be saved.'

"How, then, can they call on the one they have not believed in? And how can they believe in the one of whom they have not heard? And how can they hear without someone preaching to them? And how can they preach unless they are sent? As it is written, 'How beautiful are the feet of those who bring good news!' "

TJ swiftly turned the pages, said, "Our third reading is from the thirty-third chapter of Ezekiel, beginning with the first verse." He used the time it took the others to find the passage to say, "Here the Lord speaks through the prophet Ezekiel, using the allegory of a watchman keeping guard against the dangers of the night. As is said here, our responsibility is not the other man's response, but rather that we have ourselves responded to the Holy Spirit. It does not matter where we are. It does not matter with whom we deal. We are, each of us, called to pass on the message of salvation to all those with whom the Lord gives us contact.

"The word of the Lord came to me: 'Son of man, speak to your countrymen and say to them: "When I bring the sword against a land, and the people of the land choose one of their men and make him their watchman, and he sees the sword coming against the land and blows the trumpet to warn the people, then if anyone hears the trumpet but does not take warning and the sword comes and takes his life, his blood will be on his own head. Since he heard the sound of the trumpet but did not take warning, his blood will be on his own head. If he had taken warning, he would have saved himself. But if the watchman sees the sword coming and does not blow the trumpet to warn the people and the sword comes and takes the life of one of them, that man will be taken away because of his sin, but I will hold the watchman accountable for his blood.

" 'Son of man, I have made you a watchman for the house of Israel; so hear the word I speak and give them warning from me. When I say to the wicked, "O wicked man, you will surely die," and you do not speak out to dissuade him from his ways, that wicked man will die for his sin, and I will hold you accountable for his blood. But if you do warn the wicked man to turn from his ways and he does not do so, he will die for his sin, but you will have saved yourself.

" 'Son of man, say to the house of Israel, "This is what you are saying: 'Our offenses and sins weigh us down, and we are wasting away because of them. How then can we live?' " Say to them, "As surely as I live, declares the Sovereign Lord, I take no pleasure in the death of the wicked, but rather that they turn from their ways and live. Turn! Turn from your evil ways! Why will you die, O house of Israel?" ' "

TJ closed his Bible, lowered his head, said, "Let us pray.

"We offer up this prayer, our Father, not for ourselves. Not for today. We pray now for all of those who have never known the grace of your guiding light. Raised without the knowledge of love, they live in the arid desert of an empty heart. They walk in blindness, Father. They wallow in the trough of momentary pleasure. They move constantly from desire to desire."

He voiced the words given him by the Spirit that overwhelmed his being. There was a sense of bonding with the audience, as though he were a part of all of them, and they were all a part of something greater. United by the same Spirit that filled him. Drawn together into the body of Christ.

TJ paused for a moment to savor the wonder, and hoped desperately that he was not the only one who felt the miracle grow.

"Our brothers and sisters are lost in the world of shadows, Father. They seek to fill the void within by taking on things without. They are constantly hungry in spirit, constantly empty, constantly aware of that gnawing inner ache. Let us know the presence of your Holy Spirit, Father, so that we in turn might be able to help them. Let us offer them your holy light. Let us offer them the gift of your salvation. Let us show them what it means to live in your love."

He paused to savor the wonder a moment longer, then ended with, "In Christ's name. Amen."

He did not question when the same compelling urge drew him from the stage while the others still sat and murmured softly. By now he could tell the difference between his own basic shyness over matters of faith and the drive that now moved him to depart. TJ drew his Bible up against his chest, and with head bowed, swiftly left the room.

□　　□　　□

Congressman John Silverwood entered his office to find total chaos. Bobby waved a fistful of messages at him from his tiny alcove, talking on one phone while leaving a second one lying on the side table off the hook.

Marge sounded terribly weary for eight-thirty in the morning. "Yes, ma'am, I am absolutely positive that the congressman is aware of how important this issue is. However, with all of his other responsibilities, it's just not possible for him to speak to each caller."

He walked by her desk, ignoring her frantic hand signals for him to pick up the massive stack of telephone-message slips. He didn't need to see them. He knew what they were all about.

Bobby followed him into his office with his own pile of slips; before his assistant could speak, Silverwood told him, "I had breakfast with Ted Robinson this morning. He flew up last night, after the bomb dropped yesterday morning."

" 'Bomb' is the right word," Bobby said, running his free hand through frazzled hair. "When I left at seven o'clock last night every single phone was still ringing. Same when I arrived this morning."

"Ted told me about the reaction at home. About what you'd expect," Silverwood tried to keep his voice calm. "There weren't actually any battles out in front of our headquarters, not any that he saw. Just a lot of people milling about, shouting and waving signs and singing hymns. Said it was tough to figure out exactly who was for and who against, but it certainly did make for an interesting day."

"Calls are running about ten to one for," Bobby said, trying to match Silverwood's calm, but his bug-eyed expression betrayed him. "I hate to think what tomorrow's mail is going to be like."

"Or next week's," Silverwood agreed. "Something tells me this isn't just going to go away on its own."

"What made this TJ Case guy do it?" Bobby waved his clenched fist around the room, watched a few slips loosen and flutter to the carpet. "And the gifted children project, what about it? I wondered about that all night. I mean, the man gave up a political career, changed parties, backed you, came to Washington—all for those kids. Can you understand it? The man's destroyed any chance he had."

"That's not all he's destroyed," Silverwood said grimly. "We're about to watch the man's goose get burned to a crisp. Feathers and all."

Marge opened his door. The expression in her eyes pretty much matched Bobby's. "Norman Greenbaum's secretary's on line two. Says she's been trying to get through to you for the past half hour."

Bobby groaned. Silverwood waved him to silence, asked, "What does she want?"

"Secretary Edwards is in his office right now. They want to know if you can come over and shed some light on this issue. That's exactly what she said. 'Shed some light on this issue.' "

"They're looking for a scapegoat," Bobby muttered.

"I'm nobody's goat—not even the President's," Silverwood muttered back. Then to his secretary, "Tell them I'll be right there. Cancel my appointments for the rest of the morning." He stood, said to Bobby, "Any idea what's going on in the hearing this afternoon?"

"I'd lay you odds the thing's canceled," Bobby replied.

"You're joking."

"You think you're the only one that's got this on their hands?" Bobby waved the slips again. "Take a minute, drop in a couple of the offices. Watch a few nervous breakdowns in action."

Congressman Silverwood stared at him. "The whole nation?"

Bobby nodded. "You were right when you said this thing was a bomb."

□ □ □

Silverwood had never been inside the West Wing before; he found himself trying hard not to rubberneck. This was definitely not a time to show how green he was. To give them more space, the three men moved next door to the Cabinet Room. Outside the room's large bay windows, unseasonably brilliant sunshine played across the bare trees and brown-green lawn. Silverwood saw no one moving.

"Sometimes I wonder if Americans haven't decided that they'll settle for the mediocre, just so long as it's pure." Secretary of the Department of Education Phil Edwards rolled his cigar carefully around the edge of the ashtray, trimming the ash to a smoldering cone.

Norman Greenbaum snorted. "Pure by who's definition?"

Edwards gave his head a ponderous nod. "That's part of the problem, no doubt about it. People get so afraid of being seen as impure, they don't want to say anything at all. They're afraid to take a risk, stick their necks out. These religious whackos and their warrior tactics have 'em feeling like their backs're to the wall. They prefer to just melt into the crowd. And so the mediocre and the nut cases have a free reign."

Greenbaum turned to Silverwood, said, "Your Mr. Case doesn't seem too concerned with being a part of our team."

"He's not *my* anything," Silverwood replied heatedly, furious that this was being hung around his neck. "You think I would've recommended him if I thought he'd pull a move like this?"

"The man is plain crazy," Edwards said. "An uncontrollable maniac. The other side of the religious coin. Either they're mediocre or they're just plain whacko. That man's a menace, mark my words. He's bent on self-destruction, and aims on taking everybody within reach down with him." He set his cigar in the ashtray and eyed Silverwood. "You didn't have any idea beforehand of his being totally off the wall?"

"None whatsoever. TJ Case was very active in my campaign. He did an excellent job of bringing in the black vote. He was fanatic about the need for better education for exceptionally gifted children. That's all."

Secretary Edwards was not impressed. "Shoot, the man was in my office five minutes and I knew we had a major fruitcake on our hands. Know what he told me to do about shaping national policy? Pray. Can you imagine? The guy is something out of Loony Tunes."

"He'll be very active in your destruction, if you're not careful." The eyes behind Greenbaum's horn-rimmed glasses were hard as stone and staring right at Silverwood. "If that man's not put on a very short leash . . ."

"This is absurd!" Silverwood protested. "If I thought I was coming over here so you could pin the panic button on me, I'd have stayed in my office." He stood up. "I've got better things to do with my time than play pass-the-blame with you gentlemen."

"Sit down, Congressman." Secretary Edwards did not seem the least bit put out by Silverwood's anger. If anything, he seemed to approve. "Norm, there's not a thing on earth we're gonna accomplish by panicking. What we've got here is one fiery-eyed jerk who doesn't know how to keep his mouth in line with official White House policy. The only thing that matters now is deciding what to do with him. I for one say the solution is easy as pie. Fire him."

Chief of Staff Greenbaum was not so certain. "Do you have any idea how much publicity this thing has generated?"

"So what?" Secretary Edwards was adamant. "The guy's talking about ripping apart the nation's entire school system. Of course he's got publicity. The man's on the White House staff, he's supposed to be an expert, you think we're gonna let him stay on and just sweep this thing under the rug? I can't believe we're even discussing it. The man gets the chop. Period."

Silverwood decided the best peace offering he could give Greenbaum was agreeing with his assessment. "Calls to our office are running ten to one in favor."

"In favor of what?" Secretary Edwards' face began turning red. "In favor of the total destruction of our national system of education? You think just because a few other religious whackos agree with him, this guy Case should be left in place?"

"It's not just a few," Silverwood said.

"As of nine o'clock this morning," Greenbaum said, "the White House has received over eleven thousand calls."

"You fellows can't be serious. This guy wants to atom bomb our schools, and you're sitting here talking about letting him stay on. I don't believe I'm hearing you say this."

"I personally think we need some kind of counterproposal," Greenbaum said. "Something we can offer at the same time that the President announces Case's resignation."

An idea struck Silverwood like a bolt of lightning. "What if we could get Case to come out in favor of our own proposal?"

"You gotta be kidding," Edwards said. "The only thing I want to see that guy come out for is his funeral."

Greenbaum leaned forward. "What would make him agree to a thing like that?"

"A firm promise to put his gifted children policy into action."

"Not on your life!" Edwards exploded.

But Greenbaum ignored him entirely. "You think all this could be just a publicity stunt to put our backs to the wall?"

Silverwood had not thought of that. "Before yesterday I would have said no way. The guy's too straightforward. Now," he shrugged. "I don't see why he'd go to such an extreme. I mean, it's not like we've already axed his proposal or anything."

"No, I suppose not," Greenbaum mused. "You really think that might be enough to bring him around?"

"Over my dead body," Edwards growled. "We're not catering to the whims of some fruitcake."

Norman Greenbaum turned to Edwards, said soft and strong, "Nobody said anything about making this reality, Phil. Just calm down and think a minute. Do you really think I'd let somebody like this dictate national policy?"

Secretary Edwards grinned. "I get it. Yeah, it's great. Go ahead, Norm, promise this goof the moon. You got my full approval."

"I want more than your approval," Greenbaum told him. "I want a counterproposal we can present to the President, and the President can take to the people. Something to placate this outcry from the religious segment."

"No problem," Edwards said. "When do you need it?"

"Yesterday," Greenbaum replied. "Immediately."

"Give me two days," Edwards said. "This'll take some work."

"Forty-eight hours, not a second more," Greenbaum said, and

turned to Silverwood. "Who do you think should pitch this thing to Case, me or you?"

"Neither," Silverwood replied. "If you want it to work, get him in with the President."

—❙ EIGHTEEN ❙—

John Nakamishi walked with him as far as the main doors leading from the OEOB to the West Wing. TJ stopped there, feeling very old and very afraid.

"Whatever happens," Nak said quietly, "I just want you to know that I am absolutely certain you've done the right thing."

TJ looked back at him, thankful yet again that the Lord had brought them together. "If I'm . . . if I leave, do you think it will affect your career?"

"Probably," he said in his quiet bland voice. "I chose to join you, so I'll be suspect in their eyes. It doesn't matter, though. I wouldn't have missed this for the world."

"Nor I," TJ agreed, and stuck out his hand. "Thank you, Nak."

John Nakamishi shook his hand, smiled briefly, said, "I know what Mr. Hughes would tell you right now."

"What's that?"

"Don't be too hard on the boys. They're lost in the darkness and can't help themselves."

TJ smiled back, wondered what on earth he would have done without these friends, patted Nak on the shoulder, turned, and hurried through the cold misty morning toward the White House.

The message from Norman Greenbaum had been waiting on TJ's desk when he arrived in his office on Thursday, still high from the morning's prayer session. The President's wife had been there again, along with no less than three Cabinet members, seven congressmen, and four senators. Senator Atterly was among them; the senator had not missed a session since coming upon TJ and Silverwood at lunch, and often as not arrived with several high-ranking friends in tow.

TJ had entered his office, read the slip, and felt the jubilation from the prayer session drain away. The President's Chief of Staff wanted to see him the instant he arrived. So little had been completed, and so much was left to do. It seemed as if he hadn't even had time to really get started.

TJ left, passed under the canopy and the silver Presidential seal and entered the West Wing. He stopped in front of the guard's desk, gave his name, showed his temporary pass—the FBI clearance was still not complete, so he did not have his permanent one and could not enter the West Wing unattended. The guard ticked his name off the day sheet, asked him to pass through the metal detector, and had him sit in an uncomfortable chair stationed farther down the narrow hall.

To his surprise it was not the man's secretary but Norman Greenbaum himself who came down to greet him. "Mr. Case?"

TJ rose quickly to his feet. "Yes, sir."

"Norman Greenbaum," he said, all smiles and outstretched hand. "What a pleasure to meet you."

"It's very kind of you to come down for me," TJ said, not wanting it to go unnoticed.

"No problem. Wanted to show you something before we got started. C'm on." He turned and led him down the hall a few paces, paused, pointed out a set of stairs leading off and down to the right. "Ever had the chance to dine in the President's Mess?"

"No, I haven't."

"We'll have to do something about that," he said airily. "Real nice experience. Navy runs it, all the personnel are in uniform, very cozy atmosphere. They serve something called a John Marshall pie for dessert. Whipped cream, meringue, and chocolate." Greenbaum patted his prominent bulge, said, "Eat too many of 'em myself."

He led TJ past rows of pictures representing the President in various military settings—on the deck of an aircraft carrier, silhouetted at sunset with a row of fighter jets behind him, inspecting troops, a close-up of him in military jacket and visored cap with the Presidential seal. They walked up the stairs, down a short hallway, and entered a very elegant little sitting room.

"This used to be where people'd sit and wait to see the President. Press used it for a while too, oh, back fifty years or so ago. Couldn't fit them all in now even if we stuffed them in sideways. The President'll have photo sessions with visiting dignitaries here, or his senior staff can hold meetings here if they're looking for a more intimate atmosphere."

Greenbaum made a sweeping gesture that took in several oil paintings and a couple of glass-fronted cabinets holding ceramic figures and historical artifacts. "If you're interested you ought to come through here on a tour one evening when the President's not in. All kinds of interesting stuff."

They passed through another door, down another short hallway, then Greenbaum pushed open a soundproofed panel and ushered TJ in ahead of him.

"This is the press pool," Norman Greenbaum said, no longer smiling. "They called it that because the floor's laid over Franklin Roosevelt's old swimming pool. He had it built because the doctors told him a swim every day would help keep his body from deteriorating. You know, he was confined to a wheelchair by polio."

TJ nodded that he knew, and looked around the cramped little room. From the way it looked on television, he would have thought it to be much bigger. There were perhaps twenty rows of folding seats, maybe a dozen seats per row and very little leg room between them. Lights suspended from the low ceiling all pointed toward the narrow stage with its blue-curtained backdrop. The podium was dressed with the Presidential seal. The back of the room was slightly elevated and contained a forest of tripods and lights and television cameras. Boom mikes were stacked like mechanical logs in one corner.

"This is where it all happens," Norman Greenbaum said quietly. "Or at least, where it *should* happen."

He turned to face TJ directly, went on, "Our primary responsibility as White House staff is to help the President. The first way we do that is by making the President look good, *especially* where the media is concerned. Rightly or wrongly, the people of this nation believe what the press tell them. We have to be *extremely* careful that the media receives only the information that we want them to receive, and only the information that has been carefully screened. We have to be absolutely certain that it will portray this administration in the best possible light." He paused, his eyes boring holes in TJ. "Is that clear?"

"Perfectly clear," TJ replied quietly.

"The only way this is possible is by having one, and only one, conduit of information to the press. This is why leaks are absolutely not permitted by this administration. The President has a very strict policy with regard to leaks. Has anyone bothered to tell you what that is?"

TJ shook his head. "No, I don't believe so."

"No, that's right. You haven't been with us very long, have you? Let's see, now, how long is it that you've been here in Washington?"

"Four weeks," TJ said quietly, wishing the man would just get it over with and stop the patronizing lectures, stop shaming him like this.

"Yes, that's right. Four weeks." Norman Greenbaum shook his head. "Four weeks in Washington and you're already expert enough to go in front of national television and make a major policy statement."

There was nothing TJ could say to make the man understand, so he clenched his jaw muscles tight and said nothing at all.

"Where were we? Oh yes, leaks. Well, the President gave us very strict orders regarding leaks on his first day in office. Anyone who spoke to the press without explicit authorization was to get the boot. No matter who it was, or how important the work they were doing. Out they go."

What bothered TJ the most was that he felt totally alone. There was no answering comfort from the Spirit, no solace, no assuring Presence. Nothing. He felt empty, alone, threatened. He prayed for guidance, heard nothing in reply.

Changing gears again, Norman Greenbaum slapped a cheery hand on TJ's shoulder, said, "C'm on, let's go back up to my office and have a chat."

They entered Greenbaum's cramped quarters via the Cabinet Room. The office was shaped somewhat like a wedge of pie with the first bite taken out of the narrow end. Much of the space was taken up by a cluttered desk too large for the room. The walls were covered with framed prints of famous people and numerous diplomas bearing

Greenbaum's name. The outer wall had glass louvered doors opening out onto a small patio and neat lawn. Two seats sat facing the desk, one of them occupied by Congressman John Silverwood.

He looked up from the pad where he was making rapid notes as TJ and Greenbaum entered, did not rise, did not offer TJ a greeting. His handsome features remained set in very stern lines.

"You two know each other, I believe," Greenbaum said, going over behind his desk and sitting down.

"I've been wondering about that a lot these past couple of days," Silverwood said, his eyes still on TJ. "What did you think you were doing?"

"Let's keep this friendly, shall we?" Greenbaum waved at the empty chair, said, "Have a seat, Mr. Case."

But Silverwood was not finished. "If you want to commit political suicide, that's your choice. But it's a sad state when you repay friends by trying to take them down with you."

"That's enough, I said," Greenbaum's voice remained mild. He pointed to a narrow door set flush in the wall behind his desk, asked TJ, "Know where that leads?"

TJ shook his head, not wanting to speak.

"The Oval Office. The President sits right behind that door. Yes, sir, the most powerful individual in the world, bearing responsibility for the most powerful nation on earth. And I'm his man.

"I gave up an office ten times the size of this one, heck, my secretary's office was bigger than this. As a matter of fact, this very office used to house the President's personal secretary. I obtained permission to move in here, so I could be right at the President's side just as soon as he needed me. I took an eighty percent cut in pay and came down to Washington just so I could sit here and answer to President Nichols. What that man says is solid gold in my book. And he has told me that we are to discuss making an arrangement with you. He did not ask my opinion, so I didn't give it. If it were up to me, I'd have you out on the street so fast your trousers would still be searching for your legs. I personally have no time whatsoever for a man who doesn't respond to his nation's call of duty with one hundred percent loyalty to his President. But that's not what my President has instructed me to do. And like I said, Mr. Case, what President Nichols says, goes."

TJ could scarcely believe his ears. Were they going to keep him on? Was this why there had been no answering comfort to his desperate prayer, that it simply wasn't needed? Then why did he still feel so empty?

"Too much dust has been raised over these wild statements of yours, Mr. Case. There are a lot of people out there who feel like you've touched a very deep nerve when you started talking about their children's education. We need you to stand up for the President and his own agenda, and in return we're going to invite you to stay around and develop an educational policy for gifted children."

TJ felt his hope depart like air from a deflating balloon. Not that, please, he prayed. Don't tempt me with that.

"Now why don't you take a couple of minutes and just describe for us what it is you want to get done here."

TJ took a deep breath, struggled to gather his frantic thoughts, hoped against hope that he might be able to leave behind at least a shadow of his policy, his dreams, his life's work.

"There are two basic patterns of thought about gifted children," TJ began, repeating words he had said a thousand times before. "One states that every child is gifted in one way or another. This school of thought generally maintains that it is better to keep all children together in a sort of melting-pot approach to education. The more intelligent children stimulate the slower children to learn faster. The slower children are not ostracized by being placed in visibly slower-paced classes. Teachers are not placed in the situation of lowering their expectations for a group simply because they carry the label of slow learners.

"I disagree with this, and I feel that the most recent data supports my opinion. Our university system is not based upon the concept of treating all students the same, and I feel that latitude should be built into the grade school system as well, especially after the age of puberty. We are holding back the learning potential of our brightest children because of the unproven belief that slow learners will suffer if special classes or special schools are pulled ahead. We are punishing some of our young people for being intelligent, or for wanting to learn, or for having a deep interest in a subject that other children their age are not yet ready to tackle."

Norman Greenbaum made a couple of notes on the pad in front of him, said, "So what you're proposing is a nationwide system of special classes for gifted children."

"Classes and in some cases schools," TJ replied. "With a series of checks and balances designed to maintain an even spread across the range of race and income level. And with the opportunity given every year, through a series of national examinations, for new students to join in."

Greenbaum showed no reaction save for a brief nod of his head and another series of scribbled notes. "How long do you think it would take to put together a position paper?"

TJ hesitated, said, "No more than a couple of hours. Most of the information is already gathered, and written down in one form or another."

"Can you let me have it before three o'clock?"

"Yes, I think so."

"Good." Norman Greenbaum set down his pen, stood, brought the others to their feet with his eyes. "The President wants to speak to you at the earliest possible moment, I would say either late this afternoon or sometime tomorrow. Let me have your paper as quickly as you can, so that I can brief him in advance." He nodded once. "Good morning, gentlemen."

Outside in the hallway TJ turned to Silverwood, said, "John, I can't tell you how sorry—"

"Don't press your luck," Silverwood cut in, his voice hard as stone. "There's nothing I'd like more right now than to punch your lights out."

Silverwood turned away, said over his shoulder, "I don't care what arrangement you work out with Greenbaum. You're poison, TJ. If I never see your face again it'll be too soon."

TJ entered his office still sick at heart from the exchange with Silverwood. Quietly he instructed Nak to pull out the related files and have the papers retyped in concentrated form. The paper Greenbaum wanted was essentially complete, and had been since before TJ arrived. It was the same concept he had been working on for more than five years. Five years. A long time to carry a dream. TJ felt deeply for those children, wished there was something concrete he could do for them, ached at the very clear choice that had been placed before him. He tried not to think about the meeting with the President. Whenever it trickled into his conscious mind the fear ran through him like an electric shock.

TJ went into his office and closed the door. He stood in the middle of the floor, made a silent plea for guidance. A thought struck him, as though it had been waiting for him to ask. TJ reached for his coat, walked out, told his secretary he would be back in a couple of hours. He hoped he could find this place in Adams-Morgan where Catherine was working without too much trouble.

□   □   □

"They won't let me work with nobody but the little ones," Catherine said, as she led him down the musty-smelling hall and into the ratty kitchen. Tape held the cracked windowpanes in place, the linoleum was so scarred and pitted that the floorboards showed through, and all the appliances were rust-covered. But the place was spotlessly clean, and there was not a speck of dust anywhere.

"I'm really sorry to take you away from your work, honey," TJ told her.

"Shoot, these old bones could do with a rest. Would you like some coffee?"

"No, thank you."

"That's probably best. Last time I tried to light that stove I thought I was gonna set the house on fire. How 'bout some juice? I believe we've got some apple juice left. I swear, those children must drink a gallon a day."

"Yes, all right, some juice would be fine."

"Here, take that chair with the busted arm and set it by the window. That's probably the strongest one in here." She pulled the squeaky refrigerator door open with a hard yank. "Like I said, they won't let me work with the teenagers, though Lord knows they's just as much in need as the little ones. The thing is, they're not as trusting of strangers as the young ones are, so they won't let anybody work with them who can't give them a promise of staying at least three years."

"You look very happy, though," TJ said quietly. And she did. Her hair was pulled back and pinned tight to either side of her head, which accented her broad features and strong high cheekbones. She looked tired, and her shoulders seemed to be drooping a little as she poured his juice into what looked like a former jelly jar. But her face was alight and her eyes were sparkling. "Your expression reminds me of when our daughter was still a baby," he remarked.

That made her laugh. "Lord, have mercy, I'm way past that time."

"No, I mean, that joy on your face, it reminds me of how you used to look when you were playing with Nancy."

"Well, I don't know anything that's ever brought me as much happiness as a house full of children." She pushed the refrigerator door to, but it sprang back again. She set the glass down, took the door with both hands, and whammed it shut. The door admitted defeat and stayed put. "I swear, there are kids out there so love-starved that when I hug 'em they start to cry. 'Bout broke my heart the first time it happened. Know what that lady I worked with told me? At least they still know how to cry. They've got a special class to work with the really disturbed children. The ones who never cry. That's what they call 'em. Disturbed."

She walked over, set down his glass on the windowsill beside his arm. Catherine pulled over a second chair, rocked the back to test its strength, and eased herself down. "Forgot to make sure a chair would hold me this morning, and the thing just collapsed. Landed right smack on the floor. Children thought it was the funniest thing they'd *ever* seen. I got to laughing myself and thought I was never gonna be able to get up."

"You didn't hurt yourself, did you?"

"I'll be all right." She reached over, took his free hand, said, "Now why don't you tell me what's troubling you so."

He gave her a wry smile, said, "It shows, doesn't it."

"Lord, honey, who's been living with you for over thirty years? Now stop beating around the bush and tell me what's on your mind."

It took quite a while, not because Catherine needed to know all the details in order to understand, but because he needed to tell her. It brought the whole thing into perspective to be able to share the burden with her. Catherine listened as she always did, sitting in total silence, the attentive concern in her eyes all the assurance TJ needed to know that she was with him. She never moved, never let go of his hand, only narrowed her eyes slightly when he told her of the offer the White House presented him that morning.

"I know I can't take their offer unless the Lord guides me to do so," TJ concluded. "The more I think about it, the more certain I am that He's not going to point me in that direction. It hurts, Catherine, it really does. I've spent five years of my life working to try to help these children obtain an education that is set for the level they *need*, not the median—the average—level the school system *wants* them to have."

He rubbed a tired hand across his face. "When I was sitting in their office this morning, listening to myself talk about the plans I had for those children, I found myself wondering, was it real? Did the Lord really speak to me? Or am I just throwing away a lifetime's work on some fantasy I cooked up from stress and fatigue and overwork? Sure, I've doubted it all before. Hardly a day goes by that I don't doubt. But always before there's been some kind of sign, some answer that gives me peace and a sense that it really is divine guidance that's leading me along. Today there wasn't anything. Nothing. I don't believe I've ever felt more alone in my entire life."

Catherine sat for a moment in silence, the children's laughter a distant echo from the front of the house. Then she murmured, " 'My God, my God, why hast thou forsaken me?' "

TJ bowed his head, nodded once, felt suddenly ashamed.

She caressed his cheek. "So many burdens, so many desires. Remember what Jeremy says? It's one thing to give a problem over to the Lord. It's another thing entirely to let Him keep it. That's especially hard when we don't exactly agree with how He decides to answer us."

"Five years of work," TJ murmured.

"How would you feel if you pushed that idea through, and then found out it wasn't what the Lord wanted for those children? Wouldn't you feel just terrible? Honey, look at me. You can't tell what the Lord has in store. You're sitting in the middle of the storm, trying to peer through a driving rain and see what lies out there in the distance. You can't. It's impossible. You're just gonna have to trust in the Lord, have faith that He knows what He's doing and it's all gonna work out right."

"It's hard," he told her.

"I know it is," she said softly. "You just gotta keep in mind, honey, the Lord doesn't give anybody a burden they can't carry. And whatever happens, long as you hold fast to your faith, it's gonna work out like it should." She put her hands on either side of his face and looked deeply into his eyes. "Those aren't just words, Thomas. You know they're truth."

He nodded and she stood up, pushed on her back with her free hand, said, "These old bones start to settle if I sit down for too long. You got time for a little walk?"

He stood, said, "I suppose so, why?"

"I'd just like you to see what Jeremy's got himself up to. Let me get my coat, I'll be right back."

The sidewalk crumbled and bucked and swayed like a ship passing through heavy seas; it was a joy for the children to play on and a hazard for the elderly to try to walk on. Most of the foot traffic stayed to the edge of the street which, though pitted, was at least fairly level. The morning's misty rain had stopped, and the wind had picked up to a gusty strength that had the two of them clutching at their coats as they walked downhill. High overhead, billowy white clouds scuttled through a wintry blue sky.

Catherine pointed to the first building they passed, said, "This is the headquarters. There's a housing authority in there, legal services, the medical clinic, administration, and some of the classrooms." TJ looked, saw an ancient red-brick structure that only differed from its neighbors in that all the windows were intact and no graffiti adorned its ground-floor walls.

She pointed at a narrow alley heading off from across the street, said, "Let's turn down there and get out of this wind."

High buildings closed in on either side of them, blocking both sun and wind. TJ snuffled a couple of times, steered around a rain-filled pothole, saw scattered garbage everywhere, thought himself a million miles removed from the White House.

"All this was started just five years ago," Catherine told him, now that she didn't have to shout over the wind. "The reverend who runs it is named Tom Nees. One day he just up and quit his big Capitol Hill church, decided he wasn't doing the Lord's work preaching in some fancy place while right up the street children were going to bed hungry."

TJ nodded, remembering that Jeremy had told him about the tall white man, aged beyond his years, quiet and modest and the hardest worker Jem had ever met.

Catherine stopped, turned toward her husband, said, "Fine old church, big house, fancy car, lotsa people showing him all kinds of respect. You don't think it was tough on him, coming down here, starting off with nothing but a dream?"

"You make me feel a little ashamed," TJ said.

"Yessir, you think that man didn't have his doubts? You think he didn't wonder if maybe the Lord wouldn't just as soon he'd stayed where he was, living the nice life, tending after the needs of those rich white folks?"

"I understand," TJ said, loving her for her good sense.

"I wonder if that man would have believed what all would be accomplished in just five short years," Catherine said, looking deep into his eyes. Then, more softly, "Lord didn't say it'd be easy, honey. He just said, if I call, heed my words."

They passed from the alley into another cracked and pitted street lined with low-slung houses in various states of neglect and disrepair. The wind hit them full force, bringing tears to TJ's eyes. Catherine led him up another fifty yards, to a house whose front windows had been sealed with concrete. Signs warning of danger, condemned structure, were planted every ten feet.

"That's the one they want to start on next week, though goodness only knows how," she told TJ, then pointed across the street. "Right now they're trying to finish up the one over here."

They crossed over, were soon surrounded by the busy noise of hammers and saws and electrical machinery. Catherine stopped at the plywood barrier doing duty as a front door, peered into the gloom, saw someone and said, "Young man, do you know a Mr. Jeremy Hughes?"

TJ's eyes adjusted to the poor light to see the young black man smile hugely. "Shore do."

"Do you think we might be able to talk with him for a minute, please?"

"No problem," the youth replied, and walked to the back of the hall.

He peered up the stairs, yelled, "Hey, Jeremy! People down here wanta talk to you!"

"What about?" came the muffled reply.

The young man looked them over, still grinning. "Don't look like no heat to me, man. I think you're safe."

There was a heavy clumping down the stairs, and Jeremy came into view, limping painfully.

"Saints alive, Jeremy." Catherine was all concern. "What on earth have you gone and done to yourself now?"

"Just testin' the floor, makin' sure it'd hold my weight. It wouldn't."

"Took four of us to pull him out," the young man said, his grin even bigger. "Thought for a second we'd hafta drill through the ceilin' underneath and push. That man was *stuck*."

Jeremy turned to him, said, "You think maybe you could ask Tom to come downstairs for a minute?"

"Shore," he said, going nowhere. He went on, "Tom tol' him the next time he done a fool thing like that we're gonna stuff him on down 'tween the floors and board it up. Didn't have no more time for messin' 'round, wastin' the better part of a mornin' just 'cause Mr. Hughes couldn't watch where he put his big feet."

"I thought you had some urgent business upstairs," Jeremy replied.

"Tom says he don't see how old Mr. Hughes ever survived all those years doin' construction. Hardly a day goes by when he don't bang a head or whack a finger or break a toe or *somethin'*. Tom says the man musta specialized in buildin' houses with rubber walls. Only way he could see how the man stayed alive this long."

Jeremy searched the pockets to his paint-spattered overalls, said, "Now if I can find me my hammer I do believe I'm gonna nail me a coupla ears to the wall over there."

"I was just goin'," the young man said, and took the stairs three at a time.

"If he worked half as hard as he talks, we'd be puttin' the finishin' touches on the thirty-first floor by now," Jeremy told them.

"How *did* you survive, Jem?" TJ did not bother to hide his smile.

"I tell you what, these old houses are a builder's nightmare." He limped down the hall, opened the first door to his right, said, "Take a look in here."

What once had been a formal parlor was now partitioned into two small rooms and a minute entranceway. "House was built 'round about the turn of the century. Hasn't seen a paint brush or a nail in forty years, far as I can tell. Foundations're solid, but, man, the rest of the house was rottin' away. What we shoulda done was just tear it all out and rebuild the interior from scratch, but there wasn't enough money, so they've just had to make do." Jeremy leaned a weary shoulder against the doorjamb. "When it's finished this'll house twenty-eight homeless families, each one of 'em with their own little kitchen, bedrooms, bath, and most important, security."

"It's hard for someone who's lost everything to just start over," a voice said from behind them. They turned around, saw the gaunt white man with tired eyes and hair turned prematurely gray. "I'm Tom Nees."

"TJ Case, very nice to meet you. I believe you know my wife, Catherine."

"Yes, Catherine's been a big help to us." He eyed TJ with a look that went deep. "So you're the man in the White House."

"Not for long," TJ said.

"Yes, establishments seldom approve of someone stepping out of line. I wonder what the church today would do if Jesus Christ came and walked our streets. Crucify Him again, probably."

Tom Nees turned back to the little apartment, said, "What we're trying to do here is give people a place where they can get back on their feet. One of the difficulties of today's government is that everything has become so specialized and so fragmented that hardly anyone but an expert can tell you where to go to get anything done."

Tom went on to explain firsthand to TJ how the homeless poor spend days running from office to office, crossing town by bus, carrying their children along with them. Illiteracy means that weeks and weeks may pass trying to get the proper forms filled out. "And at the end of it they have enough to feed their children well once a day, twice if they're lucky enough to have a stove, which most of them don't," Tom said. "And perhaps enough left over to rent a room in a ratty little hotel. Not exactly the kind of place you'd want to raise your own children, I imagine, what with the prostitution and the drugs and the shoot-outs in the hallways."

His voice reminded TJ of doctors he had met in hospitals, the kind who really and truly cared for their patients, but only had so much energy to go around. They were faced with death and pain every day, and so came to accept it all as part of life. Something to struggle with and fight against. From time to time a little battle was won, but the enemy was never conquered. Never. At best, a temporary truce was achieved.

"So we give them an apartment of their own, and our staff help them take care of the paper work and get them on relief. Many of them are all tied up in court cases as well—you can't imagine some of the problems these folks are facing. Most people seem to think that a person becomes homeless, poof, just like that. It's never simple and it's always tragic. They're often good at heart but simply incapable of handling the responsibilities that society thrusts upon them—credit cards, layaway plans, monthly payments, bank loans. Things just keep adding up until one day they find themselves out on the street with no place to go."

"And it's the children who suffer the most," Catherine said quietly.

"I have trouble looking at the children some mornings," Tom Nees said, his voice low. "The pain on their little faces comes pretty close to breaking my heart."

"How many of these apartments do you have operating now?" TJ wondered.

"About a tenth of what we need," Tom Nees replied. "A lack of funds pretty much keeps our hands tied. I spend way too much time just hunting for more money."

"And it's not just the homeless," Catherine put in.

"If we're going to be really effective," Tom Nees said, "we need to be offering the same kind of services to all the poverty-stricken, especially those who haven't yet lost it all. We need more and better classes to train them in usable skills. We need more space for the children. We need a better clinic. We need to do more work in cleaning up the really bad slum dwellings, and give these people decent places to live."

"That's what he was doin' before the homeless situation started getting outta hand," Jeremy commented.

"Our first project was setting up a co-op for seventy-two families then housed in substandard dwellings," Tom Nees explained. "I won't describe what substandard means—no need to make you sick to your stomach. We should be spending our time organizing church groups and local charity agencies into building squads. We know there are people out there willing to help. We're getting more calls every week. Instead, my staff and I have to spend precious time hunting for funds."

"Have you tried working with the federal government?" TJ asked, knowing it was a leading question.

"We have," Tom Nees replied. "For five years we've been trying. I had two men working on HUD documentation for almost a year. Three projects, five hundred thousand dollars apiece." He stopped.

TJ realized the man was saying all this for a purpose, decided that he didn't mind in the slightest. "What happened?"

"We were told that our bid was so low as to be almost unbelievable. It was almost exactly half of the next lowest bid. They said that no one could build housing for what we were proposing to charge."

Tom Nees's face took on a look of utter weariness. "We invited them down. Showed them how we were using condemned buildings that the city would give us. Showed them how we had already housed more than ninety families, that we had a record we could point to. Showed them our books, showed them how the cost figures we gave were thirty percent higher than the ones done so far because we wanted to do the next ones better." He paused, finished in a dead tone, "When the first one finally came up, they turned our bid down."

"Do you know why?"

"Unions," Jeremy said shortly.

"Unions or big construction interests, we never could figure out which," Tom Nees replied. "Whoever it was, their power was strong enough to have HUD tell us that they did not wish to consider our bid a valid one. We still haven't heard about the other two. Our bids were submitted almost a year ago, and while those people downtown shilly-shally around, we're looking at people living in doorsteps and raising children in hellholes."

TJ sighed deeply, sharing the man's weariness. So much to be done, so much. "I wish there were some way I could help, I really do," he said quietly. "And I'll certainly pray about it. But I have to tell you that it doesn't look like I'm going to be around here much longer."

"You've heard somethin'?" Jeremy asked.

"I'll tell you later," Catherine replied.

"Yes," Tom Nees said, his expression turning kindly. "I've heard a little about your work, and about the furor you've caused. Well, your coming to Washington has already produced one major benefit. I don't suppose there's any harm in telling you that our friend Jeremy has become the Community of Hope's largest single donor."

Jeremy Hughes studied the far wall, muttered something about it being a drop in the bucket.

"A little shower of drops like that would put our work in an entirely different light," Tom Nees replied, smiling for the first time.

"Well, I don't want to hold you from your responsibilities," TJ said, stretching out his hand. "It certainly has been an honor to meet you."

"Remember us in your prayers," Tom Nees said, clasping TJ's hand in a hard, calloused grip. "We see miracles happening here every day, and answers to prayers almost every time we turn around."

"Especially with the children," Catherine said.

"Oh, I don't know," Tom Nees observed, another smile flickering into view. "Every day I see Jeremy leave here alive, I think another miracle's taken place."

On the way to a major intersection where Tom Nees thought TJ might find a taxi, Catherine continued to talk about the children. "The hardest part is watching them go home at night, and it doesn't get any easier with time. Not a bit easier."

TJ smiled, though his mind was busy with something else. "You don't want to bring them all home with you, do you?"

"You don't understand," she said, all seriousness and concern. "You don't know what those little childrens go home to. I hate to even use the term 'home.' It's hard, honey, I mean it is *hard* to let them go. And the more I hear, the harder it gets."

"You have to try to think about the positive things, Catherine," he said, thinking it was good advice for himself as well. "Think of all the good you're trying to achieve, and *are* achieving, and pray the Lord will water the seeds you're planting."

TJ slipped an arm around her waist. "Think about this, Catherine. Maybe the main thing God wants to do through you today is *love* the children."

She looked at him, gave him that from-the-heart smile. "You've decided what you're going to do, haven't you?"

"Woman, you change subjects faster than anybody I've ever met. I am eternally grateful I've never had to meet you in court."

"Haven't you decided?" she pressed.

"Yes, I guess I have."

"Well, are you gonna tell me?"

TJ spotted a cruising cab, waved it down. "It's very simple," he replied. "God's given me all the answer I need. I'm going to follow the example set by this preacher friend of yours, and do everything I can with whatever I have." He kissed her briefly, bent to open the door, said, "Pray for me, honey. I might be meeting with the President this afternoon."

She gasped. "The President of the United States?"

He closed the door, rolled down the window, gave her a resigned smile. "I try to think of him as the fellow next door. It keeps me from having a nervous breakdown over the thought of what's coming down."

⊣ NINETEEN ⊢

Back in his office, TJ found a carefully prepared briefing paper, complete with a table of contents and detailed appendix, waiting on his desk. He smiled as he thumbed through the document. It was exactly right. Here was his philosophy on the education of gifted children put into a practical policy analysis. He initialed the transmittal memo to the President, thanked Nak for his work, and asked him to hand-carry the package over to the White House. Norman Greenbaum would be waiting for it.

He then put a call through to Senate Minority Whip Richard Atterly. The man seemed genuinely delighted to hear from him.

"I'm sorry to disturb you," TJ started. "I can call back later if it would be better."

"I'm busy now and I intend to stay busy," Senator Atterly's dry sharp tones crackled over the phone. "Now or later won't make any difference. What can I do for you?"

TJ explained about the Community of Hope's difficulties with HUD. "They have people out there in serious need," TJ said. "There ought to be some way these things could be handled more swiftly."

There was a considerable pause before Senator Atterly said, "I suppose you know about the congressional investigation now looking into possible HUD wrongdoing?"

"I've read something about it, yes."

"Well, things over in HUD right now are frozen up tight. Staffers are so frightened for their jobs they're getting a legal opinion before walking down the hall to the bathroom."

Atterly paused, went on. "There's no reason not to tell you, I suppose. It's all public knowledge, or will be, after tonight's papers hit the streets.

"The Senate's been thinking of setting up their own investigation," Atterly went on. "I met with some of the people last night about it. I was against it one hundred percent going into the meeting. There's too much work that needs doing for us to duplicate the efforts of the House. But I was told something last night that changed my mind. It seems that several major construction groups are trying to freeze any development plans the city might have for the Adams-Morgan area. Have you ever heard of the Green Line?"

"No," TJ replied. "I don't believe I have."

"Well, if you take a look at a city map, you'll see that the Metro goes out past Bethesda, all the way to Shady Grove. Then on the other side, it runs way out to the Virginia suburbs. But right smack dab in the center of Washington, there's no Metro. There should be, of course. There's been a dotted line on the map for almost twenty years. It stands for the Green Line. The problem is, the Green Line doesn't exist."

"Why not?"

"Politics, what else? There's no money along that line. These are some of the poorest neighborhoods in Washington. The city officials have spent their money scratching the back of the biggest gorilla, and power-wise that area doesn't pack the punch of a baby chimpanzee."

TJ thought it over, said, "But I don't see what—"

"They've finally started construction on the Green Line," Senator Atterly told him. "There's a rumor that several major construction firms, along with a bank and a big local contractor, have decided to try and freeze all local development efforts. They're out buying up property like mad, speculating on what prices will do once the Metro line is completed."

"Which is skyrocket," TJ said.

"Right through the roof," Atterly agreed. "The information I saw last night indicates that there's been a major push by a couple of lobbyists to halt all HUD activity in the area. This congressional investigation and the resulting slow-down in HUD project approval has played right into their hands."

"So where does that leave us?" TJ asked.

"Let me have one of my staffers check this thing out," Senator Atterly told him. "What was the name of that organization again?"

"Community of Hope."

"Beautiful. Right where they need it the most, too. Hope, I mean. Okay, my office'll be back to you on this as quickly as possible."

"Is there any chance you could go back directly to Reverend Tom Nees? He runs it."

"I suppose so. You don't want to get publicly involved?"

TJ had to laugh. "No, I'm just not sure I'll be around much longer."

"Oh. Right." Senator Atterly seemed at a loss for words. "I'm sorry to hear that. I've found your prayer sessions a real inspiration."

"It'd be a shame if the Spirit is allowed to fade away just because I'm no longer there," TJ said. "Maybe you could use your influence here as well."

"That's an idea. Why not? Well, let me check on this HUD thing, and I'll see you tomorrow morning at least. You will be there tomorrow?"

"I don't know," TJ said gravely.

"Boy, my staffers are going to be sorry to hear about this. You sure there's nothing we can do?"

"Pray," TJ replied. "I've never known it not to help."

□   □   □

Not until Friday afternoon did the call from President Nichols' office come through.

Chief of Staff Norman Greenbaum was visibly nervous when he met TJ at the West Wing entrance. As they walked through the hall decorated with the President's pictures, Norman tried to lead and speak quietly but urgently in TJ's ear at the same time.

"When you enter the President's office you are to sit down, listen carefully, and stay quiet. Keep your mouth shut unless somebody speaks to you directly, then answer as swiftly and specifically as possible. Is that clear?"

"Perfectly," TJ replied, relieved to feel the now-familiar sense of calm replace his earlier nerves.

"The President's read your paper. He's got the facts. You're here for him to draw further information from if he feels he needs to. Do you understand?" Clearly speaking down to the lower-level official. The Chief of Staff doing his job, making sure the man understood his position at the outset.

"I do indeed," TJ replied. But the closer they came to the Oval Office, the less he was listening.

Norman Greenbaum pushed his glasses back up his nose, pointed nervously for them to pass through the lobby area and by the Cabinet Room. "I've got to tell you, Case, the President was real impressed with your concept. Real impressed. He was talking about just letting this whole publicity mess be overlooked, just so we could see about doing something with this gifted children program."

He stopped outside the Oval Office's closed door, brought his face close, said, "Secretary Edwards has had his staff working night and day on a compromise package to try and undo the damage your media blitz has caused us. He's going to want more than an apology. So is the President. You're going to need to publicly back their concept. Publicly, Case. You understand what I'm saying? It's the only way you've got a prayer of saving your hide and seeing your own policy get approval."

TJ just nodded, his eyes calmly resting on Norman Greenbaum's face, his attention an eternity away.

Evidently satisfied, the President's Chief of Staff nodded to the guard and reached to open the door.

The overwhelming sense of God's presence was with him before he even entered the room.

The President was seated by the fireplace, Secretary Edwards there beside him. The President's intricately carved desk, a present from Queen Victoria to Abraham Lincoln, was placed to the right of the door. Directly ahead were floor-to-ceiling windows looking out upon the Rose Garden.

TJ saw none of it. None at all.

The President put on his welcoming smile and stood up to meet TJ Case. President Nichols was very sure of his power and his position, a man totally at home with the authority that his office carried. He exuded the confidence and force of the leader of the world's most powerful nation.

"TJ Case! What a pleasure this is. Come on over here and join us."

TJ knew he could have broken away from the Presence if he wished, but there was no need. As he crossed the carpeted expanse, it seemed to him as though all the previous times had simply been leading up to this. They had taken place first so he might have enough confidence to allow himself to be so totally guided, so completely filled, so perfectly prepared for what was at hand.

The purpose here was utterly clear. There was no question, no *room* for questioning.

The Spirit had never been so strongly upon him, not even in that first vision. Here was Power against power, Eternal against earthly. And the outcome was indisputable.

The President stopped in his tracks, his smile evaporated, the arm fell limply to his side.

TJ's voice reverberated with the Presence that filled him. "You are forsaking the trust of your people and your Lord."

The President's jaw dropped slightly. He glanced at his Chief of Staff, who was staring round-eyed at TJ Case as though he had just sprouted wings.

"Hear what the Lord your God says," TJ continued, his voice even but firm. "Your nation and your people stand at a crossroads. You may lead them to destruction, or you may lead them to the Light. The choice is yours. Know therefore that you will either reap the benefits or rue your decision for all eternity."

The room seemed frozen solid. The President's mouth moved slightly, seeking words that would not come.

"It is not enough to rule well while following your own selfish desires. Pride and ambition are your greatest enemies, and yet in your blindness you treat them as allies. Rule for yourself and you doom your nation to destruction. Rule for your Lord and your reward shall last forever.

"All power belongs to God. He gives it to you in trust. If you do not follow His guidance, you have forsaken His trust and will pay the penalty.

"Your nation stands on the brink of salvation or disaster. Only if you allow the Lord your God to direct your vision will you be able to see and take the proper Way.

"You as their leader must do what you can to show your people this Way. If you do not warn them, and lead them by example, their blood will be on your hands.

"Seek to know the Lord's will. Profess His wisdom to all the earth. Accept His Son as your Savior, and make His teachings your foremost thought. Though you may be scorned, know that you will be saved.

"This, therefore, is your warning. Heed the word of your Lord."

TJ gave the President a slight bow, turned, and left the room.

The silence hung like a shroud. The President finally broke the quiet in a voice made hoarse by emotion, "I don't care who he is, I don't care what he's doing. I want him out, and I want him out now."

□　□　□

TJ Case arrived back in his office shaken from the contact, but not doubting. There was no room for doubt, not anymore. He was being shown the Way, and he was walking it in the name of his Lord. This was no time for fear or hesitation. He had been brought into the presence of mighty rulers, and had been shown what to say.

There was a large hand-drawn poster over Amy Lou's desk that he had not seen before. A passage from Jeremiah, done in fancy scrollwork, proclaimed, "O land, land, land, hear the word of the Lord!"

"I had a friend do it for me," she said, watching his gaze.

"It is truly beautiful," TJ said.

"Senator Atterly's assistant has been calling you every fifteen minutes. He says it's very urgent. Do you want me to get him for you?"

"Please. Is Nak around?"

"He said to tell you that the *Washington Post* wanted to do a piece on you, but when they couldn't get you they decided to interview Nak. He made them promise that if you didn't like the idea they wouldn't print it. I've got the number where they can be reached, if you want it."

"No, no," TJ smiled. "Go ahead and get the senator's office, will you?"

It was the senator himself who came on the line. "You've met my assistant, Larry Turbot?"

"No, not so as I would remember his name."

"He's the one who found out about your prayer meetings and started dragging over the rest of my staff. Anyway, he's got a friend from church who's right up there in HUD."

"Sort of a Christian underground," TJ commented, a smile in his voice.

"You'd be surprised. Anyway, his friend's done some checking."

TJ thought the man sounded excited. "Is this good news or bad?"

"Pretty good, I'd say. You can decide for yourself. It turns out that HUD has four different housing projects scheduled for the Adams-Morgan area. They've all been on hold for two years. And the other one, the one your Community of Hope people lost out on, that one was never even started. The time's run out, the contract's null and void, and it can be awarded again. Guess who the builder was."

"One of those lobbying for the slow-down?"

"Right on the button. Company called the Atlas Group, ever heard of them?"

"Why, yes I have, as a matter of fact. They competed against a friend of mine on a project back in North Carolina. There was some impropriety, and we entered suit against them. They settled out of court."

"Well, our friend at HUD confirmed that they're buying up as much of Adams-Morgan as they can get their grubby little paws on. Then they're just sitting on it, waiting till the Metro line's finished. Probably plan some massive redevelopment, you know the kind. Major high-rise apartments, shopping centers, sports halls, priced for the upper-income market. And the thing is, they've already approached HUD for financing. Looks like they're going to get it, too. If they do, those jokers will make an absolute killing."

TJ thought it over, felt a resigned sadness. "What about the people living there now?"

"Not much profit in housing for the poor," Senator Atterly said. "I imagine most of them will wind up out on the street, or shunted off to some outer area."

"That's not right," TJ said quietly.

"No, it's not," Senator Atterly agreed. "And it looks like we might have found out about this in time. My assistant's over there right now, putting a bee in their bonnet. He's wandering the halls, asking everybody he can about these projects and why they've been on hold. He's let it drop a dozen times or so that it's going to be one of the major items brought up in the Senate investigation." Senator Atterly chuckled. "I'd imagine you'd find quite a few people over there on the border of major heart attacks just now."

"So you think Reverend Nees might get his financing?"

"Here's the thing. I got a call from HUD, oh, a half hour ago. Fellow from the Contracts Award Division asks me if I was taking a personal interest in this Community of Hope bid. I told him I was interested in the whole affair, so interested I might even become the minority spokesman on the issue. But, yes, I was particularly interested in knowing why the lowest bid on three different projects was not receiving proper attention. Fellow does an outstanding job of hemming and hawing and papering over the deal with a lot of hot air, then comes out with the corker. Says they're just this afternoon planning to award the Community of Hope, are you ready for this? They're going to award them all *five* jobs."

"Good heavens," TJ breathed.

"Turns out they're all about the same, redevelopment of condemned property that the city has taken over. Range from a half million to a little over a million. Total comes to, let's see, I wrote it down, here it is. Three million, eight hundred and fifty thousand dollars. Think your people can handle five different projects at once?"

"I'm sure they can," TJ said, not trying to hide his jubilation. "This friend of mine, the one who took Atlas to court, he's a professional contractor. He's over working with them right now. I'm positive he'd be willing to act as project coordinator."

"That's fine. You want to be the one to tell them?"

"I'd love to, but couldn't you come down and let Reverend Nees thank you himself?"

"No, it's probably better if I'm not seen in the limelight on this one. I might just decide to be a Senate spokesman on that investigation after all. Let the dust settle; then maybe we can all get together and plan the next move."

"I can't thank you enough," TJ told him.

"Don't give it a second thought. I don't feel as if I've really done much at all. It's the first time in quite a while that I've felt what it's like to be the Lord's instrument. I don't mind telling you, it's given me quite a thrill."

TJ came out of his office feeling as if he were floating ten inches off the ground. Amy Lou was waiting for him. "It's Nak on the phone, sir. He's been waiting for you to get through. The *Washington Post* man wants to do an interview of you this evening also, to appear in tomorrow's paper."

It hit him then, truly like a thunderbolt out of the sky. The power of the message left no doubt from whence it came. TJ laughed aloud, thought to himself, I'm trying to climb out on every limb in sight.

"Tell Nak to bring the reporter down to the Community of Hope at 1417 Belmont Street Northwest. I'll meet them there at six. Oh, and call that young lady at the television station, Miss Sandra Hastings. They'll probably try to give you a runaround, but see if you can press them into paging her. If they do, ask her to join us as well. Tell her we have a story for her that she should really enjoy."

□ □ □

The message had already come in from HUD. When TJ arrived, he found the place in absolute bedlam. Jeremy was swinging Anna around the front office like a drunken dance partner.

"I don't know what you did, old friend, but from here it looks like solid gold."

"You're going to wring that poor girl's neck," TJ observed.

"Naw, they make 'em tough down here." Jeremy swung around so as to be able to reach TJ with his free arm. "Now why don't we go on into Tom's office so's you can tell the story just one time to everybody."

"There isn't time, Jem. The press should be here any minute."

"Press?" Tom Nees appeared in his doorway. "You've brought the press into this already? Why?"

"Tom, if TJ Case has got the press comin' down, you can bet your bottom dollar there's a good reason for it." Jeremy looked at his dancing partner, said, "You're not gettin' tired are you, miss?"

"Just try to loosen that headlock a little, would you?" She held out her hand to TJ, gave him a warm smile. "Nobody can believe what you've done."

"The man didn't do a thing except let himself be the Lord's instrument," Jeremy said. "If there's anybody who oughtta be thanked right now, it's the Man upstairs."

"Absolutely right," TJ said. "We've got just a few minutes before the press arrive. Do you think we could all join hands for a prayer?" The circle formed quickly, heads were bowed and quiet restored.

"Father, we thank you for the wonderful bounty which you have bestowed on us," TJ began. Eleven of them had joined hands in a haphazard circle that snaked around the stairwell and the reception desk. "It is truly a wondrous event, to see the unfolding of your miracles, and to know that we have had a small part to play. Let us never forget how little it is that we ourselves have done, Lord. Simply because the action has been taken by ourselves, and because we cannot see with our physical eyes that you have made our road straight, let us never assume that *we* are responsible, that *we* have made this happen.

"You have guided me to ask the press here, Father. I do not even know why this is so, or what it is that I should say. Help me, please, help us all to speak the words that you place in our mouths. Let us pass on your message, sing your praises, speak of your holy presence in our lives. Let there be no room for selfish praise or self-seeking glory. Let us speak of the One who has made all things come to pass, who has granted us this miracle of service. In Jesus' name. Amen."

People raised their heads, seemed reluctant to let go of one another's hands. Anna quoted from memory the passage from Second Corinthians, " 'God in his mercy has given us this service, and so we do not become discouraged.' "

"Amen," Jeremy chimed in.

They heard the murmur of voices rise from downstairs. "That'll be the press," TJ said. "Reverend Nees, is there any particular way you'd like to handle this?"

"Personally, I would have preferred to wait until I had the HUD agreement in writing," Tom Nees replied.

Jeremy looked at TJ, said, "Did you have a push from above on this?"

"More like a kick in the hindquarters," TJ replied.

"There's your answer, Tom," Jeremy said. "If the man's gettin' divine direction on this thing, the best we can do is hold our breath and dive on in."

They moved downstairs, where the man from the *Washington Post* was decidedly upset to find the television station there as well. "I thought this was supposed to be an exclusive interview," he grumbled.

"I agreed to nothing of the sort," TJ replied, turned, smiled, and said, "Good evening, Miss Hastings. It's so nice you could join us."

"What, is she the one who did the interview last week?" The *Post* man was irate. "I don't believe this."

Jeremy limped up. "Sport, you've got two choices. You can shut up with the complainin' and hear what the man's got to say, or you can be deposited in the street." Jeremy looked around, asked, "I'd say that was pretty clear, wouldn't you?"

"That's enough, Jem," TJ said, and offered his hand to the *Post* reporter. "TJ Case."

"Hank Weathers. Glad to know you, Mr. Case." He indicated Sandra Hastings with a jerk of his chin, said, "She in on this too?"

"It turns out I have something new to report, which is why I asked you both down here," TJ replied. "After we've discussed this, I would be happy to live up to the bargain and talk with you alone. How does that sound?"

The man grinned. "Fair enough. Thanks, Mr. Case."

"Fine. I'd like to introduce you to the director of the Community of Hope, Reverend Tom Nees."

Reverend Nees shook hands all around, said, "Why don't we troop back upstairs and get started?"

While Sandra went out to gather her crew, Nak walked over, greeted his boss with, "Do we still have jobs?"

"As of five o'clock this afternoon, nobody had told me anything differently," TJ replied.

Nak nodded, no expression. He looked over, said, "Nice to see you again, Mr. Hughes."

"Son, what say I use your shoulder to get back up those stairs. I believe I've just about worn this lady plum out."

"I think I need a neck brace," Anna agreed.

TJ listened to their slow clumping procession, waited until Sandra Hastings reappeared, greeted her crew, and walked them upstairs. "I hope it wasn't too difficult for you people to come over on such short notice."

"As a matter of fact," Sandra Hastings replied, "we'd just received a cancellation not twenty minutes before your message arrived. We were supposed to be downtown to interview the mayor about some questionable police matter, but it was put off until later tonight." She laughed. "I suppose you'd call that another of your miracles, right?"

"Why don't we wait until you hear what I have to say," TJ replied. "Then you can decide for yourself."

"If it's anything like your prayer meeting," Sandra Hastings replied, "I can't wait."

"I'm glad you enjoyed it," TJ told her.

"I don't know if *enjoy* is the right word," she said. "It certainly made me think, though. I've even found myself reading the Bible now and then."

"Just remember that as long as you don't commit yourself, you're walking along a razor's edge," TJ told her. "The only safe place in all the universe is within our Savior's arms. The longer you wait, the harder it will be to take that step."

"Amen," said a voice from behind them.

Sandra Hastings turned, said, "I didn't know you were a Christian, Mark."

The bearded cameraman gave TJ a very embarrassed glance. "That's pretty much the worst condemnation you could make, isn't it, Mr. Case?"

TJ did not try to minimize it. "We do have a responsibility to share the truth."

"Listen to the man, Sandy. You don't know how important a choice this is. When I think of how close I came to turning it down, it leaves me cold."

Sandra Hastings seemed quiet and troubled as she entered the office.

There was a brief period of small talk while the crew set up camera and lighting and mike; then Reverend Tom Nees made a short introduction to the Community of Hope, what they did, and the experiences they had in working with HUD.

He concluded with, "Yesterday morning I told Mr. Case about our difficulties. I don't know what he did, but today we received a telephone call to say that the funding has been approved. And not just for the original two projects, but for the one that was turned down, and for two more that I didn't even know were in the works."

"Wow," breathed the *Post* reporter, and was shushed by the camera crew.

"My sentiments exactly," Reverend Nees agreed. "Almost four million dollars for new low-income housing. I know the word has become so abused as to be almost empty of meaning, but this is a miracle in the truest sense of the word."

"Reverend, do you ever regret giving up the life you had to come down and work with the poor?" Sandra Hastings asked.

"Of course I do," Tom Nees replied. "In order to have these people trust me, I must live as they do. It is extremely difficult to watch my family endure that kind of poverty because of a calling I've had. Thankfully, my wife and daughter support me one hundred percent. But there are still times when I wish I could give them things, and I can't."

He gave the reporters a tired smile. "Then something like this happens. Or I see a child who came to us so abused and emotionally battered that her little face is molded into a permanent scowl, turn and hug one of our ladies, and laugh, and say that she loves her. Or I see a family who came to us absolutely broken in spirit and body and leave with the pride of having a good job and a new home of their own. And I know that I am right where I should be. There is not the slightest question in my mind. I *know* this is right."

There was a long, thoughtful silence, as TJ and Jeremy and Anna and Nak and Tom Nees watched the two reporters struggle with their own inner questions and doubts. Almost reluctantly they roused themselves, and asked TJ if he would trade places under the lights with Tom.

He did so, and with utter assurance made a compelling presentation. He described the talk he'd had with Senator Atterly, leaving out nothing but the man's name. He told them of the hunting done by the senator's assistant, and what he uncovered. He named the company, the Atlas Group. He described the change of attitude once pressure was brought to bear. And then he waited.

The atmosphere in the room had become electric. Sandra signalled to her crew, the lights were cut, and the *Post* reporter rested a weary hand.

"This is great stuff," the *Post* reporter said. "I don't suppose you could tell us which senator it was who gave you the scoop."

"That's not for me to say," TJ replied.

"I think we'll run this as a special," Sandra Hastings said, thinking out loud in her excitement. "This is fantastic. I'm going to hit the mayor with it tonight, ask his opinion."

The *Post* reporter perked up. "Yes—uh—I wanted to ask you about that."

"Tell you what," Sandra said to him. "If you'll promise to share your next HUD scoop with our television station, I'll let you tag along tonight."

"Done." The guy smiled. "Want it in blood?"

"Not in this room," Tom Nees said.

TJ listened to their antics, felt the Spirit grow within him. Why now, he wondered. Why not before the interview began? But the Presence grew until all else was secondary, until little else mattered.

Sandra Hastings turned back to him, asked, "Do you think we could have something from you as a sort of conclusion? You know, some opinion that I could run alongside what the mayor's got to say?"

"Of course," he replied, having been given the words.

The lights were turned back on, the camera focused, and Sandra Hastings asked him, "Mr. Case, as the person directly responsible for overcoming this difficult and long-standing roadblock, do you have any opinion as to the general outlook for housing our nation's poor?"

"We have arrived at a crossroads," TJ said, his voice needing no volume to put across its strength. "We must stop the impersonal, wholesale approach of public agencies' relief efforts by coupling government together with nonprofit organizations. Each need is specific. The only way to humanize the government's heavy-handed assistance is to make it a partnership with individual Christian charity."

Sandra Hastings objected, "Wouldn't this open relief efforts to enormous risks of abuse?"

"The abuse is already there," TJ replied. "It has always been there, and as the size of our government grows, so too will the magnitude of these abuses.

"Corruption will be found wherever there is a source of money as large as the government, and whenever man is ruled by greed rather than compassion. Our objective should be to set up guidelines that allow for relief to be given without strangling our ability to show compassion. We must stop making relief so faceless, and realize that money alone will not solve a person's problems. The spirit must be healed as well, and this the government can never do.

"We as a nation must stop handing over our responsibility to the government, then criticizing it for failing to do what it was never meant to achieve in the first place. Relief efforts are every Christian's responsibility. Not the churches, not the government, not some civic-minded organization allocated a budget and forgotten. Every single Christian has an obligation to his or her neighbor. Every neighbor. Regardless of race or income. Every neighbor."

Reverend Tom Nees quietly quoted the words of Christ, "He who does for the least of these, does for me."

TJ went on, "You cannot legislate hope. You cannot legislate mercy. Nor love. Nor compassion. This country, every individual, needs to reach beyond the limits of legislation. It needs to find a sense of compassionate caring. We must begin to live up to the Christian responsibility of helping one another. Only then will we see an answer to today's crises."

TWENTY

For Norman Greenbaum, the only difference between Saturday and the other days of the week was that he tried to hold himself to an eight-hour day. Sometimes he even succeeded. He was busy at his desk, reveling in the relative calm, when his phone rang.

"Norman." President Nichols did not need to identify himself. "Has Case been notified of his, ah, departure?"

"No, sir," Greenbaum replied, wondering why everything to do with this Case fellow seemed to go wrong for him. "I went over to his office as soon as it was typed up. I wanted to give it to him personally. But he'd already left for the day."

"Did you leave it there?"

"No, sir, I brought it back." In truth, Greenbaum had found himself more than a little shook up by the experience. Why, he could not explain. Even his wife had noticed and commented on it, but he shrugged it off. The whole thing, now that it was over, seemed impossible. But just the same, he'd been very glad not to find Case there. "I was going to give it to him first thing Monday, but I could drive it over to his home tonight, or call him, if you like."

"No." The President half-sighed the word, went on reluctantly. "I'm going to ask you to hold off for a day or so." He was silent a moment. "My wife, did you know she's been going to his prayer meetings?"

Greenbaum gave a silent groan, said, "No, sir, I wasn't aware of that."

"Neither was I. But it seems that one of her staff had been getting so excited about it that last week my wife decided to go herself. Now she's after me to go." The President hesitated, said, "She's been very insistent, Norman. You know what she can be like when she gets her teeth into something."

"Yes, sir, I certainly do." The First Lady was generally a discreet and reserved woman. But if she decided to press an issue she could be an absolute lioness. Greenbaum decided the President must have been catching it hard.

"So just hold off for a day, will you? I'll be going on Monday, and once I've had a chance to see this thing for myself, we'll see to our housecleaning. That clear?"

"Yes, sir, Mr. President, I understand perfectly."

"Good then. Oh, and Norman, don't mention this change of plans to Edwards, will you? I'd just as soon keep this postponement between us."

□   □   □

Congressman John Silverwood was not at all pleased. The urgent summons from Senator Erskins had wrecked his evening's plans with Sally. The next day, Sunday, was her birthday. To celebrate, he had paid a scalper a hundred bucks a seat for tickets to "Phantom of the Opera." He glanced at his watch for the tenth time in perhaps five minutes, and hoped they would finish up in time for him to make the second act.

It was very strange to see Mr. Shermann sitting in Ted Robinson's dimly lit hotel suite still wearing his sunglasses. No matter how often he saw them, Silverwood would never get used to those two-tone shades. The dried-up face, or what he could see of it, was as emotionless as ever, and the sticklike body utterly still. That could not be said for the other two persons in the room.

Ted Robinson ground out one cigarette, fished the pack out of his shirt pocket, lit another. The man's normally urbane appearance had vanished. His collar was undone, his tie at half-mast, his hair in disarray, his eyes very worried. Silverwood could not recall ever having seen him like this, not even at the close of a long and exhausting campaign.

Senator Erskins stopped his nervous pacing as the television special came to a close. He walked over and switched off the set. "All right,

Tony. We've seen the damage. Let's start talking about how we can repair it."

Silverwood dropped the *Washington Post* to his lap. He had already read the piece that morning; he was holding it simply to have something in his hands. He still did not understand what all the fuss was about. Compared to some scandals, this seemed a very minor incident with limited repercussions. And besides the fact that it revolved around Case, he could not really understand why he needed to be there. He glanced at his watch again, decided if they were going to try to hang Case around his neck, he was going to let them have it.

"Let's just wait for the drinks to arrive, shall we? Ah, here they are." Playing host in Robinson's suite, Shermann stood and opened the door to admit the waiter and his trolley. Shermann declined the man's offer to serve the drinks, tipped him, and ushered him out.

"Why don't we just allow everyone to serve himself?" Shermann gave a little wave in invitation. "Senator?"

Silverwood waited until Erskins was finished, then joined Robinson at the trolley. "Pour me a scotch, will you?"

His back to the room, Ted said softly, "I thought I told you not to get involved with this Shermann guy."

"I'm not." Silverwood dropped a couple of ice cubes in his drink. "What's he got on you anyway, Ted?"

Ted Robinson ignored the question, said flatly, "You accepted his offer, so you're involved." He rattled his ice, sipped, said, "Brother, you don't have any idea how deep you're in, do you? No idea at all."

"What's that supposed to mean?" Silverwood asked, but Robinson had already turned toward the room.

"It seems we have a very serious problem, gentlemen," Shermann began, once everyone was seated. "One which requires an instant response."

"Take that Case guy out back and shoot him," Senator Erskins growled.

"My sentiments exactly," Shermann agreed. "Unfortunately, my clients have requested that we find a different solution."

What does this guy mean by "we," Silverwood thought. All he said was, "Issue a denial."

"Oh, wise up, John!" Senator Erskins snapped.

"Please, Senator," Shermann said, and to Silverwood, "I have to admit, Congressman, that I too wondered what all the fuss was about. But you see, this Mr. Case has gone so far as to actually name the Atlas Group."

"Sue him," Silverwood said. "Force him to retract it."

"That would solve nothing, I'm afraid. It might in fact have the exact opposite effect from the one desired. If this Mr. Case refuses to bow to our pressure—"

"He'll refuse, you mark my words," Senator Erskins broke in. "These religious extremists are all the same. He'd call himself a martyr and eat it with a spoon."

"I tend to agree," Shermann said. "If that happened, whether or not we went to court, we would be tarred as guilty in the eyes of the public."

There was that "we" again. It grated on Silverwood's nerves to be classed as part of this group. "So?"

"Indeed, Congressman. So what? Most corporations have suffered through bouts of bad publicity at one time or another and survived. Unfortunately, Atlas is at present involved in several large deals. All of them are entering extremely sensitive points in their negotiations. Because of this, they require a direct, unequivocal, public declaration of their total innocence."

Here it comes, Silverwood decided. The windup's finished. Time for the pitch.

"We must therefore request, Congressman, that you go before Monday's committee hearing and declare that there is no evidence whatsoever of Atlas having ever committed any wrongdoing."

Silverwood laughed, not believing what he'd heard. "You're joking."

"On the contrary, Congressman, I'm utterly serious."

"Then you're mad."

"That may well be," Shermann replied, as dry and toneless as ever. "But it does not alter the nature of my request. Or the urgency."

"Calm down, John," Senator Erskins said. "Just think of it as part of the deal."

"I agreed to hold off during the probe." Silverwood almost shouted the words. "That's it. Nothing more."

"The deal's changed, John," Senator Erskins told him.

"They can do it. They can demand this, John." Ted Robinson sounded very tired. "They can and they will."

"Maybe from you," Silverwood said, and got to his feet. He pointed an angry finger at Shermann, said, "Just don't try it on me. Do, and I'll flay those suckers alive." He looked at Erskins, said, "Good evening, Senator."

"Sit down, John."

"Yes, do sit down, Congressman," Shermann agreed. "This is certainly a lot of fuss over nothing."

"Count me out," Silverwood replied, shrugging on his coat, resigning himself to the loss of the promised Ways and Means slot he so coveted.

He was almost to the door when Senator Erskins said, "Maybe you ought to stick around long enough to hear what happens if you don't do it, John."

Silverwood hesitated, his hand on the doorknob. Reluctantly he turned halfway around, said, "I'm listening."

"I so hoped this wouldn't be necessary, Congressman," Shermann said in his rasping voice. "I do so hate threats."

"You've got just about five seconds left," Silverwood told him.

"Very well then. If you insist. I'm sorry to have to inform you, Congressman, that the Republican party would drop its support of you entirely."

That swung him around. He faced Ted Robinson.

"It's true, John," Robinson said, his voice heavy. "And when you hear the rest you'll see there's not a thing you can do about it. Not a thing."

"This is a team effort," Senator Erskins said. "If we can't count on you in a pinch, we don't want to count on you at all."

"You'd give the district back to the Democrats over some piddling thing like this?" Silverwood nearly shouted, and thought to himself, they're bluffing. I'd go straight to the press with this and have these guys roasted alive. But it wasn't time to say that. Not quite. Let them shoot their best shot first.

"It's bigger than you think, son," Senator Erskins replied. "A lot bigger. You wouldn't believe how much Atlas supports the party, one way or another."

"I believe there is also a very promising young man the party is grooming from your district," Shermann said. "What was his name again, Mr. Robinson?"

"Arnold."

"Ah yes, that's right. Robert Arnold. The seat might not be lost after all."

"That's a risk we're prepared to take," Senator Erskins said.

"There's more, I'm afraid," Shermann went on. "Some rather compromising pictures of you and a most attractive young lady would be passed on to your local newspapers and television stations back in North Carolina. I've not seen them, of course, but I understand them to be rather—shall we say, explicit."

"This isn't happening," Silverwood whispered.

"Yes it is, son," Senator Erskins said. "And you've brought it on yourself."

In his mind's eye Silverwood watched his last defense crumble. The party would simply announce that they were dropping him because of improper behavior. Period. With the pictures it would not matter a bit what he said. No one would believe him.

"Your wife contacted a Raleigh divorce lawyer last week," Shermann went on. "I don't suppose you were aware of that, were you? No. Pity I had to be the bearer of such bad tidings. In any case, I feel sure she would bring action against you with this attractive young lady named as co-defendant."

Silverwood looked from face to face, searching in desperation. There was no hope, no hope. And the only alternative was to give up what he had taken a lifetime to achieve.

"Why don't you take your coat off and sit back down, son." Senator Erskins' mood was expansive now that the deal was done. "We need to go over the details, make sure you've got everything straight."

"Yes, please be so kind as to give us a few more minutes of your time, Congressman," Shermann agreed. "We certainly don't want to make an error on anything this big."

─┤ TWENTY-ONE ├─

That Sunday after the service, TJ walked up to where the reverend stood mopping his brow with a shaky hand, said quietly, "That was one of the finest sermons I've ever heard."

Reverend Wilkins searched TJ's face with a hard gaze before speaking. His voice rasped and grated as he replied, "Mighty kind of you to say so, Brother Case."

Jeremy was there beside him. "That story you told about the revival really hit home."

"I thought so too," TJ agreed.

Getting on toward the end of the sermon, Reverend Wilkins had been showing the strain. His face had streamed rivulets of sweat, his features starkly etched by his battle for the Lord.

"We had an actor fellow come to our last revival," Reverend Wilkins had told them. "Right famous fellow, lotsa folks've seen him on TV. Yeah. Stood up there for the benediction, gave us all the Twenty-third Psalm. Did a fine job, real nice, rolled out the words, had the people all clapping and standing and calling him on. Real nice.

"Later on, old Reverend Matthers stood up to recite the same text about our Good Shepherd. You older folks remember him, he used to preach here from time to time. Brought a lot of people to their senses, that old man did. Must be over ninety now, gettin' real shaky. Couldn't barely stand without a sister there to hold him up. Voice was all quiverin', cracked over some of the words, so weak you could barely hear him at the back of the room. Wasn't no shoutin' and clappin' for the reverend. Nossir. People were cryin' too hard to say anythin'."

Reverend Wilkins stared out over the congregation. His gaze erased away pretense, dug down deep to the heart, called people to attention. "Know what the difference was between those two men? Well, I'll tell you."

He paused, narrowed his eyes, said, "That actor fellow knew the words. But that old Reverend Matthers, now, he knew the Shepherd."

The reverend gave them a moment to let the words sink in, went on. "Lot of people out there livin' a lie, thinkin' they're close to the Lord because their lives on the outside are in order. Don't want to think what it's gonna be like when they face their Lord. All the lies gonna be stripped away. Yessir. He's gonna look at their hearts, see the emptiness, and there ain't gonna be no way for them to escape. They'll squirm and plead and point at all them holy acts, but their Lord's gonna know. Yeah. He's gonna *know*."

The silence was alive. The congregation held their breath. Reverend Wilkins kneaded the podium with work-worn hands, strained with a force that drew the tendons of his neck out like cables. He sought to physically drag them to the truth.

"Search your hearts," he said, his voice hoarse with the desire of wanting it for them with all his might. "Search your minds. Find the door. Open it. Let the Lord come in."

TJ sought some way to convey the feeling he had come out with, decided on, "They just keep getting better."

"Ain't concerned with better," the reverend rasped. "I'm concerned with bringin' people to the Lord."

Jeremy shook his head ever so slightly. "Seems to me all you can do is invite 'em, Reverend. Whether they decide to enter and sup with our Lord is up to them."

The reverend gave him a long gaze, said, "There's a lot of truth in your words, Mr. Hughes. You speak like one who truly knows our Lord."

Jeremy smiled at that. "Well, sir, I'm more like somebody who's just been lookin' awful hard."

The reverend turned back to TJ, said, "Saw the article in yesterday's paper. Saw you on the TV last night too. Yessir, real fine work you're doin', Brother Case. That all part of your vision?"

"In a way," TJ replied.

"Real fine work. Lotsa people out there in need, don't have no way of havin' their voices heard. Real important they have somebody who can point out their hardships." He mopped his brow once more, said, "We were supposed to have a lay preacher speak to the church tonight, but the man's sick. How'd you like to do it?"

TJ did not even have to think. The answer was there waiting for him. "I'd be honored," he replied. "I'd like Jeremy here to introduce me and make the opening remarks."

"You come awful close to remindin' me of a danged fool," Jeremy told him.

TJ turned to him, eyes full of calm power. "You can't argue with this, Jem."

"I can't, huh?"

"No, you can't. You can turn away from it, you can refuse it, but the invitation hasn't come from me. Now before you say anything else, you just stand there a moment and think it over."

□   □   □

Nervously Jeremy fiddled with the knot in his tie, then clenched the sides of the podium with a force that bunched his shoulders and turned his knuckles white. He lowered his head, closed his eyes, and let the shock of grayish-blond hair hide his face from view. The atmosphere was not hostile, simply reserved. Thoughts remained carefully hidden behind the caution of generations.

He raised up to the sea of dark faces, the watchful eyes, brushed the hair from his forehead, and said quietly, "I don't have much education, and I don't have the fire of your preacher here. I'm just a lowly man who made good by the grace of God, and I've tried to live as I think the Lord's wanted me to. Most times I'm not sure of what He wants. I search the Scriptures like a drownin' man grabs for a lifeline, hopin' I'll have the sense to understand His message. He's never spoken to me outright, like He did to my brother here. When I wonder about His silence, I hope it's on account of Him feelin' like I'm doin' about the best job I can."

"Amen," someone called out from the back, startling Jeremy so that he stopped, squinted, and grinned.

"Now that's about the nicest thing anybody's said to me in a long while," he said, and the congregation blessed him with a chuckle.

"I've studied the Bible pretty much all my life. Most days it seems like I've only scratched the surface. Sometimes I look at it and feel like I'm gropin' through a fog so deep I can scarcely find my hand in front of my face. Other times, like this mornin', I feel like the Lord is leanin' over my shoulder, readin' along with me. I get chills runnin' up and down my spine from the power of His message. He's right there with me, sayin', I wrote this down for you, Jeremy. I know you're a sinner, and I forgive you."

"Tell it, brother," somebody said.

"This mornin' I read how Jesus said that if a man is acclaimed here on earth, he's *had* his reward. There's nothin' more for him. He may enter heaven, yeah, but he'll do it with empty pockets and holes in his shoes. But those people who've stood firm through trial and tribulation, why, they're gonna know a wealth that's eternal. And the ones who've learned true humility, they'll sit themselves down in the back row at the holy feast, only to have our Lord and Savior take them by the hand and lead them right up front."

Catherine stood up from her place down front, turned to the congregation, pointed to Jeremy said, "Y'all just *listen* to the man!"

"I want to tell you somethin' I know for a fact," Jeremy went on after a moment. "After slippin' through those pearly gates, I'm gonna be sittin' way back in the far right-hand corner, kinda scrunched up beside a pillar.

"I'm barely gonna be able to make out our Lord up there in the distance. I'll stand up on my chair and shade my eyes and look real hard, and you know what I'm gonna see? Up there in the distance, in all those high seats of honor, know what I'm gonna find? Seated right there next to our Lord are gonna be all those downtrodden people of the world, all the simple souls, all the brothers and sisters who suffered through life because of the pride and selfishness of others."

An expectant hush fell upon the crowd. Every eye was on this gangly white man with his rawboned face and oversized hands. They sat and they waited, and for a moment the barriers were forgotten.

"So when you're up there in His presence, surrounded by His glory for all eternity, I want you to do somethin'."

Jeremy turned slightly so he could see where TJ was seated, and said quietly, "Remember me."

☐　☐　☐

After TJ's portion of the service, Reverend Wilson came up to Jeremy with an outstretched hand. "That was fine what you said up there, Mr. Hughes. Real fine."

"Never did feel like I could talk in front of folks," Jeremy replied.

"No, no, you did just fine." The reverend fastened on him with a keen eye. "You just gotta remember, sir, that black folks is just as sinful as whites. Color don't make no difference far as Satan's concerned. He'll hit us where we're weakest, and black folks've got just as many weaknesses as whites."

"I kinda doubt that," Jeremy replied.

The reverend gave him an ancient look, said, "You just take my word for it, Mr. Hughes. We's all sinners in God's eyes. Every one of us. All are in need of His saving grace. None of us is worthy. Nossir. Not one."

⊣| TWENTY-TWO |⊢

Monday morning found TJ Case marveling that he still had a job. He walked through the halls with the sensation of knowing the building, yet somehow seeing it as though for the first time. He smiled greetings to many, found a number smiling back, found others who absolutely refused to even look his way. He didn't mind. He really didn't. It was all just the ways of the world.

He was mildly surprised to find two gentlemen with earpieces stationed outside the door to the auditorium. He nodded a greeting, got stone-cold stares in return. He smothered an illogical smile and entered the room.

It was packed. There was no other word for it. Every seat was taken, and people lined the dual stairways, sitting so close together that he had to carefully pick his way down.

Bella was there at the podium. "Have I got a surprise for you."

"Good morning, Bella." He smiled at the excitement in her eyes, wished there was some way to tell her of the change he had witnessed in her. Go look in the mirror, he wanted to say. See the miraculous power of your Lord.

"You notice the two guys with hearing aids and bulges under their coats when you came in? Guess who they're here for." She glanced up behind him, said, "Uh oh. Too late. Here they come."

TJ turned, glanced up, felt himself freeze. One of the men with the earpiece was clearing a way down the stairs. Behind him walked the President and his wife.

People began turning, saw who it was, and raggedly the room came to its feet. A silent hush fell upon all who were there. Two people in the first row hastily moved out of the way and offered up their seats. It was the only time the President looked up, the only time he smiled.

While everyone was sitting down, TJ knew the Lord was with him, and his stomach began to relax. It was hard not to criticize himself for doubting, for being so afraid, for wishing he were elsewhere. The Spirit filled him with His gentle grace, and he realized a comforting sense of forgiveness for his own earthly concerns.

He opened his Bible, allowing the Spirit to direct him to the passages. He felt the Holy Spirit's presence grow until it seemed as though he were lit up like a mighty beacon. He wished the room a good morning, said, "Our first reading this morning comes from the thirty-fourth chapter of Ezekiel, taken from verses two through ten. Because this is so long, I am going to select certain segments. I would therefore ask that you all just listen to me this morning, then read the entire section later at your leisure.

> " 'This is what the Sovereign Lord says: Woe to the shepherds of Israel who only take care of themselves! Should not shepherds take care of the flock? You have not strengthened the weak or healed the sick or bound up the injured. You have not brought back the strays or searched for the lost. So they were scattered because there was no shepherd, and when they were scattered they became food for all the wild animals.
>
> " 'Therefore, you shepherds, hear the word of the Lord: As surely as I live, declares the Sovereign Lord, because my flock lacks a shepherd and so has been plundered and has become food for all the wild animals, and because my shepherds did not search for my flock but cared for themselves rather than for my flock, therefore, O shepherds, hear the word of the Lord. I am against the shepherds and will hold them accountable for my flock.' "

TJ turned the pages, understanding perfectly what was to be said, and why. "For each of us there is a position here on earth, a responsibility that the Lord in His wisdom has given us. What we do with this service, how we love our fellowman and serve our Lord, will determine our reward in the hereafter."

He looked down, said, "The second reading comes from the sixteenth chapter of Luke, verses ten through twelve:

> " 'Whoever can be trusted with very little can also be trusted with

much, and whoever is dishonest with very little will also be dishonest with much. So if you have not been trustworthy in handling worldly wealth, who will trust you with true riches? And if you have not been trustworthy with someone else's property, who will give you property of your own?' "

"It is so very important," TJ went on, "for us to recognize that all talents, all positions, all wealth, all fame—all are gifts from our Lord. We have been entrusted with them so that we might learn the lessons inherent in all such things—honesty, neighborly love, trust in our Lord's guidance, concern for that which is not of this world."

He bent his head once again, said, "Our final reading comes from the second chapter of Colossians, verses six through nine:

> "So then, just as you received Christ Jesus as Lord, continue to live in him, rooted and built up in him, strengthened in the faith as you were taught, and overflowing with thankfulness.
> "See to it that no one takes you captive through hollow and deceptive philosophy, which depends on human tradition and the basic principles of this world rather than on Christ. For in Christ all the fullness of the Deity lives in bodily form, and you have been given fullness in Christ, who is head over every power and authority."

"It is so glorious to serve the Lord," he said, wishing words weren't so limiting in sharing with them that which filled his being. "It is so absolutely wonderful. The gift of His presence makes all things complete. Nothing of this world can compare. We spend our lives running from desire to desire, ambition to ambition, forever fleeing from that inner emptiness, the aching void that we are terrified of facing and admitting that it really is there. We carry the emptiness with us, ever seeking to fill it with the trinkets of this world, and never knowing peace.

"Why? Because the peace can come to us in only one way. Faith in our Lord Jesus Christ. That is the *only* way. There is *no* alternative. In accepting Him as our Lord and Savior, we open our hearts to His glorious love. His eternal light fills the emptiness, and our hunger is stilled. And we see that there is no other way to be filled except through Him."

TJ bowed his head, said, "Let us pray.

"Oh, Lord, Heavenly Father, we thank you for this day. We thank you for your glorious gift of service, this means by which we add depth and value to our lives. We give, and in giving, we receive.

"Help us, O Father, to understand through experience what it means to have you lead our lives. Fill us with your presence, Lord. Fill us with your Spirit."

There was a sensation of reaching out, as though all were drawn together in the presence of the Lord. TJ stopped, so full of the love that swept out across the room that he could not speak. In that flood of divine love, he sensed a oneness with all who prayed with him.

"All who believe are one, part of the body of Christ. Help us to lay our fears and our barriers at your feet, and to recognize this oneness for ourselves. Oneness with each other, oneness with you. Saved for all eternity by the grace of your Son, Jesus Christ, in whose name we pray. Amen."

When all had lifted their eyes and sat in the silence that had become the usual ending for these sessions, TJ quoted the final passage of Jude from memory:

> "To him who is able to keep you from falling and to present you before his glorious presence without fault and with great joy—to the only God our Savior be glory, majesty, power and authority, through Jesus Christ our Lord, before all ages, now and forevermore! Amen."

□ □ □

Congressman John Silverwood entered the hotel suite, and flinched as Senator Erskins came swooping down upon him.

"Hey, it's our man of the hour!" He clapped Silverwood on the back, led him into the room. "Yessir, the man came through for us, just like I said he would."

Mr. Shermann eased himself to his feet, walked over, offered Silverwood his feather-light hand. "You have done us all a very great service, Congressman. I am in your debt."

"You hear that?" Senator Erskins' own hand seemed to weigh a ton as it rested on his shoulder. "Washington's senior power broker is in your debt. Son, you don't know how many people wish all their lives they could stand in your shoes."

"Your speech at the hearing was excellent, Congressman." Mr. Shermann indicated the trolley. "Would you care for a victory drink?"

"The man drinks Scotch on the rocks, water on the side." Senator Erskins was positively beaming. "Yessir, we all sat right here and watched it live. I tell you, son, I couldn't have done it better myself. Hey, Ted?"

Ted Robinson did not rise from his seat. He gave Silverwood a grim look, said, "No, it was exactly what you wanted."

"What *we* wanted," Senator Erskins corrected. "Aw, don't mind Ted, son. He's had a tough week, flying up here twice and keeping the home fires burning over the telephone. C'm on, sit down right here, let me get you your drink."

"I spoke to our clients, Congressman," Mr. Shermann said tonelessly. "They were delighted as well. They asked me to extend to you their heartfelt thanks, and to inform you that they would be backing your next campaign very heavily."

"In the strictest confidentiality, hey, Tony?" Senator Erskins walked over, set down the drink, said, "There you are, son, drink up."

"Oh my, yes," Mr. Shermann replied. "They are true professionals at the art of confidentiality. You can count on their support in whatever way necessary, Congressman, but there will be no record of this assistance. None whatsoever."

"They know and we know and they know we know," Senator Erskins said. "That's all that counts."

Congressman Silverwood sat woodenly, sipping at a drink he did not taste, turning and looking at each of the people in turn, taking in nothing.

It had been the hardest afternoon of his entire life. Nothing in memory could approach what he had just gone through. As he had sat and spoken into the microphone, saying those hated words that had cost him two totally sleepless nights, he had felt as though something inside had been torn apart.

Afterwards, as he was sitting there trying to keep his expression from folding while the television cameras were still focused on him, he saw that only three of the committee members offered any criticism of his action. Most seemed anxious to absolve the Atlas Group of any possible wrongdoing. The motion to dismiss them from further questioning passed eleven votes to three.

He had waited for the entire chamber to empty before leaving his seat. He had tried to scribble notes, to show that something urgent occupied his attention, but even the pretense was beyond him. He had sat and stared at the empty page, and felt as though blood were dripping from his forehead.

Now he listened, maintaining the outer poise and nodding in time to the voices, but all he could truly hear was the emptiness rattling around inside him. It was a wound so deep he honestly doubted if it would ever heal.

Mr. Shermann was saying, "I'm afraid the situation with this Mr. Case has not ended as we hoped. It seems that he has wormed his way so deeply into the White House power structure that even these severe breaches in confidence are going to be overlooked."

"Is Atlas still concerned about him?" Senator Erskins was suddenly very serious.

"Not only Atlas, I'm afraid. It seems that he has aroused the concerns of many of my clients. Very powerful clients, I hasten to add."

"Well," Senator Erskins paused to glance Silverwood's direction. "Does this mean that some other action needs to be taken?"

Silverwood felt himself shrivel inside. Not again, he said silently. I just can't take any more. Please. Don't ask me to do it. Whatever it is, let somebody else take over.

"No," Mr. Shermann replied, adjusting his glasses with a delicate touch. "I am pleased to say that this particular matter has been taken entirely out of our hands."

That surprised the senator. "What's that supposed to mean?"

"I'm sure I don't know, Senator. The gentlemen concerned have decided not to take me into their confidence." Mr. Shermann made a vague gesture, concluded, "In all frankness, perhaps it is better this way. Some things it is better just not to know, don't you agree?"

□   □   □

Catherine and TJ had drawn up their chairs close to the fireplace after dinner, and Jeremy was down on his knees using one of the old-fashioned corn poppers. He claimed it was the only way to eat real popcorn. When it was done, TJ tasted it, declared the man a genius. The only time he'd tried to do it, TJ said, he'd melted the pot. Yeah, well, we all got our little gifts, Jeremy replied, settling himself down. Ain't that right?

Catherine took a handful of popcorn, said, "You know what? I'd love to know what happened to those two poor fools, what were their names?"

"Preacher Jones and Father Coughlin," TJ said. "But be careful who you go calling a fool."

"Doggone straight," Jeremy said. "Personally speakin', I can look back over a long life of makin' mistakes."

"Oh, you know what I mean," Catherine chuckled. "I found myself telling the children the story yesterday. And now I want to hear how it ends."

Jeremy made an astonished face. "You been stealin' my stories?"

She reached over, patted his knee, said, "Just borrowing them, Jem. Just borrowing them for a while. Now why don't you tell us what happened."

"Well, y'all know the Father's just received his kinda original baptism, right? And old Preacher Jones, he's still stuck in the hospital, just like Saint Peter said he'd be. So the next day, he wakes up from his nap and finds a round, fifty-year-old cherub in a monkey suit sitting beside his bed. He shakes his head clear, and realizes he's looking at a Catholic priest.

"The priest's wearin' one of those little red caps perched on top of his round head. He's got on the dog collar, the vest with all those little cloth buttons, the watch chain with the gold cross bouncing on his belly, the rosary in his pudgy fingers, the works.

"He gives Preacher Jones a little smile that pushes out his fat red cheeks and says, 'Good afternoon, Mr. Jones. I do so hope you're feelin' better after your rest. My name is Archbishop Claven. I came down just as soon as I heard you wanted to speak to a man of the church.'

"The reverend starts to jump all over the man. Then he remembers Saint Peter and bites down real hard on his tongue. He takes a coupla deep breaths, says in a real low trembly voice, 'Wanna convert.'

"The archbishop positively beams. He reaches into his pocket, brings out a little black notebook and one a' those square silver pencils, and says out loud real slow as he writes, 'Mister Jones wants to convert.'

" 'And what, may I ask, is the reason for this desire to convert, Mr. Jones?'

"He doesn't say anything but, 'Had a vision.' Real short and sharp-like. Kinda eats up the words in embarrassment.

"The archbishop opens his eyes real wide at the news. 'A vision,' he says, and smiles that little grin one more time. 'Well, now, isn't that nice. And just what kind of vision did you have, Mr. Jones?'

" 'Oh, just your ordinary everyday vision,' Preacher Jones replies, squirmin' around a little at the memory.

"So the little archbishop bends over his notebook once more, and speaks the words out as he writes, 'Mister Jones had an ordinary vision.'

"Now his sayin' his vision was ordinary and havin' somebody else call it ordinary are two very different balls of wax. Especially when that somebody is a total stranger you don't care for in any particular fashion. So Preacher Jones finds himself gettin' a little hot and bothered.

" 'Just look here, now,' he says, speaking loud for the first time. 'Who do you plan on showin' that stuff to you're writing down there?'

" 'Oh, Mr. Jones, we're going to give this the widest publicity we possibly can.' The archbishop does everything but jump up and down in his seat. 'We'll send it to Rome, and we'll read it out in all the churches right across the nation, and we'll tell all the little children about it down in Central America. Yessir, Mr. Jones, don't you worry about this for a minute. This is wonderful news, how a Baptist minister has seen the light and decided to convert to the One True Church.' You can tell that the archbishop kinda capitalizes those last three words in his mind as he speaks.

"I'd like to tell you what Preacher Jones has to say about that, but I can't. I just can't. First of all, I'm not all that sure I can remember the exact order, on account of the preacher speakin' kinda rapid-like. And second, it'd prob'bly give you third-degree burns on your ears. Lemme just say that old Preacher Jones sits up straight as an arrow and lets the archbishop have both barrels right square in the face. That poor fellow does a flip and a roll off the back of his chair, runs across the floor, and claws at the door before he finds the handle. It takes him a while to get the door open, see, on account of him not wantin' to take his eyes off old Preacher Jones. Probably afraid if he does the man's gonna jump outta bed and eat him, bones and all.

" 'Course, now, soon as the archbishop's gone and the reverend has his heartbeat down below two hundred, he's awful sorry for what he's done. These two tears trickle down his face, and he kinda pleads with the ceiling real hard. Just one more chance, he says, gimme one more chance, Peter, I'll do better next time. Please. Only next time don't make him so fat and full of hisself, okay?

"You know, old Preacher Jones is so wore out by all that shoutin' that he just falls asleep, skips dinner, and sleeps right through the night. The next mornin' he wakes up, and dang if there's not *another* priest waitin' for him to open his eyes. This one's different, though. Real different. Preacher Jones decides this is about the biggest man he's seen in all his born days.

"Yessir, that fellow sittin' there waitin' for him to wake up is about six feet nine, and musta weighed in at close on two hundred and seventy-five pounds. All of it solid muscle, too. Not a speck of fat on him. Built like an upside-down pyramid, with this jaw on him that'd been just right for Samson to take hold of and mow down the enemy. Big fellow. Real big. And he ain't wearin' no smile, neither.

" 'Hear you gave the archbishop a right hard time yesterday,' that big fellow says, and it sounds like a bear's growlin' deep down inside some cave.

"Preacher Jones kinda scrambles upright and does that little yammer people make when they been shocked awake, you know, kinda, 'Hamayamahamaha.'

" 'My name's Father Prentiss,' that big fellow rumbles. 'I've come down here to take Father Coughlin's place.' Then he leans real close to the bed, gives Preacher Jones a look that freezes the man up solid, and growls, 'You can think of me as the clean-up squad.'

"The father leans back, and you can hear that poor little hospital chair moan like its back is breakin', which it probably is. 'I just finished seminary last month,' the man says. 'Thought I was going down to South America to help in one of the new missions. Then I got this call to come down here. Didn't have to think much about why.'

"The father leans forward and brings his snarl another inch closer to poor Preacher Jones and says, 'Now, why don't you tell me the real reason why you want to convert? And don't try any guff on me.'

"Well, sir, poor old Preacher Jones knows he's lookin' his last chance right square in the face. And he knows if he don't talk real quick-like this fella's probably gonna help him on his way back to where Peter's waitin' for him. So he tells him. Yep. Tells him the whole thing. All about dyin' and goin' to heaven and meetin' Peter and what Peter said and what Coughlin did and just everythin'.

" 'Bout halfway through the reverend's story, that old boy leans back in his chair and commences to chuckle. The chuckle gives way to a laugh every now and then, and 'fore long the laugh is pretty much constant. Then a nurse comes by and tells him the hospital was in a quiet zone and a surgeon down in the basement had just asked if World War Three had started up. So Father Prentiss tones it down pretty much, but he's still chucklin' and slappin' his knee and wipin' his eyes when Preacher Jones finishes up.

"When the father finally gets a hold on hisself, he asks the reverend, 'So what's he like, Saint Peter?'

"The preacher doesn't quite know what to make of that, seein' as how it ain't nothin' like what he thought he'd hear. So he stammers around and says, 'Oh, 'bout what you'd expect. Old guy, long beard, white robe, big book, that kinda thing.'

"The big fellow chuckles a little more, says, 'You sure got yourself in a fix, haven't you?'

"Preacher Jones realizes right then and there that the father believes him. And mixed in with his shame at bein' stuck in a tight place is a whole lotta relief. 'Yeah,' he says. 'Guess I have.'

" 'Seems to me like old Peter mighta had *two* reasons for sendin' you back,' Father Prentiss rumbles. 'One reason for you and a second reason for me.'

"Preacher Jones ain't real sure he understands what the father's goin' on about, but he didn't feel like he was in a position to be questionin' the man, if you see what I mean. So he just sat there, real quiet-like, and waited.

"The father thought a while, and said, 'Tell you what I'm gonna do. I'm gonna sit right here and I'm gonna tell you 'bout the church. I studied the history of the church a lot, it's a hobby of mine. And I'm gonna try and show you how it got to where it is today. How does that sound?'

"Preacher Jones ain't all that sure he wants to hear all about church history, but it's kinda hard to see himself arguin' with a fellow that big, so he says, 'Yeah, that'd be just swell.'

"So right then and there Father Prentiss commences to talk. And he talks for three solid days. I'm not jokin' nor jestin'. Three days the father sits there and talks to Preacher Jones. He's there when the reverend wakes up in the mornin' and he talks until the reverend falls asleep at night. And what's more, the preacher listens.

"On the first day Father Prentiss talks about Paul's death and the early church in Rome and the Catacombs and the lions in the arena. By suppertime he's just gotten into the conversion of Constantine, and how the church became an official body not long after.

"The next day they march through close on a thousand years, right through the Dark Ages and the Holy Roman Empire, on to the Medieval fiefdoms and past Martin Luther and the bloody Reformation Wars. And then on day three Father Prentiss finishes up with the past three hundred years before lunch, and spends the rest of the day talkin' 'bout the church of today.

"Like I said, Preacher Jones stays with him right the way through. And despite himself, the more he hears, the more interested he gets in what the father's sayin'.

"Then Preacher Jones commences to rememberin' some of the things he's said and done before he got sick. And he wonders if maybe somewhere along the line he shoulda spent a little more time studyin' before pronouncin' judgment on the Catholics.

"Not that he feels much different, mind you. He still believes the church's wrong about a lot of things. But what amazes the reverend most is that he seems to agree with a lot of what the father says. But he's still a Catholic. And a priest. And the more he listens to the fellow talk, the more convinced Preacher Jones is becomin' that the man's a truly devout Christian as well. And this surprises the preacher somethin' powerful.

"By that third afternoon the father'd gotten' kinda hoarse, but he's still pushin' on. And toward the evening he starts talkin' 'bout himself.

" 'I don't agree with a lot of what goes on inside the church,' the father says. 'Some things I hope someday I'll be able to change, but most of it I know I'll just have to swallow and accept. And it don't bother me all that much, I gotta say. It really don't.

" 'See, I figure the earthly church is kinda like clothes on the body of our Lord Jesus Christ. A lot of these criticisms I hear bandied about nowadays between churches is about like condemnin' somebody on account of him gettin' the buttons done up wrong on his shirt. People aren't seein' to the heart of the matter, far as I'm concerned.

" 'The real question is, does this particular church help this particular person come closer to knowin' Jesus Christ in his mind and heart? There ain't another thing in the whole wide world that makes any difference. If this person needs a fancy church with all them pictures and candles and stuff, fine. Yeah, and maybe that church makes a lotta mistakes in the way they worship our Lord. A *lot* of them. All right, I'm not saying they don't. But do they recognize Jesus Christ as Lord? Do they understand what the Trinity is and do they teach it? And do they help each individual to grow closer to the Heavenly Father?

" 'That's what's important for me. That's why I'm a priest. Not because I like all the fancy clothes and the ritual and that stuff. I could take it or leave it. That's kinda why I figured I'd be heading for some little mission in the Amazon or someplace, 'cause I really don't care whether all that stuff is there or not. But *some* people do. Why don't matter. Not to me, anyway. All I gotta do is to make sure those people recognize what's behind all those trappings. That they're just road signs pointing the way to our Lord.'

"When the father's finished, they sit there for a long time real quiet like. The father's quiet on account of his throat bein' pretty raw, and the preacher because he's got so much to think about.

"Finally old Preacher Jones sighs and says, real quiet and bashful, 'Think it's about time we started talkin' about me convertin'.'

"Father Prentiss reaches over and pats the reverend's shoulder with a hand 'bout the same size as the blade on an earthmover, and says with a real hoarse voice, 'Ain't no need to talk. If you're converted to Christ, we're already on the same side of the fence.'

" 'Don't recall ever having heard somebody talk quite so nice for so long before,' the reverend replies. 'Thank you for your troubles.'

" 'Think nothing of it,' the father replies. 'I'll come by and see you again tomorrow.' Then he wishes the reverend a good night's sleep, and leaves.

"But that night the reverend has hisself another heart attack in his sleep. When he opens his eyes, he's standin' there in front of old Saint Peter again, with Father Coughlin right there beside him.

"Preacher Jones nods a hello to Peter, but doesn't pay him all that much attention. He's got something more pressin' on his mind. He says to the father, 'I been wrong.'

" 'Brother, you ain't the only one,' Father Coughlin replies. 'You sure had your hands full, trying to manage that bunch.'

"But Preacher Jones don't want to hear all that just then. He's got somethin' he's just achin' to get off his chest. He tells the father, 'Your Church has got a role to play too. An important one.'

"Father Coughlin's like most preachers. Once they get started talkin'. Their mouths get in gear and don't wanna stop. He tells Preacher Jones, 'I believe I'd rather live with a cage full of gorillas than try to shepherd that flock of yours.'

"Old Peter steps forward wearin' this big grin, says, 'All right, all right, you fellows've got a whole eternity to work this out.' He kinda shooshes 'em through the gates, on account of neither one of them's payin' Peter much attention right then. Peter herds 'em along to where there are these big racks of halos and such. He leaves 'em to sort themselves out, 'cause a coupla other new arrivals popped up right then.

"Father Coughlin and Preacher Jones play around for a while tryin' on halos of different sizes and makin' each other laugh. Then Preacher Jones spots this other rack off there to one side, and he grabs Father Coughlin by the elbow.

" 'Here, Father,' old Preacher Jones says. 'Let me help you try on some wings.' "

□   □   □

"TJ! TJ! Wake up, man!"

"Honey! Can you hear me? What is it?"

Heart pounding, sweat streaming from every pore, TJ opened his eyes and focused on two very frightened faces.

Jeremy and Catherine stopped their cries, peered carefully into his face, and went limp with relief. Jeremy said hoarsely to Catherine, "Stay here. I'll call for an ambulance."

TJ struggled, managed to croak a no.

"It's all right, honey," Catherine said, her hand trembling as she stroked his shoulder. "Everything's all right."

"I don't need a doctor," TJ said, his heart beginning to slow its frantic pace.

Jeremy seemed uncertain. "I think somebody ought to see you, TJ."

"I'm okay, really," TJ said, and feebly raised his arms. "Help me up."

"You sounded like you were choking," Catherine said. "I thought you were having a stroke."

They helped him stand, stripped off his soaking pajamas, remade the bed, helped him into dry clothing. TJ was there but not there, with a calm now that touched and quieted them all. His limbs were limp, without strength, unable to support his weight.

Together Catherine and Jeremy guided him back down, settled him under the covers, and stood hovering above him.

"That must have been some nightmare," Jeremy said.

"It wasn't a bad dream," TJ said quietly.

Catherine sat on the edge of the bed, took his hand, asked, "Can you tell us about it?"

He stared at her a long time, his face aglow with an unearthly calm. He turned and bathed Jeremy with the same light, said, "My two very best friends. Not a day goes by that I don't thank God for the two of you."

Catherine stroked his forehead, asked again, "What was it, honey?"

TJ was silent a long time before saying, "You know what is written on the tomb of Martin Luther King, Jr.?"

"I don't see what—"

"Free at last," TJ murmured. "Free at last. Thank God Almighty, I'm free at last."

⊣ TWENTY-THREE ⊢

Tuesday morning TJ sat down behind his desk, basking in his sense of calm. The morning prayer meeting had been wonderful. He knew no other word for it. The President had been back, seated again with his wife, both carrying Bibles and smiling good mornings to the crowd that stood respectfully for them.

The message this morning had been on love, and the prayer had asked the Lord to join them together in the presence of His divine love. Once again a sense of glorious peace had descended upon TJ, accompanied by a love so strong that he had been forced to stop in mid-sentence. He had prayed that all had felt it, that all had sensed the power.

Nak stood by the doorway to his office, watching him quietly. "Is there anything I need to be doing?"

TJ shook his head, felt the renewed impact of last night's dream, tried to think of something to say. It all seemed so unimportant now. "I suppose we have more requests from the media?"

He nodded. "Amy Lou's typing up the list now."

"Why don't you call Tom Nees, ask if he'd like some more publicity. If he says yes, tell them all to meet us down there at five o'clock this afternoon."

"All right." Nak stayed where he was. "That was really wonderful this morning, Mr. Case. I mean it. I felt . . ."

"I understand," TJ nodded. "Thank you, Nak. I'm glad it had meaning for you."

Linda stuck her head in the door, said, "Sir, I have the President's secretary on the phone. President Nichols would like to see you right away."

TJ sighed, stood, said quietly, "It has been a great pleasure working with you three. I mean that from the bottom of my heart."

He walked up to Nak, who put out his hand, said, "Whatever happens, sir, I just want you to know that I wouldn't have missed this for the world."

"Me neither," Linda agreed.

"I'll second that," Amy Lou said, moving up beside Linda.

"You people will never know how much your support has meant to me," TJ replied, realizing they thought he was saying these things because the President was going to fire him. He decided to let it rest. "Nak, I want you to work with Bella and take over the prayer sessions."

The normally impassive face showed instant alarm. "Me?"

"Yes, you. For as long as you are here. I spoke with Bella this morning, she's willing to continue coordinating things."

The young man nodded. "All right, sir."

"Good." He forced a smile. "Don't look so sad, you people. You have got to keep in mind that I was sent up here with a mission. The important thing is not how long I stay, but that the Lord's work is done."

"We'll miss you," Amy Lou said quietly.

"May the good Lord bless you and keep you all your days, all of you." He patted Nak on the shoulder, smiled at the girls, and left.

The President's secretary was waiting for him at the guard's desk. She was an immensely professional woman, who held herself very erect and showed perfect poise as she greeted him. A simple yet elegant gray wool dress with a single strand of pearls and carefully styled gray hair carried out her aura of authority and warmth.

"It certainly is pleasant, having a little sunshine after all this rain, don't you think?" She treated him as if he were a visiting dignitary about to receive a presidential award. TJ found himself responding in kind.

She showed him into the small lobby just off the Press Pool, said, "I wonder if you would mind waiting just a few minutes. When I came downstairs the President had just taken a phone call."

"Not at all."

"I know he very much wants to speak with you. I'm sure he'll only be a moment." She smiled and left him.

As soon as she had left the room, TJ felt the Spirit come. He smiled, first because the Presence was an enormous comfort coming at such a moment, and second because there was not to be one single opportunity lost.

TJ sat down in one of the wing-back chairs, felt the calm and the power and the love spread throughout his being, found he could not stop smiling. These moments had truly been the most *complete* of his entire life. He lacked nothing, he wanted for nothing, he needed nothing more.

"Mr. Case?" The secretary stood in the doorway, smiling down at him. "The President will see you now."

It surprised him a little that there was no further buildup, no incredible surge of power, as had happened the last time. The Holy Spirit filled him with a gentle calm, a peace that surpassed all understanding. The love he had known that morning during prayer was back, and as TJ walked down the hall behind the President's secretary, he found himself feeling as though they were somehow connected. He nodded to the guard standing duty outside the President's door, and again sensed a bonding, a union that was there in the presence of the Lord.

The secretary opened the door, said, "Mr. President, Mr. Case is here to see you."

"Show him in."

TJ walked into the Oval Office, saw the President bent over his elaborately carved desk, busily signing papers. "Be right with you, Mr. Case. Make yourself comfortable over there by the fire."

"Thank you, Mr. President." Again he wondered at the absence of the forceful power as before. He was anticipating another confrontation, another stern warning. Yet there was nothing but this deep, abiding sense of divine love.

President Nichols stood up, walked around his desk, said, "You're not going to blast into me again this morning, are you?"

TJ stood to shake the President's hand. "It doesn't look that way, sir."

"What do you mean by that?"

"I speak as the Spirit tells me to speak," TJ said, feeling as though his heart, his entire being was reaching out in love.

"So when you came barging in here the other day, it was God who was telling you what to say?" The President did not seem to find the concept absurd.

"Yessir. Giving me the words, and filling me with such a power that I thought my chest was going to explode."

"Well, if somebody had tried to tell me about this last week I'd have laughed them out of the office. I tried to ignore it Friday, and being so angry with you helped. But I'm convinced it's real. I have difficulty believing I'm actually saying it, but I've learned when to trust my gut reaction. And my wife is absolutely sure you're for real, Mr. Case. I suppose you know it was she who brought me to the prayer meeting yesterday. And saved you your job, by the way. I was set to fire you after that barrage on Friday."

"Yessir, I was expecting it myself."

"And you still went on and said what you did?"

"Spoke to you, spoke to the television, and to the press." TJ wished there were some way to describe what he was feeling. His mind was sheltered in unearthly peace, like the waters of a still, deep pool. "Mr. President, I honestly do not feel like anything I have said or done here has been without the Lord's direct guidance."

The President thought that one over, asked, "What's it like?"

"It is the most beautiful experience," TJ replied instantly. "And the most natural. Sometimes when it is upon me, I feel as though the whole world could live all the time knowing this peace, if only it would put aside its selfish ways and learn to follow the Lord."

"Is that the way you feel right now?"

"Yessir, it is."

"Thought so," President Nichols said. "I've been feeling that sense of, I don't know, power is probably the best way to describe it, ever since you came into the room."

"It would be very wrong to ascribe it to me, Mr. President. I am only a human being whom God has reached out and touched. He uses me to reach out and touch others."

"I understand." The President leaned forward. "So tell me, Mr. Case, what is it I'm supposed to be doing that I'm not?"

There was a sensation of being consumed within a pillar of light. And from the Presence came the reply which he spoke. "It is time for you to choose, Mr. President. Which direction will you take? If you decide to follow the Lord, then it must be a wholehearted move. You must seek out the Lord's will on all decisions, on all actions. It must take precedence over politics, over the needs of the office, over the needs of your party, and over your future as a politician. It is a total commitment to lead this nation away from darkness. You cannot do it by executive order. You must do it by example. The people of this nation need a leader to whom they can turn for inspiration. They require spiritual as well as political guidance. An example must be set. A direction must be chosen and adhered to. And it can be done only by you, Mr. President. This is your *greatest* challenge. It is your *primary* responsibility as leader of your people."

The President turned and looked into the fire, silent for a very long time. TJ waited patiently.

Finally he shook his head, said softly, "The mistakes I've made."

"It is nothing that cannot be undone were you willing to accept Christ as your Savior and Lord and turn your life over to the doing of His will," TJ replied.

The President did not turn from the fire. "It's as simple as that, is it?" He did not sound convinced.

"The commitment of your life to God is only the first step," TJ replied. "The learning and the doing and the facing up to challenges will last for the rest of your life."

President Nichols turned back to TJ, asked in a quiet voice, "So where do I start?"

TJ replied, "Perhaps you might like to join me in prayer."

⊣‖ TWENTY-FOUR ‖⊢

Jeremy hesitated before knocking on the open door. "What you doin' in here, TJ?"

"Come on in, Jeremy." TJ finished folding up the pages, fitted them into the envelope, asked, "Do you have any idea what Catherine's done with the stamps?"

"Ain't they in that little drawer with the extra pens?"

"So they are." TJ licked and fastened a couple on the corner. "Where's Catherine?"

"She's upstairs. Didn't you hear her call?"

"No, I guess I was a little preoccupied. I wanted to finish this and get it in the mail." He pressed the envelope closed, asked, "Jem, could I please ask you to do a favor for me?"

"Sure thing, buddy."

"Could you please walk down and put this in the mailbox? I'm sorry to ask, I know it's late, but this needs to go out first thing tomorrow morning. I'd do it myself, but I honestly don't know if I've got the strength left to make it down there."

Jeremy was all concern. "You coming down with something, TJ?"

TJ smiled at his friend. "No, I'm just tired, is all."

"It hasn't been an easy road for you, has it?"

"No," TJ replied softly. "Not that easy. But it won't be long now."

"Sounded to me like the man was going to have you stay on a while."

TJ looked up at his friend, said, "Jem, if there were only some way

I could tell you how much your friendship's meant to me."

Jeremy seemed embarrassed. "Ain't no need for you to say that, TJ."

"No, there isn't, is there," TJ agreed. "You've known it all along. I just wish I knew the words to thank you for all you've done."

"Shoot. I wouldn't have missed this for the world."

"I don't mean just here in Washington." TJ's eyes glistened. "You're the best friend a man could ask for, Jem. A true brother in Christ."

"Now you just stop that before you have us both blubberin'," he said, and stuck out his hand. "Who's the letter to?"

TJ gave it to him, asked, "Do you remember Reverend Harbridge back home at the Church of New Zion?"

" 'Course I do." Reverend Harbridge had taken Reverend Amos Taylor's place at the church upon his retirement at the age of eighty. Jeremy hefted the letter, said, "You been busy, old son."

"I had a lot to say," TJ replied, and stood. "Jem, I want—"

"Now you just hold it right there, TJ," Jeremy said. "I can't think of anythin' much sillier than two grown men standin' around bawlin', and that's exactly what's gonna happen if you keep on."

TJ walked around the writing table, came up to his friend, put his arms around the man's shoulders, drew him close. Jeremy hesitated, then awkwardly embraced him back.

When TJ released him, Jeremy wouldn't meet his eye. "I'll just go get my coat," he said gruffly.

TJ was waiting for him at the front door. He held it open, said quietly, "Thank you, old friend."

"Won't be but a moment," Jeremy replied, still avoiding his gaze.

TJ shut the door, turned, and walked up the stairs. He entered the bedroom, found Catherine propped up in bed, her reading glasses perched on the end of her nose, all four pillows behind her back, the Bible open in her lap.

"Where you been, honey?" she asked.

"There was a little something I needed to finish up," he replied, walked around, and sat down on the bed beside her. TJ took his wife's hand in both of his, began playing with her wedding ring. He smiled faintly, asked, "You remember the day I slipped this on your finger?"

With her free hand Catherine took off her glasses, said, "Child, what on earth's gotten into you?"

"I was so scared," TJ said. "I don't believe I've ever been as scared in my whole life." He looked into her eyes, said, "Marrying you was the best move I've ever made, Catherine."

Her look softened. She placed her other hand on top of his, murmured, "How you do go on."

"You're the best wife a man could ask for," he said. "I just hope I've been worthy of you. I know I've made mistakes, a lot of them, but I've tried to be the best husband I could. I really have."

She gave him that deep-down chuckle, said, "I do believe I know now what my man is after."

He shared her smile, said, "All I want is to be here with you. You know I couldn't have done this without you, don't you?"

She inspected his face a long moment, growing steadily more solemn. "Is it what you told me about this morning?"

With a slow movement of his head, TJ nodded once. His eyes never left hers. "Are you sure you want to go through with this?"

Catherine had to swallow before she could reply, "I didn't think the time was coming so quick."

"It's the Lord's timing, Catherine, not ours," TJ told her, his voice as soft as his eyes. "There are still the children, honey. It's your choice."

She gave a heartfelt sigh and set her head back against the pillows. Wrapping her fingers around his, she drew their hands up close to her heart. "I can hardly believe this is real."

"I love you with all my heart," TJ said.

She drew him to her with a violent strength. "You're my man," she said.

With a soft and silent beginning, that quiet, holy Presence filled the room, so gentle, so gradual, that at first it was hard for either to believe that He was truly there.

"Honey!" Catherine held her husband close with excited fingers. "What is it?"

His voice was sure, the words the last he ever spoke.

"The Lord is here," was all he said.

The light grew beyond the power of human vision, and with it grew a love so total, so complete that there was room for nothing else. All was light. All was love. All was eternal.

□   □   □

Jeremy had his hand on the mailbox slot when the blast rocked him. People screamed up and down Connecticut Avenue as windows shattered and cars swerved in their paths. Jeremy leaned on the mailbox for support, his hand still clenched to the letter, and let the sobs wrack his body. He ignored the cries and the running footsteps and the sirens and the people. He stood where he was and bowed his head and cried for what he knew had happened.

When he could, he turned around, the tears streaming down his face, and said to no one in particular, "I believe I'll just deliver this letter in person."

╼┤ EPILOGUE ├╾

They made fairly good time, all things considered. The motorcade leaving Washington in the early morning darkness was over a mile long. Jeremy and Nak rode in the first car with Reverend Wilkins and TJ's eldest daughter, who had come up to accompany them home. The lights on the squad cars up ahead continued to blink in through the front window, hurting Jeremy's eyes. The funeral service was to be held at noon, so they left at four in the morning, which was fine with Jeremy. He hadn't slept much the last few days.

For reasons Jeremy could not explain, he had decided to drive rather than fly the bodies home. There was something solemn about the process of driving his friends on their final journey. It just seemed to fit better than putting them in a plane and flying them home. Much better.

The telephone had rung constantly. Although the blast had almost completely destroyed the back of the house, Jeremy insisted on sleeping on the sofa in the living room. He ignored the detectives and the yellow police-warning tape and the curious onlookers. TJ's secretaries brought him sandwiches and words of encouragement.

Two phone calls had stayed with him through it all. The first had come from Congressman John Silverwood. The man had sounded totally shattered, his pain so sharp that it had cut its way through the fog of Jeremy's own grief. I can't talk to TJ anymore, the man had said time and again. I know it's too late for that. Jeremy had struggled for words that might have eased the man's agony. The Lord is here with us, he had said. At that Silverwood had completely broken down. I don't know how to talk to Him either, he had told Jeremy. Over the phone Jeremy prayed for the man's relief from sorrow, feeling the words had been aimed more at himself than at the congressman.

The second call had been from the President of the United States. It had come early in the morning after another sleepless night, and Jeremy had not been able to respond. The man had seemed truly bereaved, but before Jeremy could share in his sorrow, the President promised a full inquiry into the cause of TJ's death. Jeremy had felt himself return to his familiar numbed state as he thanked him and hung up as quickly and politely as possible.

Most of the phone calls were from people who wanted to be a little closer to the center of their grief, who needed details of the funeral service. Jeremy told everyone when and where the service was to be held, when the procession would leave, and suggested that everyone just fly down. But by three-thirty in the morning of their departure for Raleigh, there were over four hundred fifty cars parked as far away as Dupont Circle, all waiting for the motorcade to get underway.

Jeremy was pleased to see Senator Atterly's limousine directly behind the hearse, completely filled with friends from the Community of Hope. The senator spent the entire trip down discussing various ways that he might be of further assistance. His staff filled two more cars farther back in the line.

Almost as soon as the motorcade crossed the North Carolina border, dawn broke upon a cloudless sky. By the time the mourners arrived at the Church of New Zion, the day had turned warm and spring-like. The procession was by then national news, and had been buzzed a dozen times by low-flying television helicopters. It passed through Raleigh as though guided by remote control. Patrol cars guarded every major intersection, and officers replaced stoplights to wave them on through.

The Church of New Zion had done what it could to prepare. There was no way the church could hold the crowd, no way at all. So all the pews had been carried outside and set in careful rows. Behind them were placed all the folding chairs the church could possibly find. At the front was the altar and low stage used for revival meetings, with a space reserved before it for the two coffins.

Thankfully, it had been a mild winter—so mild, in fact, that it had seemed to many as though autumn had simply drifted into an early spring. The dogwoods encircling the churchyard had grown fresh leaves, and now the first blossoms were beginning to appear. In the sparkling spring sunlight it seemed as though the motorcade was pulling up to a brilliant field of green, crowned the entire way around by snow-covered trees.

As pallbearer, Jeremy helped carry the coffins up through the long line of local mourners. There was almost total silence, broken occasionally by the sound of quiet weeping and the sporadic birdsong. Jeremy kept a tightly clenched jaw and willed himself to hold fast to his composure. As soon as the caskets were set in place he fled to the distant perimeter, only to be recruited by a frantic Nak. He was trying to help the police and sort out the press, keeping them to the separate line of chairs set underneath the dogwoods. Jeremy didn't mind lending a hand. It kept his mind occupied. It also gave him a chance to console a teary-eyed Sandra Hastings and send her up into the mourners' section. By the time he had corralled all the photographers and cameramen seeking pictures of the three senators, nine congressmen and two members of the President's Cabinet who dotted the crowd, Jeremy was feeling much more in control.

Jeremy stood between the press section and the main gathering, watching people reaching over the rows to shake hands, seeing many shared hugs, murmurs and tears. He was in no hurry to move. A man in a hurry needed someplace to go.

"You're Jeremy Hughes, aren't you?"

Jeremy turned around, saw an overweight woman with bright red hair and weepy eyes. "Yes, ma'am, that's me."

"I'm Bella Saunders. I've heard a lot about you."

Jeremy held out his hand, said, "TJ's talked so much about you I feel as if I've known you all my life. It's a real honor to meet you, Miss Saunders."

"Call me Bella. Please. Everybody else does." She dabbed at her eyes with a tattered tissue, said brokenly, "I feel as if my whole world's been shattered."

"Know just how you feel," Jeremy replied. "Would you care to sit with me, Bella?"

"If you don't mind sitting next to a fat old woman who's gonna bawl her eyes out."

"I'd consider it a privilege," Jeremy replied. "Besides, it'll keep people from payin' too much attention to me. C'm on, I think there's some chairs up front where we're supposed to sit."

Bella held back. "Oh no, please, not where everybody can see me."

But Jeremy was very insistent. "Make TJ proud of you, Bella. That's the only thing that's keepin' me goin' right now. Remember all he did for you and make him proud."

She took a shaky breath, said, "All right, then. Let's do it now before I lose my nerve."

They walked forward together, heads erect, jaws set into firm lines. They nodded to the people around them, sat down, looked straight ahead.

Jeremy asked her, "Do you want to join them?" He pointed with his chin to where a long line of people toured slowly around the two closed coffins. Some people reached out and touched the lids; others just looked down sadly, many were crying. Bella shook her head in a brief sharp jerk. "Couldn't bear it," she said.

"Mr. Hughes? May I sit here?" It was a very red-eyed John Nakamishi.

"Why sure, son, set yourself down. You two know each other, don't you?"

"Yessir. Hello, Bella."

"Hello, Nak." She said to Jeremy, "After all this, I've just got to find something to do to keep myself going. I've been wracking my brains, but all the ideas I have don't seem very meaningful. I need to do something, though, something to keep it alive."

Jeremy did not need to ask her what "it" was. "You've got that prayer session, don't you?"

"Sure, Bella," Nak agreed. "We need you."

"It's not enough," she said firmly. "I want to do more. But I can't see myself getting involved with some little church group that gets together twice a week and talks about their kids."

Jeremy thought it over, asked, "You ever heard of the Community of Hope?"

"I don't think so, no."

"That's a great idea, Mr. Hughes," Nak affirmed.

"Looks like it's about time," Jeremy said, suddenly having difficulty with his voice. "Tell you about it later, Bella."

Reverend Harbridge approached the podium, looked out over the gathering, said gravely, "There's a big question in everybody's mind about why this had to happen to such a godly couple. Don't know how many people've come up to me, asked how the dear Lord could let this be."

He reached into his inner coat pocket, came out with a few papers, unfolded them, set them on the podium. With studied slowness he spread them out flat, said, "I believe the best thing to do is to let Brother Case answer that for himself.

"Our dearly departed brother was kind enough to leave precise instructions with our friend Brother Jeremy as to just how we are to proceed today. These were written the evening of their homegoing."

He stopped, waited, let the words sink in. The crowd gave voice as the import of this message went home.

"We will therefore follow the wishes of Brother Case as closely as we can," Reverend Harbridge went on. "We will start by singing his and Sister Catherine's favorite hymn, 'Just As I Am.' Y'all be sure that those who don't know the words have the hymnals."

There was no organ to guide them, nor was one needed. Voices lifted and rang out in the fresh spring air, mingling with the breeze and the light and the birdsong. Jeremy found himself unable to sing. He stood and listened and recalled the words, and felt their power reach down and touch something deep, very deep inside.

> Just as I am, without one plea,
> But that Thy blood was shed for me,
> And that Thou bidd'st me come to Thee,
> O Lamb of God, I come, I come!

Jeremy felt a weight lean heavy on his side. He lifted an arm, settled it gently across Bella's trembling shoulder. He did not look down. He could not do so and keep control himself.

> Just as I am and waiting not
> To rid my soul of one dark blot,
> To Thee, whose blood can cleanse each spot,
> O Lamb of God, I come, I come!

The power of the voices pressed gently against Jeremy's heart, made his head ring like a Sunday-go-to-meeting bell. Nine hundred voices raising hearts and minds in unison, chiming words for two who could not hear them, singing and drawing close and filling the emptiness with song.

> Just as I am, though tossed about
> With many a conflict, many a doubt,
> Fightings within, and fears without,
> O Lamb of God, I come, I come!

Jeremy sought to escape the pressure in his chest by looking beyond the congregation, inspecting the encircling dogwoods. Their white blossoms floated on the breeze like earth-bound clouds. He took a shaky breath, decided he would never be able to hear that hymn again.

> Just as I am, poor, wretched, blind;
> Sight, riches, healing of mind
> Yea, all I need in Thee to find,
> O Lamb of God, I come, I come.

The music pried with gentle fingers at that inner door Jeremy thought he had sealed tightly closed. Loving power reached within, stroked and calmed and showed that it was possible to let it out, let it pour and flow and heal. He raised his eyes to the unseen heavens, did not bother to wipe his face.

> Just as I am, Thou wilt receive,
> Will welcome, pardon, cleanse, relieve;
> Because Thy promise I believe,
> O Lamb of God, I come, I come.

> Just as I am, Thy love unknown
> Hath broken every barrier down;
> Now, to be Thine, yea, Thine alone,
> O Lamb of God, I come, I come!

After they were finished, Reverend Wilkins came to the podium. "Be seated," he said, and the gathering became silent. "I have a letter here from Brother Case. He wanted his dear friend and brother in Christ,

Mr. Jeremy Hughes, to read it. Brother Hughes asked me to do the honor. It seems that Brother Hughes lacks my experience in handlin' the sorrows that this world tries to set upon us."

His face set in a somber expression, Reverend Wilkins drew out the paper and unfolded it. "This is not a long message, so I hope you folks can pay careful attention. Real careful. It is the last gift of a man who gave his life in service to his Lord." Reverend Wilkins looked up. "Are you people listening to me out there? Are your hearts good and open?"

"Say it, brother," someone called.

Reverend Wilkins paused again to search the crowd. "Lord, Lord, I do pray you will open these people's minds and hearts. Let them listen, Lord. Let them hear. Speak to them, Lord. Speak to them."

The gathering became a little restless. Those who did not know the Washington preacher wondered about him saying a prayer with eyes wide open and glaring out at the people. Those who knew him wondered also, for there was a light in his eyes that few had ever seen burning so intensely.

Reverend Wilkins adjusted his reading glasses, flattened the page with his hand, and began, " 'Dear friends, dear gathered brothers and sisters. Last night I was taken up to the mountaintop and shown where I would be traveling to, and when. It was a divine vision, the most wondrous of all, and like all visions it only has meaning if it is used for the glory of our Lord.'

" 'I know of no way to give the vision more meaning than to share it with you here today. Why? Because I am going home, brethren. As you read this, I am standing in the presence of our beloved Lord. There is no need for grief, not for me and not for Catherine. We are home, the only home we have ever known.' "

Reverend Wilkins stopped and stared out at the audience, said, "We'll probably never know this side of Jordan why the Lord told TJ ahead of time. Maybe just so we would know the evildoers are not in charge. TJ and Catherine didn't *choose* death—their *choice* was to simply rest in their heavenly Father's strong arms." Reverend Wilkins paused another moment then went back to the page in front of him.

" 'How many of you feel as if you do not belong? How many wish there were some way to know peace of mind and happiness? Brothers and sisters, I tell you that so long as you search only in this world, you will not find it. But it is there. Your home is waiting for you. Lasting peace is there for all of us to know. All we have to do is turn away from the things of this world and seek that which is unseen.'

" 'This, then, is my gift. It is the fervent prayer that each one of you will turn from your self-centered seeking and come to know the Lord. Ask Jesus into your hearts. I beg you from beyond the grave. There is nothing more important. Nothing more urgent. Seek the Lord with all your hearts, with all your minds. Your home is not here, the possessions of this world cannot satisfy your endless hunger.'

" 'Search along the false paths of what you see with your eyes and touch with your earthly senses, and you will know only bitterness and sorrow. Seek what is *real*. Seek what is *eternal*. And know that the Lord's bountiful mercy is there, ever waiting for you to open the door.'

" 'I do not say goodbye, my brethren. For if we are truly united in Christ, we will be together soon. The time of suffering and sorrow is so short, the time of joyful reunion truly eternal. Think of that when the world tries to darken your heart's eyes and draw you from the narrow path. Remember that reunion awaits you. I wish there were some way I could show you what that word means. Reunion with your Lord. Is that not an awesome vision? Reunion with the Master, the Supreme Being. He awaits you. *He awaits you.*'

" 'The peace, the joy, the love that you may know on earth is only a glimmer of that which will be yours once you are free of this world. So do not mourn our passing, I beg you. We are free. Mourn for the godless. Cry for all of those who are still trapped in the world of suffering and torment.' "

Reverend Wilkins stopped, looked up, and gave extra emphasis to the final words, " 'Cry for all of those who will never know what freedom means.' "

Reverend Harbridge stood, took his place at the podium, said, "Let us pray.

"O, Lord, look down upon us, we pray, and open our hearts to your holy Word. Show us, Father, that our lives are not in vain. Let us learn what it means to see death as a passage, an open door into what is real. Help us to cling to this truth, O Lord, throughout all the lies and temptations and trials and sorrows this world of shadows tries to heap upon us. Let us hold fast to the truth. Keep our feet upon the Way, O, Lord. Give us the clarity of vision to see what must be done, and the strength to see it through to the end. Right to the end, Lord. Right to the end, right into your open arms, into the palace of eternal light. This is our prayer, O, Lord. We do not pray for Brother Case and Sister Catherine. We know they have gone home to their reward. Our prayer is for those they have left behind. Help us, O, Lord. Help us to find our own way to you. This we pray in Christ's holy name. Amen."

⊣ ACKNOWLEDGMENTS ⊢

The lessons I learned and the friendships I forged during the research and writing of *The Presence* continue to be a blessing. I would once again like to thank the officials and staff members of the many organizations involved, including the White House, the Old Executive Office Building, the Department of Education, the California Governor's Office, the Prison Fellowship, the Community of Hope, the North Carolina Democratic Party, and many others.

A special thanks to Reverend Paul McCommon and his wife Ruth, whose wisdom and energy in doing God's will is a constant source of inspiration.

Ten years on, my debt of gratitude to Bethany House Publishers and my admiration for its members grows ever deeper. Thank you, Gary and Carol Johnson, for showing early confidence in my writing. And thank you for this wonderful reaffirmation in the way of a new edition of my first novel *The Presence*.